To Cha...
all best,
Dennis Ment...

EXCESSIVE FORCES

A **Pittsburgh** Police Thriller

EXCESSIVE FORCES

A **Pittsburgh** Police Thriller

Dennis Marsili

WORD ASSOCIATION PUBLISHERS
www.wordassociation.com
1.800.827.7903

ISBN: 978-1-59571-631-6
Library of Congress Control Number: 2011920232

Designed and published by

Word Association Publishers
205 Fifth Avenue
Tarentum, Pennsylvania 15084

www.wordassociation.com
1.800.827.7903

The author dedicates this book to those law enforcement officers who have faced their inner demons and fought the good fight – God bless you.

CHAPTER 1

Indifference.

After a few moments of contemplation the word struck his mind with the spontaneity of a popped balloon. It happens like that sometimes. He will be searching his mind for the right word and it will just appear to him with an unprovoked suddenness. Fascinating, he thought, how, with little effort his brain computes all the possibilities—analyzing and comparing until settling on the appropriate selection. Strange how the mind works, he thought. There were still some lingering doubts however, so he took another few seconds and mulled the term over to make sure it was right. This was important because the emotion had to be identified properly. Therefore, per his standard procedure, he defined the word in question before making his decision final. *Indifference*—a lack of interest in or concern over some matter or subject. Right? he asked himself. Sounds right, he answered, pleased that he had found the right word.

At first he had considered the word "ambiguous," but it didn't seem to capture his mood as succinctly. He reasoned that the word

1

ambiguous refers more to a "state of confusion" rather than a feeling of unconcern or lack of interest. Although there was an element of confusion in his mind, this feeling was overshadowed by the sincere lack of interest that he was experiencing. No, ambiguous didn't fit and he had to find the exact word that truly epitomized his current emotional state.

Taymond Diaz sat, deep in thought, staring out through the open car window into the dark night. He stroked the chin hairs of his perfectly groomed goatee, as was his habit when carrying on these introspective exercises. Yes, I'm indifferent, Diaz affirmed to himself. I am indifferent to this work that I find myself in at this time. I could take it or leave it, and I am leaning more toward leaving it.

Maybe I need to set a time frame on this job, six months or possibly one year? His mind wandered from thought to thought, one theme giving impetus to the next, like runners handing off a baton in a relay race. Lord knows that I have put enough applications and resumes out there. Something has to hit soon, he reasoned.

Many of his friends had already begun their career journeys, most finding choice positions with large companies. Some of them had to relocate to other states since the local economy was so poor-especially those who were looking for high-profile employment with six-figure salaries and clear opportunities for corporate advancement. Compared to his friends' careers, Diaz was somewhat ashamed of his job. That was the perfect word for it too—*job*. It wasn't a career.

Diaz was somewhat successful in hiding the nature of his occupation from the out-of-state friends, but he couldn't do anything about the ones still around. Although the local friends were polite about it, he knew that privately they looked down upon the fact that he was now a police officer with the Pittsburgh Metro Police Department. Trying to rationalize, he figured his situation was temporary until something better came along. As far as middle class jobs went, the pay wasn't all that bad, he thought. Still, he had to admit that when you got right down to it, the influential corporate positions held by his fellow collegians were simply in a much higher stratum than riding around in a patrol car all night.

"Radio to 7-33. See the man at the corner of Matilda and Dauntless streets about a domestic dispute. No weapons involved. Verbal at this time," exclaimed the voice of a female police dispatcher from the in-car speaker, shaking Diaz from thoughts of *indifference* toward his job.

"7-33, 10-4," replied a male police officer, who was in a separate squad car, confirming the call.

"23:04," the female dispatcher announced the time, 11:04 p.m., in military fashion.

"Radio to 7-32. Meet the resident at 1933 Aurora Street. Report of a broken window," said the same dispatcher, relaying a second call to a different police unit.

"7-32, 10-4," answered that officer, another male with a gravelly voice.

"23:05 hours," reported the dispatcher, giving the time of call.

And so it went as Diaz listened, or tried to. He couldn't believe the steady stream of calls. He had never realized that there were so many people calling the cops. The calls ran the gamut from the violent to the mundane—robberies, stabbings, bar fights, domestic disputes, prostitution, and drug dealing. Then, on the opposite side, were your run-of-the-mill calls - dog bites, vehicle accidents, landlord tenant disputes, and even stolen lawn ornaments. No calls

3

for shooting incidents yet. Diaz wondered when he would answer that type of call.

While staring incredulously at the radio in the squad car, which continued to spew out call after call for help, Diaz's thoughts were interrupted by the voice of his training officer, Guy Ruggerio.

"This place was owned for years by this big black lady named Suzy, even before I started on the force," offered Ruggerio.

"We used to call her 'Ole Susanna.' She was a great old broad. She was from Georgia, originally, and would take a little dip of Copenhagen once in a while. She used to make us soul food— black-eyed peas, collard greens, and chicken fried steak. Damn, it was good. Suzy passed away a few years ago. Now, two Middle Eastern guys bought the place and it's just not the same. Suzy used to make the best coffee in this zone, but I guess this stuff isn't that bad," he said, taking a sip from his white styrofoam cup with a nostalgic sigh. "You ever try espresso?" Ruggerio asked his rookie partner, who seemed to be mesmerized by the car radio and still stroking the dark hairs of his goatee.

"What's that?" Diaz answered, initially missing the question.

"Don't worry. Before you know it, you won't even notice the calls. Somehow, your mind will be trained to block out the noise until your own car number is called. Then it will register," Ruggerio said, understanding what the rookie was thinking about. "I know it sounds hard to believe, but it will happen sooner than you think. One day it will just click and the drone of the constant calls will just be background noise like your FM radio—until the dispatcher calls your number, of course."

Diaz was still wondering what he had gotten himself into with this police work thing. It's just temporary, he reminded himself as he re-directed his gaze out of the squad car windshield. They were parked in a small area situated on the side of a steep hill, one of the many mini-mountains common to the landscape in Western Pennsylvania. The area is known locally as the West End Overlook, which even at nighttime presents a stunning view of the city, beginning in the foreground with an area called "The Point," where the Allegheny and Monongahela Rivers meet to form the Ohio River, the famed "confluence." For some reason, every sportscaster who covers a nationally televised event in Pittsburgh feels compelled to use this word "confluence" when describing to the television audience the aerial view of the city and the convergence of its three rivers. Diaz would agree that it was eye catching the way the rivers seemed to surround the downtown skyscrapers like a moat around a medieval castle. The scenic panorama before him slightly dispelled the image he had of this city of a gritty old steel town.

He looked back over at his training officer and observed how the dark back drop, along with the glow emanating from all the dashboard electronics gave his face an eerie, ghost-like quality, especially with the burn scars that were evident on the right side of his neck and part of his face. Diaz wondered how Ruggerio had gotten these scars, but was not going to ask. The texture looked as if a sheet of wrinkled cellophane was stuck to his skin. His skin tone varied throughout the scar, deep red along the wrinkle lines, with a lighter flesh tone in the spaces between the creases. He noticed how the scar rose up from Ruggerio's uniform collar to a spike type formation near his right ear, then descended downward like the side of a steep mountain along his jaw line and neck, back under his dark blue uniform shirt. Diaz took a sip from his own cup and decided to answer his partner's original question.

"Yeah, it's a little too strong for my taste. But I do like coffee. I learned to drink it in college, when I had to pull all-nighters," he explained.

Diaz could feel the coffee working on his bladder already and wondered why they were drinking hot coffee on a steamy July night, anyway? Like it wasn't hot enough outside. Diaz looked out the windshield at the sparkling city below. He had to admit it really was a beautiful sight and could see why his partner liked to sit in this spot.

"So, Diaz - that's Hispanic. Are you Puerto Rican or Mexican?" Ruggerio, who was very Italian, had the stereotypical Mediterranean look — short in stature, the dark, deep-set eyes, pronounced nose, and, especially visible this time of year, the dark tanned skin tone. Even though Ruggerio's hair was buzzed, Diaz could tell that it was jet black. When the two first met, he was immediately curious about Ruggerio's burn scars. It appeared to have been a pretty severe injury and Diaz was dying to ask him how it happened, but proper etiquette prevented him from approaching the subject.

Diaz had seen many Italians in Philadelphia. But even though Pittsburgh was much smaller, it had a large Italian population as evidenced by the preponderance of vowel ending names on the police roster hanging in the station house. Sizing up his new acquaintance, Diaz wondered how this guy would handle himself in a fight. Ruggerio was short, but appeared to be in good physical shape. Still, Diaz was concerned. He resigned himself to thinking that if they got into something tonight, this guy wasn't going to be much help. Diaz would take care of any situation alone, if necessary.

"I'm half Puerto Rican and half African American," Diaz answered, thinking at the same time that it was way too early in their relationship to broach such a personal topic. After all, they had met a mere thirty minutes earlier. Since then, all they had done was go to what used to be Suzy's for two free coffees to go. The coffee tasted horrid to Diaz, like rocket fuel. Those Middle Easterners must like their coffee strong.

Robust. That sounded like a good word, *robust*. Isn't that how those coffee connoisseurs describe the taste of coffee, he thought to himself. Ever since college Diaz had been afflicted with a habit – or *ritual* – of needing to find the most appropriate word for whatever situation he found himself in. It was a holdover from a classroom exercise in college as he worked toward his psychology degree. He continued the exercise after graduating because it made him feel more cerebral as he mixed with the blue-collar world.

"I love Hispanic food. Does your mother cook a lot?"

"Do you mean Hispanic food, or just cook in general?" asked Diaz, feeling a little more agitated at having the ethnic thing brought up again. Hasn't this guy ever seen a Puerto Rican before, he asked himself?

"Hispanic food. Does she cook a lot of Hispanic meals?"

"No, but we eat a lot of fried chicken and black-eyed peas. You know, *soul food*," Diaz said with contempt. Then he thought, what a hick I got here. I bet he hasn't been east of the Alleghenies his whole life. I must look like some exotic creature to him. An *anomaly*, would that be right? he wondered silently.

Ruggerio saw that he crossed some invisible ethnic boundary. He started the police car and pulled out from the parking spot where they had been sitting for fifteen minutes. This was Ruggerio's routine every night on the midnight shift. He liked to move around to different parking locations each night to keep the bad guys guessing. This spot was one of his favorites, though, and why he chose it for this trainee's first night. He knew that this Diaz guy was originally from Philadelphia, and Ruggerio wanted to introduce him to Pittsburgh by showing off the city from her best side. From this west side vantage point, high atop one of the many hills in the city, you can cast your gaze over the bright twinkling lights of the tall downtown buildings. In the foreground and acting like a natural mirror was the Ohio River, reflecting the illuminated images of the buildings in its rippling waters. It was peaceful, and when he rode alone it gave him time to reflect and sometimes pray, if he felt the need.

Gaetano "Guy" Ruggerio was a ten-year veteran of the force. He was well respected by his peers, earning him the task of training new recruits, of which Taymond Diaz was his newest.

Ruggerio pulled out and began patrolling their zone of the city. He saw that he had touched a nerve with Diaz and wanted to create a distraction so he could change the subject. He sensed something was bothering Diaz. Of all the rookies he trained in the past, none acted like this on their first night out. This one seemed distant, like he had something on his mind but was afraid to say it out loud. He also knew that it was time to move after sitting in the same spot for over ten minutes. He was not one of those officers who sat parked for long periods of time, only to move when he received a call. He was paid to patrol and look for crime—not just respond to it after it had already been committed.

In an effort to lighten the mood, Ruggerio said, "Man, is it hot tonight. This humidity will surely make the natives restless." The second he said it he knew that he had made a gaffe. He realized that the "natives" reference could be taken as a racial epithet.

"I'm sorry man, I didn't mean…" he said, trying to save face.

"I know. Don't worry about it," Diaz replied.

"Can we start over?"

"Sure," said Diaz.

"So, what made you join the force?" asked Ruggerio.

"The city was recruiting minorities and thought that I just might qualify," Diaz said with a smirk.

Ruggerio let out a chuckle, relieved that the tense moment seemed to have passed.

"Since this is your first night, let's just start by teaching you the streets. You'll need to find your way around the streets first before you can get into the police work side of the training." Then Ruggerio did exactly what Diaz had done earlier and what most cops do. He sized up his partner for physical prowess. Diaz definitely had an athletic build, Ruggerio thought, so handling himself in a fight should not be an issue. Ruggerio was surprised that the department was permitting trainees to keep their goatees. Then again, has chin hair ever affected how a police officer performed his job?

Just then, they both heard loud explosions reverberating into the police car. BOOM! BOOM! BOOM! ... Boom, boom, boom, boom! The last four shots discharged in such quick succession that they almost seemed to be on top of one another. The officers could hear these shots so clearly because of Ruggerio's habit of leaving the car windows down a few inches, no matter what the weather conditions were. In Diaz's view, all this habit did was hamper the efficiency of the air conditioner, which was cranked up to maximum in an attempt to make the bulletproof vests both officers were wearing seem less suffocating.

There were multiple shots, fired in rapid succession, Ruggerio counted six, but knew that there were more. Then exploding into the radio was the desperate voice of a male officer, the one with the gravelly voice.

"7-32 to radio. I got shots fired on the 1000 block of Euclid Street."

"10-4. Car 7-32 requesting back up on the 1000 block of Euclid Street. He hears shots fired," the female radio operator announced.

The gunfire seemed so loud that Diaz thought the shooter or shooters were standing just a few feet away. He couldn't understand why but he actually thought he could feel the sound waves from the gunfire transmitted through his body like the aftershock of an earthquake. He had never felt anything like that before.

"Listen, you stay with me no matter what happens, OK?" Ruggerio wasn't concerned about hurting anyone's feelings now. It was time to put on his trainer's hat and take charge.

"OK," was all Diaz could get out of his mouth, which was getting very dry.

BOOM! BOOM! BOOM! More shots and this time, Diaz actually saw orange colored muzzle flashes as they appeared to splash off the sides of brick buildings in the distance with each round fired. The source of the gunshots was on the opposite side of the buildings, so Diaz could not see the shooters, although he saw the flashes of their corresponding explosions delayed by a millisecond.

This audible illusion was created by sound waves bouncing off the walls of the buildings in this once thriving business district. In urban environments, acoustic conditions tended to amplify the sound of gun fire to make the weapon being used sound much louder than it ordinarily would in an open field for example, thereby giving the impression that the firearms being used were of a larger caliber than they actually were. Diaz was afraid, afraid of this ominous light and sound display and of the fact that they were heading directly into the fray. His hands began to shake. Ruggerio put the window down a bit more and pitched the coffee out, as did Diaz.

"Unit 7-21 to radio. I am two blocks away and will be backing up 7-32," Ruggerio spoke into the radio.

"10-4, unit 7-21. Unit 7-21 will be backing up unit 7-32," repeated the female dispatcher, announcing to all cars that unit 7-32 would have at least one car as back up. Ruggerio pushed the accelerator and propelled the marked Chevy Impala around the corner toward the sound of the shots.

Along with the shaking hands, Diaz could feel his heart rate increase, so much so that it felt like it was pounding up in his throat. Those shots sounded so damn loud, they had to be from a shotgun or something like it. He had heard shots like these in an urban area before, but not this close to the actual scene. He had been born and raised in Philadelphia but moved to Pittsburgh when his father, an ordained Baptist minister, had been transferred to the area three years ago. Diaz had actually lived outside of Philadelphia in an upscale neighborhood. His experience with gunfire was limited to just one incident when he and some friends heard shots when they were bar-hopping in the city one night. This time however, he was not just a simple bystander annoyed by the disruption but very soon could be an actual participant.

"7-32 to other units. The shooter is a black male wearing a long white t-shirt and baggy, dark colored jeans. Last seen on foot running north on Euclid Street toward 11th Street. This from a wit on scene," relayed the officer.

Ruggerio hurriedly pulled the patrol car between two buildings into a small parking area covered with limestone gravel. He slammed the brakes on and turned the wheel, causing the car to slide on the stones. Diaz's body was pressed against the passenger side door by inertia as the Chevy slid to the right. Pieces of the gravel in the lot ricocheted off the under carriage of the car and sprayed out from the two right side tires as the car came to rest shrouded in a cloud of limestone dust. Ruggerio cut the engine.

"Don't turn your radio on until you need it," he instructed Diaz. "This is where they run through. Stay behind me and watch my back." Both officers exited the car and started running toward an alley that ran behind the buildings.

"Draw your weapon," Ruggerio whispered to Diaz. He complied and nervously pointed the .40 caliber Glock pistol toward the ground while holding the firearm with both hands, just as he had been taught. Diaz could feel his bowels begin to loosen at the thought of having to shoot someone or be shot at. He had experienced fear before, but never to such a degree.

Ruggerio, seeing Diaz handling his weapon in the proper manner, gave him a reassuring smile and nod. He was glad to see that Diaz took the handling of his firearm seriously, because many officers, even veterans, did not. The academy did its job with this kid, Ruggerio thought. This also gave him some comfort that he just might not get shot in the back tonight by this rookie. Even though it was obvious that Diaz was a bit overwhelmed, Ruggerio could see that the training was kicking in and overriding the fear.

"Find some cover and stay behind it unless I tell you different."

Diaz nodded, affirming the instructions.

He could only nod his head, too afraid to speak, thinking that his voice might crack with fear in front of his training officer, revealing just how afraid he was. Diaz could not believe that he was reacting this way. When he had fights or when he played football in high school, there was always some level of nervousness. But he had never been this anxious before. He thought that with his academy training, at which he excelled in all physical requirements, coupled with his Philadelphia upbringing, he was well prepared to handle anything he ran into on the streets. To be this afraid made him ashamed, especially after seeing how calm Ruggerio was.

They reached the end of the gravel parking lot where it met with the pavement of the alley. Diaz looked down the alley and saw some working streetlights, which made this section of the alley partially visible. He also could see directly across the alley from where they were standing a battered white picket fence. Parts of the fence were long gone and the portion that was still standing was leaning inward toward an open area where weeds had grown as tall as five feet. It was obvious that the property had been let go for quite some time. A worn footpath passed down the middle of the high weeds. At the end of the path was an abandoned old two-story steel-mill era house that had somehow eluded the wrecking ball. The windows were boarded up, and rubbish was scattered among the weeds and throughout what used to be the backyard.

On either side of this property, block buildings sandwiched the old house. The back walls of both block buildings met the edge of the alleyway, leaving no open ground to run through except for an unseen passageway made between the old house and one of the neighboring buildings. In the alley a dumpster sat askew behind the southernmost building, in a diagonal position that partially blocked the alleyway.

Ruggerio pointed to a telephone pole standing near the corner of a building on their side of the alley. This could be the cover that Ruggerio mentioned. Diaz went behind the pole and crouched down. At that point he could hear running footsteps that got progressively louder. Before his mind could comprehend that someone was rapidly approaching them, a shadowy figure emerged from between two buildings, a distance down the alley and began running at full speed in their direction. When the figure passed under one of the few functioning streetlights, he saw that this individual fit the description of the shooter that had been given out over the radio. Diaz raised his side arm slightly, while Ruggerio was flat against the wall of a building opposite Diaz and in front of him. Ruggerio peered around the corner and assumed a stance that demonstrated that he was poised and ready to challenge the suspect.

Action was imminent and Diaz needed to swallow; he could feel his heart pounding in his ears. Images of shooting someone began to flash in his mind. The sound of rubber soled athletic shoes rapidly pounding on asphalt echoed down the alley. He could hear hard and labored breathing, as the running man got closer. Diaz began to ask himself, when will Ruggerio make his move? What if this guy gets past Ruggerio? What should I do, shoot him? The footsteps were nearly on top of them and Ruggerio was still not moving. What is he waiting for? Go, go, Diaz willed him to move. He could see Ruggerio with his right foot back a short space from his lead foot, and on the toe, similar to a runner in the starting blocks. His legs were bent slightly and his hands, which held no firearm, were in front and above his waist. He was ready to pounce, but he wasn't moving.

Diaz looked back at the running man and saw him suddenly veer toward the weed-infested property. Before he could look over to where Ruggerio was standing, Diaz saw a blur come into his peripheral vision. It was Ruggerio running with his upper body leading the way and his shoulders lowered, just like a linebacker about to tackle a running back squirting through a hole in the defensive line. Diaz rose up a bit in anticipation of something going wrong. He wanted to be ready to react.

The shooting suspect grabbed on to a fence post to swing himself in the direction of the foot path, slowing down to make the turn. This was Ruggerio's opportunity to move in. He closed in from the blind side and like Jack Lambert, he tackled the runner and brought him down into the high weeds. He hit the runner so hard that Diaz could see the white bottoms of the runner's athletic shoes as his feet came off the ground from the crushing blow.

Just as he briefly felt a sensation of relief from seeing Ruggerio take the shooter down, Diaz saw another runner appear in the alley. This one was dressed differently than his partner – a dark, oversized basketball jersey hung down to his knees over a white T-shirt of the same length. He was coming at them at full speed, exactly like the first runner. Just then Diaz remembered Ruggerio's instructions. "Watch my back!" His eyes darted in Ruggerio's direction in the vain hope that Ruggerio would tell him how to handle this new threat. But he was occupied wrestling with the first shooter in the weeds. Diaz would have to handle this on his own. His hands shaking from anxiety and with the fear of events going drastically wrong, he raised his weapon and pointed it at the running figure. Diaz could wait no longer.

"STOP! POLICE!" he shouted.

The runner, stunned by the surprise challenge, slid on the loose pebbles in the alley. Both legs went out from under him and the runner went down on his back end with a thud.

Diaz moved in. "Don't move! Let me see your hands. NOW!" he demanded.

The frightened runner, still lying on the asphalt, raised his hands.

"Don't shoot me. I don't have anything yo," he exclaimed, his voice shaky with fear.

"Roll over and put your hands behind your back," Diaz ordered. The runner complied.

"I don't got nothin'. Don't shoot. I'm not resisting," he implored.

Diaz was breathing heavily as if he had just finished a hundred yard sprint, but in actuality, he had only moved about ten yards from his cover location. He tried to holster his weapon, but it took him three tries to find the holster. He attempted this without looking, keeping his eyes on the suspect, as he had been trained to do, but he found it much more difficult to do in a real life situation than in training. He finally had to look down at his holster to find the right spot and inserted the barrel of his sidearm to secure it. Then he moved in and placed handcuffs on the suspect.

After Ruggerio had handcuffed his own suspect, he looked over to check on his rookie partner.

"You OK?"

"Yeah," he replied breathlessly, kneeling on the back of his arrestee.

"Let's bring them over to the squad," Ruggerio instructed.

They walked their prisoners over to the police car in the gravel lot and instructed both suspects to sit on the ground so the cops could collect more information.

Then he and Diaz called for unit 7-32, the officer who had initiated the call, to obtain a summary of what occurred. That officer reported he had three victims down by gunfire at his location. The next step was to attempt to have the suspects who had just been apprehended positively identified as the shooters. This was of course contingent upon on how severely wounded the victims were and if they were willing to cooperate with the police. In the likely event that the witnesses were not able or not willing to identify the suspects as the shooters, Ruggerio wanted his arrest scene protected so that he could go back and look for any evidence that the suspects may have dropped. He did not want to just turn these two loose without filing any charges against them, especially after taking the kind of risks he and Diaz had taken. After all, what kind of message would that send to the rookie he was training? There already were enough lazy cops on the force. He did not want to create another one right out of the gate.

After leaving an officer to stand by where the arrests were made to protect the scene, Ruggerio and Diaz took their suspects to the 7-32's location. Upon arriving at his location, the gravelly-voiced officer advised that the victims had suffered only superficial wounds and were not in serious condition. As predicted by Ruggerio, the wounded parties were not able to identify the suspects. The initial reporting officer then provided the background on the motive for the shootings to Ruggerio and Diaz. It all emanated from a long-standing feud between the shooter's brother and one of the victims; apparently one individual had somehow disrespected the other. As petty as it sounded, this motivation was somewhat typical of many acts of urban gun violence; the value of respect was highly regarded on the street.

And so to even the score the aggrieved party waits, in some cases several months, for the right opportunity and takes a few shots at the one who insulted him. But in this case, it was not the actual aggrieved party, but his brother. Like this example, most of these cases escalate to the point where the grievance affects all members of the group. Therefore a fire fight could erupt between any particular group members at any time. In the urban setting, life in the eyes of some members of our society is truly cheap.

Victims, usually involved in drug dealing, will rarely assist police even if they have been grievously injured by the perpetrator. The code of the street is that the police are the enemy and if you cooperate with them you may be retaliated against. If you have a problem with someone, you or your crew will take care of the situation—not the police.

Since the victims were of no help, Ruggerio and Diaz went back to the scene of the arrest. The suspects were placed in separate cars, so they could not collaborate on a story. They were not officially under arrest at this point but being held pending further investigation.

"I know that I saw something in my guy's right hand just before I tackled him," Ruggerio told Diaz as they looked around the area for any discarded evidence.

"I have to piss. Where can I go?" Diaz asked, realizing that he hadn't taken care of this necessity.

"Over there," Ruggerio pointed to a spot in the alley behind a dumpster. Ruggerio stood by so no one would disturb Diaz while he relieved himself.

"Wow, sounds like a horse going back there," Ruggerio joked. He wanted to loosen the kid up a little. He could see that Diaz was still tense. Diaz chuckled while he zipped up and thought that Ruggerio didn't seem to be a bad guy after all. He seemed to know what he was doing and he put one hell of a hit on that guy.

"Did you ever play football?" Diaz asked.

"No, just a lot of backyard stuff."

"That was a nice tackle you put on that guy. How did you know that he was going to cut through there?"

"In this section, they like to run into that alley and hit the path where the high weeds are. After the weeds is a small opening between the buildings that leads to the front street. Across the street is a hillside that leads to a residential area where most of the drug dealers live. If he would have made it through that opening we never would have caught him," Ruggerio explained.

"You are going to get an 'A' for today. You did exactly what I told you to do - you watched my back by confronting that second runner. That's the result when partners work as a team. We get the bad guys and no one gets hurt. Good job."

"Thanks," replied Diaz.

Back at the arrest scene, Diaz could see officers using their flashlights to search the ground for discarded contraband in the dimly lit alley. Officers were checking under parked cars, on low rooftops, in catch basins, behind dumpsters and in areas with high vegetation. The items they were looking for could be anywhere and would be relatively small. The dark conditions meant finding any evidence would not be easy.

Ruggerio walked up behind an officer who was looking behind a dumpster with his flashlight. Ruggerio turned his flashlight around so that he was holding the lamp end in his left hand and the six-inch long shaft was pointed forward like a sword. When he got close enough he made a thrusting motion with the flashlight into the rather large buttocks of the searching officer. "Corn hole!" Ruggerio taunted. The officer jumped and shouted out, "WHOA! You jagoff! You almost made me swallow my chew."

It was Officer Toby Tobias, Ruggerio's best friend. Since the first day they had met on the force their personalities clicked and they had been friends ever since. Toby's most common trait would be that he almost always had a generous pinch of Copenhagen tobacco protruding from under his lower lip. He did not disappoint on this particular evening.

Ruggerio gave the introduction. "Toby, this is Taymond Diaz."

"They call me Tay." Diaz shook Toby's hand.

"I shouldn't have done that. Now my flashlight smells," said Ruggerio.

Toby spit out a stream of brown liquid from his mouth. Then looked over at Ruggerio and said, "One of these days I'm gonna turn around and clock you one if you keep pokin' me in the ass like that, you jagoff."

"What's a jagoff?" asked Diaz.

"That's Pittsburghese for jack-off. Don't ask me why," Ruggerio shrugged.

"Did the guy have a gun or did you arrest another innocent person, Guy?" Toby joked.

"I saw something in his right hand. It should be in the weeds somewhere," answered Ruggerio.

Officers were searching the weeds but the property had been neglected for so long that the grass had grown nearly to eye level.

"We may need a metal detector," noted Ruggerio.

Just then the voice of Detective Curt Faust boomed in the alley, "Who's the asshole that caught this perp?"

They called him "Mad Dog" because of his explosive temperament and his aversion to legitimate police work. He was apparently mad that an officer had taken some initiative and actually caught a criminal, thus forcing him to do his job. Although Faust was ten years older, he and Ruggerio had been hired together. But as the years passed, their careers took different paths. Faust was highly ambitious and got close to the right people very early in his career. Faust worshipped at the altar of the old boys club and played the game for all it was worth. He was on the fast track and shot up through the ranks to his present position as a homicide detective.

Faust and Ruggerio had a history, based in an incident five years prior. Faust had been a patrol sergeant at the time, was working on Ruggerio's shift one early morning. Faust, who had never been an active officer as far as making arrests, happened to make one this night. The arrestee was a small frail black man about fifty years old, a local drunk who was a regular on the street. His name was Lonnie Washington and Ruggerio and the other officers on the midnight shift knew him well. Ruggerio and the other regular midnight officers knew that Lonnie was harmless, just a nuisance to them at times.

Lonnie might be seen on any particular night, sleeping on benches or urinating in doorways, never out to hurt anyone. In fact, the most serious thing about Lonnie was his propensity to have a bowel movement anytime or anywhere he felt like it. The officers who knew Lonnie would always take an extra look down at the ground before taking a step around him. More than one officer had experienced one of Lonnie's calling cards squished into the treads of his boots.

On the night that the Faust/Ruggerio feud started, Faust was working an overtime shift with Ruggerio's midnight crew. Since Faust's political contacts afforded him the luxury of a permanent daylight shift, he normally didn't work with Ruggerio. Not being a regular on this shift, he did not know Lonnie as well as the other officers.

On this particular night, when Faust arrested Lonnie, Lonnie had taken another crap, this time in the alley behind the restaurant where Faust ate his free lunch every day. To Faust, this was like

someone taking a crap in his own living room. Faust knew that if
he didn't take some action and the restaurant owner thought that
a vagrant was squatting behind his business, the free lunch practice
might come to an abrupt end. So he dutifully made Lonnie clean
up his mess, arrested him, and brought the poor wino to the station
for processing.

If Faust wasn't pissed off enough already, at the station he noticed
that Lonnie had gotten some feces on his handcuffs. Ruggerio
was at the station with two other officers when Faust exploded
on Lonnie. He grabbed the still handcuffed one hundred and ten
pound wino by the throat and lifted him off the ground, pushing
him against a wall with his feet dangling in midair. Faust was a
weightlifter and bragged to everybody on the force about how
strong he was. So, lifting the skeletal body of Lonnie Washington
was not very difficult.

Ruggerio saw that Lonnie could not breathe, but wasn't sure
if he should step in. Interfering with another officer in this type
of situation can be a dangerous thing. The mediating officer could
be tagged with the reputation as a bleeding heart cop, and this
would not sit well with the more abusive cops like Faust. This
type of label could make life difficult within the department for
the interfering officer.

Faust was also laying a heavy dose of profanity on Lonnie while
he was choking the life out of him.

"You motherfucker, you got shit on my cuffs. I should kill you
right now, you fuckin' asshole!"

Ruggerio could see the rage in Faust's eyes, much too wicked
and exaggerated for the situation. Lonnie was starting to lose
consciousness and Ruggerio could see his eyes rolling back in their
sockets. He was getting worried not just for Lonnie but for himself

also. He was imagining himself in some future courtroom sitting on the witness stand at Lonnie's homicide trial, testifying about what he saw when a suspect arrested for public drunkenness was choked to death in the police station. He didn't like the thought of some prosecutor asking him why he idly stood by and watched the whole incident play out without lifting a finger to stop it. Of course, no one else in the area was moving to stop it, so Ruggerio made the decision. He grabbed Faust by the arm and said, "OK, Sarge. That's enough."

Faust flailed his arm free from Ruggerio's grip. "Don't you touch me you greasy Dago."

To most full-blooded Italians like Ruggerio, that word Dago is a hot button. And also like most Italians, Ruggerio had a pretty bad temper when provoked. Having lifted a few weights in his day also, Ruggerio grabbed Faust by the collar and pulled him off of Lonnie. Lonnie fell to the floor unconscious as his head struck the ground with a thud.

Faust turned and began cocking his right fist back to deliver a punch to Ruggerio's face. Ruggerio, moving quickly, side-stepped Faust's punch. Simultaneously, he swept Faust's feet out from under him by using his right leg and kicking backward from behind at about knee height. In the same motion, he grabbed Faust by his throat with his right hand and pushed backward, laying Faust flat on his back on the floor. Some other officers stepped in at this point and held the two from engaging any further.

The incident was not reported since Ruggerio didn't really do anything wrong and probably would have had to file excessive force and assault charges against Faust. He was not a snitch and did not bring the incident to higher command. But Faust wouldn't let it go and rejected Ruggerio's attempts to patch things up. In fact, Faust kept promising to finish the fight that, in Faust's eyes, Ruggerio had started. Thus the feud perpetuated and like most feuds that are not settled, it festered and eventually turned from mere dislike into hatred.

Back at the arrest scene, Ruggerio answered Faust's rhetorical question, "I'm the asshole who was doing his job," he said defiantly. Ruggerio was not one to take anything from anyone. Besides, he had Faust pegged from the start; he was the classic bully, all talk no action.

Faust acted as if he didn't hear the statement and started to walk away.

"Just what I need, another case to add to my fifty other ones. Just let these assholes shoot each other," he said to the other detective who was with him.

"What's that guy's problem?" Diaz asked Ruggerio.

"You mean besides being a class-A number-one asshole? He and I don't get along. He probably knew that I was the one that made this pinch. That's why he came in here breathing fire, just to see if I would take his shit."

"What is the problem between you two?"

While they continued to look for the missing gun, Ruggerio told Diaz the story about Lonnie and how ever since that day, he and Faust had been enemies.

Just then, Toby called out, "I got it. It was in the seam of the dumpster lids."

"How the hell did it get there?" asked Diaz.

"I guess when I hit the guy it flew out of his hand and landed on top of the dumpster," Ruggerio concluded, shining his flashlight on the gun that was nestled between the black plastic dual lids on the dumpster. The gun was black and was nearly invisible against the plastic covers.

"Just goes to show you the weird things that can happen out here, right kid?" Ruggerio hit Diaz on the arm, playfully. "Toby, call Inspector Clueless over so he can collect the gun," Ruggerio requested, referring to Faust.

"Sure you don't want to ask him? I am sure you guys want to sit down together and have a private meeting about this case," Toby joked, following with another long brown stream of tobacco juice spit on the ground.

"Just go get him, dick-weed," Ruggerio said.

"Hey Guy!" another officer called out to Ruggerio. "We found some crack on the guy your partner caught."

"Good, two for two. Not bad for your first night," Ruggerio smiled at Diaz. "Let's go to the station and start the paperwork."

CHAPTER 2

Bang, bang, bang, bang. The pounding at the door could hardly be heard over the thumping rap music playing inside the fraternity house. Two frat brothers sat in the living room, smoking marijuana and listening to hip-hop. They looked at each other when they heard the pounding.

"Only cops pound on a door like that. Hide the herb!" one of the brothers said with urgency. This was a black fraternity at the university, and the campus police had visited several times before as they had most frats. The harsh pounding on the door seemed to say, you better get this door open or it is coming off the hinges. Both brothers scrambled around to find a good hiding spot, but before they could spray air freshener around the room to mask the odor, the door was opening.

An affluent-looking white man, wearing a light blue golf shirt, beige Dockers and brown leather loafers, stepped in. He looked to be about fifty years old. What was left of his once-blond hair was concentrated around the perimeter of his head. He was obviously not a cop. With his style of clothes and tanned skin, he screamed high society. He looked panicked and his eyes searched desperately for someone. The man saw the two frat brothers in the living room and watched as one of them went over to the stereo and turned the rap music down.

"What you doin' runnin' up in here like that?" one frat brother said.

"Where's my daughter, Lauren Wilkes?"

"Man, we don't know no Lauren Wilkes. You got the wrong house. Now get on out of here!" said the second frat brother, the one who had lowered the music.

"Her boyfriend is Jamar Dickson. Now I know this is his frat house. Where is he?" the father said, moving closer to the boys.

Thomas Wilkes was not a fighter, even though he was known as being a ruthless lawyer. Grilling witnesses on the stand until they shed tears was not the same as taking on two twenty-year-old college kids in peak physical condition. Nonetheless, he was finding his daughter, even if it meant taking a beating from these young studs.

Lauren Wilkes had been dating a black man, Jamar Dickson, and Thomas Wilkes did not approve. It wasn't so much that Dickson was black but that he didn't seem to have the prospects ahead of him that Thomas Wilkes wanted for his daughter. Dickson was enrolled in pre-law courses, but was a semester away from being expelled for academic reasons. Since he knew the dean of the school, Thomas Wilkes had been able to get a peek at Dickson's grades. The dean and Wilkes both belonged to the same country club.

Lauren Wilkes is in her third year of college, but attended a small private college nearby. She lived at home while taking her courses. She had met Jamar Dickson at a mixer and they had been dating ever since. On the previous night, Thomas Wilkes had told his daughter that he did not want her seeing Dickson any longer. She stormed out of the house and Thomas knew where to go looking for her the next day when she didn't return home. Dickson was taking summer classes to make up some courses that he had failed during the regular session. He was living at this frat house, another bit of inside information Thomas was able to get his hands on through his connections.

"We don't know any Jamar. Now you get your white ass out of here," said the first frat brother. He lifted his shirt up a bit and placed one hand slightly into his waistband, as if he had a gun concealed.

Thomas began to think that he might have overstepped his bounds. Maybe this was a situation for the police. He immediately backed up. "OK, but this isn't the last you will hear from me."

"Just get on out of here and go back to Cracker Land. You don't belong here," said the frat brother who hadn't made the gun gesture.

Thomas went outside, quickly scampered to his BMW and pulled away from the curb. The frat brothers, watching the old white guy run to his car, doubled over with laughter at their successful ploy.

After playfully bumping into each other while still laughing and giving congratulatory high fives, the first brother began to mock Thomas by trying to imitate the white man's voice, "This isn't the last you will hear from me." More laughing and playful hip checks as the two friends enjoyed the moment.

Then the second brother, while still chuckling, said to the other, "Cracker Land, where did you get that from—a 50 Cent movie?" The first brother replied, "Yeah I wish I knew some gang signs. Hey, you think he would ever believe that I hold down a 3.8 QPA and you're an English Lit major?"

Upon hearing this statement, the first brother quickly developed a serious expression on his face and then exclaimed, the way a teenage girl might, "OH! I gotta get this down in my journal." Thomas went to the end of the block and called the campus police, who arrived in a matter of minutes. He explained the situation but because his daughter was of legal age, there wasn't anything the police could do. With his legal background, though, Thomas realized that maybe he could get the police to act after all.

"Officers, while I was inside the frat I could smell a heavy odor of marijuana and one of the boys inside motioned as if he had a gun in his waistband. I'll even sign a statement and have my name placed on a search warrant." Thomas knew that they would have to act now.

One of the officers surprised Wilkes by his next question.

"Sir, were you permitted entry into the house or did you walk in uninvited?"

Thomas Wilkes didn't think a cop, especially a campus cop, would be this sharp. Thomas knew that if he told the officer how he made entry, without being invited inside, that his observations of smelling marijuana smoke and the gun gesture would be inadmissible in court. It would be the equivalent of an illegal search by a police officer, and, in actuality he would be admitting to committing the crime of trespassing. Therefore, in order for the police to use his information, Thomas had to lie.

Of course for Thomas Wilkes, lying was second nature. He has been coloring the truth to get his way in court for years. Besides, Thomas rationalized, I did hear the boys yell something. It could have been "come in," for all I know. He smiled to himself. How ironic, he thought. Things that I have been accusing cops of doing for years, I'm now doing myself. But in my case, I know that this is for the best.

"Yes, officer, one of the boys said, 'come in,' when I knocked on the door. When they saw that it was me they must have realized that I might report the marijuana use, so they told me to leave."

"OK, sir. Before we do anything, I want a written statement completed," the officer requested sternly, realizing that he was being placed into a possibly precarious situation.

"No problem, Officer," replied Thomas.

Thomas completed the statement in his car. The officers approached the frat house after both agreed to try to reason with the frat members first. The campus cops knew what was going on. This Wilkes guy only wanted his daughter back home. They could have gone to the station to fill out a search warrant, taken the warrant application to a district justice and had the warrant issued, but that would have taken about two or three hours. The officers reasoned that most likely they would have found maybe an ounce or so of marijuana, if they were lucky—nothing of much consequence. The gun thing was probably made up by Wilkes to make the situation sound more urgent than it really was. The cops both knew some of the frat members of this house and they were not the way Wilkes was portraying them. Both officers agreed that Wilkes's statement was less than creditable. No reason to stick one's neck out if all he wanted was to locate his daughter. Why waste the time with a bogus search warrant?

At the door, the officers explained the situation to the two boys Thomas Wilkes had met earlier. They said that Jamar Dickson did live there, but neither was sure if Dickson was in his room at the time. The officers asked to enter and check Dickson's room. The frat brothers agreed and showed the officers to Dickson's room on the second floor. The officers could hear Rhythm and Blues music from inside the room. The heavy oak door was closed, but the officers could still smell marijuana smoke filtering through. They stood there a while and listened, in no rush to knock just yet. They could hear a girl's voice in the room, but no sounds of danger or distress. They knocked on the door.

"Who's that?" Dickson said from inside.

"Campus police. Open the door," one officer responded.

The officers could hear shuffling around in the room, well aware that the occupants were hiding or ditching the dope. The police didn't have to knock. They could have just gone inside the room when they first detected the odor of marijuana, but the officers choose not to at that point. They were there for a different objective and they wanted cooperation from Dickson, so they decided to take the soft approach again.

Once they heard what sounded like an attempt to hide or destroy evidence, they both knew they had to make entry before all the dope was discarded or hidden. Besides, cooperation sometimes requires a little incentive, and a possession of marijuana charge could provide the cooperation they were looking for.

The officers opened the door, which wasn't locked, and found Dickson and Lauren Wilkes throwing small plastic baggies filled with green vegetable matter out of the window. One officer grabbed Dickson and threw him onto the bed. The other took Lauren by the arm and moved her carefully but firmly away from the window. Jamar Dickson complained, "That's illegal! You pigs can't come in here like that! Do you have a warrant?"

Lauren made her feelings known as well. "Take your damn hands off of me, you dumb-ass pig!"

"Just relax. We're really not here for the dope, and we were invited into the house. We could smell the marijuana smoke from outside your door, Mr. Dickson. We don't need a warrant," one of the officers said, trying to enlighten the wide-eyed pre-law student. Dickson bounced to his feet. His machismo dictated that he had to save face in front of his girlfriend and demonstrate that he could not let a cop manhandle him--especially a white cop!

"Don't you put your hands on me again," Dickson threatened.

"Listen," the big cop who had pushed Dickson said, "we don't want any trouble. We just needed to talk to Ms. Wilkes."

Dickson had his chest puffed out; his hands were down at his sides and clenched into two rigid fists. He was trying to show his manhood, like a dog baring its teeth to protect its territory.

"You don't come in my crib and not have a warrant. I'm pre-law. I know the rules. I want you out!" Dickson shouted.

The big cop was losing his patience, but knew that he should try to calm the young man down. At the same time, he reasoned that if this kid didn't settle down in the next few minutes, he was going face first onto this bedroom floor. "Mr. Dickson, give us a few minutes to explain and we will soon be out of your hair."

Dickson was not backing down. In fact, he moved a little closer to the bigger officer. Another step and the officer would have to take some action. In this confined space, he couldn't permit someone to get that close.

"Dickson, I'm warning you, just back off a step or..." That was it. Dickson made the final move that sealed his fate for this day. Before the big cop could finish his sentence Dickson closed in to about three feet to the officer. This was just too close for the officer to be tactically safe. He needed to make a move. He knew that he could make an arrest because there was still a baggy of dope sitting on the bed in an upside down frisbee, just like when the cop was in school in the eighties.

The bigger officer reached out toward Dickson and grabbed his right arm. He put Dickson in an arm bar and easily wheeled him down to the floor, face-first. Dickson was really not a fighter and the cop could see this in his eyes. The officer had been in a few scraps in his day and could size up an opponent. After a while, an officer can usually predict when he will have a rough time with an arrest. But in this situation, the officer didn't see much of a fight coming from Dickson.

Dickson only wanted to make a stand for his girlfriend's sake. His true intentions were to submit eventually to the officer's commands. So he was shocked that the officer was actually going to arrest him. He didn't think that he pushed the officer too far. He had intended to back down soon, figuring he had made enough of a show to convince his girl that he was a man and was not afraid of the police.

The officer manipulated his arrestee to put Dickson's hands behind his back and handcuffed him in expert fashion.

"You assholes leave him alone. My father is an attorney we will have your jobs for this!" Lauren warned.

The second officer saw his chance to set the girl straight. It was moments like this that cops live for. "Is that right? Now who is your father?"

"You'll find out, damn rent-a-cops!" she said with contempt.

"Let me guess. Could he be Thomas Wilkes, attorney at law, who is standing outside on the sidewalk by his BMW right now?" It was obvious that he was enjoying this moment.

Lauren now understood the real reason why the cops were there, so she closed her mouth and sat down in an easy chair behind her. The officers secured the marijuana and began to walk the two young people out of the room.

The big cop asked Dickson as he was walking him down the hallway from his room, "Whose dope is this, Jamar?"

"Fuck you, man. I don't know what you're talking about," Dickson said defiantly.

"OK, we will just have to charge both of you with it. That's called constructive possession, in case you haven't gotten to that part in your studies. Might as well make this a learning experience while we're at it, don't you think Jamar?" the bigger cop cajoled.

"OK tough guy. It's my dope. Let her go," Dickson allowed.

"Good enough. I can respect that," the big cop said.

The cops walked both parties through the frat house and out the front door. Lauren was crying, now that her boyfriend was going to jail, but she still kept haranguing the police.

"You dumb-asses couldn't find a real job, so you had to be rent-a-cops. Leave him alone. Why don't you go pick on real criminals? We weren't bothering anybody."

Then she saw her father outside standing by his car. The crisp, polished, black paint on the Beamer showed bright in the sunlight, almost as shiny as Thomas's scalp.

"I'm not going home with you, Dad. They're going to have to lock me up, too."

Thomas went over to Lauren and tried taking her by the arm. "Lauren, don't make a scene now. You need to come with me." He was speaking to as if she were twelve years old, not twenty.

The officers put Dickson in the back of their patrol car. Lauren began banging on the rear window, shouting, "Jamar, I love you."

The officers took Lauren by the arms and moved her away from the police car. They figured the best thing to do now was to get into their car and drive off and leave Thomas Wilkes to take care of his daughter. The bigger officer was driving the car and looked back in his rearview mirror to see Lauren kneeling in the middle of the street, waving at the car and crying Jamar's name as they drove away.

Jamar Dickson was fuming as he sat with his hands cuffed behind him in the back of the police car. These damn white pigs had manhandled him and made him look weak in front of his girl. Lauren's father had brought the police to his frat house, which proved to Dickson that he was a racist. He could not believe the lengths Thomas Wilkes had just gone to in order to get his precious daughter away from the dirty black man. His mind raged with hate and anger at his situation and the people who had unjustly put him here. Dickson's thoughts evolved to images of his own father and the years of neglect and uncaring treatment that Jamar had experienced with him.

Dickson figured that his father would not care in the least to hear that his son had been arrested and treated so unfairly. If Jamar called his father now for help with these criminal charges, he would only say that Jamar deserved what he got, and to be man and handle the situation himself.

Jamar Dickson's father, Rudy Dickson, was a self-made man. He grew up in the Hill District of Pittsburgh and fought his way out by working hard in school and earning a scholarship to Carnegie Mellon University. He achieved a computer science degree and landed a job at the best high-tech firm in the region. He quickly moved up in the ranks and now sat on the board of directors. Rudy

Dickson was a millionaire several times over and wanted his son to follow in his footsteps.

This was not to be. No matter how hard he tried, Jamar could not live up to his father's expectations. Rudy was severely disappointed; he thought Jamar wasn't trying hard enough and that his son was just plain lazy. Jamar tried computer science, but flunked out after two semesters. Then, he attempted engineering, but that ended with the same result. Now, it was pre-law and it was only a matter of time before he either dropped out or was expelled for poor grades.

Jamar Dickson didn't care, though. He had never wanted to go to college. His true passion was to be a musician. He loved playing the drums and wanted to play jazz music in a rhythm and blues band someday. But, in an act of tough love his father got rid of Jamar's drum set when he was fifteen, promising to give them back when his grades improved. That would never happen. Even though he was intelligent, Jamar was just not interested in academics. He hadn't played the drums since and hated his father ever since for taking them away. He could still feel the hurt as if it were happening all over again. Someday, Jamar promised himself, he would find a way to hurt his father just as severely.

Taymond Diaz wheeled the squad car around the parking lot of the police station as he and Ruggerio were leaving to begin their patrol shift. It was late August and nearly two months since Diaz had joined the force and started riding with Ruggerio. At first, Diaz was not sure if he would like this job. He felt very apprehensive about working as a cop. He felt the same way about his training officer and many of the other officers in the department. Diaz felt uneasy being a minority working in a largely white police department located in a largely white region. In Western Pennsylvania, the Hispanic population was very small—and Diaz's mixture of half Hispanic and half African-American was even more scarce.

Slowly however, Diaz came to see Ruggerio and his fellow officers as being essentially colorblind and eager to help him learn the ins and outs of police work. Although a few subtly racist remarks were made from time to time, Diaz became more at ease as the days passed. Ruggerio told him that being Italian was not exactly popular either, even in this day and age. Pittsburgh has a large elderly population and some of the old ethnic prejudices still emerge from time to time. But he assured Diaz that most of the guys who work the street could care less what color their back-up is, just as long as they do their jobs.

Ruggerio was glad that the city was recruiting minorities. The department was severely lacking in this area. He wondered if the department would be open to promoting minorities to higher positions in the department, especially positions in the investigative branches. Right now most detectives were white; many of them were finding it very difficult to gather credible information from minority citizens during their investigations of violent crimes. An increase of minorities in these positions would make the investigators more approachable to the community where these crimes typically take place.

But Ruggerio was not too optimistic about this happening, because detective positions were highly coveted and almost exclusively awarded to those who played the political game, officers who sought to further their police careers by supporting candidates behind the scenes as they campaigned for regional offices. This was how Curt "Mad dog" Faust had gotten to his lofty position in the department.

Guy Ruggerio could not see himself selling out like that to get promotions, even though moving up in the department would help to level the playing field with Faust. He knew that receiving favors from politicians always had a price tag, and he could not stomach having to do someone's dirty work. Better to stay in uniform and keep his self-respect.

The disadvantage to having little political influence, while engaged in a feud with a vengeful psycho like Faust, is that you have to sit back and take all the abuse that is dished out. Some of the trivial jabs that "Mad dog" had directed at Ruggerio largely concerned irrelevant infractions of departmental policies. Using his political allies, Faust leveled minor charges against Ruggerio like leaving his patrol zone without first receiving permission, or hanging out too long in a coffee shop on a cold winter night even though there were practically no calls. The topper of them all was when he accused Ruggerio of exceeding his duties by investigating a rape incident.

Faust made the allegation against Ruggerio that he was doing the job of a detective when he conducted several interviews while completing his preliminary investigation into the rape of a fourteen-year-old girl. Of course the charges were summarily dismissed, but Ruggerio still had to go through the aggravation of a hearing before several department supervisors to clear his name. This was the routine year after year as the simmering feud between the two officers continued. Ruggerio had to take these types of things in stride. When Faust saw the chance to take a shot, he took it without letting conscience slow him down. But as the years and the list of allegations leveled by Faust against him piled higher, Guy

Ruggerio was starting to feel the effects of being the target of so many attacks. It was only a matter of time until something had to give on the embattled cop.

"Hey, Guy, I hope this isn't too forward, but I have to ask you something," Diaz asked delicately.

"Go ahead, unless you're going to ask me if I like show tunes," Ruggerio said with a chuckle.

"Nah. I've heard from some of the other guys that this Faust guy really hates you. Is he like that with everyone? I just want to get along with everyone and I wanted to know if I need to watch my back around this guy."

"Don't worry, kid. You'll be OK. Just do your job the way you think is right. If anyone has a problem with that, then just keep your distance. You can't please everyone. If there is one thing about this job, it's that you're going to make enemies no matter what you do. A guy like Faust has an inferiority complex. He needs someone to put down because it makes him feel better about himself. If it wasn't me, someone else would be his punching bag. I actually feel sorry for him, to walk around with that kind of hate has to be a miserable existence. I mean, what kind of life is that to wait around for the next opportunity to take another shot at your enemies? Guys like Faust have so many enemies; he has to keep watching his back all the time. He is probably always on edge, waiting for the day when someone will come up and blind side him with some charges of their own."

"It has to be tough for you to have someone against you like that. He sure has some connections, from what I hear," Diaz said.

"I won't lie to you. There are times when I have been tempted to cozy up to one of those bigwigs to get some political juice myself so that I can return some fire to that bloated bag of gas. But

I calm down and realize that I wasn't raised that way. My place is out of the spotlight where I can work the street, help people when I can, and then go home to my wife. As long as I have that, I am just fine," proclaimed Ruggerio proudly.

Diaz thought to himself, is this guy for real or is he putting me on? That kind of corny, "I want to help people" is sixties flower-child stuff. The irony was that Diaz felt the same way; he just didn't think he would meet anyone else on the force who would actually say it out loud. Since he's been riding with Ruggerio, Diaz is freer to act on his feelings. Maybe Guy really does take his job seriously?

Diaz noted an example that he had witnessed during his time as Ruggerio's trainee. One particular night on a drunk and disorderly call, Diaz saw Ruggerio show more patience than he ever thought possible. The drunk simply refused to listen to Ruggerio's requests. He told the drunk to come down from the porch where the boozer was sitting, smoking a cigarette and had recently vomited. The homeowners had called when they saw a strange man sitting on their porch. The drunk told Ruggerio that he wasn't leaving the porch, and that Ruggerio and the other cop were the ones who were trespassing.

It took Diaz a few minutes to figure it out, but he finally realized why Ruggerio had not gone up on the porch, snatched the intox squatter up and arrested him. The truth was revealed after some insightful questioning by Guy.

Ruggerio asked the intruder where he lived and the color of his house. The drunk said it was green. This house where the subject was now located had light blue siding, which may have looked green at night to a bleary-eyed drunkard. The defiant intox had simply gone to the wrong house by mistake in his impaired state. Ruggerio found his correct address on the drunk's driver's license and the two officers escorted him home. He even thanked them for their courtesy as they left.

Diaz came to admire and respect Ruggerio. After observing him interact with members of the community, he realized that this is what a cop is supposed to be like. His personal conception of the ideal police officer was a community advocate, an extension of the neighborhood, co-existing with people as a common stakeholder as they collectively strive for success. He did not expect to actually meet an officer who mirrored his own ideals, let alone to be partners with him. It must be divine intervention. Diaz's father would have thought so and maybe he would be right. Maybe God orchestrated this arrangement to show Diaz his true calling?

CHAPTER 3

Thomas Wilkes peered out the windows of the French doors that lead to an in-ground pool in his backyard. He was pleased to see that the sun was still shining. The forecast was partly cloudy with a chance of rain today, which, in Western Pennsylvania, is the forecast almost every day. He was looking forward to a round of golf that he had scheduled at the country club and hoped that the rain clouds would not interfere. Thomas had on his lucky Arnold Palmer golf shirt, the one he'd worn when he beat Judge Holmes and won a thousand dollars. The judge was a law school classmate of Thomas's and they'd had a friendly rivalry ever since—with a degree of seriousness that made their meetings a little more interesting.

Thomas Wilkes was fiercely competitive and couldn't wait to get another chance to wax Holmes at golf again. He remembered how mad Holmes had become the last time, losing by only one stroke. This time, the stakes were increased to fifteen hundred dollars—but the money wasn't important to Thomas. It was seeing the look of utter frustration on Holmes's face as he wrote out a check to pay his debt. That was what Thomas really enjoyed.

Thomas Wilkes loved to show his dominance over other people, especially in the courtroom. The moment a jury came in and delivered a not guilty verdict acquitting one of his clients, he struggled to hold in his overwhelming joy. And with equal delight, he enjoyed the look of total despair on the assistant district attorney's face when such a verdict was read. Thomas could almost hear his opponent asking himself, how did I lose? The evidence presented was overwhelming, so how could the jury find this defendant not guilty?

Meanwhile, little would the prosecutor know that Thomas Wilkes usually had the deck stacked before he even entered a courtroom. To win a case, Thomas had several options – using a judge who was a close friend, paying off a key witness to alter his story, or, in extreme cases, rigging the jury. He had exercised all of these tactics in the past.

Just like today. Thomas had the caddy waiting in the wings at the country club. For two hundred dollars this caddy, Thomas's favorite, would make sure that he worked in his round with Judge Holmes. The caddy had made all the necessary preparations so that Thomas's golf ball would not be found out-of-bounds. If Thomas couldn't find his ball, the caddy would have one ready in his pocket to be dropped in a moment's notice. Just like the last time.

Just then, Thomas heard something hit the side of the house. It sounded like a stone thrown against one of the second floor windows. He looked out the living room window on to his perfectly landscaped lawn. He thought he saw something moving in the shrubbery. Thomas first thought that it could be Dickson because, after all, Lauren's second floor bedroom window was located on this side of the house. He decided to wait him out and keep watch on the area.

There! There it was again. Thomas saw the trees rustle. Then an arm making a throwing motion. A black skinned hand emerged from the sleeve, then the crack against Lauren's window.

"That fucking darkie just can't get enough," Thomas said aloud to himself. He grabbed the phone and called 9-1-1 to report a prowler. Thomas couldn't believe how stupid Dickson was, coming right to the house in broad daylight.

Wait a minute! Thomas originally had told Lauren that he would be golfing at one o'clock and it was now two. Lauren was not aware that the judge had called earlier and asked to have the tee time changed to three o'clock. Of course, since she slept until this time every day, she wasn't up to see that her father was still home.

Lauren Wilkes and Jamar Dickson knew that they had to be discreet. Lauren was aware that while her father was out of house, he would have his private detective watching to ensure that she did not sneak out to see Dickson.

Thomas was pretty proud of this strategy. First, he placed an order against Dickson for him to stay at least a hundred yards away from Lauren and the same distance away from their house. Getting a domestic protection order was extremely easy, but just in case, Thomas had the order worded to make it appear as if Dickson was causing Lauren physical and mental harm. And to add some extra juice, he used the minor pot arrest at the college to make it look like Dickson was a drug dealer. Thomas also had his private investigator place listening devices on the phones. The detective had been ordered to follow Lauren around while she went to school and back. In the time since the pot incident at Dickson's college, the PI had not seen Lauren and Dickson meet. However, he had seen her use a pay phone yesterday. The PI's report on that phone call speculated that the couple might have been arranging a clandestine meeting.

Thomas was still on the phone with the 9-1-1 operator while he played out in his mind the scenario of how Lauren had orchestrated this meeting with Dickson.

"Can you describe the prowler, Sir?" the female 9-1-1 dispatcher asked Thomas.

"I can do better than that. His name is Jamar Dickson. He is my daughter's ex-boyfriend and there is a protection order against him, which he is in violation of at this time."

"Can you provide a physical description so I can advise the units proceeding to your residence, Sir?" the operator said with monotone efficiency.

"Yes, of course. He is a black male, about five-nine, thin, about 22 years old, with short, black hair. I cannot see him right now, so I can't tell you what he is wearing."

"Yes sir. Thank you. Please stay on the line until the units arrive," the operator requested.

"Sure. No problem."

Suddenly Thomas saw Dickson emerge from the well-groomed shrubbery. He walked nearer to Lauren's second floor window and shouted up to her.

"Lauren, are you up there? Come to the window, Baby!"

"He just approached the house! Where are those damn cops?" Thomas snarled to the 9-1-1 operator.

"They are pulling up now, Sir. Which side of the residence is the suspect located?" she asked, again with no emotion.

"North side. He is wearing a blue jacket that is opened and a red and blue striped shirt and brown slacks. Hurry or he'll get away!" Thomas was insistent. He wanted Dickson to suffer for so brazenly defying a court order and violating his personal property.

Thomas saw a uniformed officer circling around the east side of his house approaching the side where Dickson was still standing and calling up to Lauren, in a more muffled tone. He appeared to be speaking with her.

Stupid cops, Thomas thought. The moment Dickson sees the one circling around he will run the other way. Actually he can run in any one of several directions and still get away. Why did they only send one guy? If Dickson gets away, I'm calling the chief of police and heads will roll. Besides, I pay enough taxes. The one day that I need the cops, they have to screw it up. How can you bungle something as easy as this? Dickson is practically asking to be caught.

What Thomas did not realize was the officers had set up a little trap. One officer would smoke out the suspect, while two other officers would stand by waiting for the suspect to come running along one of the escape routes. In reserve was a K-9 officer driving in his car on a parallel street, just in case the suspect eluded the first officers nearest the house. Simple as it may sound, the plan was eloquent in execution. The officers really didn't need much time to set this plan in motion. These particular officers had performed this maneuver hundreds of times, usually on midnight shifts involving much more desperate and dangerous criminals than Jamar Dickson. Since the officers did not know how dangerous this suspect could be, the safest course of action was to expect and prepare for the worst.

Dickson thought he heard something around the corner of the house.

"Hurry up. You know that I can't be here," he said to Lauren, who was leaning out her open window to tell him that she was coming.

Then Dickson saw a face look around the corner. The officer did what is known as a "quick peek." The officer had taken a quick glance around the corner of the house to minimize his exposure. But Dickson saw the officer and ran in the opposite direction.

"West!" the officer shouted to his colleague, alerting him that the suspect was coming his way.

The officer on the west side was behind a tree and saw Dickson approaching. But the front yard was expansive and gave Dickson a great deal of room to maneuver. He was running through the front yard on a line that was a good thirty yards from the officer behind the tree. This distance gave Dickson a greater advantage over the officer.

Although this particular officer thought he was in pretty good shape for forty-three, Dickson was much younger and wasn't carrying around ten extra pounds of equipment. In addition, strange as it may sound, Dickson actually had what might be considered an advantage of being the hunted one. Like in the wild, the prey being chased can garner up the extra energy to out run or out-fight their pursuers when their lives are in the balance. It's the physiological effect from the adrenalin dump known as the fight or flight response.

The officer had to make a move and hope for the best.

"Police! Stop!" he ordered as he quickly advanced to close in on the running suspect.

Dickson's eyes widened with shock. He hadn't expected to see someone coming at him from that direction, but he quickly recovered. Spurred on by this sudden rush of adrenaline, Dickson jetted passed the officer and kept on running through the front yard. He ran out on to the street then headed south, away from the two officers pursing him.

Immediately, the officer who had previously been on the west side of the residence radioed the route that Dickson was taking to the K-9 car. The K-9 officer was two blocks south of Dickson. He immediately took his dog out of the car, a ninety-pound five-year-old German shepherd imported from The Netherlands named Max. Max and his handler were closer than blood brothers. And Max absolutely loved chasing bad guys. In fact, the handler had to quiet Max down so he could hear the radio and the direction of the running suspect over Max's yelping. The dog became so excited at the possibility of going on the hunt that he couldn't contain himself. Max had been around long enough to know all the signs and was well aware that the game was afoot. When he heard all the radio chatter, coupled with his handler's anxious tone, Max knew that action was imminent.

The handler gave a Dutch command for Max to settle down. *"Regel, Maxy, regel."* (Easy, Maxy, easy.) Max had been trained in The Netherlands and only knew his commands in Dutch. So, Max's handler had to learn these commands while training with his new partner. He opened the back door to the K-9 sport utility vehicle, marked "Caution Police K-9 Unit."

Max's handler was Quinton O'Neal, a red-haired Irishman with a bushy, whisk broom-like mustache that he grew to camouflage some of the freckles that covered his face and almost his entire body. O'Neal had always been self-conscious of all the freckles, starting back in grade school, when the other kids used to tease him. Quint would seek out activities that let him cover up as much skin as possible—like football, which allowed him to express himself while practically covering his whole body in padding and a uniform.

Quint was good at it, too. At six-two he was an ideal choice to play as a lineman on his high school football team. So good, in fact, he received a football scholarship to West Virginia University, where he had played until injuring his knee, thus putting an early end to a promising career. Depressed, Quint left school and returned home to Pittsburgh to decide what to do with the rest of his life.

When the Metro Force had started hiring cops, Quint jumped at the opportunity. Like football, being a police officer seemed to fit Quint's personality. He'd be relatively anonymous by blending in as one member of a large organization. At the same time, he'd put his physical attributes to good use—even with the bad knee.

After joining the force he had been assigned to work the midnight shift, being junior in seniority. It worked well for Quint. Fewer people out and about on the streets, which made him feel more relaxed than during the hustle and bustle of the other shifts. Even though he had outgrown most of his insecurities, some self-doubt still lingered and the relative solitude of the midnight shift suited him. Quint didn't have a large circle of intimate friends. When he was asked to become a K-9 handler, he eagerly accepted, subconsciously realizing that he was filling the void that a close friend would have been in his life.

After Quint popped the cargo door open, he quickly hooked the lead on Max's collar, while the dog panted and jostled. Then he told Max to come out and gave him another command in Dutch to be ready. The chasing officers relayed over the radio that the suspect was still headed south. Quint knew that a runner usually would not run in a straight line for long. So he decided to move in with Max to close the gap and try to cut down the angle before this perp decided to turn right or left. Quint led Max away from the SUV to the street and commanded his partner to stay close and settle.

"*OK Maxy regel, regel.*" Quint stroked Max's fur to help calm the dog.

As he and Max moved toward the direction of the chase, Max was getting more excited. He was barking now and the fur on his back between his front shoulders was raised up to make him look larger. An instinctive reaction that harkened back to Max's ancestors, the intent was to make the dog's body appear larger to intimidate adversaries. Froth was forming at the corners of his mouth and spraying out the sides when he barked and jostled his head up and down.

Quint then told Max to get ready. "*Klaar Max.*"

Max was highly trained and his demeanor was just right for the situation. He didn't need to be jazzed up to be ready for action and he was still firmly under the control of his handler and would obey any command. If Quint saw that the suspect was apprehended, he would command Max to stand down and the animal would return to a calm but alert posture as he had been trained to do. On the other hand, if necessary, Max would engage in mortal combat to protect his handler from any threats. There was a deep-rooted companionship between a dog and its handler, especially in police work.

Quint suddenly saw Dickson coming as expected and started running with Max toward Dickson.

"Police! Stop or I will release the dog!" It was required that this warning be given to the suspect in the hope that he would come to his senses and stop before a police dog was unleashed. Even though no human can out run a conditioned and well-trained police dog, Quint had never seen a running suspect heed the warning to stop, and Dickson followed this trend. Since this was a felony criminal trespass, it was permissible to use a police dog to capture the suspect. Since police dogs have the potential to inflict severe injury on suspects, they are not permitted to be used for apprehending criminals suspected of less serious crimes.

Quint gave the retrieve command. *"Max win terug!"*

Max shot free of his handler like a bullet from the barrel of a gun. Max wasn't barking now. He was completely focused on his mission to catch this running suspect. The instinct to chase and catch prey is what he was born to follow. Built powerful and low to the ground, Max's legs were kicking up turf in the well-manicured lawns of this upscale neighborhood. Quint watched for a moment in awe at the speed and agility of his dog and the way he deftly maneuvered a sharp corner around the side of a three-story bricked mansion, and out of his sight.

Quint ran trailing behind to catch sight of Max and Dickson. As he made the corner of the house that Max had just turned, Quint knew the chase was over. He could hear the all-too-familiar sounds of Max gnawing on the downed runner. Max was trained to close in on the suspect and jump at the closest available arm, take hold and not let go until commanded to do so. Quint had told the officers who regularly worked his shift the release command, since Max had worked with these officers for some time now and would obey them. This would be critical in the event of Quint becoming incapacitated for some reason and unable to give this command.

As he turned the corner, he saw Max clamped down on Dickson's left arm, pulling at it as the suspect was writhing on the ground and screaming in pain.

"Get him off me! Oh God, get him the fuck off me!" Dickson was screaming and crying at the same time.

"*Ult!*" (Stop!) Quint then gave the command and Max released immediately, moved back and squatted down in a ready position. He was ready to pounce again just in case the suspect still had some fight left in him and sprung up to attack. Quint caught up and held Max by his collar. Dickson was not yet handcuffed, but didn't look to be in any shape to harm anybody. He was crying in pain, holding his mangled arm into his chest as he lay rolling around on the grass.

"Fuckin' cops. You get off on this, don't you?"

"You just lay still and don't try to get up or the dog will automatically attack. That is what he is trained to do," warned Quint. Max let out a succession of fierce barks to remind the suspect that he was there and ready to respond, if needed.

The two other pursuing officers arrived and quickly, but gingerly, handcuffed Dickson while he was still on the ground. They searched him for any weapons while Dickson let loose with a string of verbal insults and threatened to sue for excessive use of force. Having heard it all before, the veteran officers quietly and professionally secured the suspect, careful to protect his rights.

Quint praised Max. *"Goede jongen Maxy, goede jongen."* (Good boy, Maxy, good boy.) Quint used a high-pitched voice. It sounded weird, he knew, but it helped calm the dog.

Max did his job to perfection and deserved praise. It kept him motivated for the next call to duty. To an uneducated observer, Quint's praise of the dog might seem sadistic, but this couldn't be further from the truth. Quint really didn't enjoy when Max actually bit a suspect and drew blood, because this put Max at risk of being infected by any number of diseases. In addition, now that there was a confirmed bite, Quint would have to go back to the station and complete a litany of reports explaining this incident, which would probably take up the rest of his shift.

Although necessary, he couldn't help but to view this tedious exercise as a real pain in the ass. Couldn't one detailed report cover the incident? Quint reasoned.

Quint was snapping Max's leather lead back onto his collar when he heard a door slam closed behind him. The owner stormed out of his house and into his backyard, where Quint, Max, and the others were standing. He was short and pudgy, about sixty years old, wearing brown leather sandals with no socks. His blue gym shorts had bleached white legs sprouting out of them, and he wore a white pullover polo shirt with a wide horizontal blue stripe across the chest. As he approached the officers, Quint could not help but think that the man walking toward him looked like a giant billiard ball with legs.

"What the fuck happened here! Look at my yard! Do you know how much this grass cost me to put in? This isn't cheap K-Mart grass seed that I have here! Look at what that damn dog did to my sod. The city is going to pay for this," said the bloated and pompous man.

"Look, Bud, we just caught a trespasser in your neighborhood. The damage to the yard could not be helped. An officer will take the information down on the damage and restitution will be ordered from the suspect," explained Quint. Max barked a few times before he was quieted by his master.

"First of all, I am not your Bud. My name is Chester Walton. Just ask your mayor; he knows me. The police chief, too. Now, I want all your names and badge numbers. I'll make my own report. I can get action much quicker than you could on your best day."

Quint and the other officers, who were still in the yard waiting for a paddy wagon to arrive, were fighting to control their tempers. This was quite a challenge since they hadn't even had an opportunity to come down emotionally from the arduous foot chase they had just experienced. Regardless, they managed to maintain their composure. Not only had they dealt with all manner of violent criminals in their careers, but they had seen their share of ungrateful citizens as well.

The officers gave their names and badge numbers, knowing that this 8-ball looking jerk wasn't going to remember them anyway, since he wasn't writing any of this down. Just then, the wagon arrived and Dickson, still whimpering from his wounds, was loaded into the vehicle.

"You'll be hearing from me sooner than you think," exclaimed 8-ball. Quint was the first to use the name for Chester Walton. Even though the moniker wasn't an exact correlation, it just seemed to fit.

"OK, 8-ball," Quint said quietly to his fellow officers as they walked away from the ranting citizen. The other two officers snickered at the accuracy of the moniker. All three officers could still hear 8-ball grumbling as they began walking back to their squad cars.

The result of this lack of appreciation turned Quint's elation on the good job that Max had done to frustration over being reamed out by this ungrateful civilian. He was looking for an outlet to vent his anger when he realized an opportunity for a little pay back. He knew that after an exciting chase, Max was going to have to relieve himself. Few things do more damage to a yard than dog urine, especially Max's. Quint knew this all too well as his mind flashed to the sight of his own backyard with the burned-out, yellow spots of grass that he constantly had to repair. Just then near the front door of 8-ball's house, Quint saw a better target than the guy's front lawn. Several beautiful azalea bushes positioned right in Max's field of fire, so he steered Max in that direction and gave him the go sign.

"Ga pipi door Max." Go ahead Max, pee.

Max let out a stream of steaming yellow fluid, hitting the azalea perfectly. The golden shower left at least three plants soaked with Max's unique marker. Finished, Max turned away from the plants and instinctively but proudly kicked backward with his hind legs, tearing up more of 8-ball's precious sod.

"Goede jonden Maxy, goede jonden!" (Good boy Maxy, good boy!) Quint scratched Max vigorously under his chin and behind his ears. Max turned his coffee-colored eyes up toward his master and gave him a lick of affection. Max's tail was creating quite a wind as he wagged it back and forth, his mouth agape and tongue hanging out, a dog's version of a human smile, relishing the attention and praise. Both partners walked off toward their vehicle, the black and tan police dog strutting proudly, having pleased his master by catching a bad guy and settling the score with an arrogant jackass.

Jamar Dickson sat quietly in the back of the paddy wagon, his arm aching from the dog bite. Along with the physical pain, he began to feel depression increasingly overwhelm him as he contemplated his situation.

For police prisoners, this is a common syndrome. Officers often witness arrestees playing out their final acts in the melodramas of their lives. When their freedom is taken away, even if only temporarily, prisoners often feel that there is nothing left. The arrestee has dealt with or tolerated his other emotional and personal problems up to this point. But when one of life's most precious privileges is taken away, namely his freedom, he sometimes has an overwhelming feeling of defeat. Couple this with the impaired judgment of being intoxicated, a common condition of arrestees, and the result can be suicide. This is why law enforcement personnel need to take away all items that could help someone take his or her own life while in custody.

Dickson took an introspective inventory of his life during his ride in the wagon. He realized that he really had no one in the world who really cared about him; his parents viewed him as a failure and had given up on him. His girlfriend was unreachable because of her father's disapproval of him. Everything Dickson had tried in his life had ended in failure and now he didn't even have his freedom. Even the color of his skin was wrong, he thought, giving these cops a reason to harass him, beat him, and even use a dog to attack him. All because he was a black man dating a white girl. Whitey can't let this happen, he reasoned, it makes it look like they can't please their own kind. If it were a white guy, the cops probably would have told him to leave and not to come back again, and that would have been the end of it.

Dickson wanted to die. If he'd had a gun, he would have shot himself right there in the back of the wagon. He could shoot himself in the mouth and have the bullet come out the back of his head, spraying brain matter all over the back of the wagon. Then the cops would have to clean his blood and brains off the walls of the metal prisoner box in the back of the vehicle. A disgusting job that no one would want to do. At least it would force them to get their hands dirty for a change, instead of sitting in a car all day eating doughnuts and getting fat.

The wagon pulled into the hospital emergency parking area and the officer got out and opened the back door for Dickson to exit. They walked into the emergency room and the officer and Dickson were shown to an examining room. A second officer walked in soon after. To Dickson's surprise, he was black.

"Hey brother. You see how they done me wrong?" Dickson asked, looking for a little sympathy.

"First of all, I'm not your brother. Second, if you hadn't run, this would not have happened to you," said the black officer, admonishing Dickson.

"Is that right, Uncle Tom? I guess you sold out for a badge and gun. You enjoy lickin' whitey's shoes for your paycheck?" shot Dickson indignantly.

"Listen man, I don't need to prove myself to you. I choose to make an honest living and support a family instead of making my money from slingin' dope and creating a bunch of drug addict zombies. If that is an Uncle Tom, then that's what I am. I'd rather try to better the neighborhood that I grew up in than add to the problem," said the officer, repeating a statement he had made many times before. He didn't mind because he was secure in his beliefs.

"Man," said Dickson, "they really have you brainwashed."

A nurse came in and began cleaning and dressing Dickson's wound. The doctor, who arrived shortly thereafter, manipulated Dickson's arm to size up the extent of the injury. Dickson winced a few times and then suddenly let out a short yelp.

"It may be a fracture. We need some x-rays taken," ordered the doctor.

After going to x-ray, Dickson was taken back to the initial examining room where the officers were still waiting. He had a hairline fracture to the radial bone in his left forearm. It needed to be put in a cast immediately and the procedure could take a few hours. The officers were not too keen on hanging around waiting for this guy to be discharged. And they knew all too well that in the ER, a few hours could turn into the whole shift spent watching the huge, institutional-style clock on the waiting room wall. They weren't exactly holding Charles Manson here, so they decided to do what cops have done for decades – have someone else make the decision. The officers called their sergeant and asked him what they should do. His answer was just what they had expected.

"Tell the hospital to call us when he is discharged and we will go back and pick him up. Since he is only looking at criminal trespass and resisting arrest, and the only other thing on his rap sheet is simple possession of marijuana, you guys are of more use to me answering calls. We are already backed up ten calls. Get on the street as soon as you can," relayed the sergeant.

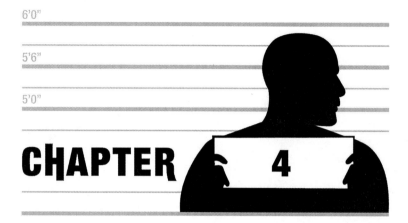

CHAPTER 4

Diaz walked into the roll call room about to begin his midnight shift. He saw Ruggerio and Tobias sitting in the middle of a cluster of about thirty chairs, talking and laughing uproariously about something. There were several other officers milling around in the room, other members of the midnight shift waiting for roll call to begin. Diaz went over to them just as their laughing jag was waning.

"What's so funny?" Diaz smiled.

"Toby just told me a joke. Go ahead," Ruggerio said, encouraging Tobias to repeat the joke.

"OK. A guy and his wife get pulled over by the police. As the cop is asking for the guy's driver's information, the wife says, 'He can't give you his license because it is suspended.' The guy shouts at his wife, 'Shut up!' Then the wife tells the officer, 'His insurance is cancelled, too.' The guy yells at his wife again, 'Would you keep your damn mouth shut.' The wife still doesn't listen. 'Oh, and his registration has been revoked.' The guy loses it, 'You dumb bitch. Why can't you just keep quiet!'

"The cop then asks the wife, 'Does he talk to you like that all the time?' The wife says, 'No, only when he is drunk.'"

Diaz breaks up with laughter at the old cop joke, one that has been continually dusted off and told to rookie cops for years.

Just then, Faust came into the room and sneered in Ruggerio's direction. Ruggerio automatically transitioned into defensive mode when Faust was in the vicinity because he usually was the victim of a verbal sneak attack and he wanted to be on guard to return fire. Ruggerio knew how important it was to his credibility in the department to counter all of Faust's assaults. If he didn't, then the other members of the department might take what Faust said as gospel. In a business where credibility is so important, Ruggerio worked hard at keeping his intact.

Faust walked by Ruggerio and Diaz, but stopped near three officers, clustered near the shift sergeant's podium. The officers were acquaintances of his. Faust whispered something to them, his voice rising intermittently so Ruggerio could hear and catch the drift of the conversation. It was of course another attack on Ruggerio.

"Yeah, he missed a whole bag of crack that the guy threw," said Faust to the others in a hushed tone, but loud enough for Ruggerio, Diaz, and Tobias to hear.

One of the other officers glanced quickly in Ruggerio's direction, but quickly looked back at Faust when he caught Ruggerio's eye. Faust was chuckling, but the three other officers were not. In fact, they looked a bit self-conscious, as if thinking, "Why are you saying this? Don't you know he is sitting a few feet away and can hear you?"

Ruggerio knew what this was all about. Faust wanted to embarrass Ruggerio in front of Diaz, his trainee. The event he was referring to had happened on Diaz's first night on the force, when the two cops had arrested two suspects running from a multiple-victim shooting scene. Before Ruggerio and Diaz apprehended the two suspects, one of them had allegedly thrown a bag of crack on a roof while he was running from the scene. But neither Ruggerio nor Diaz had seen this happen because the suspect ditched the crack before rounding the corner to the alley where Diaz and Ruggerio were waiting. They had no way of knowing about the crack.

But, facts never worried Faust when it came to attacking his enemies. He saw a chance to go at Ruggerio and he took it.

"Some training officer. I wouldn't let him train my dog," Faust said still chuckling. One of the officers in the group turned and walked away, realizing that this was getting out of hand.

Toby saw that his friend was getting upset. "Let it go, Guy. Let it go. Everyone knows what he is. He's just trying to bait you."

Diaz straightened up and remained silent, waiting to see what Ruggerio's response would be. In his mind, he thought that Ruggerio shouldn't let such an audacious attack go without defending himself.

Ruggerio knew that Toby was just being a friend and didn't want to see anything bad happen. Both veteran officers knew that Faust had connections in the department who could make Ruggerio's life difficult. Ruggerio was thinking the same thing— that he should just let it go. But, no, this needed to stop and the only way was a direct confrontation.

"Hey, Faust. You're a detective, aren't you?" Ruggerio said defiantly.

"What is that supposed to mean?"

"Well, you would think a detective would be more observant." Everyone in the room fell silent and waited to see how this would play out. They could tell that Ruggerio was leading up to something, but the punch line was a mystery to everyone, including Faust. The officers in the room, all accustomed to verbal confrontation, could see that Faust was surprised by Ruggerio's comeback. They could also see that Faust was afraid, even though he was trying to hide it. These people could smell fear in a person like an animal does in the wild.

"What the fuck are you talking about?" Faust retorted, giving his best effort to look fearless but coming up a bit short.

Ruggerio saw it, too. Faust was scared, like the stereotypical schoolyard bully who acts tough but can't back it up.

"Well, one would think a detective could cover his tracks better, no?" Ruggerio paused briefly for effect and then continued. "Next time, it would be a good idea to dust off your knees after leaving the lieutenant's office." He delivered the line with great confidence, then sat back and waited for Faust to respond. Ruggerio was relaxed and smiling, his facial expression projecting fearlessness that gave the impression that he was ready for whatever Faust had to offer, including a physical altercation.

Faust's face went red with anger and confusion. He stammered a bit and tried to conjure up something to say. Ruggerio's defiant appearance and "go ahead, make my day" attitude rendered Faust unsure of himself. All he could think to do was use his rank in the department as leverage.

"You listen. You better respect my rank or I will write you up for insubordination!" Faust's booming voice echoed down the hall into the other offices, one of which belonged to the shift lieutenant.

Ruggerio knew that he had him on this one. How could he write Ruggerio up for something that Faust had initiated?

"Go ahead and write me up, or don't you have the balls?" Ruggerio said with ultimate confidence.

"You just keep disrespecting me and you'll see what I can do to you."

But Ruggerio wasn't taking it anymore, even if it meant severe political consequences. This was going to end right here and now with this prick.

"You would get respect if you earned it, but you don't. You sold your soul to get to where you are and a person like that don't deserve to be respected."

Ruggerio's words hit the bull's eye dead center. The other officers in the room silently agreed, some even nodding their heads.

Before Faust could respond, the lieutenant stormed in like a hurricane. "What the hell is going on in here? Faust, I could hear you all over the building. Get back to your office!" he commanded. Then looking at the patrol officers he said, "You guys get roll call started and get out on the street!" The confrontation was quickly over and the group quietly settled into their seats for roll call. As Faust left the room, he and Ruggerio exchanged stares of resentment.

After four hours, the doctor finally arrived to complete the process of placing an immobilizer on Dickson's injured arm. The splint was made of nylon with metal inserts to keep the fractured area of the bone rigid. The black nylon splint was wrapped around Dickson's left thumb, palm, and wrist, and then it ran up his arm, covering the fractured area up to the elbow. The doctor told

Dickson to stay put while he ordered some pain medication. After that, he would be released.

Alone in the exam room, Dickson saw his chance. He peered out of the curtain that was drawn over the entrance to the room. The ER was busy as ever and the staff was scurrying about, attending to their duties. Dickson heard his doctor ordering vicodin for his pain and the nurse removed some small envelopes from a cabinet and started to make her way to Dickson's room. He quickly ducked back inside.

"Here are two vicodin tablets for the pain." The nurse placed a small envelope containing the pills in Dickson's hand. "Take them about one hour from now. That is when the meds we gave you earlier should be wearing off. Now, this is a powerful pain medication. It should last about four hours. Here is a prescription for twenty pills. Take two every four hours as needed. Don't take any more than two pills every four hours, and whatever you do, do not drink any alcohol while on this medication," she said sternly. "OK? I will call for the officers to come back for you. Sit tight until they get here."

Dickson put the pills in his pocket, along with the prescription. He had to get out of there before the cops came back. He needed to do something, but didn't know exactly what. It had to be dramatic so that he could show his persecutors that he wasn't going to take their abuse anymore. One thing he was sure about though, he couldn't do anything while sitting in jail. He had to make a run for it.

He looked out of the room again, drawing the curtain back ever so slightly. He saw his nurse with her back to him, dialing a number on the phone at the nurse's desk. Just then, the sliding glass automatic doors to the ER swished open. Paramedics rushed in a patient lying on a gurney. There was an oxygen mask over his face. Another paramedic walked quickly alongside the gurney and called out to the nurse who was on the phone. "Code blue! He just went into cardiac arrest!"

The nurse pushed the disconnect button on the phone and punched some other numbers to page the doctor. "Code blue in the ER! Code blue!"

This was his opportunity. Dickson slipped out of his examination room and walked quickly—but not too quickly—toward the exit. He was out in the parking lot before anyone noticed a thing. He began to run toward the street and then down an alley to put some distance between him and the hospital.

He turned around after running about one hundred feet down the alley and didn't see anyone following him. He had made it. Now, he could plan his next move. He needed to show his father, Lauren's father, Lauren, and the cops that he was going to fight back. In one sensational act he thought he could demonstrate to all his detractors that he wasn't going to sit back and take it anymore. But what could he do? he thought. What could this act be that would show them all that he was not a punk?

He felt a sharp pain. His broken arm reminded him of the cops and the dog that they had sent after him. The pain reminded him of his other problems. He thought about his failure in school, and Lauren's father using his influence to keep him and Lauren apart. He thought about how his own father and how he had not been able to live up to the image that his father had of him. Dickson's pain wasn't just mental; he felt it deep in his stomach. He had no one to turn to now. He was experiencing a helplessness that he had never experienced before and he wasn't sure how to deal with it.

If I only had some weed or a little coke to snort, he thought. That might take away some of the hurt and help me forget. But, the few small-time pot dealers that he knew were not in this part of town. He remembered the pills in his pocket and the nurse's firm warning about not drinking any alcohol. That would set me right, Dickson thought. Pop these pills with a little Johnnie Walker and I'll be gliding in space. If I OD and die, then no one has to worry about me causing them any problems or disappointments anymore, he concluded.

He needed some money first, if he was going to buy some alcohol or dope. The cops had taken his wallet, with his credit cards and his ATM card. Maybe he could take the money he needed? Yeah, Dickson thought. Folks have been taking everything away from me; now it is my turn to start taking. The first person I see, I am going to rob the sucker—especially if it is a white person. I've had enough of whitey taking from me. Dickson was determined to get revenge.

His life had been sent into a tailspin that he could not get out of, and he needed to punish the people responsible for his failures. Any white person would do, but he especially wanted a white person who was loaded and privileged like Lauren's father —or even his own father.

He walked around a corner toward a small parking lot in the middle of the block, and as if by destiny, he saw his target—a white guy getting out of a Jaguar. He was a short, chubby man with a wisp of gray hair barely covering his head. An easy target, thought Dickson. It was dark now, and the artificial light showed only a few people on the street; none of them seemed to be looking in Dickson's direction. He approached his target, but the man walked by Dickson, not paying any attention. As he passed, Dickson wheeled around from behind and reached out to the man's collar with his right hand and placed the index finger of his splinted left hand in the small of the man's back.

"Don't you say anything, asshole, or I will shoot you," Dickson commanded, making sure the victim knew that it was not an idle threat.

"OK, what do you want?"

"Your money, you stupid fuck. Now, throw your wallet on the ground."

The man did exactly as he was told.

"Now, take off. Don't look back at me or I'll put a cap in your ass," Dickson said with authority. Then, he caught view of the man's cell phone attached to his belt.

"Drop your cell too, next to the wallet. Don't break it, whitey, or you'll pay." Dickson felt powerful and in control. He liked it.

"OK, you can have it. Take anything, just don't shoot, please," the man said with a shaky voice. He dropped the phone gently next to the wallet. "Can I go now?" he asked, like a schoolboy asking the teacher for the hall pass.

"Get your honky ass out of here and don't look back!"

The victim ran as fast as he could to get away and made it around the first corner but then stopped suddenly. Even though he had been warned not to, he had to look back. He slunk back toward the parking lot and saw Dickson rifling through his wallet and greedily stuffing cash into his pocket. Dickson threw the wallet down and took off down the street in the opposite direction, but not before the victim was able to get a look at Dickson and what he was wearing. This information would be very useful later when he filed a police report.

Diaz could see Ruggerio's Italian temper rising up in him from the confrontation with Faust. Ruggerio was jerking the squad car around as he negotiated the nighttime city streets.

"You know this is exactly what he wants, for you to be jacked off right now," Diaz said.

"I know, but it's so fucking frustrating to have an enemy who is nearly untouchable the way Faust is. He can just sit back and take pot shots at me whenever the mood hits him without worrying about any consequences." Ruggerio's tone was absent of the familiar training officer authoritarian style that Diaz was used to hearing. He realized that Ruggerio was talking to him as an equal and a friend, searching for a sympathetic ear.

"I'm sorry I forgot I was in Pittsburgh. I should have said, 'you know he wants to JAG you off,' not jack you off." Diaz looked over at Ruggerio with a smile, hoping that this would lighten the mood and help his partner forget about Faust for a moment.

Ruggerio began to chuckle. "You're learning. I'll have you guzzling Iron City beer and swearing at the TV during Steelers games in no time."

"Only if they are beating the Eagles," said Diaz, relieved that Ruggerio seemed to relax somewhat.

Just then the radio dispatcher called Ruggerio's car number. "Radio to car 7-21."

"7-21. Go ahead radio," Diaz answered.

"Car 7-21, return to station and see Lieutenant Marks."

"10-4."

"Looks like Faust is not done with me tonight," Ruggerio said.

"What do you mean?"

"The Louie is Faust's drinking buddy and his connection to the chief of detectives. I don't think this will be a 'shake hands boys and let bygones be bygones' type of meeting," Ruggerio said with a sense of trepidation.

Not knowing what else to say, Diaz tried to calm his partner. "Well, maybe not. I'll go in and tell the Louie what I heard. Maybe that will help?"

"Remember, you're on probation still. The last thing you want to do is stick your neck out," Ruggerio told his partner. "But thanks, just the same."

As they wheeled into the station, Tobias was standing at the entrance waiting for Ruggerio. He seemed agitated, pacing back and forth and spewing tobacco juice into the grassy area between the parking lot and the walkway.

"I can't believe this! I'm coming in with you, Guy. I'll tell him what happened. That bushwhacking creep attacked you for no reason. I heard it. I'll tell the boss!" Tobias said in fierce defense of his friend.

"I appreciate it Toby, but you know it won't do any good. You'll just get your name put on Faust's and the Louie's hit list, then you will be in the same boat I am." He then turned to Diaz and pointed with his thumb in a hitchhiking motion. "This hero wanted to do the same thing." Ruggerio was proud of his trainee and knew he was going to make a good cop. "I appreciate it, guys, but let me go in and take my lumps. I'll be back in a minute." Ruggerio walked into the station and his two friends waited impatiently for him outside under the dimly lit entrance to the station house.

When Ruggerio walked into Lieutenant Mark's office, he was surprised to see one of the officers sitting there whom Faust had been talking with in the squad room before the argument started. Ruggerio sat down in front of the lieutenant's wooden desk, a few feet away from Faust.

"Ruggerio, I called you in after I spoke with Faust and Tanner about the commotion in the squad room. Now, Tanner confirms Faust's account about what happened." The lieutenant was talking as if he already had his mind made up about this situation. It was obvious that Ruggerio's position was not going to be taken into consideration. Just as he thought, the fix was in.

"Faust wasn't talking about you. He was talking about a movie he saw and was describing it to Tanner and the other guys there. You have to watch your temper, Ruggerio. Just because you and Faust have a problem with each other, don't automatically assume that he is trash talking you."

Ruggerio needed to say something at this point. He couldn't just sit there and take the rap. It went against his nature to take this kind of injustice lying down.

"Wait a minute, this is a farce …"

Ruggerio was interrupted in mid-sentence by Marks. "I don't want to hear it. I have the facts and you were in the wrong. Now, let me finish what I was saying."

Then Ruggerio did the interrupting. "I was in the wrong? This guy tried embarrassing me in front my trainee. I can't have that happen. It destroys my credibility as a trainer."

Marks interrupted him again. "I'm not interested in what you assumed he was saying about you, and if you interrupt me one more time, you will be immediately suspended without pay. You understand?"

Ruggerio nodded his head. It was futile. He would just have to sit back and take this load of shit.

"Now, you are going to receive a letter of reprimand in your personnel file for disrespecting a ranking officer. I am letting you off easy. I could suspend you. Now, go back out on the street and don't let this happen again."

Ruggerio could see Faust smirking, sitting in his chair totally relaxed with his elbows on the arm rests and his fingers peaked in front of his face, trying to cover his smile. It was too much to take. Suspension or no suspension, Ruggerio could not just sit there and let this happen without saying something. But, just as he opened his mouth to speak, Marks brusquely stopped him.

"No, the matter is over. Now, go back to work. You can appeal it through the union, if you want, but I don't want to hear it now."

Dickson sprinted out of the parking lot and down the sidewalk until he saw an alley he could duck into. He checked out the wad of cash and counted his take. Seventy-four dollars and the cell phone—that was it. But it didn't really matter. He felt a wild rush from the experience of actually being in control of someone for a change. He felt empowered and wanted to do it again. Not just for the money, but also for the feeling it gave him. He stowed the money and phone in the pocket of his jacket and left the alley for the sidewalk. He thought for a second and then retreated back into the alley. He took off his jacket and reversed it so the interior was now on the outside. It was a reversible, so the outside, which was previously blue, was now light beige. Now, when Jaguar man gave the cops the robber's description, the jacket color wouldn't match what Dickson was wearing. He was careful to zip the jacket up and cover the red and blue striped shirt underneath, just in case this had been noticed. Dickson was proud of his quick thinking, believing that this little trick was sure to fool any punk-ass cop he might come across.

He reemerged from the alley and began the hunt for his next victim, almost giddy with anticipation. He scanned up and down the street for police. He saw a squad car driving through an intersection and thought that Jaguar man must have called 9-1-1 and that the cops were already looking for him. Best to get off the street for a while, he reasoned. Spying a bar across the street, he decided to duck into it and get that drink he wanted. The pills were starting to wear off, anyway. The pain in his arm was increasing, so this would be a good time to take the extra vicodin.

Dickson's first victim had to put his hand against the wall to keep from falling. He tried to run again from the corner where he had just peeked around at his attacker. He willed his legs to move, but they wouldn't go.

I could have died, he said to himself, visualizing bullets piercing his body from behind. He felt a warm sensation in his lower extremities and he froze for a moment as he tried to understand what he was feeling. He was trying to put it all into perspective.

Oh no! he thought. It just can't be! He felt wet. He had pissed himself and was just realizing it. His left leg was soaked from the crotch to the knee. Just then, a passerby saw that he was having difficulty.

"Are you OK?" the woman asked.

The robbery victim abruptly turned away in an attempt to hide his embarrassing condition. "I was robbed," he could only think to say.

"Oh my! I'll call the police for you." The young black woman took out her cell phone and gave the 9-1-1 operator all the information, including a description of the suspect as told by the victim.

A few blocks away, riding on routine patrol, was Max the German shepherd police dog with his partner, Quint O'Neal. They were working a double shift because budget cuts had forced the department to cut back on manpower. This town always seemed to be in crisis, the K-9 officer thought to himself.

"You know that Max?" Quint said to his partner, who was riding in the back of the police SUV. Max picked up his head at the mention of his name. Part of the reason K-9 handlers become so passionate about their animal partners is that they treat the dogs almost as human partners, and the dogs return this respect to their masters. A dog can't express opinions, so the chance of the two having arguments is not very likely. Sure, a dog can and will do things to make his handler mad, but the two will always make up later. There is an undying loyalty extended from the animal toward its master.

"You know," Quint continued, "my whole life, this town has been in financial crisis. I never saw the heyday of the big steel mills. The economy is always bad. Nothing new seems to come into this area. What do you think?"

Max was listening with intensity, cocking his head to one side as if he was trying to understand. When Quint would ask Max what he thought, the dog, recognizing the inflection of a question, would routinely make a sighing sound and creep forward a few inches toward his master, just to let him know that he heard him. Quint saw this through his rear view mirror, smiled at his friend and passed a dog treat back to Max. Just then the radio squawked, announcing the robbery call that involved Dickson's victim. Quint and Max were close by and acknowledged the call to the dispatcher.

When Quint arrived at the scene, he immediately recognized the victim, who was still with the black woman who had stopped to help.

"Well look at this, Max." Max had been panting heavily and wagging his tail ever since his partner answered the radio. He knew they were going on a job and he was ready.

"You see him, Max? Its 8- ball from early today." Max barked, as if he was answering his partner. "Sometimes the chips fall just right. What do you think, Max?" Max barked again.

Quint took the information from 8-ball about the robbery. Neither party acknowledged their previous relationship. 8-ball was too embarrassed. Seeing the piss stain down his pant leg, Quint didn't see a need to inflict any more humiliation; he was satisfied that this creep had gotten his just desserts. Quint put out the description and other details over the radio for the patrolling cars to look out for the robbery suspect.

However, there was one officer that still had not squared with old 8-ball yet, and that officer was Max. Making sure that his partner was also duly compensated, Quint let Max out of the car to sniff around the area. He said that he wanted his dog to try and locate the escape route of the robber. But really, Quint just wanted an excuse to get Max involved.

Knowing that dogs are attracted to the smell of urine, he figured Max would eventually make his way to 8-ball's crotch and at that point, Quint would let Max do the rest. It took a few minutes; the whole time 8-ball was asking if he could leave. But Max started to pick up the scent and crept closer to the urine smell.

"Hey, what's he doing?" asked 8-ball. "The guy ran *that* way."

"I don't know, he must have caught his scent on you," said Quint, tongue in cheek.

Max's nose was working feverishly. He started at 8-ball's feet and before the man could turn away, Max raised his nose toward the source of the scent. Max hit pay dirt and in one quick motion zeroed in on the urine smell and slammed against 8-ball's groin. The man went down like a bag of dirt, shouting in pain as he hit the pavement.

"Max!" Quint shouted, a little too late. He pulled Max away from the collapsed 8-ball with the lead he was holding.

"I don't know what he is doing. Sorry, Sir," Quint apologized sarcastically.

"Uuuuuuh! That damn dog!" screamed 8-ball, still lying on the ground holding his privates.

"Wait a minute! Now I see why he did that. You pissed your pants, Sir," Quint said, in the best phony surprised voice that he could muster. "No wonder. Sorry again, Sir. Well, do you need anything further?"

8-ball shook his head no. He just wanted to get the hell out of there. He wasn't about to complain or ask for any more assistance. Quint loaded Max up in the car and was getting ready to take off before 8-ball started asking for badge numbers again.

"OK, Sir. We will let you know if we find out anything," said the K-9 officer.

8-ball was getting up on his feet and started toward his car, holding his balls with his left hand and waving at the officer with his right, as if to convey his defeat!

It was getting near midnight and the streetlights were buzzing from above as they burned to illuminate the city. Dickson was looking for another victim. Maybe this could be my new lifestyle, he thought, the gangster or thug life. That's how everyone thinks of me, anyway. Lauren's father, my own father, the cops, I'm just some bad-ass gangster to them, so why not act the part? Besides, it's the first time I have felt good about myself in a long time.

Dickson saw a patrol car at an intersection further up the street. The cop slowed the car a bit as he passed through the intersection. Dickson's paranoia convinced him that this was the same cop car he had seen passing by earlier. Now he was definitely going into the bar across the street. Milligan's Pub read the green neon sign in the window above the front door.

Dickson darted across the street. Inside the bar, he scanned the room. A dark colored wooden bar was situated against the opposite wall. All but two of the rickety bar stools were empty, one at the opposite end and the other near the center. There were some booths on the near wall, but Dickson could only see the back of one person's head. Salt and pepper hair—more salt than pepper. They were all old white guys, including the bartender, and all of them except for the guy in the booth stared at Dickson as if he were an alien creature that had just dropped from the sky.

Dickson wanted to leave, but thought that it was not exactly safe on the street right now. He would take his chances here. Maybe he could put on his new thug persona and put these old heads in their place before they tried anything with him. He tried strutting like he had seen on a hip-hop video once, and made his way over to the bar. Dickson could feel all eyes burning into him. He kept reminding himself, I'm a thug, act like one. Dickson stepped up to the bar.

"What can I do for you?" the bartender asked with a tone of apprehension in is voice.

What Dickson did not know was that the bar patrons had watched him walking on the street before he came into the bar. This was a predominately white area of town and a black male walking the street was quickly noticed. Had the police officer passing through the intersection noticed Dickson, he or she most definitely would have stopped him, especially after 8-ball's description had been broadcast to all patrol cars in the area.

"Yeah, *dawg* how about some Johnnie Walker?" Dickson tried to sound like one of the urban gangsters he has seen in the movies. He could see the other patrons were mesmerized by his presence. Their right hands clutching drinking glasses or bottles, cigarette smoke wafting up toward the tarnished copper-plated ceiling, mouths slightly agape and wide eyes fixed on Dickson, waiting to see what he would do next. The bartender came over with the drink and Dickson threw out a ten-dollar bill that he had stolen from 8-ball earlier. Dickson had the feeling that he was pulling off the stunt and that the old heads in the bar were buying his act, but their stares were becoming uncomfortable. Dickson felt a jolt of pain shoot through his arm. He remembered the pain pills in his pocket. It was time to use them. Turning away from his captive audience toward the window, he took the pills from his pocket and slipped them in his mouth. He reached for the Johnnie Walker to wash them down. His throat burned, but the rush to his brain felt good and took his mind off the pain in his arm.

He looked back at this audience of three, still frozen in the same positions. "What you all looking at? Never seen a black man before?"

Two of them quickly averted their gaze away from Dickson, stunned by his directness. The bartender busied himself with cleaning some wine glasses, even though they were already clean. No one in this old-man Irish bar had ordered wine since one unfortunate well-dressed black man some time ago. This professional looking gent had quickly realized that he wasn't welcome at Milligan's and made his escape without finishing his drink. His wine glass had been ceremoniously pitched into the trash and all in attendance raised their drinks in celebration.

The Milligan's faithful were going to do the same to this new invader, another smart-ass who needed to be taught a lesson. He should stay where he belonged, in his own neighborhood where he could sell his drugs and shoot up his drug rivals all he wanted, and leave good people like them alone.

One of the old guys at the bar, the one closest to Dickson, known to his friends as Ace, felt compelled to say something. "This is just a neighborhood bar. Don't you think that you would be more comfortable somewhere else?"

Dickson was fuming now. With all that had happened to him in the last few months, he couldn't even go into a bar and have a drink without being hassled. He could really feel the combination of the pills and the booze hit him now. The pain in his arm was just about gone, but he could feel the muscles in his legs begin to weaken. He needed to sit on the bar stool just to feel a little more stable. Dickson wanted to confront the old head, but first he needed another drink. He looked over at the bartender, who was still trying to look busy re-cleaning glasses.

"Yo! Another Johnnie, please." Damn, he thought, he slipped back into his real self for a moment. Don't be polite, Dickson admonished himself.

He turned back to Ace. "Listen, you all just mind your own business and I'll take care of mine," he said, taking a sip from the fresh glass of Johnnie Walker.

"This *is* our business," Ace said, taking a stronger tone in his voice. "Now, you be a good boy and finish your drink and go on your way." Looking more agitated, Ace's eyes narrowed and his left hand squeezed into a fist at his side.

Dickson was beginning to worry a bit about a confrontation with these guys. He was outnumbered here. He wondered just how effective his feigning of a gun had been earlier. Maybe it would work now, too? He needed to sell it convincingly, along with the gangster image he was portraying.

"Listen to the old head making threats," he said tauntingly. Dickson raised his glass again and finished his drink, then abruptly reared back and hurled the glass in the direction of the other old guys sitting across the bar. The glass missed the patrons and smashed against the wall behind them, near the old guy sitting at the booth. The old dude in the booth hit the floor and crawled under his table, shaking with fear. Another patron who had not said anything to Dickson ducked behind the bar. He took hold of the bar rail above him and raised his head just above the level of the bar top to see what Dickson was doing.

Ace stood up with both hands clenched into fists at his sides, defiantly staring at Dickson. Dickson knew that he had to stay in character, so he reached toward his waistband as if he were going for a gun.

"Now, who wants to be a hero?" Dickson shouted at Ace standing and facing him. The bartender slowly retreated. Dickson moved toward the door, still holding his hand near his waistband, hoping that this would freeze everyone until he could make his getaway.

Dickson saw the bartender moving and shouted at him. "Hold it right there, asshole!" Ace was still standing tall with his fists clenched. He turned his head slightly toward the bartender, while keeping his eyes on Dickson.

"Joe?" he said to the bartender.

"Yeah?

"Get me my shillelagh."

Dickson did not know what he was talking about, but the regulars at Milligan's knew. It was code for the revolver that was stored behind the bar.

Dickson figured it probably meant a weapon of some kind. He kept up his slow creeping shuffle toward the door, still play-acting that he had a gun in his waist.

"You get that, Joe, and I'll put a cap in your ass," Dickson said, hoping that the bartender would heed his warning.

"J-o-o-o-o-o-o-e," Ace said, trying to keep Joe focused on the shillelagh.

"I don't have it. Johnny took it to clean." Joe told Ace out of the corner of his mouth, trying not to let Dickson hear.

"That's right, Joe. You play it smart and no one gets hurt." Dickson knew that he had the upper hand and decided to teach this old white racist asshole a lesson.

"OK, old head, cracker, racist. Now you are going to apologize to me for being so rude." Dickson's confidence was enhanced by the effects of the pills and booze in his body. His brain began to feel fuzzy and he was slightly wobbly in the legs. He thought it best to make his escape while he could still stand.

"Apologize? You can go to hell!" Ace slammed his fist down on the bar.

Dickson was feeling a bit woozy and reached for the door handle, "Anybody follows me and I'll pop a cap in their head, you got it?" Then he opened the door and took off down the street, looking back occasionally to make sure that no one was following. He ran a few blocks, wavering and stumbling but still on his feet. He would turn occasionally to check behind him but no one was trailing. He came upon a small park with tall trees and benches and sat down to rest. His vision was starting to blur and he felt increasingly unsteady. Dickson's mind was working overtime. His thoughts were cluttered and overlapping as flashes of the last few months raced into and out of his consciousness. Just slow down and relax, he told himself—but he couldn't. The medication, fueled by the alcohol, inhibited rational thinking.

Dickson used 8-ball's cell phone to call Lauren. Maybe she could pick him up. It took him three attempts but he finally called the right number. If her father picked up, Dickson would just disconnect the call. He would never know it was Dickson since the number would not look familiar.

"Hello?" Lauren answered the phone in that sweet voice that he loved.

"H-e-l-l-woe." His diction was slurred. Dickson cleared his throat to give it another try. "Lauren, it's me," he said much clearer.

"Jamar, what's the matter? You sound strange," she asked, quizzically.

"Lauren, I need you. I am in some park. Can you…"

Before he could finish, Lauren's father broke in. "I told you to leave us alone." Click. The call disconnected abruptly. He must have taken the phone right off of her. Man, Dickson thought, he must have radar to find out that fast that I was calling her. That bastard. Now what am I going to do? He sat there looking into space, contemplating his plight. He watched as two lovers walked by him hand in hand, oblivious to him. That used to be Lauren and me before her father screwed everything up, he concluded. I have nothing, nobody, no place to go. Dickson dropped his head down on his chest and closed his eyes in despair.

"What's the use? I should just walk out into traffic and end it all," he said out loud to himself. His thoughts were still clouded. "Or, how about the bridge?" he muttered into his lap, with his head hanging down on his chest. "Yeah, the bridge."

Dickson took off, not sure where the nearest bridge was. He walked along a footpath through the park.

"What do you think they will do with Guy?" Diaz asked Tobias.

"Nothing, just chew him out a bit."

"But it was obvious that Faust created the situation. Guy was just reacting and defending himself," Diaz insisted.

"I know it and you know it, but the reality is that if you are in with the clique you are untouchable. And if you are out of the clique you are always wrong. Let me tell you, Faust is definitely in the clique," Tobias explained.

"That doesn't make for a very comfortable work environment."

"Only for those who sell their souls and join up with the good old boys who run the city." Tobias spit a brown stream of tobacco juice into the grass. "For them, life is very comfortable. The only requirement is that you have to check your conscience at the door before you can join."

The metal-framed glass-front door crashed open and hit the outside block wall. Ruggerio emerged from behind it, cussing and muttering under his breath.

"Get this," he said with hands flailing about. "He was talking about a movie and I made an assumption that he was talking about me. Can you believe this shit? How stupid do they think I am?"

"Of course, the LT backed Faust up one hundred percent, right?" Tobias asked cynically.

"One hundred percent. He wouldn't even let me defend myself. Son-of-a-bitch!" Ruggerio threw his hands in the air in frustration.

"A movie?" Diaz said incredulously. "It was obvious what he was trying to do."

"Yeah, and I fell hook, line, and sinker. You think that I would have learned by now how this game is played," Ruggerio lamented.

"I thought we were all supposed to be on the same side," said Diaz somewhat naively.

"In a perfect world, Kid. You know what they say; a policeman's worst enemy is another policeman." Tobias turned his head and delivered another load of tobacco juice into the lawn. Then Tobias asked the inevitable question. "So what did you get out of it?"

"A letter of reprimand for disrespecting a ranking officer," Ruggerio said with resignation.

"You gonna appeal it, right?" Tobias inquired.

"I doubt it. You know, they have the union in their back pocket. If I appeal, they might just fire me."

"How can they fire you if you appeal?" asked Diaz.

"Well, they can. In a disciplinary appeal, the penalty can be reassessed and they can make the punishment more severe," Ruggerio explained.

"That doesn't sound very fair. Even criminals can appeal without their penalties increasing," observed Diaz.

"That's the game. It's all about contacts. The better your connects are, the better treatment you get," Tobias explained, taking the chew out of his lip and flicking it into the grass. "We better get back on the street before the Louie sees us out here."

Ruggerio tossed the car keys to Diaz. "You drive." He walked toward the lot where their squad was parked. Tobias grabbed Diaz's arm and held him back until Ruggerio was beyond earshot.

" Keep him out of trouble tonight, if you can. I will try to stay close," Tobias instructed the rookie.

"OK," was all that Diaz could say. He didn't want to linger and let Ruggerio know that they were talking about him.

As Diaz navigated the squad car through midnight traffic, Ruggerio sat next to him in silence, staring out the passenger window. Feeling a bit uncomfortable, Diaz decided that he needed to break the ice.

"Listen, don't let them get to you. Those kind of guys aren't like us. They're motivated by greed and power and will step on anyone who gets in their way," Diaz said.

"I know you're right, and I tell myself the same thing constantly, but it still gets to me," revealed Ruggerio. "The feelings of frustration and helplessness are hard to overcome, when you know that the deck is stacked against you. I just sit back waiting all the time…" He paused, mid-sentence and tried to stifle a sob.

Diaz said nothing as Ruggerio regained his composure then finished his thought. "…just waiting for the next hit, knowing that when it comes that there is nothing I can do to protect myself."

Diaz thought for a moment. "Maybe…" then he hesitated.

"Maybe, what?" Ruggerio asked.

"Maybe you might want to think about moving on."

"I have and I just might have to if this continues. But being a cop is all I ever wanted to do. If they would just leave me alone."

"I've seen guys like Faust before. They don't stop. They have an inferiority complex and they need to tear others down so they can feel good about themselves," Diaz said.

"You hit the nail on the head there. But understanding why Faust is like he is doesn't really help my situation," Ruggerio continued. "I can remember loving this job. I couldn't wait to get to work. One time, when I was a rookie like you, I went on an accident call. Two-vehicle collision, nothing major, no one was hurt. But when I got there, I saw a little kid crying and hugging his mother while they were standing outside of their wrecked car on the side of the highway. I walked up to them and this little kid, probably about five years old, broke from his mother's arms and ran toward me, throwing his arms up for me to hug him." He stopped to remember the moment. "Its times like that, when you can give a little comfort that makes this job worth it."

Diaz didn't know what to say; he was stunned. He knew that Ruggerio liked being a cop, but he didn't realize how much. That was probably why Ruggerio was so good at his job. Ruggerio truly looked upon his profession as some type of calling that he had to answer, like a priest or one of those foreign missionaries who live with natives for years and help them grow corn or something. Those kinds of people who have a sincere desire to help their fellow men. *Divine vocation,* Diaz thought it was called. He wondered what it would be like to feel that kind of passion for something.

Ruggerio is... Let me see, Diaz thought to himself, trying to come up with the perfect word to describe him. He is *devoted.* Yeah that's it, devoted. Devoted or obsessed, he wasn't sure at this point. One thing was for sure; Ruggerio had a fire in him to be a great cop. It was either something to envy in a person or was it a curse when dealing with no-win situations like this one with Faust.

The radio erupted and shook Diaz and Ruggerio from their thoughts.

"All cars in the Highland Street area be on the lookout for the following male suspect thought to be armed with a handgun. Patrons of Milligan's Tavern report that a black male was inside the establishment and threatening them with a firearm. The male was to have left on foot, last seen headed toward Bartlett Park. Male is described with medium complexion, approximately five-seven to five-nine, one fifty to one seventy pounds, wearing a beige lightweight jacket and brown slacks. The firearm was described as being black in color, no further description. Any units coming in contact are asked to stop and hold for questioning and to use caution." The female operator conveyed the information with a steady professional cadence.

"That park is a few blocks away," Ruggerio said to Diaz, seemingly in better spirits, but still brewing inside. "Take the next right then kill the lights," he told his trainee.

Diaz glanced over at Ruggerio, curious about his partner's mood. He could tell that Ruggerio was still tense by the way his right hand was balled up into a fist on the dashboard in front of him. This doesn't look good. Maybe I should call Tobias, he contemplated. But Diaz didn't want to offend Ruggerio. He hoped Tobias would back them up. He had said that he would stay close.

The suspect in question was Dickson, of course. The bartender, Joe, coached by Ace, had called the police. Ace encouraged Joe to get creative in his description of the events at the bar. They had never actually seen a gun on Dickson, but instead had decided to place one in his hand anyway. Besides, Ace told Joe, all them blacks carry guns, so it's not really lying. Anyway, that is the only way to get the cops' attention.

"Brown slacks," Diaz thought out loud.

"Yeah, what about it?" asked Ruggerio.

"Brown slacks. That was the same description of the robbery suspect from the previous shift. I read it on the alert sheet before we left the building," Diaz was proud of himself for following Ruggerio's advice to read the alert sheet before every shift and take notes. Ruggerio opened his own notebook and checked what he had written. Diaz smiled, glad to see that his training officer followed his own advice.

"The coat description is different. The alert sheet has the robber wearing a blue coat, not a beige one," Ruggerio reported.

"Maybe he changed," Diaz speculated, wanting his instinct to be correct.

"Yeah, that's possible," Ruggerio said thoughtfully.

"Brown slacks, that's unusual," Diaz remarked. "Usually you hear brown Dickies or work pants, like the bangers wear, not brown slacks. Sounds more like Dockers or something," he said, hoping that he made sense.

Diaz turned right and then cut the lights.

Ruggerio did not respond to Diaz's analysis of the unusual clothing description, except to say, "uh-huh." He was still holding his right hand in a fist on top of the dash.

"Pull up to the curb," Ruggerio told Diaz.

Diaz brought the patrol car to a stop.

"We can see the whole park from here." Ruggerio's eyes scanned back and forth, neck straining over Diaz like a wolf scanning for prey. His burn scar was exposed by the way his body was turned. Diaz could not help but to compare his partner to a wounded wild animal, still ready to fight.

Suddenly, Ruggerio fixed his gaze on something and then narrowed his eyes as if he was trying to focus his eyes to make something out. Diaz looked in the same direction, but he couldn't see anything in the darkness.

"There he is. Kill the engine." Ruggerio sounded determined.

Diaz looked out again. This time he saw a form walking toward them on a poorly lit footpath made of brown brick and meandering through tall oak trees and shrubbery in the park. The figure was about a hundred yards away, making it hard to distinguish, especially in the darkness.

"How do you know that's him?" asked Diaz.

"The slacks. This guy has dress pants on. There's enough light to make them out. And they go up to his waist, like Dockers. His jacket is bunched at his waist, where the elastic is and I can see where his pants are belted. This isn't a gangbanger wearing low-ride Dickies. One other thing. He is staggering like he's drunk." He said it all without taking his eyes off the suspect in the distance. He spoke in a hushed tone as if he was talking to himself and not directly to Diaz.

Diaz was nervous, not only about the potentially armed suspect that they would inevitably be challenging soon, but even more about how his partner was going to handle this situation. Again, he thought about getting some help but this time he said it out loud.

"Maybe we should call for backup?" he said, tactfully.

"Go ahead," Ruggerio answered. Then, without another word, he opened the passenger door, never removing his eyes from the approaching suspect.

"7-21 to radio. Possible suspect from Milligan's Tavern on north side of Bartlett Park. We are going to attempt to stop him." Diaz made the call, lowering the volume on the car radio to lessen the chance of alerting the suspect.

Ruggerio walked tentatively in front of the squad car and across the street, then crouched down near the base of a thick oak tree. The suspect was walking slowly, staggering from side to side.

Diaz waited for the acknowledgement from the 9-1-1 operator, then slowly and quietly exited the cruiser. He knelt down next to Ruggerio, his breathing and heart rate beginning to accelerate. He already had his gun out, prepared for anything. Diaz watched as the suspect stumbled his way along the path under a row of street lamps—not all of which were working. He couldn't see a gun in his hand, but the guy matched the description given over the radio perfectly.

The path ended about fifty yards up the street, connecting to the same street where Diaz had parked the squad car. Between them and the border of the path was a large open field, distinguished only by several randomly placed trees and some lighted lamp posts. The opposite side of the street was lined with parked cars that probably belong to the occupants of the adjacent row houses. It was more like a big alley than a street. At the end of this roadway that ran along the edge of the park, Diaz could see cars traveling in both directions into and out of this part of the city.

They were on sort of a demarcation line between low and high crime areas. On the opposite side of the park were mainly residential, middle-class communities. This side, however, was the beginning of a crime-ridden area, filled with housing projects and low-income rental units. Drugs, prostitution, and rundown rental properties – they could all be found here. But something looked strange to Diaz. There were no people milling about tonight. No one was out on their porches, or on the streets. No drug dealers were hanging out by their expensive and tricked out rides—though he saw some parked near the curb. They were apparent, even in the darkness, from the shine off all those chrome rims.

"Where is everyone in this neighborhood?" Diaz whispered to Ruggerio as he watched the suspect stop and rest next to a tree.

"Lookouts. The lookouts probably warned everyone when we drove up," Ruggerio surmised.

It was quiet, so quiet that Diaz could hear the suspect muttering something to himself, although he couldn't discern what he was saying. Then the gunman cried out loud enough for Diaz to hear.

"You dirty son-of-a-bitches, leave me the fuck alone," the gunman pleaded, looking up at the sky.

"OK," Ruggerio whispered to Diaz, about to lay out the plan of attack. "You flank out to the left through the park. Move from tree to tree until I signal you to stop. I will go along the line of parked cars and make the challenge, alright?" He wanted confirmation from Diaz before they moved.

"OK, but don't you think we should hold off until back up arrives?" Diaz was still worried about his partner's mental state and wanted other officers around. He'd hoped that another officer would intervene and relieve Ruggerio from becoming directly involved with the gunman.

Ruggerio's only reply was, "Let's go."

Diaz felt very uneasy and just wanted to observe this guy until extra officers were on scene. But he had no choice. He had to abide by his training officer's directions. There was no other option available to him. He just hoped that the incident would conclude without violence.

CHAPTER 5

"What the fuck is going on? Can we all go back out yet?" the short black girl with the southern drawl said to the man watching at the picture window.

"Shhhhh," he answered, holding his index finger to his pursed lips.

The girl staggered across the darkened room, bumping into a wobbly coffee table with her leg as she made her way over to the window to see what the man was looking at outside. Neither one knew the other's real name, only their street names, a common situation on the street. The girl crouched down slightly to peer out the window next to the man whom she only knew by the name "G." She also had a street alias. Since she was a refugee of hurricane Katrina from Louisiana, she had been pegged with the name New *Ho*leans. It didn't matter that she was actually from Baton Rouge rather than New Orleans. The name was eventually shortened and everyone knew her as New Ho.

She and G had hooked up into a little partnership for this evening. New Ho would entice some unsuspecting "John" into thinking that she was turning tricks. When the "John" was hooked, New Ho would walk him into a secluded place in the park where G was waiting in the bushes with a .38 snub nose revolver—a little item stolen by G that very evening from a friend's house. He would bring the gun back when he was finished with it and hope that his friend wouldn't realize the gun was missing.

After introducing the "John" to his .38, G would then relieve the poor frightened man of all his money. After making two quick scores, New Ho and G bought themselves five rocks of crack and went off to have a little party. G knew about the abandoned row-house next to Bartlett Park, where they could light up their rocks in private.

New Ho and G heard the alert from the lookouts that "Five-O" was coming. Five-O was street slang for the police. A dated reference to the old police television show, *Hawaii Five-O*. In urban drug areas, lookouts are always posted to watch for the cops; when they are spotted an alert is raised so the dealers and junkies can vacate the street before the arrival of the police. When one of the lookouts shouted, "Five-O!" in a few seconds the street was devoid of any humans—except for Dickson of course, who was still staggering along the footpath toward the bridge.

G had been plastered to the window ever since he heard the "five-o" call. Cops made G nervous; he was on parole and if he were caught with any contraband at all, he would go back to prison for two more years. Add armed robbery on to that and he could get a total of seven. He hated cops because in his last experience, for no reason they had given him a bad beating when they arrested him. G figured if any of the cops came toward the abandoned house they were in, he just might use the .38 to get away. He had checked earlier and the gun was fully loaded.

"What's going on?" New Ho whispered.

"Just keep quiet. The cops are after someone," G said quietly.

He could see two officers kneeling down next to each other behind a big tree. They were intently watching a brother who was obviously high or drunk, staggering along the brick walkway in the park. G was somewhat relieved that apparently the cops weren't there for him. He had worried that they may have responded to a complaint by one of the victimized "Johns" he and New Ho had robbed earlier. Comforted by the belief that he was not the intended target of the two cops, G watched the scene playing out before him, one that was all too familiar to him from childhood memories.

G was new to Pittsburgh, having grown up in public housing projects in Erie, Pennsylvania. He had found himself in Pittsburgh after being placed in a halfway house just before being released on parole. He quickly came to realize that Pittsburgh was no different than Erie; cops were cops no matter where you went, he reasoned. As a boy, G had witnessed numerous clashes between the police and members of his neighborhood. Of course, in the minds of G and his friends, the police were always in the wrong. The members of G's community always perceived police practices as excessive or corrupt. To G and his friends, the police were the most visible means of oppression employed by a government bent on keeping the black population from rising in society.

Prompted by the resurgence of these old memories, G caressed the wooden handle of the snub nose in his waistband, and imagined gunning down both cops outside the window. He felt himself sweating copiously and noticed his heart was pounding in his chest. He realized that the cocaine in his system and the anger at the police were the cause of these symptoms.

"Motherfuckers," G said under his breath. He considered the scene before him. They are probably going to shoot that young brother, he reasoned.

"What are they doin' out there?" New Ho asked, her eyes half closed from the effects of the drug.

"Cops are after a brother in the park. Just get over there and keep quiet," G ordered. New Ho obeyed by plopping down on the broken down couch backed against a far wall.

"We need to score some more money G," she implored, still whispering.

"Just wait and shut up. I'll tell you when we go again," G commanded.

He watched as one cop fanned out to the left, darting from tree to tree holding his handgun in front of him, pointing it at the ground as he moved. The other was bent over, creeping slowly in the direction of the young brother. He was staying in the darkness of the sidewalk in front of the row houses and moving along the line of the cars parked next to the curb. He could see that this cop was holding his gun out too. G thought to himself that this poor messed up young brother didn't have a chance.

Helpless and frustrated, G wanted to do something about the situation. He didn't know what, but he had to do something. He couldn't just stand there and let this thing happen right under his nose. With these thoughts racing into his drug induced mind, G jerked the snub nose out of his waistband and held it down at his side, grinding his teeth at the thought of cops gunning down another black man for nothing.

It seemed as if the earth was shifting under his feet. With every step he took, Jamar Dickson found it difficult to judge where the ground would meet his feet. To keep upright, he needed to walk very slowly and deliberately. Even though he was being so deliberate, he would still lose balance and stagger occasionally. The pain pills and alcohol had kicked in at full force now, wreaking havoc with his physical movements. On top of not being able to walk straight, Dickson's vision was becoming significantly blurred. He could discern that he was on a footpath, but to make out the edges of the path was difficult. On one step, his foot landed half on the bricked path and half on the grass, which was uneven and caused him to stumble. He would have fallen to the ground if it weren't for a nearby oak tree, which he grabbed onto and was able to stay upright.

While contemplating his inebriated condition, Dickson reasoned that if it weren't for the discriminatory treatment of several authority figures recently, he would not be in this position. He considered people like Lauren's father and the police, all elitist bigots, having to reassure themselves that they were important by abusing and oppressing people like him. Even though he didn't come from a disadvantaged home, he felt that he was still looked upon with disdain by the "white upper class majority" due to his skin color.

Even his own father had bought into the idea that you had to play the game like the good old white boys. Dickson was visualizing his father, with his fat-ass white friends, lounging in the country club, puffing their twenty-dollar cigars and sipping expensive brandy. He could just hear his father deftly avoiding the necessity of having to answer the question, "How's your son faring these days Rudy?"

"Oh, he is doing just fine, trying to find himself you know. He is trying out a few different courses of study before he settles on one particular field," Dickson imagined his father saying to a group of saggy-jowled old men, quickly changing the subject to the latest hot stock rumor. Dickson wondered how his father was going to explain to his pals about his son jumping to his death into the Allegheny River. He was sure that his father wouldn't even shed a tear; in fact, he would probably be relieved. No longer would he have to be tormented by his son's failures and disappointments. In essence, Dickson was actually doing his family, not to mention Lauren's father, a favor by killing himself. As he stood there, hugging a tree trunk to keep from falling, the images of those who had tortured him throughout his life flashed in his mind. The anger boiled up inside of him until he had to release it by shouting.

"You dirty son-of-a-bitches, leave me alone!"

Then a thought entered his mind. Lauren! What about her? What would she think when she heard that he killed himself? She wouldn't know the actual circumstances of what made him commit suicide. Dickson decided that he had to try calling her again to explain why suicide was the only answer. Dickson couldn't see the numbers on the touch-tone pad, so he simply pushed the call button twice to call the last number dialed.

The phone rang but no one picked up. He was about to disconnect the call when he realized that Lauren had an answering machine. Dickson decided that he would leave her a message, even though there was a chance her father would erase it before Lauren could hear it. Dickson talked very lowly and slowly so his words could be understood, explaining his reasons for ending his life and freeing her from the tension and strife he was causing between her and her father. It was at this point when Diaz and Ruggerio heard the gunman muttering under his breath, words that they could not make out.

Dickson disconnected the call when he finished and replaced the phone in his pocket, then continued on his mission. He had reached the end of the footpath and could see the bridge in the distance. Only the top of the superstructure was visible over the roofs of some buildings, but he knew that he was headed in the right direction.

He staggered again as he misjudged the height difference from the footpath edge to the asphalt of the roadway, but he caught himself and maintained his balance. He decided that he should use the parked cars to lean on as he walked down the roadway toward the river and the bridge. His mind was becoming so cloudy that he wondered if he was going to make the bridge at all. He willed himself forward, determined to make it all the way. Jamar Dickson dramatically concluded in his drug-soaked mind that oblivion would be his salvation from the troubles of this earthly life.

Diaz moved as fluidly and quietly as possible, trotting across the roadway onto the grass of the park grounds, and then stopping behind a large oak tree. Breathing was becoming a little more difficult as his tension level started to rise. Conversely, Diaz also realized that he wasn't nearly as nervous as on that first night when he and Ruggerio had responded to the shooting call. Since that time, Diaz had experienced and resolved numerous incidents, many of which involved the possibility of physical danger. He rationalized that since he had successfully managed himself through so many of these types of situations, he must have received a kind of inoculation from the fear response, enabling him to approach these situations in a more relaxed state.

Diaz first peered out from behind the tree to get a read on where the suspect was. He spotted him about to walk out onto the roadway. Then he checked on Ruggerio and saw him creeping along the line of cars parked next to the curb. He was using the cars as cover, since they were situated between him and the gunman. Diaz checked on the position of the suspect again; seeing that his back was still to Diaz, he felt it would be safe to pick out another large tree to move toward. While he crept along, careful to hold his firearm out in front of him, he constantly kept watch on the suspect, occasionally peeking down at the terrain in front of him so as not to trip. After making it behind his next source of cover he repeated the same technique to move again. The suspect stopped and leaned against the car that was parked third in line from the intersection with the main roadway at the end of the park. He appeared to be resting or trying to get his bearings. Diaz checked his hands again but, to his relief, did not see any weapons. He looked over to check on Ruggerio and could see the top of his head and part of his back as he continued to move along the parked cars.

Diaz decided that he needed to move a few feet closer, so he selected another tree and made his move. As he did, Diaz turned his gaze away from Ruggerio's direction and back to the perp. In doing so, he missed his signal to stop where he was.

Ruggerio watched as Diaz was moving quietly toward another tree. He tried giving him the halt sign by putting his non-gun hand up, palm out, but Diaz was concentrating on the gunman. When Ruggerio turned to look at the suspect, he was relieved to see that his back was still toward Diaz's position, seemingly oblivious to the activity taking place all around him.

But then…"CRACK!" Diaz's foot found a dried twig on the dark ground and the snapping of wood caused such a loud sound that the gunman wheeled around to look in the direction of the noise. He moved so fast that he lost his balance and slid down the side of the car he was leaning against; his rump landed on the pavement.

Ruggerio's heart stopped for a moment; he quickly looked in the direction of the sound and saw that Diaz had frozen in place, stunned at having caused such a loud noise. Ruggerio snapped his head back toward the suspect and quickly raised his weapon in the same direction as a precaution, but he couldn't see the suspect any longer; he had disappeared from sight. Ruggerio began to panic at the thought of losing the suspect's position; he quickly lowered his torso behind the car that he was positioned next to and scanned the area to relocate the suspect.

G was also startled when he heard the cracking twig. By reflex he nearly pulled the trigger on the .38, but caught himself in time when he realized the source of the sound. G saw how the cop on the sidewalk next to the parked cars had reacted, raising his gun quickly as if he wanted to shoot the poor brother on the street.

The young man was so messed up that he went down on the ground like a chump. That nigga ain't got a chance, G thought to himself. G wanted to call out to him on the street, but he knew that if he did his own freedom was in jeopardy. With few options, G had an overwhelming feeling of powerlessness. These emotions triggered more old memories from his youth.

He had seen this thing happen before, as a kid. The Erie cops had gunned down a young black man on his block in broad daylight. They shot him so many times he must have had five pounds of lead in him. After it was done, those honky ass pigs stood around together, drank coffee and laughed with each other over their big kill for the day. G would never forget how nonchalant the cops had been about killing someone. It was one of his first lessons on the cruelty of the world. Unfortunately, he would experience much worse as he grew to adulthood, most of it from his own mother and her various man friends.

G was not about to let that happen again; he had to stop or disrupt the inevitable killing of this young man somehow. Then, he realized what could help the young brother escape the two cops tracking him down—or at least keep their heads down. He could squeeze off a few rounds from his snub nose, making the cops dive for cover. This might give the young nigga time to run away. G could duck out the back of the abandon house and take a few alleys toward his friend's house where he could then deposit the snub nose. Everyone is happy and the young buck is still alive and kicking for another day. Except for the cops. They would have to find someone else to blow a few holes in tonight.

When Jamar Dickson had called Lauren's house she heard the phone ring but didn't dare answer it, because her father had threatened to take her Mercedes away from her if she spoke to Dickson again. She liked Jamar but she *loved* her Mercedes. The thought of bumming rides or walking to her classes at school was just too humiliating. Besides, Jamar was starting to get a little too intense for her liking anyway; every time they were together he was complaining about his dad or how everyone was abusing him. She thought it was time for her to move on. Maybe she could scope out the guys at the medical school building when she went back for classes.

Lauren had been in her second-floor bedroom when she heard the house phone ring. Since the answering machine was on the first floor, she could not hear Jamar leaving his message. She hadn't heard her father pick up either and she knew that he liked to screen calls at this hour of the evening. She decided to walk out of her room and check out the machine. If it was Jamar she could erase the message before her father heard it. When she walked out of her room, her father was still in the shower, so she felt safe to check for voice messages.

To Lauren's relief, she discovered that the recorded message left on the machine had not yet been played by her father. Lauren pushed the play button and Jamar's intoxicated voice came over the speaker at a volume level of eight—much too loud. Lauren was startled at first by the loud volume of Jamar's voice, then by the content of his message.

"*Lauren I love you and I can't live any longer if we can't be together. Tell your punk ass father that he did this to me. I am leaving on my final journey. Maybe in the next world I will be more acceptable to others?*" He disconnected after this short but direct proclamation. Lauren was panicked that Jamar was actually thinking about killing himself. She didn't know what to do, should she call the police? She didn't know where to send them. Telling her father wouldn't do any good. He would be glad to hear that Jamar was committing suicide. Lauren then noticed that the phone number that Jamar called from was on her caller ID. She quickly realized what she had to do. She would erase the message and call Jamar back and talk him out of this foolish idea. If she did it fast enough her father would never know.

Dickson just wanted to rest for a bit before making off for the bridge, his final destination here on earth. He was looking forward to seeing what eternity would be like. He made his way over to a light colored four-door sedan that was parked next to the curb, third back from the intersection. Dickson supported himself by placing his hands on top of the driver's side front fender area, almost mimicking the old pat down search position that police would use.

He thought about calling Lauren again. He needed to hear her voice once more. At this point there was no need to worry about her father answering the phone. Dickson wasn't going to ever see him again anyway. Still feeling unsteady from the drugs, and with his backside toward the park, he faced the car and pressed his body against it for support. Dickson retrieved the cell phone from his pocket with his right hand and placed it in his left, even though this was the hand that had the nylon brace for his broken arm. He needed his free hand to punch the re-dial button on the touch pad. But before he could open the flip phone cover to access the number pad he heard something that interrupted him.

"CRACK!" The sound of a twig breaking. Startled, Dickson wheeled his body around toward the direction of the sound. As he did so, his upper torso turned faster than his legs and his center of gravity shifted to his right side, causing him to lose balance and stumble. Dickson started to fall and made a desperate attempt to reach out with his right hand and grab hold of something on the car to keep from falling. He found nothing to hold onto but the smooth side of the car. Dickson slid down the side of the car and hit the pavement with a thud.

He looked up to see a figure standing still in the open and shrouded in darkness. The figure was barely visible, due to slim fragments of moonlight that filtered through the leaves of the tall oaks. He righted himself into a sitting position and watched as the figure moved toward one of the trees in the park. Dickson saw something familiar in the way this form moved, as if whoever it was had been stalking him. His suspicions were confirmed when a beam from a distant street light reflected off of something shiny on the stranger's left chest.

"COPS AGAIN!" he screamed in his head. Dickson could not allow himself to be abused again by the police. He couldn't let them have the satisfaction. While scrambling to right himself into a sitting position, Dickson noticed that he was still holding the cell phone in his hand.

Looking down at the cell phone and the brace on his arm, the memory of the attack by the police dog flashed in his head. Dickson began to feel several emotions simultaneously. Anger, confusion, and paranoia were exaggerated by the mind-altering chemicals saturating his brain. His impaired thinking gave him a new idea for a course of action that would take care of all his problems. The idea popped into his brain like the throwing of a light switch. *"I will use the pigs for my way out!"* After all, he had already successfully faked having a gun once, why not another time? If he really sold the stupid pigs on it, maybe they could save him the trouble of jumping from a bridge. It shouldn't be too hard, he thought; cops are always ready to use force and if anyone knew about police excessive force it was Dickson. He again noticed the cell phone in his hand and decided that he would use the cell phone to threaten the cops, using it to mimic a handgun. A trigger-happy pig could do the dirty work and Dickson would be free of discrimination, hatred, and bigotry.

To Dickson, this felt like the ultimate answer, the end of his quest. Then, abruptly, something fired in his brain, a synapse that ignites decision making. His mind cleared suddenly, the fog from the drug stupor seemed to be lifted, all inhibitions were removed, and he felt free. Jamar Dickson knew that this move was the right thing. He hadn't felt like this in years. His thoughts were perfect and rational, or so it seemed to him in this impaired condition. He was on autopilot with no failsafe mode, all other distractions or secondary thoughts were blocked, and nothing would stop him. His physical actions became robotic and his face fixed into a trance, eyes squarely aimed at the cop. Dickson began to rise up and move toward his destiny.

Taymond Diaz was moving very effectively, he thought, constantly scanning his surroundings as he moved from one cover position to the next, all the while edging closer to the target. He found himself next to another of the ubiquitous oak trees on the grounds of the park, but this one was little more than a sapling and did not provide good protection against bullets. Diaz saw that the gunman had stopped and was leaning against a parked car with his back to him. It was a good time to make another move to a more suitable cover position. He quickly found a thicker tree approximately ten yards to his left.

As he was making this final move, his foot fell on a twig, creating a loud cracking sound. In a hypersensitive condition, Diaz thought the sound waves were loud enough to fracture glass. In alarm, he froze in place for a few seconds. Still with his foot on top of the broken twig, he looked up at the gunman to see what his reaction would be. Diaz then observed the surreal scene as the suspect spun around in surprise, like a movie stuntman who had just been shot, then lose his balance and collapse to the pavement. The eyes of the two men met for the first time. Diaz realized what was meant by a condition he had been instructed on in the academy, the "thousand yard stare." A phenomenon experienced by battle weary solders and emotionally disturbed persons, it refers to a mental state that operates on a separate plane from reality. A person in this condition is very dangerous and highly unpredictable. He or she has lost the capability for logical reasoning and has no regard for his or her own physical well-being or the well-being of those who might want to interfere.

Diaz felt a shiver of fear race up his spine, tingling at the base of his neck as he looked into the eyes of the suspect. It seemed as if Dickson was gazing right through him and beyond to some object in the distance. The suspect's eyes were fixed laser straight, with an unblinking stare and a facial expression completely devoid of emotion. Diaz concluded right there in those short few seconds that this encounter was not going to end without violence.

Even though he hoped that it wouldn't come to that, he knew, unequivocally, someone was going to die.

He saw Diaz frozen in place and wanted to shout over to him to get moving and put some cover between him and the suspect. But Ruggerio waited for a second to see what Diaz would do. Maybe he was stopped for some reason? Ruggerio still could not see the suspect from his position; he couldn't provide covering fire if it became necessary, so he decided to move. He decided to slip between the front and rear ends of the two cars parked near him so he could quick peek out from the driver's side rear quarter panel of the lead car to get a read on the suspect. Ruggerio quietly moved a distance of about four feet, between the cars, then crouched behind the taillight assembly. He used the quick peek technique to relocate the suspect. He darted his head out from cover only far enough to see where the subject was, then just as quick, jerked his head back to the original position behind cover. He sighed in temporary relief to see that the gunman was in a sitting position, apparently distracted by something in his hand. He was not focusing on Diaz nor was he a threat at that time.

Mentally shaking himself out of his own trance, Diaz regained composure and decided that he had an opportunity to move to cover while the gunman was still on the ground. Diaz moved quickly to get behind the tree he intended to use for cover. After safely making it to the large oak, he relaxed a bit, then crouched down in a baseball catcher's stance to make himself a smaller target. Since he had not been directly threatened at this point, he continued to point the barrel of his firearm at the ground and not at the suspect—even though he would have been justified to do so with the reports that this subject was carrying a firearm.

She hit the "erase all messages" button on the answering machine and picked up the receiver to dial the number Jamar had called from. Lauren was in a mild panic because she knew that her father did not take long showers, "a waste of water and money" he would say, the tight wad. Lauren was confident that she could convince Jamar to stop thinking about suicide. He was so impetuous, and she knew what buttons to push to make him come around to her way of thinking. All she had to do was agree to meet up with him somewhere and he would be back to normal. Of course she would not go through with the meeting, remembering her father's threat about the Mercedes. Lauren would handle that situation by making a believable excuse to miss the meeting and keep doing the same routine until Jamar got tired of the exercise and would leave her alone.

Lauren looked at the number she had written down and punched the numbers into the handset. In the meantime, she dreamed of asking her father to buy her a new car. A sports car this time, but the color had to accent her blond hair. Maybe red, she pondered as she hit the "send" button.

G didn't want to fire the gun from inside because New Ho would probably scream at the loud explosion. The sound would be muffled anyway, which would not provide the effect he wanted—to make the cops duck for cover. Before he could decide on where to pop off the rounds, he needed to do something about New Ho, so she wouldn't be in the way.

"Listen, you go in the back room and wait. I'll be right back with some money for you. OK baby?" he told her, figuring that the incentive of money would motivate her to cooperate without complaint.

"A-w-w-ight, but hurry. I'm starting to Jones y'all." She sauntered back down a hallway into the back room and out of sight. Now G could deal with these pigs.

G was standing in the living room of the abandoned row house, looking around for an open window where he could stick the gun out and fire for effect. The only window in the room, however, was the one he had used to observe the cops and the young man. G thought that there had to be an open window somewhere close by, since he had heard the snap of that twig so clearly. He moved from the living room area through a threshold that divided the living room from the front entrance. Inspecting the front door, G saw the reason for the sound quality in the house. There was a pane of glass missing from one of the windows of the door. It was a cheap hollow wooden door that had a series of four diamond-shaped windows clustered in the top half. The windows were designed in a diamond pattern, but one of the panes was missing, popped out of its frame. Probably squatters had removed the window to come in and use the abandoned house for the same reason G and New Ho were using it now. G noticed a slipshod nail job on the jamb side of the door. The property managers must have nailed the door shut, apparently a half-hearted attempt to discourage others from using the same entryway. To G's advantage, the neglect of the property owners not replacing the popped out window, provided him with the gun port that he needed to put a scare into the cops. All he had to do was wait for the right moment.

Ruggerio was still behind the car in a squatting position when he saw the suspect stand up and lean his back on the same car that he had fallen next to. He was preparing himself to make the challenge, to order the subject to submit to arrest. But then he stopped himself upon seeing the gunman slowly raise up his left arm and point in Diaz's direction, as if he was holding a gun.

Diaz peeked around the trunk of the tree and to his horror saw the gunman standing and pointing what appeared to him to be a gun in his direction. Diaz quickly jerked his head back behind cover and took a deep breath, trying to think what he should do next. He silently cursed Ruggerio for not waiting for backup.

Dickson's mind shifted into overdrive; visions of Lauren, his father, and his mother crying at his funeral played out before him. The future scene of the cops standing trial for murdering him flashed in his mind. These images made him smile in vindication and with the knowledge that it was his turn to show his transgressors the error of their ways.

When he raised the cell phone, with the stubby antenna pointed out like the barrel of a snub nose handgun, he saw the cop duck his head back behind a tree. He was scaring the cop but the cop wasn't getting ready to shoot him. Dickson felt that the cop needed some encouragement. He shuffled a few feet to his right to get a better angle on him behind the tree, still leaning on the car to keep from falling.

"Come on you bitch. Come out from behind that tree," Dickson punched out the cell phone in front of him, toward Diaz to emphasize his statement. "Stand up like a man. Are you afraid to die?" Dickson taunted Diaz, who still crouched behind the tree.

G saw the young buck stand up and point what looked like a gun at the cop behind the tree. He also saw the cop kneeling behind the car to the young man's rear and knew that the young nigga was as good as dead unless he did something. The time had come. G put his gun hand out of the diamond shaped opening and pointed the gun straight out.

Due to the elevation of the house and the door behind which G was standing, the barrel was pointed several feet above Ruggerio's position and behind him. The dynamics of the sound patterns that would be produced from the round that G was about to fire would be plausible enough for Ruggerio to believe that the round was actually coming from Dickson's position. But that would not be the only selling point convincing Ruggerio that Dickson was shooting at Diaz.

G squeezed the trigger of the snub nose and the round discharged, causing the barrel to spit out an orange flame, blinding him temporarily. The bullet whizzed through the air, flying through the park and burying itself fifteen feet up a tree on the opposite side of the park. G wanted to make the cops duck down and stay down so the young buck could run. Or maybe he would drop down also so he wouldn't be shot. He figured that a second shot was needed to produce this effect from the cops and the young man. So immediately after the first round went off, he quickly pulled the trigger on the next round in the chamber. This time, the hammer had fallen on a cheap reload, a round that had not been primed correctly and the bullet did not fire. G decided that it was time to make good his escape while the cops were trying to figure out where the shot came from. He ran through the house, catching a glimpse of New Ho standing in the hall, where she could easily have seen what G had just done. But he couldn't worry about that now. He needed to get out of that house and away from the area as soon as possible. As for New Ho being a witness, he thought, she didn't know his name anyway. Any questioning by the police would only provide the street name of G, and there were hundreds of black males in the projects with the same street name.

Ruggerio observed as the suspect turned his body slightly in his direction, giving him a view at what the subject was holding in his left hand. In the darkness it was hard to tell exactly what the object was, but it certainly could have been a snub nose revolver. He didn't know it at the time, but the cast Dickson was wearing on his arm from the dog bite assisted in creating the illusion that he was holding a firearm in his hand.

Ruggerio had the P and the O of the word POLICE out of his mouth when he heard the report of a gunshot. It sounded a little weird and for a millisecond he didn't believe that the gunman had fired the shot. But when he saw a flash of light from the suspect's gun hand, he knew that the gunman had shot at Diaz. Or at least he thought so. What Ruggerio didn't know was that the flash he saw was the cell phone light that flickered to indicate an incoming call. This call was the one Lauren placed to Jamar's cell phone, to talk him out of his suicidal intentions.

Ruggerio instinctively squeezed the trigger on his .40 caliber Glock semiautomatic pistol and as the round exploded, the firearm kicked back in the two-handed grip he employed. He was confident that his aim was true and that the bullet would find the target. Ruggerio was ready to follow up with another shot, but held back when he saw the gunman's body lurch forward from the impact of the bullet, the projectile hitting home on the left side of his back.

CHAPTER 6

The bullet that Ruggerio fired smashed against one of Dickson's vertebrae in his back. This bullet is designed to mushroom out when it impacts a solid object, to prevent the round from passing entirely through a human body and continuing on its flight path—endangering any innocent bystanders who might be in the area beyond the intended target. The bullet did exactly what it was designed to do, but after impact, fragments of the bullet broke free from the main body of the projectile and penetrated into various surrounding organs. A few metal fragments perforated the main artery to Dickson's heart. The results of the shot were twofold; first, Dickson's frail body was thrown forward from the force of the bullet, and second, the severe bleeding caused by the damaged artery produced death within a few seconds.

Another effect was that the cell phone in Dickson's hand flew out and forward, bounding and skipping on the ground and coming to rest under a parked car. The impact with the ground caused the call that Lauren placed to be disconnected. On Lauren's end, she heard one ring then a dial tone. Almost immediately she could hear her father coming out of the shower. She decided that she better replace the hand set and make her call to Jamar later.

Dickson's phone had momentum behind it, which caused it to tumble and roll under a parked car. The phone bounced up and came to rest inside the curb-side rear wheel, wedging itself in the concave space between the hub and the rim. Diaz did not see this since he was still behind the tree when the shots were fired. Ruggerio did not see it either since his angle would have placed three parked cars between himself and Dickson's body, blocking his view. In fact, Ruggerio had to step out from behind cover, partially into the street, to see Dickson lying on the ground. He also wanted to determine if the suspect was definitely down and no longer a threat. In a few moments it was obvious to Ruggerio that the suspect was dead. No movement was observed from the suspect's limbs nor could he see his chest rising or falling. Diaz took a peek around the tree trunk and saw Ruggerio still pointing his weapon at the subject, as the body lay motionless on the pavement. Diaz aimed his weapon at the suspect also as a precaution, in case the gunman gave one last effort to shoot at the officers. He watched as Ruggerio slowly and cautiously moved, still covering the suspect with his weapon, until he was standing next to the downed assailant.

Police squads were coming in from all directions, most following procedure by arriving with their lights out. They had not been informed about what had just happened and believed there was still an armed suspect in the area. Ruggerio was close enough to re-holster and then cuff the suspect, per procedure.

Diaz saw Ruggerio check for a pulse at the carotid artery of the body. Finding no signs of life, Ruggerio called out to Diaz, "No pulse, but call for an ambulance anyway."

Diaz switched on his portable radio and called out to all responding cars.

"7-21 to base. Be advised we have one suspect down, requesting an ambulance. All cars come in code-four."

Code-four was the call sign to indicate to other units that the scene appears safe. After completing the call, Diaz also holstered his weapon and walked over to Ruggerio. He found him scanning the pavement and mumbling, "Where is the gun, where is it?" Then he asked Diaz, "I need a flashlight. Do you have one?"

"No, Guy. I left mine in the car. It has to be here somewhere. Just wait until one of the other guys get here. Someone will have a light," Diaz said reassuringly.

Tobias was one of the first to arrive, huffing and puffing from the short jog he had just made from his parked squad to their location.

"What happened?" he asked Ruggerio first.

All he could say was, "I can't find the gun. Do you have a light?"

Tobias clicked on his light and began to scan the area for a gun but couldn't see anything, even when Ruggerio directed him on where to search. Within seconds, more officers arrived—including the shift sergeant, who took Ruggerio to the side to receive a briefing on what had occurred. A crowd of onlookers began to gather, mostly black folks from the neighborhood. Within minutes, as the word spread about another black man killed by the police, the crowd grew larger and larger. Along with its size, the gathering became proportionately more unruly and agitated, hurling invectives at the police who were maintaining a perimeter around the scene.

The sergeant, who had already called for the detectives to respond, placed a second call for more security, relating in his radio message that the crowd was becoming increasingly hostile. Due to the crowd control problem, the officers conducting the search for the missing gun had to stop their efforts to concentrate on the people encroaching on the crime scene. Bottles started to rain down on the officers attempting to hold the line on the perimeter. The officers, who were still too few in number to disperse the onlookers, had to maintain the demeanor of a holding action until reinforcements arrived.

Ruggerio watched as he saw young black men and women shouting at the officers with hate-filled faces. The content of their angry shouts was varied but the meanings were similar; they were accusing the police of being nothing more than murderers. Eventually the crowd united in their efforts and began to chant the familiar mantra that became popular during the riots that followed the acquittal of the LAPD officers accused in the Rodney King beating trial.

"No justice, no peace! No justice, no peace!" the crowd chanted in unison. The sergeant told Ruggerio to stay put; he would be back after he helped deal with the crowd.

Ruggerio's head started to spin and his heart sank in his chest; despair showed on his face like a death mask. This is how Diaz found him when he walked over to console his training officer.

"How are you feeling Guy?" He realized the minute that the words came out of his mouth that it was a stupid question, but what else do you say, he thought to himself.

Ruggerio didn't respond at first. He simply looked up at Diaz from his sitting position on the bumper of a squad car. Then he mustered in a weak, whispering voice, "I can't believe that we haven't found the gun yet."

Diaz reassured him, "We will, we just have to wait until the crowd is dispersed."

Ruggerio was looking up at Diaz with an expression that conveyed a desire for reassurance, then he asked Diaz, or more accurately he implored, "You heard the shot, didn't you?" Ruggerio's voice trailed off at the end of his question as if he had trouble breathing.

Before Diaz could answer, Ruggerio jumped off the bumper and darted around the squad car holding his hands to his mouth. Near the back bumper, out of sight of the crowd and the other officers, Ruggerio vomited onto the pavement.

Diaz quickly moved to Ruggerio's side and placed his hand on his partner's shoulder as he was still bent over the rear quarter panel of the squad.

"Listen, there had to be a gun. We both heard the shot. There is nothing to worry about. We will find the gun when the crowd is under control. Just relax. It will be OK."

Ruggerio started to straighten up to face Diaz, wiping his mouth by using his left hand to grab the right short sleeve of his uniform shirt. "The shot we heard, it sounded funny, like it came from somewhere else," Ruggerio was whispering to Diaz so no one else could hear. He continued, "I am not so sure this guy even had a gun."

Diaz replied, "No. I saw something in his hand. I know it." As he was saying this to Ruggerio he began to ponder the possibility of the object in the shooter's hand being something other than a gun. As he replayed the scene in his head, Diaz began to second guess his initial conclusion. But what about the shot they had both heard? It had to be a gun, he rationalized to himself.

"Just relax. We will find the gun and everything will be fine. Come on, come over here and sit down. Take it easy." Diaz comforted Ruggerio.

Tobias walked over to the two officers and saw that his friend Ruggerio needed some bucking up.

"Hey Guy, this is a hell of a way to get some time off. You couldn't fake an on-duty injury like everyone else?" he chuckled. His smile was distorted from the tobacco plug in his lower lip. Becoming serious, he leaned against the front of the car next to Ruggerio and said, "Hey, damn good job. You dropped that sucker with one shot before he could hurt anyone. You did your job Brother, and don't let anyone tell you different." He spit, then continued, "I mean it," placing a hand on his friend's shoulder.

"Thanks Toby," was all Ruggerio could muster. He had a nagging feeling that something was wrong with the shooting. He kept replaying the events in his mind and it seemed that all the elements were there for a clean shoot, but there was something missing and he could not figure it out.

"Toby, something is not right," Ruggerio confided to his friend.

"What's that?"

"I saw a flash of something in his hand and then I heard a pop that sounded like a gun, but they seemed to be out of sync, like they didn't belong together.

Tobias turned to Diaz and asked,

"Did you hear a shot?"

"Yes, it was gun. I am sure."

Then Ruggerio, still whispering stated, "Yeah but the flash in his hand, I don't think it was a muzzle flash." As he said this he moved closer to Tobias's ear to keep others from hearing.

"What about that?" Tobias asked Diaz.

"That I did not see. I ducked behind a tree when I saw him pointing the gun at me," Diaz related.

Tobias turned back toward Ruggerio. "You got nothing to worry about. You were definitely justified. Even if it wasn't a gun you certainly had enough cause to think that it was. I mean, what else were you supposed to do? Wait until your partner or you get shot before defending yourself?"

As Tobias was finishing his remark the sergeant returned and told Tobias to go back over to help with the crowd, who were still chanting. Some were now pointing at Ruggerio and calling out, "That's him. That's the one… Fuckin' killer!"

The sergeant then turned to Diaz and Ruggerio, "You two. Come with me to my car."

They both walked with the sergeant to his vehicle, parked on the opposite end of the crime scene. The crowd intensified their chanting and ranting as Ruggerio walked past the rowdy bystanders.

"They're gonna hide him now and make up their story," one said.

Then another remarked, "He don't have to worry. It will be covered up. But what about this poor nigga's family!"

Still another said, "He'll probably get a raise for knocking off another nigger."

The path the sergeant was taking to his squad passed near the body of Dickson, still lying on the street. Someone had taken the cuffs off of the body, to help appease the sensibilities of the crowd, who had made numerous comments about the degrading connotation implied by the handcuffing of a mortally wounded black male. As Ruggerio passed the body, he had to look down at Dickson in curiosity. He could see the deep red colored stain of his blood coming through the light-colored jacket. Ruggerio felt his stomach turn over again, and for a moment he thought that he was going to puke again. More officers were arriving every second and the crowd was slowly getting under control.

At the sergeant's car the sarge turned to Ruggerio with his hand out palm up.

"I need your gun," he asked Ruggerio. This was standard procedure. Ruggerio didn't think anything of it and did as asked.

The sergeant turned to Diaz and asked for his gun also. He complied without complaint but thought this was strange.

Then the sergeant explained, "The detectives just want to make sure that all bases are covered. They want both guns examined to make sure who fired the shots at the suspect."

Ruggerio felt a sharp pang in his stomach when he heard the word, detectives. He realized that Faust was working this evening and might be the investigator assigned to this shooting. He knew that the case would be investigated by the district attorney's office but one of the metro detectives would also be assigned to assist. He thought if that detective was Faust, what better way for him to get at Ruggerio than to screw up this shooting investigation.

The sergeant ordered another officer to take Ruggerio and Diaz to the station house for interviews. Ruggerio knew this was standard procedure also but didn't want to leave, fearing that Faust was on his way to the scene and would be able to tamper with evidence unchecked if he wasn't there to monitor him.

He called out to Tobias, who was walking near them, "Toby, don't let Faust screw up this scene!"

Tobias nodded his head in acknowledgement, but had to direct his attention to a young bystander who crawled under the yellow barrier tape to run through the crime scene. Tobias grabbed him by the arm and began escorting him back behind the line. Just then, as Ruggerio and Diaz were following the sergeant toward the car, Ruggerio heard someone's cell phone chirping in the crowd. It made him look in that direction by reflex and his eye caught the blinking of the light from the cell phone. The small light was very pronounced due to the dimly lit conditions. Ruggerio saw a glimmer of hope in the light he had just seen. A cell phone! He thought the gunman had a cell phone in his hand, not a gun! With that he turned around to alert Tobias, "Toby!"

Tobias was still escorting the male back behind the line and did not hear Ruggerio.

He tried again, "Toby!" This time, Tobias heard him over the noisy crowd and looked in Ruggerio's direction. "Look for a cell phone. He had a cell phone."

Ruggerio felt a tug on his arm. It was the sergeant. "Let's go, Ruggerio. The dicks are waiting."

After getting a confirmation nod from Tobias that he understood about the cell phone, Ruggerio and Diaz loaded into the squad that was assigned to take them to the station. The police car they were riding in pulled away from the scene as two officers, on either side of the squad, held barrier tape up so the vehicle could pass underneath. Immediately after the squad car cleared the crowd, two more bottles crashed to the ground on either side of the police car. It was a parting message to the killer cop from the embittered throng.

Faust alighted from his unmarked squad car and made his way over to the sergeant in charge at the scene to obtain a briefing. As he approached the sergeant in charge, Faust thought to himself that this could be the moment he had been waiting for to deal with the little punk who had been a thorn in his side for so long. He could finally expose Ruggerio for the inept cop that he was. He didn't deserve to wear the uniform. He was a damn midget, for God sake. But oh, did the people in the community love him. "Is Guy Ruggerio working?" was a question Faust would hear on the street from black and white people alike. Especially if the person he was talking with was a damn dago. They almost without exception asked about, "Gaetano," using his Italian name, which really pissed Faust off. Then the little prick, Ruggerio, was always coming to the detective division with information from snitches on the street, making Faust look bad in front of his fellow detectives.

In Faust's view, the police could not expect to be community partners with the public, therefore to receive respect from the citizens the police had to be feared by the public. That was the only way order could be maintained in the neighborhoods. Coddling civilians was simply being naïve. The public hates the police and has no intention of cooperating; it's us versus them. This was the law according to Faust and if anyone from the police department didn't subscribe to his view, they were bleeding hearts who caused more pain than healing. Not to mention creating an atmosphere where a cop could get himself hurt or even killed. If people don't fear the police, it makes them more likely to shoot or attack them. This was how Faust saw the role of the police in the community. Needless to say he was not exactly a proponent of "community policing."

The sergeant at Bartlett Park explained how the shooting had taken place to Faust. Then he described how the crowd situation forced his officers to delay their search of the area for the gun that was reported to have been possessed by the assailant. He theorized that someone in the crowd could have grabbed the gun off the ground before the officers were able to maintain a proper cordon around the crime scene. The sergeant assured Faust that all was under control now and that he had enough manpower to handle the crowd.

Upon hearing from the sergeant that no weapon had been found, Faust produced a smile on his face that he tried, but could not suppress.

"Sounds like the little grease ball screwed up," Faust said with glee.

The sergeant, looking puzzled at the detective's demeanor and unsure why he had made this comment, shrugged his shoulders in reply. "Don't know. Maybe. Both officers did hear a shot, so a gun had to be involved."

"Not if they both concocted a story to try and cover-up that there wasn't a gun involved at all," retorted Faust.

"That doesn't sound like Ruggerio, but you never know I guess. I have to relieve some of the guys. Let me know if you need anything," the sarge said as he started moving away to attend to his officers controlling the scene.

Faust walked over to view the body and wait from the other members of the homicide unit to arrive. Standing next to the corpse was Quint, the very K-9 officer who had arrested Dickson earlier in the day and taken the robbery report from 8-ball. The

K-9 officer observed the interior color of Dickson's jacket and the cast on his arm from Max's bite. He surmised that the dead guy may have been the robbery suspect from the incident he had handled. When Faust came over, he asked Quint, "Do you know him?"

"I can't really see his face in that position but I think my dog got a bite on him earlier in the day and he may be a robbery suspect from an incident that I handled today. If it is him, he might have a cell phone from my victim on him. That would confirm it," Quint reasoned. As he thought about it further, he concluded, "I don't know where he would have gotten a gun though. He was taken to the hospital by one of the wagons. They left him there to be treated for the dog bite but he escaped before our guys could go back to pick him up."

Faust scanned the body with his eyes, careful not to touch it since the coroner and the crime scene photographer had not processed the victim yet. He did not see a cell phone in the victim's hands or any bulges in his pockets, indicating that it may be under him. Playing the scenario out in his mind, if Quint was right and this guy didn't have a gun, the cell phone could be important. It could provide an "excuse" for Ruggerio to justify the shooting by claiming that he thought the cell phone looked like a gun in the hands of the suspect. But if there was no cell phone found at the scene, this version of the incident would be dismissed by the DA.

To give himself some privacy to look for the phone, Faust told the K-9 cop to help with the crowd and that he would let him know if he found the cell phone. Quint acknowledged the request and moved off to assist the other officers, but not before shooting a glance back over his shoulder at Faust with a puzzled look. Quint was suspicious but wasn't sure what was up.

Faust flicked on his mini-flashlight and checked the body again for the phone, this time physically going through the victim's pockets and looking under the body. To hell with the coroner, he concluded. Not finding it on the corpse, he began to search the surrounding area by passing the beam of the flashlight in a sweeping motion under the parked cars. If this phone actually existed, he knew that he had to find it quickly to dispose of it before the other members of the homicide unit and the DA's investigators arrived. If it was under one of the parked cars, it would be easily found with the help of the light, but he didn't see anything at all. He was about to widen his search when he saw the blinking of a light from under the car he was crouching behind.

Faust moved fast to kneel under the rear part of the car and saw the light of the cell phone winking at him. He realized why he had not seen the phone before with the beam of his light, because it was not lying on the ground but wedged inside the passenger side rear wheel. On all fours, Faust crawled under the car and was just barely able to reach the phone and grab hold of it. He shut off the power to the phone while he was still concealed between the parked cars, then shoved the phone into his blazer pocket. He stood up, his left hand still shoving the phone inside the breast pocket of his sport coat, and nonchalantly looked around to see if he had raised any suspicions. With no one paying him any attention, he felt that he had gotten away with snatching the phone undetected.

As he brushed the road dirt from his knees, he grimaced to himself, recalling Ruggerio's comment about dirt on his knees earlier. Faust, still feeling apprehensive, took another three hundred and sixty degree look around to make sure that he had gotten away with what essentially amounted to the criminal offense of "tampering with evidence." Just as he was about to give a sigh of relief, his eye caught a form in the front window of a house across the sidewalk and to his right. His head snapped back to get a look at the person in the window. It was a black female staring straight at him, but in the dark he could not make out her face. Faust switched on his mini light and directed the beam in her direction. The bright light made her turn away and shield her eyes with her hand, but Faust was still able to get a clear view of her face.

He didn't recognize her but now he had to find out who she was in case she had seen what he had just done. With the beam still on her Faust saw the woman dart away from the window and back inside the house. He was about to run after her but was stopped by another member of the homicide unit who had just arrived and called out his name. Faust made an effort to burn the image of the black girl's face in his brain so he could try to locate her later. When he felt that the image of the girl's face was secure in his memory, he turned toward his colleagues to collaborate on the investigation, planning to dispose of the cell phone later.

Hours later, after he cleared the Bartlett Park shooting scene, he heaved the cell phone off the side of the Andy Warhol Bridge into the Allegheny River. No one would ever find this most crucial piece of evidence in the investigation of a police-involved shooting and death of Jamar Dickson. This would not be the only death attributed to this incident, however.

After most dramatic incidents that the police experience, officers tend to cluster and exchange with each other their own tidbits of information relating to the major players in the event. Especially after an officer-involved shooting incident, officers like to console one another in an attempt to bring some normalcy to the environment, almost like a funeral setting. The co-workers of the "officer involved" talk about him in a tone as if he were actually the dearly departed. "He was a good guy. I remember one time when we chased some car thieves together," or "I wonder how his old lady is going to take this?" would be some of the comments officers would make.

This event would be no different. The officers back at headquarters were standing in groups in front of the police station house, the common topic of conversation being the Bartlett Park shooting, as it was starting to be called. What was different however, unlike most police shootings, which are overwhelmingly deemed to be justified, the facts were not as clear cut in this case. The circumstances from this incident could cause an officer to have some doubts about the validity of the officer's lethal use of force. Tobias was there and could hear some of the comments.

"I heard that they didn't find a gun," he heard from one cop.

"The dicks were saying that he and his training partner made up a fairy tale that they both heard the perp fire a shot, but no spent round was found," said another.

Tobias was getting worried for his friend. He had heard at the scene that the spent bullet had not been found. Neither was the gun. He tried to look around for the cell phone that Guy had told him about, but all his efforts failed to locate anything. Tobias could never believe that Ruggerio would make up a story. He had heard Guy say on more than one occasion, "If you honestly believe that your life or that of another is in jeopardy, then lethal force will be justified. It is when you try to fabricate a story that you get yourself in trouble."

Tobias was attempting to keep his thoughts rational but could not help thinking that Ruggerio may have had something when he said that Faust was out to screw him. Maybe Faust did something at the scene? he thought to himself. I just can't believe that Guy would make up such a stupid story. First of all, he considered, Ruggerio and Diaz would have to get together and talk about fabricating the part with the single gunshot that they both heard. Tobias really didn't think that they had enough time to collaborate on this story. The backup officers were right there within seconds. Second, both officers said that they saw something in the perp's hand. Ruggerio would not have told me out loud for everyone to hear that he wanted me to look for a cell phone, if he wanted people to believe that the perp actually fired a shot at Diaz. Ruggerio would also realize that the crime scene guys would look very suspiciously upon the fact that they could not find a spent round near the location where Diaz was positioned.

No! Tobias concluded, in a sort of epiphany. Guy and Diaz were definitely not lying. But he still had an uneasy feeling about something. A thought was germinating in Tobias's mind that Ruggerio was being set up.

Quint came over to Tobias and was able to corroborate his suspicions. "Hey Toby, you're a friend of Ruggerio's aren't you?"

"Yeah."

"I don't know who else to tell this to, so I am going to have to trust you," the K-9 officer said in a hushed tone. He took Tobias by the arm and walked him over to a more secluded area, closer to the parking lot where the squads were located and most officers had deserted.

"Listen, I took a report of a robbery earlier today. Ruggerio's perp was the robber. One of the items he took from the vic was a cell phone. I told one of the dicks that, but they didn't find it. Now, it's possible that the creep threw the phone away, but from what I have heard about how this shooting went down, a cell phone in a person's hand can look like a gun in the dark," he concluded.

"Which dick did you tell this to?" Tobias asked, already knowing the answer.

"The first one that was there. The heavyset one, with the face that looks like an orangutan."

"Faust!" Tobias replied, displaying a facial expression indicating that a new angle to the situation had just been revealed.

"Yeah! I heard one of the other dicks calling him by that name," Quint confirmed.

"Something is screwed up here. Thanks, Man. I owe you." Tobias patted Quint on the shoulder.

"You didn't hear it from me, OK."

"You got it, Brother. Thanks again." Tobias walked away to contemplate his next move.

CHAPTER 7

The morning sun streamed into the room through the spaces between the slats of the vertical blinds, the bars of light giving the interior a prison cell like appearance. Ruggerio was lying on his couch when he awoke, eyes squinting from the light. As he rose up he groaned in discomfort due to the severe hangover he was suffering from. His head felt like a high pressure steam pipe that needed the relief value opened.

After five minutes of sitting motionless in this position, he looked around at what was once his and his wife's living room. The putrid smell of vomit filled the air, and swarming flies feasted on remnants of food in old pizza boxes and take-out containers. Newspapers and empty beer cans were strewn about the floor. He was sleeping full time in this room, using the couch as his bed. It was more convenient for him so he could use the puke bucket that he routinely placed next to him on the floor. Ruggerio needed the bucket most nights, now that he was drinking heavily, in a vain attempt to ease the pain he was feeling. The room hadn't been cleaned since his wife had left about two weeks earlier.

Since the shooting incident, two and a half months previously, Ruggerio had endured a steady bombardment of disappointing setbacks and discouraging developments surrounding the event. He had watched on television as local African-American groups conducted street protests against police violence, in response to his killing of young Jamar Dickson. Local black community leaders railed against the police and the maltreatment that African Americans were suffering at the hands of the cops. Several of these activists called for the indictment and conviction of Ruggerio on charges of murder and abuse of power, as a first step in diffusing tensions in the community. The recurring theme was that the white officer, Ruggerio, had summarily executed a young black man for no other reason than the color of his skin. After a few days with no reaction from the city on criminal charges, the protests progressed to violence. Police, adorned in riot gear, hurling teargas canisters at unruly crowds, had become a common sight on the nightly news. Images of burning buildings, reminiscent of the Rodney King situation in Los Angeles, were becoming more frequent as the days went by without a ruling from the district attorney's office. The front page of the paper had repeatedly showcased the incident and its aftermath, proving once again the old adage, "if it bleeds it leads."

Along with the protests came a barrage of death threats, some of which were disturbingly graphic. A few more serious individuals even went so far as to deliver their messages via air mail, i.e. through Ruggerio's back kitchen window, attached to a brick. Of course this occurred only after the police protection had been lifted from his house. This decision took place as soon as the indictment for homicide was filed against Ruggerio. The city decided that it wouldn't be proper to spend taxpayers' money on police protection for an individual accused of homicide. At this time, the Ruggerios decided that his wife should go to her parents' house in Ohio for her own protection. She didn't want to leave her husband, but Ruggerio insisted. After long discussions and the delivery of a second air mail message, this one in the form of a Molotov cocktail, Sally Ruggerio decided it was best to leave.

Sally and Guy Ruggerio had been brought together five years earlier in a way common for police officers. Sally was an ER nurse and had become acquainted with Ruggerio from his regular appearances at the hospital on police calls. By virtue of their occupations they were predestined to have numerous opportunities to see each other, the reason that there are so many marriages between cops and nurses. They were married shortly before the incident that had caused Ruggerio's burn scar.

Sally was petite, fair skinned, blonde, and pretty, contrasting with the dark appearance of Guy Ruggerio. He wondered at times if seeking out a light-skinned mate had been intentional on his part. They were a couple that epitomized the saying, opposites attract. Sally was fun-loving and outgoing, with a large group of friends. Ruggerio's personality was more reserved and serious; he usually limited himself to one close friend instead of numerous acquaintances. His persona suited his career choice.

They had no children and were noncommittal on when they would start a family. The couple even had suspicions about their ability to become pregnant; they were both devout Catholics and practiced the Vatican-approved rhythm method, which was infamous for its unreliability. After a few years of using this method, in which Sally had yet to become pregnant, they both assumed that a child would not be in their future. The couple concluded that either one or both of them was sterile, or that in their case the rhythm method was working perfectly. They decided to leave the possibility of a child in God's hands.

Since the shooting incident, Sally had begun to work part-time at the hospital to spend more time with Guy. But no matter how much time she devoted to him or what distractions she attempted, to shake him from his depression over the shooting, she was unsuccessful. Along with the threats of violence that entered their household, Sally Ruggerio could not stand seeing her husband self-destruct any longer. She felt that she had to leave and hope that Guy would come through this with the help of his friends Toby Tobias and Taymond Diaz. She took a leave of absence from work and went to her parents' home in Ohio.

Since Ruggerio was under indictment and free on bond, he could not leave the state without being considered an absconder. He considered a hotel but that was out of the question due to the cost. He couldn't stay with family or friends either and burden them with the constant threat of violence following him wherever he went.

When he turned to the police union for help with alternative housing, they decided that they could not provide any assistance beyond legal aid. Ruggerio saw Faust's fingerprints and that of and his cronies all over this decision. The union was not obligated to assist members in cases that were likely to be lost causes. Of course this clause in the by-laws was conveniently utilized by the union leadership whenever the requester was devoid of the proper political connections. On the other hand, this provision would have been ignored for someone that did have these contacts, someone like *Faust*.

As far as the legal assistance the union was providing, it left much to be desired. All one needed to hear was the nickname for the union lawyer Ruggerio was assigned and it was clear that the fix was in. The lawyer's name was Clive Lloyd, and his nickname around the courthouse was "Let 'em die Clive." It would be funny if it wasn't so pathetic. An obvious conspiracy was in motion to ensure that Ruggerio would be persecuted for the crime he was accused of, and it did not take much imagination to figure out why it was happening.

Ruggerio had it figured. There were two basic reasons why he was doomed to be convicted of homicide and have his life destroyed forever. First, was the obvious reason. Faust hated him and Faust was crazy. Acting on his prejudice, he could use his vast political connections to influence certain key figures in furthering the case against Ruggerio. The other reason was not so apparent to those outside the city government but clear to Ruggerio. The current city administration was in the middle of a tough re-election campaign and desperately needed the black vote since the challenger to the incumbent mayor was an African-American. In an effort to appear sympathetic to the black community and also to quell the violent protests, Ruggerio was being made the scapegoat. He had been cast in the role of the sacrificial lamb. When this realization came to him, the heavy drinking began in earnest and steadily became heavier and more severe.

Ruggerio went into the bathroom and splashed some cold water on his face for some temporary relief from his alcohol-induced misery. Why did I do it? he thought to himself as he looked into his own face reflected in the mirror above the sink. With water dripping from the tip of his nose, he questioned, why didn't I wait for back up as Diaz suggested? I let my emotions get to me, just the thing I tell the trainees not to let happen. Now I am going to be tried and convicted of homicide. My life is over, because I was too wrapped up in my personal battle with that jerk Faust.

Ruggerio tightened the fingers of his right hand into a fist as the anger and frustration began to build. Still staring at himself in the mirror with the self loathing and disappointment roiling inside of him, his body began to shake uncontrollably. Images of Faust and his faceless compatriots backslapping each other and laughing with glee at Ruggerio's predicament were flashing before his eyes. Both hands tightened into white knuckled balls. His teeth clamped shut and exposed like a mad dog, growling at the face in the mirror. He took note of the ugly burn scar that covered the right side of his neck and part of his face. It disgusted him, and he said to the face in the mirror, "Fuckin' Frankenstein-looking motherfucker."

His whole body quaked with self-loathing and anger at himself for giving his enemy such an opportunity. In such a state Ruggerio's internal pressure valve had given way. He reflexively attacked the source of his anger by punching the face in the mirror and smashing the glass. It took only a few seconds to realize that he had cut his right hand seriously and the blood began dripping in the sink and on the floor. After wrapping his shredded hand in a towel, he lowered himself down, sat on the closed toilet lid, and began to cry.

Approximately one month after the Bartlett Park shooting, Faust had finally tracked down the elusive New Ho. He had discovered where she frequented after literally arm-twisting some of his old street informants. Unlike the stereotypical portrayal of police on television, good cops don't physically abuse informants for information. Officers would rather treat an informant with respect. This ensures a good relationship between the two and a continual flow of information. As the saying goes, "you get more flies with honey than vinegar."

Faust set up surveillance near the location of a bar where New Ho regularly picked up her johns. The bar was called "Bottoms Up," a most unimaginative name for a strip club. Faust smirked at this name, realizing that if he wandered into any town in the U.S. of significant population, he would probably find a strip club with the same name. Faust's preparations were so elaborate that he even impressed himself, if that was possible. His first order of business was to acquire the drug that he would use to murder New Ho. This was easily accomplished simply by cruising the streets while on duty, then shaking down a few drug users under the guise of looking for information. Faust took their heroin kits and informed them that he would properly dispose of the illegal narcotic, then warned them that next time, he would charge them with possession if they didn't give him some information that he needed for any one of a number of investigations.

Having accomplished this, he started his arm-twisting campaign for information on the whereabouts of a skinny black whore who might hang out in an abandoned house near Bartlett Park. It only took him two nights to discover her name and that she usually turned her tricks here at the "Bottoms Up" club. He also learned that she sometimes used a partner named G to rob johns in the park. This confirmed her identity to Faust. Good police work, if he said so himself.

With this information and the heroin junkie's shoot up kit: needle, spoon, and rubber circulation band, he was ready to move on to the next phase. Faust sent away for a fake driver's license in a doper's magazine. For his purposes, this phony ID would suffice. Then he scanned his own vehicle insurance card into his computer and printed out an altered specimen with the same false name that he had on his new identification. Having collected these necessary documents, Faust took a bus to a town approximately forty miles away from Pittsburgh called New Hope. Here, he sat outside of the first car rental agency he could find and waited until he saw the right pigeon that he could dupe. He found a pimply-faced twenty-something kid standing behind the rental agency sales counter. It was probably his first job out of high school, renting out cars in this small town that had maybe two traffic lights. The younger the better, Faust thought. He will be more likely to be influenced to leave off some identifying information on the rental agreement, in exchange for a few extra dollars.

Faust didn't just pick this town out of thin air. He had good reason for renting a car from this location. The small town of New Hope was well known in the Pittsburgh metro department. Drug users from this town routinely rented cars from here and drove them to Pittsburgh for two main reasons. One reason was that the drugs these users needed were more readily available and at a significantly cheaper price in the big city of Pittsburgh rather than at home. The other reason was if one ran out of money for the next fix, a simple transaction known as a "Rent-a-Rock" could be utilized. Drug dealers, ever on the lookout for transportation that could not be traced back to them, were more than eager to give a user a few rocks of crack cocaine in exchange for the use of a rental car. The drug users from this town were famous for this type of transaction in Pittsburgh. Therefore, if someone copied down the registration plate of the car Faust rented, it would not raise much suspicion and it could not be traced to him since he used the phony ID to rent the car. Just in case some cop got a little too nosey.

To eliminate any future physical description linking the renter of the car to Faust, he had put on a getup that made him look more like a junkie. A slightly torn and soiled white T-shirt under an unbuttoned long-sleeve flannel shirt was a typical junkie fashion. The long sleeves were mandatory, better to cover the supposed track marks. To complete the disguise, he put on a false mustache while standing outside of the car rental agency. To match his ID, it was the same mustache that he wore in the fake ID photo that he took of himself, with a self timing camera. When he saw that "pimple face" was alone in the agency, he went in to make the deal. After fifteen minutes and a little kicker of twenty bucks for the kid, Faust was driving a Ford Taurus out of the lot, headed for his meeting with New Ho.

Back at his surveillance point near the "Bottoms Up" club, waiting for New Ho to appear, Faust began to take inventory of all he had gone through to pull off this deception. He started to wonder whether this was all worth the risk just to bring down the little grease ball that he hated so much. He began to weigh the pros and cons of following through with his cleverly conceived plan. If he left the whore New Ho alone, could he gamble on the possibility that she really didn't see him grab up the cell phone from the street on the night of the shooting? No, he answered, quickly discounting this possibility. He could never be sure if she had or hadn't seen him. Besides, the way she had been looking at him and then ran away when he pointed the flashlight beam at her, he was sure that she saw what he had done. Faust knew what junkies and prostitutes were like. The first time she would get popped on a drug possession charge or scooped up in a prostitution sting, she would use whatever juicy information she could to get out of the arrest. He could foresee New Ho standing at the booking counter in the station, spilling her guts in an attempt to negate the charge. With this thought, he concluded that he needed to follow through with the plan.

His thoughts continued to the on-going feud he was having with Ruggerio and why he found it so necessary to finish off the little dago. Just the thought of Ruggerio made Faust's blood boil. Especially that night when Ruggerio had stopped him from trouncing that alcoholic nigger's ass. He couldn't live with that memory without getting even.

Faust thought back to his own childhood, to images of his abusive father slapping his mother around after an all-night drinking binge. There was the time that his dad broke Faust's nose after a high school football game, angered by his son's performance. Faust, who was his team's offensive tackle, missed numerous blocking assignments, which resulted in several sacks of his quarterback.

Faust didn't want to admit it but this feud with Ruggerio was somehow linked to his relationship with his father. Faust was really just using Ruggerio to settle the score with his abusive, and now deceased, old man. He wasn't astutely cognizant of it, but his father's behavior instilled in Faust the need to always be on top and never to be taken advantage of by anyone, especially a midget like Ruggerio. He knew this obsession to get even with Ruggerio was more *complicated* than the unfinished business of a station-house fight, but he wouldn't allow his thoughts to go there.

There she was! He sat up in the seat of the Taurus as New Ho staggered out of the club. Faust figured that she used this spot because it was fertile territory to turn tricks. Men exiting a strip club were sure to be horny, thus more likely to pick up a skanky ho for a quick BJ. Faust cranked the ignition and the Taurus fired up. After slipping the gear shift into drive he eased out of the parking spot, which was down the street from the club. He waited until she reached the corner and he pulled up next to her, the passenger window already down. Faust leaned over to his right and called out to New Ho.

"Hey baby, want to party?"

"Y'all the police?" she asked leaning into the open window. New Ho, like many other prostitutes, still believed in the falsehood that undercover officers were forbidden by law to lie about their profession.

"No way. Do I look like a cop to you? I just want to have a good time." For emphasis Faust opened his palm to let New Ho see the balled up twenty-dollar bills in his hand.

That was all she needed. New Ho opened the passenger door and climbed inside. She took over the proceedings from there, having consummated hundreds of such transactions in the past.

"Drive on down to the next light, then makes the right," she instructed with her southern drawl. Her speech was slightly slurred from having had a few drinks in the club.

"Whatever you say, Baby," Faust complied.

It was just getting dark and the headlights from the cars passing in the opposite direction were blinding New Ho as she was trying to get a look at her prospective john.

"I don't think I have ever seen y'all round here before?" she proclaimed.

Faust didn't say anything, not sure if he should say that he was new in town or not. He couldn't feel it but his mustache was starting to peel away from his upper lip. He had sat in the car for so long and the heat of the day caused his lip to perspire so much, the adhesive hold on the false stash was loosening. Faust made the right then New Ho told him to make another turn, bringing them closer to Bartlett Park.

"Where y'all from anyway?" she asked suspiciously.

"New Hope," he said, giving the name of the town where he had rented the car, deciding that this would be believable.

"Y'all from New Hope then," repeating what Faust had just said.

Faust's mind began to panic, thinking that she was getting suspicious. Then he came up with a diversion to get her off track. Faust reached into his shirt pocket and removed the heroin stamp bags that he had taken from the junkies. He then opened his palm next to New Ho and said, "Let's get the party started."

New Ho's eyes lit up like Christmas morning.

"Whatever you say, Baby," she said, now sure he wasn't a cop, since cops wouldn't offer drugs when making prostitution arrests.

"Just pull over next to the dumpster on the next street and park," she told Faust.

By coincidence it was the same dumpster that Ruggerio and Diaz parked near on the night of the shooting. Faust did as told and they both exited the car, New Ho explaining that she had a quiet place they could go. She directed him to the rear of the same

146

abandoned row-house that she and G had used as their safe house on the night of the shooting.

New Ho took a sturdy plastic plasterer's pal from behind some overgrown weeds and used it to stand on next to the window. Using the over-turned pail, she climbed on top of a dumpster which positioned her next to the boarded up window. She then removed the plywood sheeting that covered the window opening. The three-feet by four-feet sheet of plywood was loose and propped up on the window ledge so it appeared as if it was still nailed to the window frame. They both climbed into the house and walked into the living room area.

"OK, you got a spoon?" she asked Faust.

He removed the spoon he had taken from a junkie and handed it to New Ho, along with one stamp bag of heroin. She carefully opened one of the stamp bags and emptied its contents into the scoop of the spoon. She reached for a clear plastic bottle of water that she had placed in the living room earlier. New Ho poured a small amount of water into the spoon full of powdered heroin. She then lit a cigarette lighter and placed the flame under the spoon for heat, which would eventually liquefy the heroin so it could be drawn up into the syringe.

At this point, Faust's mustache had been loosened further by the act of climbing through the window opening. New Ho looked up at him and, with the assistance from the lighter's flame, she got a look at the strange way his mustache was hanging from his lip. The events of the shooting incident of which she was a partial witness began to flood into her mind. She recognized him as the cop who had picked something up from the ground just outside of the house. New Ho hadn't known what Faust picked up from under the car that night, but she knew that he had done something wrong. She realized this from the way he looked all around after he placed the object in his jacket pocket. She quickly deduced that he was there to silence her from repeating what she had seen. Being from the New Orleans area and having had numerous encounters with dirty cops, New Ho was experienced in the ways of corrupt law enforcement.

She quickly sized up the situation and decided that she should make a break for the window and at the same time, take out the razor blade she had in her pocket to assist in her escape. Most prostitutes carry some type of sharp edged weapon, usually a razor due to its small size and effective cutting ability. In this line of work one encounters some rough customers, along with those who need some encouragement to pay up after services have been rendered.

New Ho threw the lighter, spoon and heroin in the face of the cop as a diversion and in the same motion made her move toward the window. Faust, caught off guard by the sudden reaction took part of the heroin in his eyes, but quickly recovered. He got to her just in time to keep her from jumping out of the window. As he pulled her back into the darkness of the house, New Ho retrieved her razor. She had melted the end of a toothbrush and inserted the blunt side of the razor into the soft molten solution, then let it harden in place, similar to shanks made by prisoners. As Faust spun her around so he could face her, New Ho slashed at him with the razor, catching the writer's palm of his left hand, as he reached out to grab hold of her. Faust recoiled back in surprise at the unexpected attack. Grasping his injured hand with his unaffected one, he could feel the warm blood oozing from the wound.

Again New Ho attempted to run for the window but Faust was on her before she could make it. This time, he slammed her down to the floor and held her there, then removed his Glock service weapon and pointed it at her head, thinking about just finishing her this way. He decided to stick with the plan and replaced his pistol back in its holster.

"You're under arrest," he said and began to place handcuffs on her.

"You fuckin' bastard. Help me!" New Ho shouted knowing that he was going to kill her. "Help me. He is going to kill me, please somebody!"

Faust was having trouble getting the handcuffs on her due to New Ho's valiant efforts to fight back. Television again creates a fallacy when cops are portrayed easily slapping handcuffs on suspects with little effort. In reality, when a subject resists arrest during handcuffing, it is extremely difficult for a single officer to control both hands of an arrestee in order to place the cuffs on them, even if the arrestee is a woman.

Faust decided to forgo the cuffs but he needed to shut her up before someone responded. He decided to use a choke hold and cause her to pass out. Faust slid his right arm under New Ho's chin and put her neck in the crook of his arm. By sandwiching her neck between his bicep and his forearm, he could put pressure on both sides of her neck. Faust knew from training that if you can cut off the blood flow to the brain on both sides of a person's neck, unconsciousness will soon follow. Within seconds, New Ho was out cold and her screams for help were silenced. She was now at his mercy and Faust was able to follow through with his plan to silence her. Constance Lebeau, New Ho's real name, would die a junkie's death. Not because of her reckless lifestyle, but because she had the unfortunate luck to become unwittingly entangled in a deadly feud between police officers.

The last few months had left Diaz's head spinning. Every morning when he woke up, he wondered if all the events that had taken place were just a bad dream. First, the weird circumstances of the shooting in the park, and the lack of corroborating evidence. Then the conclusion of the DA investigators that he and Ruggerio were lying about how the shooting occurred, the result of which being suspension without pay for Diaz, and Ruggerio being formally charged with homicide. A similar fate was possibly awaiting Diaz with the district attorney announcing on television that charges against the rookie partner of Ruggerio were still being considered. Diaz had to get his own attorney, since he was being considered an accomplice.

The district attorney's investigators, who had charged Ruggerio with homicide, were trying to convince Diaz to save his own skin and testify against Ruggerio at trial. They told him and his attorney that conspiracy charges would eventually come down and that it was just a matter of time. If that happened, he might as well forget about ever returning to duty again. In addition, they told Diaz that he likely would end up serving some time in prison, with the outcry from the public over this case. Even though he was black himself, a prison sentence for the co-conspirator in this homicide would be demanded by public opinion. Larger forces were at work here, the savvy investigators cajoled. The mayor's office, the police commissioner, black civil rights organizations, the ACLU, hell even the U.S. Attorney's office in Pittsburgh was investigating to determine if federal charges should be instituted for civil right violations, as one of them told Diaz.

To his credit and largely due to his strict and righteous upbringing, Diaz held firm to his story in the face of this overwhelming pressure—even though his own attorney confessed that he had doubts about the accounts of the two officers and that maybe Diaz should consider the offer from the district attorney's office. The deal was, as stated to Diaz, that if he changed his story and testified against Ruggerio, he would receive probation for lying on an official document. The probation would be arranged so when he successfully completed the term, his record would be expunged and he could return to duty. Diaz answered his attorney and the DA's investigator in the following manner.

"I would rather spend ten years in prison than to change my story and send an innocent man to jail for doing his job and trying to protect my life. It's not the easy way, but it's the right one."

He then walked out of his attorney's office and went to work with Tobias to prove Ruggerio and himself innocent.

The bar was dark and smoky; a heavyset woman was sitting at the bar playing video poker with a cigarette dangling from her mouth. She occasionally sipped from a watered-down glass of whiskey that was gathering condensation on the countertop. The room was quiet enough that Tobias could hear the electronic blipping sounds of the computer poker game. He dug out a hefty chew of Copenhagen and wedged it in his lower lip as he watched the door from the table where he sat. He sat with his back toward the wall, like most cops would, so he could see the door. It was a weeknight, so the number of patrons was on the light side, with one man sitting at the bar, on the opposite end from the woman playing poker. There was a seedy-looking older couple eating chicken wings and swilling beer with great gusto at a table closer to the bar than where Tobias sat.

He took a pull from his own bottle of Iron City beer and enjoyed the cold liquid as it flowed down his throat. Notwithstanding the way the man and woman were devouring those wings, they were actually starting to look good to Tobias as he watched the couple pitching meatless bones on top of a large pile in the center of the table. He thought twice as he looked down at his ample belly and realized that he had already had dinner with Ruggerio earlier.

He had brought a pizza over to Ruggerio's house in an effort to try to cheer him up and get his mind off of the pending legal proceedings. It was all for naught. Ruggerio was obviously in such deep depression that Tobias insisted that he go to the department shrink for counseling. Ruggerio had agreed, but Tobias suspected that he was just trying to avoid the subject.

Just then the full length glass outside door opened and he saw Diaz walk inside then stop immediately after clearing the threshold. Diaz looked around the small expanse of the barroom and quickly saw Tobias waving him over to his table. The eyes of all the patrons, including the burly bartender, burned holes into the young athletic looking black-Hispanic, who self-consciously sat down with Tobias.

"What's the matter? You couldn't reserve a table at the KKK meeting hall?" he asked Tobias, with a nervous smile on this face.

"Sorry, Tay. I didn't think through the meeting place very well," Tobias explained.

"How's Guy? Did you see him tonight?" Diaz asked.

"Not good at all. I demanded that he see the shrink. He said that he would, but I think he was just appeasing me. We need to do something fast. I am afraid that he is headed down a bad road."

"I know what you mean. I saw him yesterday and I got the feeling that he has lost all hope. Does he have any guns in the house?"

"Sure he does. I tried to get him to stay with me but he won't budge. The best thing we can do now is find a way to prove that you guys are telling the truth. That's why I asked you here. We are waiting for a friend of mine that works homicide. He ran the cell phone number of the phone that Dickson was supposed to have on him at the time that Guy shot him," Tobias said.

"What do you think that will prove?" Diaz asked.

"We don't know until we find out, right? It might give us a lead to help establish that Dickson did have this cell phone and at least we can show the possibility that Dickson could have had something in his hand that looked like a gun when he was shot."

"Why don't the DA investigators do this? Isn't that their job?" Diaz wondered.

"After what they tried with you, do you trust them with this investigation?" Tobias reasoned.

"You have a point," Diaz agreed.

"Since you brought it up, what we are doing right now is against regulations. I want you to know this before we go any further. This is technically an unauthorized investigation and we could be fired over this if we are found out," Tobias said with a serious expression.

"Listen, my chances of getting back onto the force are pretty much shot. I think the Pirates have a better chance of winning the NL pennant," Diaz said with a smirk.

"Geez, you really aren't giving yourself much of a chance when you put it that way." Both officers laughed, which gave them a respite from the tension in their desperate circumstances.

Tobias went up to the bar and bought Diaz a cold bottle of Iron City just as a shortish, dark-haired man with a barrel-like chest walked into the bar. With the same scanning motion that Diaz had used, the man searched the bar for a familiar face. He was wearing a light brown blazer with a loosened striped tie and dark slacks, looking almost as out of place as Diaz. The man had a dark complexion, with a powerful appearance, and looked as if he were stuffed into his shirt. Diaz saw the man and Tobias joyfully greet each other next to the bar. They shook hands robustly and the short man pushed a thick thumb into Tobias' protruding lower lip, and said, "Still chewing that shit I see."

Tobias gave a crooked grin to the man who was obviously the homicide detective that he had been talking about, and then waved him over to where Diaz was sitting.

"Tay, this is Joe Massimo, another southern dago like Ruggerio," Tobias said, making the introduction.

"I'm Sicilian to be exact. Let's get it right," corrected Massimo.

Massimo stuck out a beefy and hairy right paw to shake Diaz's hand and all three officers sat down. Massimo pulled out a vertically folded stack of papers from his inside jacket pocket and was about to explain what he had, when Tobias stopped him by raising a hand in a halting gesture. "Let me crank up the juke box to cover what we are talking about. You never know who might be in here," he said as the two other men nodded in agreement.

Tobias dropped some money into the machine and punched in some random numbers, then returned to his seat. The music kicked on to the tune, "Do You Really Want to Hurt Me?" by Boy George. Both Massimo and Diaz looked at Tobias and laughed. Massimo said, "What are you going to play next, 'Girls Just Wanna Have Fun'?"

"OK, OK, just get to the phone records funny man," Tobias said with his crooked grin. After the laughter died down, Massimo flattened out the paper work that had the call records of the cell phone that Dickson used in his last hours on earth.

"I can make this real simple. You guys want to talk to a girl by the name of Lauren Wilkes. Here is her driver's license info that I got from the DMV. Dickson called her several times just before Ruggerio iced him," Massimo stated.

"How do you know that he talked to her?" Diaz asked.

"Well, I traced the number on the call records to a Thomas Wilkes, Attorney at Law. I then did some asking around about this Wilkes guy at the court house. All those attorneys know each other. I found out that he has a young daughter and that she was seeing a black guy but old man Wilkes had been trying to separate the two of them. It turns out that daddy Wilkes has been a royal pain in the ass to our young love-struck mister Dickson. He had him arrested on minor drug charges at the university—while his daughter was also there, by the way. And on the day of the shooting, Dickson was on the Wilkes grounds and the old man called the cops again. That is when your K-9 pal took a bite out of crime and Mr. Dickson's arm. Does that answer your question my young and inquisitive friend?" Massimo said with a generous smile and a meaty but friendly slap on Diaz's back.

"Not really. Did he actually talk to her?" Diaz asked pointedly.

Massimo gave Diaz a smile, realizing that he had given a lot of information but really hadn't answered the original question. He looked at Tobias and said, "This one has some *cogliones* on him," he said while mimicking as if he were holding two bocce balls in his hands.

"It looks that way according to the records." Massimo pointed a fat knuckled index finger to a line on the call detail sheet that indicated "Duration of Call, 20 seconds."

"Twenty seconds on this call, minutes before the shooting. And one other little interesting tidbit, if I had to guess, this call right here." He pointed at another line on the sheet. "At 0033 hours, which went unanswered is probably the exact moment of the shooting. You see here, she called Dickson and no one picked up." He reclined back in his seat and let the revelation sink into the two cops.

"We need to talk with her," Tobias said, in a serious tone.

Tobias looked over at Massimo and gave him a smile so wide that his tobacco almost spilled out of his lip, then said, "You, my beefy Italian friend, are drinking on me tonight. Sorry, I mean Sicilian friend."

He was just two years removed from college so Diaz was able to mix right into the hustling mass of coeds scrambling around between classes on the tree-lined sidewalks of the campus mall. It was well into the fall semester and Diaz was waiting for Lauren Wilkes to walk by. She was scheduled for Economic Theory from 10:30 to 12:00 noon at Stiller Hall. It was 12:05 and she didn't have another class until 1:30, giving him an hour and a half to talk to her about her ex-boyfriend Jamar Dickson. Tobias had gotten her class schedule from Massimo, who, it turned out, had a contact on the university police force who supplied him with her schedule and the other inside information on her relationship with Dickson. Massimo had introduced the topic to his contact simply as a request for some background information, "Just tying up loose ends," he had said. He didn't want too many alarm bells sounding.

Tobias had said that Massimo had the contacts, which along with other traits, made him a good cop. And since he was a good cop he knew how far he could go with his involvement in this unauthorized activity. Tobias respected him for sticking his neck out and providing good information for them to follow up. He relayed his gratitude to Massimo for helping so effusively that Massimo's reply to Tobias was, "Hey, Ruggerio and I are pisans. We help each other out and I just can't say no to that ugly mug of yours when you ask for a favor."

As Diaz paced up and down on the sidewalk in front of Stiller Hall, he rehearsed the cover story that he and Tobias had developed. It was important that Diaz not reveal to Lauren Wilkes, unless absolutely necessary, that he was a police officer. This was necessary if they were to keep their investigation secret from the department brass. Diaz was to play the part of a college student. He was even carrying his old book bag that he had found stored in a box at home, to fit the role. He would strike up a conversation with Wilkes and wait for the right moment to bring up her relationship with Dickson, and then see where it went from there. Tobias had said, "not to be racist, but she has an eye for black guys, and since you might be considered halfway decent looking, she might take a liking to you."

"You sure know how to give a compliment," Diaz joked.

He recognized her leaving Stiller Hall and followed as she made an immediate right turn onto the sidewalk. Massimo had given Diaz a picture of Wilkes from her DMV photo and it did do her justice. Her picture displayed a bright toothy smile in a tanned face, framed by long straight blonde hair and bright blue eyes. Diaz trailed her as she and someone who appeared to be a girlfriend walked together, passing the tall rectangular buildings that paralleled the maze of walkways on campus. Diaz kept a good thirty yards back, which was more than sufficient with all the other students milling about, to keep from being noticed.

He followed them into a coffee shop and waited behind the two girls while they stood in line to buy cappuccinos. Diaz watched as the two took their coffees and moved to a table inside. Diaz ordered a regular coffee without cream, a habit that he had picked up from Ruggerio. As he waited for the clerk to pour his drink, Diaz took a glance over his shoulder at Wilkes. Their eyes met and she gave an alluring smile that he read as a promising sign. Diaz took his drink and sat down at a high table near the window. To look the part, he took out an old college text that he had brought with him and cracked it open. He was positioned, so he could see Wilkes' back over the top of the book.

The shop was full of students, some grabbing a quick drink and hustling off to their next class, others leisurely reclined in leather easy chairs, sipping lattés while pecking away on notebook computers in their laps. Diaz caught Wilkes turning around in her chair and looking in his direction. He decided to meet her stare but this time give her a return smile to see what would happen. It worked! She gave him the same toothy smile that he had seen in the driver's photo. Well, we have something here, he thought. Now he just needed to get her alone for a one to one. Surprisingly, as if on command, the friend got up and took her drink with her and walked out of the shop, looking in Diaz's direction and giving him a leer that said, good luck pal. It was time to make his move so he picked up his book bag and coffee, and walked over to the table where Lauren Wilkes now sat alone.

"Excuse me," he said. "Aren't you Lauren?"

"Yes, yes I am. And who might you be?" she replied with excitement.

"Lance. I am a friend of Jamar's. He used to talk about you often. I am sorry about what happened," Diaz said with sympathy.

"Thank you. Would you like to sit down?" she asked.

"Sure. Thanks. I hope I am not disturbing you?" he said sincerely.

"Not at all. So how well did you know Jamar?" she inquired.

"He was in one of my law classes. What a terrible thing to happen to him, these cops are out of control. That is why I'm a pre-law major. If we can't fight back on the streets then maybe we can in the courts," Diaz said, going out on a limb. He had heard from Massimo that Lauren Wilkes had a mouth on her and did not have much affection for the police.

"That is very courageous. I only wish that you could be a lawyer now and prosecute the killer that shot Jamar in cold blood," she said with conviction.

That was it, the opening he needed, Diaz thought.

"I really didn't hear many details. You know how reliable the newspaper accounts are. I think they are controlled by the city administration anyway. What do you know about how the shooting took place, if you feel comfortable with my asking?" Diaz asked tactfully.

"No, not at all. I really don't know much about it, other than Jamar did not have a gun. As a matter of fact, I have never seen him with a gun. He was a gentle soul, something like you," she said as she cupped her chin in the palm of her hand, resting her elbow on the table and flashing her smile at Diaz.

Diaz thought, get back on to the story. She is starting to flirt with you.

"So why was he in that area near Bartlett Park?" he asked.

"I don't really know. He was feeling very depressed. My father had broken us up and he was upset about that and just being arrested earlier in the day."

"When was the last time that you talked with him?" Diaz figured this might encourage her to talk about the phone calls near the time of the shooting.

"As a matter of fact, no one really knows this, but he called me and left a message on my phone just before the shooting," she said in a hushed tone as she leaned in toward Diaz.

"What did he say?" Diaz asked as his heart raced with excitement, hoping that the next words out of her mouth would somehow help him and Ruggerio.

"You are awfully interested in this aren't you?" she said with an air of suspicion.

Diaz had anticipated this and was ready with an explanation.

"I know, and I am sorry if I seem forward, but I did like Jamar as a friend, so I am concerned about what happened to him. And this is good practice for my future law career. I only hope that my clients will be as attractive as you are," he said hoping that she takes the bait and is not turned off.

She smiled and looked down at the table in mild embarrassment.

"Well, to tell you the truth, Jamar was very suicidal that night. His message said that he wanted to end it all and go into the next world, something to that effect," she said.

"So you never talked to him?" he asked.

"No, I tried calling him back but he never answered."

There was a moment of silence between the two. Diaz figured that this was the extent to which Lauren Wilkes could help. Now he had to extricate himself and keep his cover intact. He took a quick glance down at this watch, a gesture to set up his exit plan.

"Lauren, I am sorry about Jamar. I have to get to a class, but maybe we can talk again. Would that be OK?" he asked in his best humble voice.

"Sure!" she said exuberantly.

"Here, this is my cell number." She wrote out the number on a napkin and handed it to Diaz, making sure to touch his hand as she transferred the note.

"Thanks, I'll call you." Then he got up and made his way for the door, trying to control his excitement about what he had just found out about the last hours of Jamar Dickson and anxious to tell Tobias this new information.

A few weeks after Diaz was wooing Lauren Wilkes at the university coffee shop, Tobias was back at work answering service calls on a daylight shift. So far on this relatively warm December day, he hadn't handled anything exciting, just a neighborhood dispute concerning limited street parking. They never get it through their heads, Tobias thought, a public street is open for everyone and anyone to park. People still think that the space on the street in front of their house belongs to them exclusively. Unique to Pittsburgh is the practice of placing chairs on the street to save one's parking space. Astonishingly enough, this custom is somewhat honored by the city natives. But when it comes down to the letter of the law, the street is still public domain and the chairs have to be moved.

After he settled this dispute, Tobias went to a house where a frazzled mother couldn't convince her fifteen-year-old daughter to go to school. This was a typical call. Even though the first half of the school year was nearly done, some kids just couldn't bring themselves to go to school. Usually there was an underlying reason why the kid didn't want to go and it normally was not just because the child was lazy.

In his experience, Tobias had seen that some kids were teased incessantly and/or experience repeated physical threats from fellow students, the proverbial bullying syndrome making school a nightmare for the child. Complicating the situation was the unwritten code among teenagers that prohibited alerting parents or others in authority to this situation. Instead of asking for help, they would simply refuse to go to school.

Others might suffer from severe learning disabilities that have escaped the inquiries of school officials. The student may be too embarrassed to ask for help or maybe they have and their parents (in most cases their single parent) does not believe them and simply thinks that the child is making excuses to get out of class.

In this particular case, Tobias was able to get out of the young girl that she was pregnant and she was having morning sickness and did not want to suffer the embarrassment of puking in class. He was able to convince her to tell her mother with Tobias present so that they could go for counseling.

When he cleared this call, Tobias resumed a normal patrol and was leisurely cruising through a mixed business and residential area. The main street was a blend of low-rise mom and pop stores with a few intermittent residential buildings crowded in on the same street. Tobias was thinking of Ruggerio and was figuring on calling soon to check up on him, as he did every day since the shooting. He was suddenly taken from his thoughts; when looking down an intersecting alley, he saw what appeared to be a fight between two males about mid-block. Tobias stopped the squad and reversed the vehicle so he could drive down the alley toward the disturbance. As he entered the alley, he grabbed the radio mic and called in the incident, requesting backup since he was a single officer unit. As he quickly traversed the ground to reach the location of the disturbance he could see what he quickly surmised were two homeless black males engaged in a fight. The aggressor was apparently slashing at the defender with some sharp edged object, possibly a knife or a broken bottle but it was hard to tell from the distance and the angle. Both men were in ragged clothing. The attacker had on a black muscle shirt that exposed his thin, rope-like triceps, and loose-fitting light brown pants. He looked to Tobias to be about mid thirties. The defender was also thin, wearing a long-sleeved blue sweater with light brown and yellow horizontal stripes and a pair of worn-out looking blue jeans. He looked older due to the hints of gray in his close-cropped but unruly hair.

When he was braking and nearly to a stop Tobias observed two things, first that neither male noticed that a car was approaching and second that he recognized the older male. It was Lonnie, Ruggerio's friend. It was the very same Lonnie that was the igniter of the feud between Faust and Ruggerio.

Tobias jumped out of the car while the attacker was still swinging his right arm at the defender, as if he had a weapon and was trying to slash his opponent.

"Police. Hold it!" Tobias commanded.

The attacker turned toward Tobias, who was standing on the opposite side of the police squad from the aggressor. He could now see the attacker was holding a broken bottle that he had been trying to slash Lonnie with. Tobias pulled his Glock .40 and pointed it at the attacker and ordered him to drop the bottle, which he did immediately. Upon hearing the bottle smash on the pavement, Tobias's tension level, which had spiked at the possibility of shooting someone, was now significantly reduced. He felt that it was safe enough now to re-holster his weapon.

As quickly as he had dropped the bottle the attacker began explaining what had happened and why he was fighting with Lonnie. Lonnie, who looked quite relieved also at this point, simply moved over to a cement step positioned at the rear door of a bakery business and sat down.

"Hey, Man. This drunken fool took a crap right next to where my bed was, the damn fool. I stepped right in it when I woke up. What would you do?" Both men looked dirty and disheveled, unshaven for days and Tobias could smell the body odor from both of them, even though he was still on the opposite side of his car. When the man mentioned his bed, Tobias was sure that he meant an area on the street that he would use to sleep every night. Probably an old mattress thrown on the floor of an abandoned building somewhere, Tobias figured. He had to chuckle a bit though. Lonnie, he thought, still crappin' up a storm.

"What you laughin' at?" the attacker said to Tobias, seeing that he was amused by the whole situation.

"You damn cracker. You think this is funny." Tobias quickly took the smile off his face and reached again for his Glock. He only placed his hand on the butt of the gun at this time and didn't feel the need to pull the weapon, since the man did not present a lethal threat at this point. But Tobias was on guard; he knew from experience the signs that a subject was preparing to become aggressive. By the look on this guy's face and the stance that he was taking Tobias had to be prepared.

Just then the attacker, still incensed and probably emotionally disturbed, leaped onto the hood of the squad. Then he charged at Tobias, snarling through clenched teeth as he advanced. He was like a tiger in the wild, pouncing on its prey, Tobias thought. His next thought was that the fight was on!

When it came right down to it, this type of street fight was just like in the wild where the penalty for losing the battle is instant death. A fight to most people gives the connotation of a school yard brawl, or a bar mêlée, where the fight ends when the loser gives up. Conversely, a street fight between a perp and a cop is more like a no holds barred death match, a primitive, muscle-straining, hernia bursting duel, with possibly lethal consequences. The major concern for the cop, if he or she loses this battle, is the frightening possibility of the assailant taking the officer's gun. Many officers are killed each year from this exact circumstance.

Tobias had been here before and had always come out on top, no matter what it took, although it had been a while. He also realized that this guy had probably been here before too—and on any given day anyone can be beaten. Especially with an EDP, police acronym for Emotionally Disturbed Person, it didn't matter how small or big they were; a true crazy doesn't submit easily.

Tobias had to rely on experience and training; in situations like this, the value of these attributes rose to the surface. Tobias knew that he could not even think about losing; losing was not an option. The way Tobias figured it, to lose a street fight was to lose your life.

So, just like in those past battles, Tobias was not going to lose, no matter what. He was well aware there were no rules at this point, if winning the fight took a dirty trick or violent maneuver, he would use it and get out of this alive.

However, he made the decision not to pull his Glock and shoot the advancing attacker, for two distinct and logical reasons. First, he and every other cop on the Metro force had Ruggerio's shooting and its aftermath fresh in his mind. No cop wanted to go through what Ruggerio was experiencing after shooting an unarmed suspect. Second, this attacker did not have a weapon. Even though it was possible, with the correct articulation of facts, that using lethal force against this type of attack may be legally justified, this would be quite a gamble, because using deadly force in this case was still a legally gray area and could open him up to severe liability. Besides, he was supposed to be a professionally-trained police officer, skilled in hand-to-hand combat, right? Little did the public know that most cops never receive any further self-defense training beyond the academy level. So Tobias decided to forgo the firearm and use his hands. Moreover, it was starting to piss him off that this punk would even try to fight him straight up.

The aggressor lunged at Tobias off the hood of the car like a puma. His arms were extended out and he was flashing his long, dirty, and sharp fingernails, leading the way directly at Tobias's face. Tobias skillfully parried away both the right and left hands of the attacker, with his own left forearm, but he could not get out of the way of the attacker's body as it crashed down on top of him. Both men went to the ground and the fight resorted to a wrestling match in the grimy alley. Tobias grabbed the guy's head and put him in a headlock, then tried to roll him over and pin him to the pavement. But this perp was stronger than he looked. He resisted the maneuver and popped his head out of the hold that Tobias had on him. Now he was up on his feet and began to strike Tobias in the back of the head with bony fists. Tobias, still on the ground was in a bad position and taking blows to the back of his skull. Then as he spun his body around to face the threat, he began taking hits to the facial area. He tried and was somewhat successful in blocking some of the flying fists coming at him, but a few did connect.

The big advantage to having a winning mind set at a moment like this was it enabled a person to clear his mind of negative thoughts and concentrate on what would work to survive. Toby Tobias was a fourteen-year veteran street cop and one kick-ass brawler, to be perfectly blunt. Tobias remembered a training video entitled, "Fighting from the Ground" that he had purchased himself in an effort to improve his self-defense ability. Tobias recalled a technique from the video, tailored for this situation when an officer was forced to fight while lying on the ground.

The first step was to position the feet toward the assailant. Tobias did this by quickly spinning around on his left side and swinging his legs around, putting them between him and the attacker. Then the technique stated that he should support his upper body by placing the ground side arm propped up onto the elbow. At the same time he would retract his legs inward slightly, toward his own torso, with one leg elevated and prepared to strike out at the attacker. Tobias first had to kick away his attacker with both feet as the assailant tried to advance and get on top of him.

The aggressor was pushed backward by Tobias's thrusting legs. But this EDP was undeterred and started another charge at Tobias. This time, Tobias was ready; his grounded elbow and lower leg provided him a strong base to push off from, and his opposite leg was cocked and ready to strike when the target came into range.

The training video instructed him to strike at the forward knee joint, which would cause the most pain and quickly disable the attacker. When he came within striking distance, the attacker's left knee was his lead leg and prime for Tobias to strike. He saw the maneuver unfold in his mind before it even happened, which gave him confidence in its success. Tobias pushed off from the ground and jabbed out with his right leg, which happened to be his strong side. He connected perfectly with the attacker's left knee and immediately his adversary wheeled around, screaming in pain and grabbing his affected knee. He crumpled to the ground, totally incapable of continuing the fight. The technique worked to perfection and the fight was over just that fast.

Tobias wanted to go over to the would-be aggressor and pummel him further but just as he rose up from the pavement two backup squads arrived. The officers ran over to Tobias and he explained why there was a screaming man on the ground. One of the officers said that he would transport the prisoner to the hospital for treatment, while Tobias got all the information from Lonnie. They asked him if he needed any medical attention. Tobias said he was OK and wanted to get to the paperwork as soon as possible. The squads pulled out and Tobias could still hear the prisoner complaining about his knee that it was definitely broken. He even heard the guy say, "That damn dirty cop shot me in my leg!" This put a smile on Tobias's face but then he felt a stab of pain coming from his left elbow. He figured that when he had used it to push off the pavement for his kick, he must have bruised it. Now that the adrenalin was gone, he could feel the injury.

Tobias went over to where Lonnie was, still sitting on the cement step at the back door to the bakery.

"What happened Lonnie?" Tobias asked.

"It was just like he said, I took a crap and he stepped in it. What else can I say? When nature calls, I answer. I have a condition you know, divertitis; it makes me shit a lot," Lonnie explained, mispronouncing diverticulitis.

"I know, Lonnie. Don't you remember me? Tobias is my name. I used to work with Ruggerio," Tobias said.

Lonnie's face lit up with the sound of Ruggerio's name. It is not often street urchins like Lonnie received kindness. When they do, most—not all, but most—remember the source.

"You know Rug-g-e-e-o-o?" Lonnie could never say Ruggerio's name properly.

"Yes. We used to work together. We took you to rehab? Remember?" Tobias was about to give up, realizing that Lonnie's brain was probably so damaged by alcohol abuse he could hardly remember his own name.

"Yeah I remember. Ah, Tu-u-b-is is your name. You guys are good cops. Too bad about what happened to Rug-g-e-e-o-o," Lonnie said.

"Yeah, that is true Lonnie, maybe he will come back. OK let's get you to a shelter or something." Tobias needed to get going and start on the charges at the station.

"You know I heard some things about that boy that Rug-g-e-e-o-o shot the other day," Lonnie said, stopping Tobias in his tracks.

"Yeah, what was that?"

"I heard that a girl and a man saw what happened. They was in a house watchin'."

"What girl and what man?" Tobias probed.

"The girl is dead. She was from New Orlins, Louzzeanna, I think. The man, he is a nasty one, always messin' with people. They call him G," Lonnie explained.

"G. There are a lot of people they call G. Do you know anything else about him?" Tobias was starting to get excited. This could be promising.

"G from Erie. Yeah, that's him. G from Erie, I heard someone say that about him," Lonnie said, satisfied with himself.

"What about the girl Lonnie, the girl from New Orleans. What happened to her? You said that she was dead?"

"They found her the other day, floating in the Allegheny I heard," Lonnie said.

It clicked in Tobias's head. It was on all the local television news programs, along with the continued protests outside of city hall to prosecute Ruggerio. The report stated that a known prostitute was found dead in the river. Yeah! He remembered, and some of the officers that were talking about it, called her, New Ho, short for New Orleans... could be, he thought.

"Lonnie, did they call her New Ho?" he asked hopefully.

"Yeah! You got it. That's her name," Lonnie said excitedly.

"You didn't happen to hear how she got into the Allegheny?" he asked.

"Don't know. Probably hopped up on H and thought she could fly off the Clemente Bridge, I expect," Lonnie reasoned.

"Do you know where I can find this G from Erie?"

"You don't want him. He is no good."

"It might help Ruggerio, Lonnie. Where can I find him?" Tobias was desperate.

"I don't really know, but I do know that he likes to rob people. Uses a hooker to bait them, then robs 'em when they have their pants down. Nasty one, he is," Lonnie editorialized.

Tobias took out a business card from his back pocket. Most cops carry business cards with their contact information on them.

Tobias wrote his cell phone number on the back of his card and handed it to Lonnie.

"Here. If you see G, I want you to call me on my cell phone. The number is on the back."

Lonnie looked at him as if he were asking Lonnie to perform some indecent sex act on him. On the street giving information to the police, any information was considered snitching. Snitching is a mortal sin in these circles, unless you can get something in return. Tobias saw he was going to have to offer some inducement for Lonnie to comply.

"There is a bottle in it for you if you find him for me, OK? And it would really help out Ruggerio," Tobias said putting on his best salesman demeanor.

Lonnie's eyes lit up and he took the business card.

"If it will help Rug-g-e-e-o-o."

Tobias was excited he has something to work on now, a real witness. His next stop would be back to Massimo so he could have another chance to help his "pisan."

Driving back to the station, Tobias was busy making cell phone calls to everyone that was needed in unraveling this predicament that Ruggerio and Diaz were involved in. First, he called Ruggerio, knowing that any little glimmer of hope in his situation was important to tell him right away. He became a little worried when he only got his voice-mail, so he left a message. He tried to sound upbeat and hopeful in explaining that there may be a new angle to investigate in his case. He didn't want to go too far for fear of giving him false hope. The new information had been provided by a dyed-in-the-wool alcoholic to start with, and it needed to be corroborated before it could be deemed legitimate.

The next call would be to Massimo. He wanted him to snoop around and find out about the death of the prostitute New Ho. Something sounded funny to him about this. As he considered this death, he went through the circumstances step-by-step, just as a good investigator should. Tobias had the qualities of an astute detective, if he would have been interested, which he wasn't.

"A," Tobias said aloud. "Heroin junkies normally don't have hallucinations. They only want the dope to keep from being sick. But some do commit suicide so that is a possibility. B, jumping from the Clemente Bridge is not a sure way to kill yourself. The height isn't far enough," he reasoned. "C, isn't it a coincidence that one of the possible witnesses to Ruggerio's shooting is now dead so that she can't be interviewed." This was the most curious coincidence. "And what do cops say about coincidences? There are no coincidences."

He was beginning to feel the aches and pains in his left arm and leg from the fight he had just been in and considered, though he was only 35 years old, he might be getting too old for this business. He made the call to Massimo and asked him to check out the file on the New Ho suspicious death and to check around about this guy, G, from Erie. Massimo was his usual accommodating self and gleefully agreed to find out what he could and get back to Tobias as soon as possible. Tobias told him that he was on his way to the station to do some paperwork, so if he had anything to come downstairs and let him know. Massimo already knew about Tobias's fight. Police officers gossip more than a women's bridge club, and let him know this by commenting with a chuckle, "I heard about your back alley dance, not bad for a fat Jew."

"OK muscle head. I still got some chutzpah but I think that I am going to smell like Ben-Gay for a while." They both laughed and ended the call with Massimo telling Tobias that he would get the information as soon as he could.

Tobias called Diaz and told him the new information from Lonnie, thinking that he also could use some good news. Tobias noticed that Diaz was feeling frustrated at not being able to really get involved with clearing Ruggerio, while being on suspension since the shooting. When he set out on his undercover mission and gleaned the information from Lauren Wilkes about Dickson's suicide run, it made Diaz feel useful. But now he was sitting at home watching day time cooking shows and eating too much. He wanted to get back into the game. Tobias could hear this in his voice when he was talking to him over the phone. But he didn't want Diaz to get in any trouble, especially since he was still on probationary status as a new officer. Tobias disconnected the call, feeling helpless that he couldn't give Diaz another assignment in the case to clear him and Ruggerio.

Later at the station house, Tobias was standing at the printer, waiting on the paperwork concerning the fight he had just been in, to spit out of the machine. The paperwork, which included all three pages of his incident report, two pages of his criminal complaint, one page of his sworn affidavit, one page of evidence inventory (the broken bottle that the attacker was using to try to cut Lonnie with), one page of an equipment damage form (his uniform had been ripped during the mêlée), and two pages of his use of force form (in which he had to describe his tactics and why he used them). Massimo, tie undone as usual, sleeves rolled up but minus the blazer this time, came walking over to him and grabbed Tobias by his tender left elbow.

"Hey I got …"

"Ow!" Tobias said, flinching.

"Sorry. I didn't know we were so delicate. Anyway, I got something for you. Let's go where we can talk," Massimo said in a hushed tone.

Both officers went into a break room and closed the door. Massimo poured them two cups of coffee and carried the white styrofoam vessels over to an old beat-up wooden table where Tobias was sitting. He was looking over his pile of papers, making sure his report was suitable and thinking that his body felt a lot like this break room table looked. Tobias looked up at Massimo when he put the coffees down and said, "OK, what did you find out?"

"This hooker, 'New Ho.' It looks like homicide to me. First of all, the cause of death was drowning, but that isn't the interesting part. The autopsy report shows that she had contusions on either side of her neck, right where the carotid arteries run to the brain. What does that make you think?" he quizzed Tobias.

"That's almost like a police choke hold," Tobias said.

"Exactly, my dear Watson," said Massimo. "And there's more. She had a high concentration of heroin—but not enough to kill her."

"OK, but she was a heroin junkie, so that isn't unusual," Tobias answered.

"That is true, but from what I hear she was a nickel and dime hooker living from stamp bag to stamp bag. The level of 'H' listed in her toxicology report would have run a pretty penny, possibly too expensive for her budget. What I am saying is, it is possible someone other than her put that heroin in her. Maybe I am reaching, but it's just something to keep in the memory banks," he concluded.

"OK, anything else?" Tobias asked, feeling that Massimo wasn't quite finished.

"Oh but there is my inquisitive companion," he said with a flare.

"Just spit it out, Miss Drama Queen," joked Tobias.

"The lab found a bit of foreign blood on the late Miss New Ho. It was on the back of her shirt, the outside part. She didn't have any injuries that would have left blood there, and the blood type was different from hers. Dump the body into the river in the hope that the blood smear is destroyed and the contusions on her neck are concealed after a few weeks in the water. Add all this up and I call it murder. What do you think?" Massimo said, leaving Tobias to consider these new revelations.

Tobias sat still for a moment and looked up to the ceiling, processing the information. After a short while, he leveled his gaze into Massimo's eyes, and with a serious voice and expression to match he simply said, "Faust."

"I quite agree my dear Watson. Let us away, there is a criminal afoot," Massimo said comically.

"OK Mr. Holmes, what do we do next?" Tobias asked.

After a little strategy discourse between Tobias and Massimo, on what steps they should take in the crusade to clear Ruggerio and Diaz, both cops walked out of the break room and headed back to their respective duties. Tobias watched as Massimo strode up the old wooden stairs of the station house. He was in a hurry because he didn't want anyone to become suspicious about his extended absence from the detective squad room. Tobias could hear the creaking wood of the stairway every time Massimo's foot fell on a step. The station house was right out of an old Hollywood movie. The building dated back to the 1950s and had not changed in design much at all. The front entrance still had the old hanging globe lights, with "Police" painted on them. Inside, the raised wooden desk where the desk sergeant used to sit was still there. Now this was covered with bullet resistant glass and a civilian receptionist instead of a cop sat at this desk.

Tobias was turning the corner from the hallway to go back to the patrol muster room where he was going to hand his reports from his alley brawl to the shift sergeant, when his progress was abruptly blocked by none other than Detective Faust himself.

"Hold on there cowboy," Faust said, holding up one hand like a traffic cop. "Where do you think you are going?"

"To the squad room. Why, what's up?" Tobias said curiously.

"I hear you had a little use of force incident this afternoon. I hope you have all your paperwork in order. We won't want any IAD trouble messin' up your case would we?" he said cynically. IAD referred to Internal Affairs Division, the part of the police department that investigates officer misconduct, such as excessive use of force cases.

"Don't worry, everything is in order. Can I ask why you are so interested in a measly assault on an officer case? I mean, don't you have other things to worry about?" Tobias, not one to be intimidated easily, was hoping Faust understood the meaning behind this question.

"Not right now. I just don't want to see you get jammed up on a Conduct Unbecoming rap or maybe Conducting an Unauthorized Investigation violation. You know that could ruin a cop's career like right quick. Not that I think you need to worry about anything.

I'm just saying, it is good to be careful. Maybe you can let Massimo know this, too."

He paused for a brief second, and then continued as he moved a little closer to Tobias for effect. "Listen, Ruggerio murdered that kid and Diaz lied to cover it up. They are going down, and you don't want to go with them, do you? I'm just trying to keep the peace, that's all." He said the last sentence halfway turned toward Tobias as he walked away. It was a planned maneuver to prevent any back talk from Tobias. It seemed Faust was good at starting a confrontation but lacked the nerve or will to finish. He wanted to throw a little fear into Tobias and maybe get him to think twice before he delved any deeper into Faust's illicit affairs.

The problem was, that Faust didn't really know Tobias, and wasn't used to dealing with a stubborn Jew like him. Faust was the quintessential schoolyard bully. He used his size and forceful tone to intimidate people, and it usually worked. But when someone stood up to him this bravado quickly disappears. He detected some defiance in Tobias' previous retorts, so he didn't want to chance any further counter attacks from him. Faust also didn't want him to detect any signs of weakness, which would dilute the essence of the threat, so a quick hit and run was in order.

What Faust would soon find out about Tobias was that his demeanor was similar to that of his Israeli brethren, who responded to threats by becoming even stronger and more determined. So when Faust hurriedly scurried up the stairs to the detective squad room, Tobias didn't get angry. He simply smiled to himself and felt a wave of calm come over him. At first he didn't understand this relaxed state, but he quickly realized that Detective Faust just made a colossal mistake by delivering this ill-advised threat. Tobias quietly thanked Faust for inadvertently confirming once and for all that he, Faust, really did commit some yet-to-be-discovered infraction concerning the Ruggerio shooting. More importantly, that he was worried Tobias, Diaz and Massimo were going to expose his conduct and call him to account for it.

"Thank you, dumb shit," Tobias said quietly to himself.

At the end of Tobias's shift, he arranged to pick up Diaz and head over to Ruggerio's house to try to lift his spirits. On the way Tobias told Diaz that he didn't think they should relate all the new information on G to Ruggerio until they had a better fix on G's location.

"You know Guy, he will go out beating the bushes to try and find this dude, and we can't have that," said Tobias to Diaz.

They couldn't believe what they saw after Ruggerio opened his front door to let them inside. Ruggerio had on a navy blue, cotton sweatshirt that had light colored specks of crusty old food on the front of it. For pants, he wore dark grey jogging pants, made of the same material, which he probably hadn't changed in a week. On his feet, he wore what used to be white cotton tube socks, now soiled from overuse, especially the bottoms, which had the tell tale darkened marks on the heel and balls of the feet. He hadn't bothered to pull them up, so when he walked the toes of each sock flapped in the air with every step. He had let his hair grow and it was uncombed with one side flattened to his head. He hadn't shaved in probably three days. Of course, where the burn scar ended, the beard began, creating an irregular and unsightly hair line down his neck. His eyes looked drawn with bags under each. He had the look of soldiers that had seen excessive combat, and just didn't feel anything anymore. To Tobias he was a man on the brink of collapse and he knew immediately that if he didn't provide Ruggerio some nugget of hope that he may not see his friend alive much longer. He also realized that they were going to have to tell Ruggerio the news about a possible witness, even though they have no clue where to find this guy, or how they would go about locating him.

Walking into the living room area where Ruggerio apparently was living full time, they saw a disaster area. It was a scene of scattered newspapers, old food take-out boxes, crushed beer cans, and a sweat-stained pillow lying crumpled on one end of the couch. They all sat down, Ruggerio holding his head as if suffering from another hangover and staring down at the floor leaving his two guests unacknowledged. Tobias broke the silence but began his words in a soft tone as if they were at a viewing in a funeral home.

"Hey, Guy, I have some good news for you."

Diaz snapped his head in Tobias's direction with a puzzled look on his, but didn't say anything out loud.

Tobias continued, still speaking in the funeral voice as Ruggerio kept his gaze fixed on the living room carpet, or a portion that could be seen through the discarded debris. "We may have a witness to the shooting."

Ruggerio's head shot up and his eyes met Tobias's. He even displayed the semblance of a smile.

"Now, that got your attention," Tobias said in a satisfied tone.

"Who is it? Did he hear the shots and see the kid point the cell phone at Diaz?" Ruggerio said with the excitement of a child on Christmas morning.

"Well we haven't located him yet, but we have some people out looking." Tobias exaggerated a bit, but he didn't want to tell him that they were pinning their hopes of finding G on Lonnie the wino.

"Who is this guy? Do we know anything about him?" Ruggerio asked in anticipation.

Tobias gave him all the information they had gathered on G and told him that they were going to hit the streets and start asking around about him, hoping not to scare their potential witness away. Tobias knew that telling Ruggerio was a risky proposition but he had no choice, after seeing what condition he was in when he opened the front door. Witnessing his positive reaction to the news, Tobias knew that he had made the right decision. Now he had to deal with Ruggerio's desire to get involved, and he wasn't sure how he was going to handle this part.

"OK, I can hit up some informants that owe me. Maybe they know this G from Erie. I've never heard of him," Ruggerio said with determination.

"Are you sure that you should get that closely involved? You know that word will get out that you are asking around and the brass will come down on you hard," Tobias said, trying to be gentle with the subject.

Diaz, who had remained silent up to this point, felt the need to add his assurance that everything was being done that could be done. "Don't worry Guy. We will find him. We got Massimo asking around too."

"He is a good detective. If anybody can find this guy, Massimo can," Ruggerio said with confidence. He added, "But I need to do something. I can't stay here and drink myself to death. I have to feel like I have a purpose. Don't take that away from me. I don't care if the higher ups find out. What else can they do to me anyway?"

There was a short silence as Tobias looked into Ruggerio's pleading eyes.

Tobias said the only thing he could say, "OK, but we all go together, and no one freelances, alright?"

"No problem. When do we go?" Ruggerio said as a relaxed expression transformed his face.

CHAPTER 8

The plan was that Massimo was to take a less obvious profile in the Ruggerio investigation, as it was starting to be called by the department rumor mill. Massimo was a courageous cop, but he had two kids in college along with the usual family bills, and could not afford to lose his steady paycheck, not to mention a pension that was eight years down the road for him. So, it was agreed that the best way he could help in locating the mysterious G was from the privacy of his own desk. Massimo, a detective, had at his fingertips a larger database of department information on arrestees and other criminal subjects than did the patrol division. In addition, he could tap into other state and federal sources of information, such as the Department of Motor Vehicles, the Department of Corrections, and the Administrative Office of the Common Pleas Court, not to mention a statewide database of all persons arrested by state and local police in the last ten years. He also had contacts with the Welfare Office, the Social Security Office, and the Pennsylvania Parole Board.

Along with these bureaucratic searches, Massimo would fire up the phone lines and call his collection of informants that he had accrued over the years. Any good detective works hard at cultivating and maintaining informants as his careers progress. Massimo was no different; in fact he figured that if he were to find G, the most likely method was through information supplied by informants.

He also knew, due to the lifestyle of street informants, making contact with them was not as sure and easy as communication between regular citizens. Street informants don't have the means or the mores of people in the noncriminal world. For example, they don't have normal business hours—they don't work nine to five or eight to four. Those involved in the drug world are nocturnal; both dealers and users sleep most of the day and awake at night to engage in their business. Massimo knew that he would be making most of his calls in the evening hours, when these informants were out conducting their activities. They usually don't have access to a computer, so e-mail is not really an option. Street informants don't usually have a home phone number, so calling a home base is not going to work. However everyone on the street has a cell phone by necessity.

The cell phone is the great device that greases the gears of the drug trade. Most drug dealers have two or three cell phones, a tactic that makes pinning them down to one phone a little more difficult for law enforcement. By contrast, drug users, who are usually also the street informants that police use, typically have only one cell phone. The great difficulty is that since addicts are always money strapped, they often fall behind on phone payments and are constantly defaulting on their accounts. Therefore, phone numbers almost never stay constant for street informants, confounding law enforcement when they attempt to reach out for information.

On top of all these difficulties, Massimo knew from experience that street people are by their nature suspicious and never actually answer their cell phone when they see a foreign phone number or anonymous phone call on their caller ID. Since he was calling from a secure phone line, his number would come up restricted and he would probably have to leave voicemail messages, then wait for return calls which usually don't occur until the next day, or in some cases several days later—if at all. He figured that on this first night the street information would probably be lean, but this first step was necessary. He needed to get the word out that he was looking for a "person of interest." This phrase has become a part of police lexicon since the Oklahoma City bombing incident.

While Massimo was busy burning the phone lines and tapping away at the computer, the other three cops were set to initiate the second half of the strategy to find G. This part of the plan had two phases; the first was simply that Tobias, Diaz, and Ruggerio would hit the streets and talk to as many people as possible to gather information on G and/or his whereabouts. If they did not see any results after giving this tactic enough time, phase two would begin. In this part of the plan, Diaz would play the major role in gathering information by going undercover into the drug scene. Since his was a relatively fresh face on the street, he was mostly unknown to the users and dealers as a police officer. In addition, as Tobias had delicately put it, since he was black he could blend into the scene more effectively.

With the plans laid out, the three cops piled into Tobias's personal car, a 1994 dark gray Chevy Lumina, the Tobias family's second car. Since it was a well-used vehicle, a beater as they call it on the street, it fit in well with the other crack head mobiles cruising around looking to score. All three were dressed for the part, in oversized pullover hoodies and jeans. Since it was a cold winter night, Tobias put his hood over his head just like the junkies do.

Street code dictates that you should keep the face covered; always maintain anonymity if possible. Cops get to know their beats and become very familiar with the names and faces of the drug addicts and most of the dealers from the repeated encounters they have with these subjects. If a cop sees a known junkie cruising around, he will be sure to stop him and check him out, so it is better to keep your face concealed as best as you can, if you are out trying to score some dope.

Ruggerio had a Pittsburgh Steelers ball cap on, which he had chosen because it was predominantly black in color and helped conceal his face in the darkness. Diaz was a special case; since his mission was possibly twofold, he had been instructed to dress the part of the drug dealer character. He also wore his hoodie over his head to conceal his face, as a person in his role would do. He rode in the back seat of the Lumina, in the center position just like a dealer would do, so he could easily exchange the drugs and the money with the two front seat occupants.

The last part of the plan was what to do if they actually discovered who G was and where to find him. Tobias had to include another trustworthy soul on the force, someone willing to potentially place his career on the line to help out Ruggerio. The K-9 officer, Quinton O'Neal, who had tipped Tobias off to the cell phone that Dickson was using at the time of his death, was a good friend and could be trusted. Quint was on duty and would be working the 4-12 shift all week long. He agreed to attempt a legitimate police encounter with G if Tobias was able to locate him. Tobias said that he would call Quint on his cell and give him the details of G's whereabouts when he was discovered. The added advantage with a K-9 officer was his four-legged friend that could out run any fleet footed crack head on the street.

With all bases covered, the three undercover cops hit the street in search of the elusive G. Ruggerio contrived the approach that they would use when inquiring about G. They would pull up to a prospective junkie and ask about G's whereabouts, explaining that he owed them some money on a deal and they wanted to collect. After several attempts using this line, they quickly discovered that this information was going to be difficult to come by. The plain clothes cops found themselves repeatedly trying to get out of being involved in three party drug transactions proposed by the junkies they were talking with. Every time they tried asking about G it was the same reply,

"No I don't know him, but if you give me a ride I can hook you up with some rocks as long as I get a pinch off of you."

They had to turn away offers to purchase such items as stolen televisions, CD players, DVDs, GPS units, Playstations and even guns—all hot commodities on the black market. One time a hooker said she would do all three of them if they gave her a twenty piece. After declining this offer, Diaz commented to his partners as they drove away, "That shit must take a powerful hold on these people to make them debase themselves this way."

For him, it seemed to be a personal epiphany regarding life on the street. Reverting to his habit of finding the right word to describe the circumstance, he thought to himself, *debase*. That was a good word.

"It'll make you a slave to the drug. A junkie will steal whatever from whomever to get the next fix. Sometimes they might even kill to satisfy the addiction." Ruggerio paused for a moment indicating that he was about to say something further on the topic.

"I think I might be experiencing a little of what they go through myself," he concluded. Out of decency, the other two didn't respond, but quietly agreed with his assessment.

Tobias broke the tense silence by changing the subject. "This is getting us nowhere. All we are finding out is that you can buy just about anything you want on the street in this city. Tay, what do you think about trying your hand at acting?"

"I'll do the best I can. I have both your cells on my speed dial so if I need you all I have to do is hit a single number," he said nervously.

"Good, don't push too hard, patience is the name of the game when trying to get information while you are undercover," Ruggerio said, relapsing into his training officer role.

Tobias was wheeling the Lumina around the city streets, watching junkies and dealers ducking in and out of shadowy nooks and crannies between buildings in their efforts to keep out of sight but constantly on the alert for potential customers or the appearance of their favorite dealer. He thought to himself that the drug problem can never be solved in society with so much demand and the unlimited quantity that is available in this country. He realized that working out of uniform gave him a much different perspective on what the city's mean streets were really like.

Ever since the night of the shooting, G had been afraid and he didn't like feeling that way. It made him feel weak, and that was not his way. He had survived prison, although he would never go back—never. He had survived his home life, including many assaults by his mother's so-called boyfriends. He had survived the street and all the dangers associated with this life. He lived always with the possibility that death could be just around the next corner or at the next drug deal, or when committing the next armed robbery or when breaking into the next house or business, or when being stopped by the next cop.

He really became afraid after hearing about New Ho being fished out of the river. He was convinced that the cops had killed her trying to cover up the bad shooting that took place in Bartlett Park. He was also convinced that he was next on their target list and that they were out hunting him right now. Having a crack habit, which tends to distort one's view of reality, did not help his growing sense of apprehension.

Since the shooting incident he had been keeping a low profile on the street, only coming out late at night, in the very early morning hours around 4 a.m. G knew that detectives didn't usually work this late and if they did, they would not be very active. He also knew that patrol cops had a tendency to reduce their activity at this hour, just killing time before end of watch. So he would come out at this time to cop some dope, make a few snaps, as the dopers would say. In other words, hook up some customers with some dealers. In exchange he would get a few rocks of crack from the dealer. After chancing a few of these type deals he would head back to his crib to smoke up the rock and hope that it would hold back the hounds of addiction until the next day.

The apartment he was staying in was a stroke of luck, he thought. He was staying with a mentally disabled person by the name of George. He didn't know his last name. On the street people rarely know last names; most of the time even the first name is fictitious. George was a black man with the mentality of a twelve-year-old. He was eligible for government assistance so he could pay for a place to live and some other meager necessities of life. George lived on the second floor of an apartment house that had a black and white couple living on the first floor. He was white, she was black; they were both drug addicts and they stole from George every chance they got to support their habits, until G came along and protected George from the couple downstairs. In exchange for his protective services, G could live at George's apartment rent-free.

This was the way of the street, survival of the fittest, just like prehistoric times before man walked upright and supposedly civilized the world. This instinct remains instilled in humanity, remnants of an uncivilized past, but still a significant part of our being. Today G was George's protector, but if he needed to, G could turn on George in a second and take whatever he wanted. Whether this innate viciousness of mankind manifests through street people or between two police officers vying for superiority, this trait is not confined to social class or station in life.

G knew that this arrangement was not going to last forever and that the police would catch up with him sooner or later. He figured that there was an arrest warrant out for him by now anyway from the parole board, since he hadn't seen his parole officer in months, as his conditions required. He needed to get out of this town and go somewhere where he was not known. Maybe Cleveland, or Philly, maybe New York City. A nigga could mix right into the crowd in those cities, he thought.

But he needed some money to get out, a score that could carry him all the way to one of those towns where he could get lost. He still had the gun that he'd used on the night of the shooting. He never returned it, thinking that it could come in handy. He had even been able to obtain two additional .38 rounds for his revolver to replace the one he'd shot in Bartlett Park and the one that malfunctioned. Now he was glad that he had kept it because he decided that the way he was going to get some money to get out of

Pittsburgh was to rob a store, one with a lot of cash on hand. To do this, he would have to go out during daylight hours and risk being seen by the police. It was a risk, but it was one he had to take in order to make good his escape to a fresh town and survive the urban jungle for another day.

After three days of Massimo's phone calls and computer research, and after the three patrol officers spent the same amount of time beating the streets to find out where G was, they still had very little success. Massimo was largely finished with his end of the investigation; the phone calls had been made, the messages left. Now he waited for return calls and hoped some useful information would come back.

Both Massimo and the patrol cops received scant sightings and loose, unconfirmed information from their collective sources concerning G. Yes, some people had heard of him, some had even smoked dope with him, but with the vagaries of the drug life, all junkies and dealers are about the same in concealing their true identities. Details like what someone's name is, where they live, or what they did before becoming a crack crazed addict, are not important to junkies. Only finding the next fix or how to get the money for the next fix is important. So the information that police officers need to find a person is not easily obtained.

However, good old-fashioned police work, even in this technology-driven era, still is based on gathering every scrap of information from all possible sources. From this patchwork of information, deductions are made and conclusions can be reached toward the ultimate goal of solving a case. In this instance, after three days of hard work, both at the street level and from computer-generated data, the officers had the following:

Several drug addicts who had gotten high with G gave a good physical description of him. The potential witness to the Ruggerio shooting was described as being 5'10" tall, with close cropped hair and a goatee, about 160 pounds, and approximately 35 years old. The most vital piece of the description was G's distinctive tattoo. Like many other cons who do serious time in prison, G had a tattoo done while in the joint. Proud of his street moniker, G had the initial tattooed on his left forearm in Gothic script.

How the three plain clothes officers obtained this description, which would later turn out to be critical information, was due to a mixture of frustration and deception. When rolling up on addicts and simply engaging them in conversation was not really getting them anything more than a scant physical description, they decided to have Diaz try his acting ability again. The first time he went out, he may have been suffering from stage fright and therefore received the cold shoulder from the addicts. On the third night out, he lost the newness of playing an undercover role and was ready to "hit the ave," as they say.

Diaz put on a black nylon head rag, like the other dealers, flipped up his hoodie on his Fila pullover, and tried out the "drug dealer strut" that he had practiced all day at home, alternately swinging his arms out in front of his body, and then quickly drawing a straightened arm way back behind his rear end, mimicking the ultra confident march of the street-level drug peddler. Ruggerio and Tobias were sitting in the Lumina down the street as they watched Diaz sauntering away from them, but with strict orders not to leave their sight.

"He is a quick study, this kid," Tobias said to Ruggerio.

"He is going to be a good cop, as long as I didn't get him fired by that damn shooting," he answered.

"We are going to find this guy and get you two cleared. I know it. Don't worry."

Easy for him to say, Ruggerio thought to himself, but he was appreciative that Tobias had said it. Not to mention being overwhelmed with gratitude by the incredible risks that Tobias, Diaz, and Massimo, and now Quint were taking for him. He felt that he needed to say something to show his gratitude.

"Hey, Toby," he said.

"Yeah?"

"I really appreciate what you guys are doing for me. I know that you could get into a lot of trouble, and I want you to…"

"Hey," Tobias stopped him from going any further because he knew it was difficult for men to talk this way with each other. He already knew that Ruggerio was thankful for their efforts. "After we get this cleared up, you are going to owe me big time, Brother. I want a steak dinner at Ruth's Chris Steakhouse, and not the cheapo sirloin—the filet dinner," he said jokingly.

"You do realize I am off duty without pay, don't you? How the hell can I afford a dinner at Ruth's Chris, you greedy bastard," Ruggerio replied, smiling.

"All you got to do is work a couple overtime shifts and you got it paid for… Geez, and you guys call us Jews cheap," Tobias said as Ruggerio abruptly stopped him.

"Look!" He pointed out the front windshield in the direction where Diaz had last been seen.

The figures were in a badly lit portion of the street, but it was unmistakable that Diaz was fighting with someone on the sidewalk. The two officers in the car jumped out and ran toward the scuffle.

They could see Diaz jostling with a white male. Both men were latched onto each other, holding one another's coat sleeves almost like two hockey players trying to pull the other's sweater over his head. Diaz, the stronger of the two, pushed his opponent backwards to knock him off balance. Diaz maneuvered his right hip side by side with the attacker's. He lowered his center of gravity as he had been taught in the academy to perform a hip throw. With one motion, Diaz lifted with his legs and pulled his opponent over his right hip, sending the man sailing through the air then crashing down on the pavement of the sidewalk. Just as the would-be assailant hit the ground, the two backup officers arrived and all three men held the white male down.

"Get off me, Man!" he said.

"What happened?" Tobias asked Diaz.

"This jerk tried to rob me. He pulled a knife on me," Diaz said in response.

"Let's get him in that alley," said Ruggerio, thinking that maybe this creep had some information they could use and wanting a more discreet place to question him.

They picked up the attacker, dragged him over to a nearby alleyway, and then pinned him up against a brick wall.

"OK you slimy fuck. We are cops and you just assaulted a police officer," Tobias said, showing him his badge.

"Now you can do five years for that, you know. That means State Penn, where the other cons will use your hole as their personal Disneyland, you get my drift," Ruggerio said bluntly.

"I didn't know he was a cop. I'm just a crack fiend. I thought he was a dealer. I don't have no money, I just wanted a rock is all!" pleaded the addict.

"Maybe you can help us and we may not have to charge you. What do you think?" said Ruggerio, his breath showing in the cold air.

"Yeah, sure. Anything you guys want," said the junkie, his eyes wide open with fear.

"You know a guy they call G, from Cleveland?" Ruggerio asked, testing the junkie to see if he would lie just to get out of this jam.

"I know a G from Erie. I don't know any G from Cleveland," he said, realizing what the game was.

"OK, maybe it is the same guy. What does he look like?" Ruggerio was handling the questioning now, with Tobias helping him hold the junkie against the wall and Diaz watching for any bystanders.

"I don't know, ah," he stopped and thought for a moment. "He has a scruffy goatee and usually smells like cat piss. He is a junkie too. Maybe he sells a little on the side."

"Where is he?" Ruggerio asked.

"I don't know. I haven't seen him for weeks," the junkie said, seeing that his information was not pleasing the officers.

"He has a tattoo, yeah, on his arm," he added nervously.

"What kind of tattoo?" said Ruggerio.

"It's the letter G in Celtic. I know 'cause I'm Irish and the tattoo is in Celtic lettering."

The junkie immediately knew that he had hit a homerun when he saw the two cops holding him look at each other. Then the fat one asked, "Which arm?"

"His right forearm."

"OK, what's your name, Man?" Ruggerio asked.

"Louie," the frightened junkie replied, hoping that he was about to be released.

"Last name too, Dopey," Tobias added.

"O'Reilly."

"OK. That doesn't sound made up. Get out of here," Ruggerio said sarcastically as both officers released the crack head and collectively pushed him out toward the street. The last they saw of him was a figure sprinting down the avenue, rubber soled tennis shoes pounding on the pavement.

Ruggerio looked at Tobias and mockingly said, "'OK, you slimy fuck?' Where did you get that line?"

"Alright, I got a little dramatic. We got the info didn't we?"

"Yeah, and it might be something we can actually use. Let's go tell Massimo what we have," Ruggerio said.

Ruggerio went over to Diaz as they made their way back to the Lumina.

"Good job, Man. You OK? Listen I want you to know that I really appreciate everything you are doing. Sorry I got you into this mess," Ruggerio said apologetically.

"I know it sounds weird, but I am having the time of my life," Diaz said with a broad smile on his face.

He could never quite understand why, but when the snow fell like it was falling now, it seemed to silence all background noise. It was very calming. Big fluffy quarter-size flakes drifting down, visible in the night as they descended through the beams of street lights like paper confetti. Ruggerio watched from inside Tobias's car as the flakes crashed and quickly melted against the glass of the windshield, warmed by the car's heat.

· It was the night after they had received the information from the junkie O'Reilly. The three amigos, as they were calling themselves now, were back on the crusade attempting to locate the elusive G. Ruggerio put his window down a few inches to let some cool air into the car. He was starting to sweat from the combination of his layered clothing and the hot air blowing out of the Lumina's heater.

As he looked out the front passenger window he thought about similar nights when he would be working and enjoying the calmness of the snow fall. It was getting close to Christmas and some of the houses in this lower income neighborhood already had holiday decorations adorning their homes. He thought, and even prayed a little, what a Christmas gift it would be if they could find G and obtain the information that would clear his name and Diaz's also. Still gazing out of the car window, watching what weathermen call a snow shower, he could see the ground beginning to be covered by a blanket of white. Ruggerio actually felt relaxed for the first time in months, but this feeling and the calm winter night he was experiencing wouldn't last much longer.

One reason Ruggerio was feeling so good was that he and the others finally had a solid lead on their quest to find G. From Massimo's efforts they felt that they actually had his real name, Jacque Gerald Holland. When Ruggerio heard this last name he thought that his nickname should be "Dutch" not "G." But "Dutch" wouldn't be very street-worthy if your way of life was drug dealing and committing violent crimes.

They got G's real name when they went back to Massimo with the information from the Irish crack head, O'Reilly. With this new information, Massimo was able to work with his contacts and find G's identity.

Massimo relied on his experience, which told him that a drug dealer/junkie who comes to Pittsburgh from Erie probably is on the run from an arrest warrant and has a good chance of being on parole. So he contacted the Erie office of the Pennsylvania Parole Board and gave one of the supervising agents G's description as provided by the three amigos. The agent promised to check on this information and get back to Massimo as soon as possible. The next day, they had G's full name, description, photograph, and criminal history from the Erie parole agent.

The story of Jacque Gerald Holland was a typical one that police and parole officers see time and time again. Holland was popped several times for dealing crack cocaine and other crimes, which included theft and armed robbery. The robbery was the crime that sent him to state prison. After serving five years, he was released on parole. After lasting a whole three months without any violations, G made the typical mistake that nearly 80% of people make when they are on parole. His urine came up dirty for cocaine. Fearing that he would go to jail again, G decided to run instead of waiting for the parole officers to come and arrest him.

The Erie parole office had all the information that Massimo needed to confirm that his G, and the one that Erie was looking for, were the same man. The tattoo was actually in Gothic script, not Celtic, and on G's left forearm as stated on his bio sheet, not his right. Information from junkies is infamous for being inaccurate, but in this case O'Reilly was close enough. The officers from the beginning didn't think O'Reilly's tattoo description was accurate since none of them had ever seen a Celtic script tattoo before on a black guy. He even had the scruffy goatee in his parole board photo that was e-mailed to Massimo, along with the warrant for this fugitive.

Armed with this photo of Holland, Ruggerio and the other two cops were showing it to whoever walked their way. So far, there weren't any bites. Either, the people they asked didn't know G, or didn't want to admit that they knew him.

Someone upstairs must have been listening when Ruggerio prayed for a miracle however. He was about to receive an early Christmas present. Tobias heard his cell phone chirping. After answering and ascertaining who was calling, a smile began to form on his face.

"Hey Lonnie, what's up?" he said into the phone, causing Ruggerio to stop breathing for a second.

"You do? Where?" Tobias said in response.

"He found him. Did he find him?" Ruggerio asked.

"OK. You stay right there. Don't move. We will be there in five minutes. Remember Lonnie, you got a bottle coming so stay where you are," Tobias said, knowing that the added incentive of alcohol should make Lonnie comply.

After Tobias disconnected the call, he simultaneously put the car in drive and began explaining what he had earned from Lonnie.

"He found G on the North Side in a second-floor apartment, living with a retarded guy," he said as the Lumina lurched out from their parking space.

"Good old Lonnie. I bet he was taking a crap in an alley when he saw G," Ruggerio said, giggling with excitement.

"Call Quint so he can meet us in the area somewhere," Tobias told Ruggerio. Ruggerio immediately grabbed his own cell and punched the key for Quint's cell. Of course Quint was 9 on the speed-dial, 9 for K-9.

After hanging up with Quint and agreeing to meet at a supermarket parking lot on the North Side, Tobias wheeled his Lumina toward the bridge that hooked up with this part of the city. After crossing the river, Ruggerio and Diaz watched out the window in anticipation of seeing Lonnie waiting on a sidewalk. They were to meet him on a side street off the main drag in this part of town.

This section was a largely Afro-American area and a high crime area, which meant that two white guys with a black male in the same car might attract some attention from the police. That was why Tobias told Lonnie to meet off the main thoroughfare and out of sight as much as possible.

Tobias cut around a corner to turn onto the side street where Lonnie was waiting. He was so anxious to catch him that he didn't realize how slick the streets were getting with the snow. He took the turn a little too fast and the Lumina fishtailed in the middle of the street. Knowing how feebleminded Lonnie could be, like most alcoholics, Tobias wanted to find him before something distracted Lonnie, causing him to forget about their meeting and leave the area. This nervousness subsided when he pulled toward the curb at mid-block and saw Lonnie emerge from the darkness of a doorway and wave toward the car.

"How did you know it was us?" Tobias asked Lonnie as he walked up to the driver's window.

"Who else would be drivin' around here with two white guys in a car but cops? Who dat in the back? You arrest somebody?" Lonnie asked, looking at Diaz.

"No, he's a cop too. How you doin' Lonnie?" Ruggerio stated.

"That you Ruggio? Man, it's good to see you. How you doin'?" Lonnie said, showing a toothless smile.

"Good, Man. What do you have for us? We are in a little bit of a hurry," Ruggerio said, getting to the point.

"OK, your man G stays up there a ways on Monitor Ave with a retarded guy named George," he said, blowing stale alcohol breath into the car. "Listen, I don't like standin' where somebody might see," he said, looking around the area.

"OK, get in the back. You can show us where he is staying," Tobias said, but then realized something and quickly stopped Lonnie as he was reaching for the back door handle. "Wait! You're not brewing up a healthy shit now are you?" he asked Lonnie, fearing for his cloth car seats.

"No I went just before you-all got here," Lonnie exclaimed proudly.

"OK get in, but hold your cheeks together until we drop you off," Tobias said while Ruggerio and Diaz giggled under their breath.

"Don't say drop," Diaz whispered to Tobias and Ruggerio before Lonnie got in the car.

"Show Lonnie the picture, Tay," Ruggerio said.

Diaz put the photo of Jacque Gerald Holland into Lonnie's lap and directed his mini flashlight beam on it so he could see. Before Lonnie could respond, Diaz recoiled a bit from Lonnie's body odor.

"Yeah that's the dude they call G from Erie," Lonnie said immediately.

"OK, where do I go?" Tobias asked.

"Go up two blocks and make a left onto Monitor," Lonnie instructed.

Tobias did as he was told and soon found himself on Monitor Ave. He cruised slowly so Lonnie could point out the house.

"That's it right there, with the green roof over the porch," Lonnie stated. "OK, do I get my bottle now?"

"Yes you do. Good job Lonnie," Ruggerio said, handing him a twenty-dollar bill.

"Take me around the corner will you, and leave me up the street. I think the state store is still open," Lonnie said, rubbing the twenty between his hands like it was a good luck charm.

He was watching when Lonnie got out of Tobias's Lumina on this North Side of the city and he was watching when they picked Lonnie up two blocks away and drove him here. He saw the three off-duty cops, two of whom were on suspension, showing a piece of paper to locals as they walked by and apparently asking them questions. He knew what was taking place. He had done the same thing while investigating crimes. But the difference was, he was performing his duty and his actions were sanctioned by the department. What he was witnessing would be grounds for termination for all three of these rogue cops. The official term used for this type of activity according to the department policy and disciplinary manual would be "conducting an unauthorized investigation."

Faust parked about one block to their rear as he saw Lonnie jogging away from the Lumina and disappeared as he made a turn onto Main Street. In this part of town, most of the businesses were located here on this street, including the state liquor store where Lonnie was headed. He waited for the Lumina to pull out from the curb and readied himself to follow it. It was amazing, he thought, that they didn't seem to notice he had been shadowing them all night. Well not that amazing. He was a trained detective and he had to remind himself that these were three numbskulls he was trailing, so it wasn't really all that surprising. He could sense that things were coming to a head, that what he had just witnessed was going to alleviate all his problems very soon. A devious smile spread across his face.

Faust now had the proof he needed. All he had to do was have another witness observe this activity so that formal charges could be filed against these three jerks. It was for the good of the department, he reasoned. These creeps had no business being cops, if they couldn't act the way real cops do.

For Faust, real cops have to stick together, not go traipsing around on personal crusades. Real cops back each other up, even if it means bending the rules a bit and violating someone's rights, or taking a vital piece of evidence from a crime scene so that a bad cop will be thrown off the force. It was for the greater good, he rationalized.

Moreover, it was necessary out here. The deck is stacked against the police from the courts to the civil rights activists. Just like the night with that shit bag drunk that Ruggerio defended. Instead of backing him up, that little dago helped out the nigger drunk instead. No! he thought, convinced of his motives, they have to be stopped before they rat out other decent coppers.

Having again verified his sense of purpose, Faust flipped his cell open and punched in the lieutenant's office number. Raising the phone to his ear, he watched the snow shower outside his car begin to wane to a light flurry.

While listening to the lieutenant's phone ring, Faust contemplated the scenery. I hate snow, he thought. In Faust's view, snow was a nuisance, inhibiting free movement and making vehicle travel dangerous. There was nothing good about the frigid white precipitation, though other people say it looks pretty. The snow lay on the ground, got mixed in with road salt and antiskid, and then was pushed to the side of the road by the plows, to make a dark gray mass of frozen shit. What is so damn pretty about that? he wondered.

"Lieutenant Marks!" He was jolted back to the present when the lieutenant answered his phone.

"Yes, Sir. This is Faust. I have something you might want to see," he reported with a sinister sneer.

G was standing across the street, watching, waiting for the right moment to strike. He was standing inside a darkened store front so he couldn't be seen clearly from the street. It was near closing time and he reasoned the liquor store would have the largest amount of money for the day at this time. He had been watching for the last three evenings and knew the routine of how the employees closed up the store at night. There were always two employees at the end of the night. One would wait on the last few customers while the other was in the back, tallying up the day's profits. After the last customer was taken care of, the cashier would lock the front door as the patron exited. Then at exactly 8:45 p.m., a police car would pull up to the front of the store and the employee who had been working on the deposit in the back of the store would emerge and get into the cop car to be taken to the bank. It was the same all three nights, and the same employees were working tonight. All G had to do was wait for the right time, and take the clerk to the back room at gun point, as quietly as possible. He would have the man who was counting up the receipts turn over all the money. G could then take off through the back door and return to George's apartment before the cops could start looking for the robber.

He had the route that he was going to take back to George's house all mapped out. G even did a dry run one night and timed himself. It took him a little over two minutes to go from the back of the liquor store to the front of George's apartment house. The route would take him through some backyards and over a few fences, but it was well within his physical ability to accomplish. G was proud of his precise planning and was excited now to put his strategy into action.

At about 8:30 p.m., there were still a few customers in the store; G thought that this was probably the right time to move. The street seemed quiet, with very little traffic moving and only a few drug dealers active this early in the evening. They would periodically appear on the sidewalks when an addict came by to purchase crack. Then, quickly, the dealer and the addict would vanish.

The dealer might jump in and out of a parked car or a nearby building that would serve as his base of operation. The junkie might drive up or have someone else drive, jump out of the car to make the deal, then scamper back to the car and jet out of the scene. Or, since the addicts spent almost all of their time in the neighborhood and had knowledge of every footpath, abandoned house, and unsecured store front in the area, they could use this knowledge to duck in and out very quickly on foot. The philosophy was, as little time spent in the open as possible made being stopped by the cops less of a risk.

Lonnie hastily rounded the corner onto the main drag, eyes half squinting from the attack of snowflakes. As he made his way to the liquor store, Lonnie held the twenty-dollar bill in both hands, guarding it as if it were a Fabergé egg. He could almost taste the whiskey he was about to buy with the twenty that Ruggerio had given him. Lonnie's mouth was salivating in anticipation of the liquid gold flowing down his throat. He loved the feeling when this magic potion began absorbing into his system. No rotgut tonight, he thought, Black Velvet whiskey is what I'm gettin'… "And I ain't sharing it with nobody!" he said out loud and with conviction.

Lonnie was still over half a block away when G emerged from his lair and crossed the street, gripping the .38 in his coat pocket. He had on a woolen pea coat that he had purchased for ten dollars from the Salvation Army store, just in time for this cold western Pennsylvania winter that had descended upon the city.

With his non-gun hand, he held the collar of his pea coat over his face to guard against the cold air and hide his appearance at the same time. He was halfway across the street when he saw through the large plate glass windows of the state store the last customer headed for the front door, a brown paper bag wrapped around his recent purchase. A few paces behind, the cashier walked in tandem toward the door to lock it just like every other night. G couldn't believe his luck; the timing appeared to be working out just right for him.

Lonnie could see nirvana just ahead; the lights were still on in the store and it lifted his spirits to think that he would be in time before the store closed for the night. Out of the corner of his eye, he caught sight of a figure crossing the street ahead of him, also headed toward the state store. Must be another boozer hurrying to secure his own bottle of hooch for the night, Lonnie thought. The wind whipped up and slapped Lonnie on the face, causing him to turn slightly in response. He thought about the Black Velvet and how it would keep him warm tonight. As he turned his gaze back toward the direction of the liquor store he saw the other boozer reaching the front door ahead of him by some thirty feet just as another person left the store. Then he saw the boozer ram his body hard against the front door, forcing it inward. Immediately, he heard loud shouting coming from inside the store. The front door slammed closed so hard, that Lonnie thought the full-length glass in the metal-framed door would shatter—but it didn't.

The customer who had just left the store wheeled around to see what the commotion was, but after a quick look he turned back toward the street and began running as if the devil himself was chasing him. He went right past Lonnie like he wasn't there. Lonnie stopped dead in his tracks and turned to watch the running patron dart around him without saying a word of warning. This wasn't unusual to Lonnie, because on the street the motto is, "look out for yourself," very few spare compassion for their fellow man. Without having to go and look, he knew exactly what was happening; the damn store was being robbed, again! Just when he was about to buy a choice bottle of hooch for himself. That's a wino's luck, Lonnie thought as he turned back in the direction of the store.

Lonnie stood there for a moment, contemplating what to do, knowing full well that leaving the area was the smart move. But for some reason—he couldn't figure out why—he had to go see what was happening in that store. Maybe it was the unrealistic thought that this really wasn't a robbery and he could still make his purchase.

Or, could it have been that when he saw what he thought was a boozer crossing the street, he subconsciously recognized the true identity of this person and needed to confirm this by getting a better look? Whatever the reason, Lonnie chose the more dangerous path of moving toward the store and taking a look through the glass at the scene inside.

He wasn't moving. G screamed at him again. "GET THE FUCK INTO THE BACK!" he shouted at the frozen liquor store clerk.

The man was quivering at the sight of G holding a gun on him and shouting unintelligible instructions. He had just gotten to his feet after having been violently knocked to the floor when G came crashing through the door. G had thrown all of his body weight against the metal-framed glass door, forcing it inward and hitting the store clerk in the chest and sending him flying backward to the ground. The clerk, a white male in his forties, had recently been transferred to this store and had never been robbed before. He was petrified with fear and could not get his body to move, nor was he able to understand what the robber was saying to him.

During times of extreme stress, the body goes through unusual changes. One such anomaly is that the hearing ability of a person can become severely reduced. As in this case, the clerk could distinguish that the robber was yelling something at him and gesturing with the gun, but damn if he could make out what this maniac was saying to him. So he remained there, standing in front of this John Dillinger wannabe, unable to move or clearly hear what was being shouted at him.

G was still holding the collar flap of his pea coat over the lower portion of his face with his left hand, and with his right hand pointing the .38 at the store clerk, who was doing an impressive imitation of a statute. He knew that he didn't have much time and that the back room clerk would be either coming out to see what was going on or dialing 911 very soon. He had to make a move and couldn't think of anything else to do but to whack the terror-stricken clerk over the head with the butt of his gun. He hoped that this would knock him out so he could move on to the back room and the money man.

What G didn't realize though, was that the money man was already out from the back room and with his own gun. This second clerk was ready for this type of crime and at that moment was pointing a well trained shooting hand at G's center mass.

Lonnie crept up to the edge of the plate glass window of the state store. Since it was a store front in the middle of a block of other store fronts, most abandoned and closed down years ago, Lonnie had his front side pressed against the wall of the adjoining building. He leaned his head to the right to look through the glass and into the liquor store. His first thought was, there goes my Black Velvet. He could tell that another robbery was taking place and he knew what would happen after the robbery was over. The cops would be called and the store closed for the night. No further sales would take place.

"Damn!" he said aloud.

Even though Lonnie was positioned well to the rear of the robber, as he pointed a gun at a frightened store clerk, the robber must have heard Lonnie's remark because he turned his head slightly in his direction. It was enough of a turn that Lonnie got a look at his face. To his horror, Lonnie immediately recognized the infamous G from Erie, the very same guy that had earned him the twenty-dollar bill that was now in his hands. To Lonnie's dismay, he felt sure that G recognized him too and that wasn't good.

Lonnie figured G for a stone cold killer. A wino's life is tough enough, and Lonnie did not relish the thought of constantly hiding from this maniac. Thus, Lonnie abruptly changed his priorities from a quest for a bottle of whiskey to how fast he could run to the corner of the block and get the hell out of there. He was off and running, hoping as he ran that Tobias and Ruggerio were still parked in the spot where they had dropped him earlier.

Lonnie raced for the corner as he pumped his arms and legs up and down, his cheap hard-soled shoes clippety-clopping on the concrete sidewalk. Snow pelting him in the face, he would occasionally turn to look back to see if G was following; he was relieved to see that no one was there. But this relief quickly turned to frustration when he made the corner and found that Tobias and Ruggerio were gone. Lonnie stopped on this side street, bent over, hands on his knees, huffing and puffing, feeling his lungs burn and wishing for a drink to calm himself down.

As he was catching his breath, Lonnie was trying to figure out what he should do next. He was sure G had seen him looking through the window of the liquor store. G would come after Lonnie to silence him as a witness, he was sure. Lonnie had been on the street his entire life and knew what kind of person G was. Lonnie was good as dead unless he had G arrested.

It hit him then; he knew where to find Ruggerio and Tobias—at G's house. Since he had just shown them where G was staying, they were sure to be watching the place and waiting for G to come back. He took a suck of wind into his lungs and started jogging down the street toward G's house, where he was sure to find Ruggerio and be saved from this predicament.

G brought his attention back to the trembling store clerk standing in front of him. He knew that someone, he didn't know who, had seen what was going on from the store widow, but there wasn't anything he could do about it right now. He had to stay focused and carry out his plan. G lunged forward, raising his gun hand high in the air and coming down hard with the butt end on the top of the clerk's head. The clerk, who simply stood there paralyzed by fear, felt the shooting pain of the blow reverberate through his body like an electric shock. He went down in a heap and remained conscious, but only barely. Later, he would be an excellent witness to the events that were about to take place.

Seeing that he had effectively taken the cashier out of the way, G turned to make his way toward the back room and deal with the employee who had all the money. As G turned in the direction of the back room, he was greeted with an unpleasant surprise, the business end of a .380 Colt semi-automatic pistol pointed right at his chest from about ten feet away. Store clerk number two, a black male about fifty-five years of age, who had been the victim of several other robberies in the past, had bought the weapon four months ago for protection. He has been practicing with it since that time and was just waiting for the opportunity to use it in a situation like this one.

One detail that clerk number two didn't take into account when he was firing all those rounds from his slick new pistol into a paper scoring target, was that target practice is not the same as shooting at a real person. Especially when the person you are facing is also holding a heater. What was even more disconcerting to clerk number two was that this particular criminal had no such inhibitions or moral dilemmas when it came to taking a life; it was very clear from the expression on the robber's face that he meant business.

G began to move forward, gun trained in the direction of the clerk, who was using a display rack of vodka bottles as cover, another bad move. G, feeling quite exasperated with what seemed to be one obstruction after another, decided to go for broke and start firing at this guy. He could sense his opponent's lack of will, since he hadn't shot at G up to this point.

POP, POP went the .38 in G's hand, vodka bottles shattering, sending glass flying and liquid from the broken bottles spilling onto the floor. G never stopping his forward progress, taking a step toward the clerk with each round fired. The frightened state store employee moved back away from the exploding vodka bottles and turned his head away from the flying glass, hoping that none of the .38 rounds found their mark. Unfortunately, one round had hit home and passed into the clerk's abdomen. He staggered back toward the wall, slamming against it, then looking down and grasping the leaking wound in his stomach.

Determined to end this as soon as possible, G fired another round, hitting the helpless victim in the left chest area. The clerk recoiled from the second impact and staggered to the side, trying in vain to get away from this maelstrom. Severely wounded, with imminent death in his thoughts, the clerk's instinct for survival finally triggered. He raised the Colt and squeezed off two quick rounds. One round clipped G on the left side, ricocheting off a rib bone and fracturing it in the process, then quickly exiting near his back. The second round missed him completely and exploded a bottle of Lambrusco on a back shelf. G doubled over the affected side of his body and moved to retreat from the man firing the Colt. He went behind another display rack and knelt down to survey the situation.

As he groaned in pain and tried to staunch the flow of blood from his side, he began to realize that this wasn't going very well. He needed to make sure the other guy was out of action. G tried to stop himself from groaning so that he could hear if the clerk was moving in his direction. He gritted his teeth through the pain and listened. Not hearing the man moving, he decided to take a quick look over the display rack and see what the clerk's status was. Peering over the top of the rack of various bourbons and brandies, he could see the legs and feet of the clerk protruding from behind the service counter. It looked as if he was down and not going to be any further trouble, but G had to make sure. He carefully made his way over to the man and could see that he was most likely dead. Just to make sure that he couldn't use the gun anymore, G grabbed the Colt from where it was lying on the floor next to the crumbled body. As he straightened up, G felt a bolt of pain shoot through his body from the gunshot wound in his side and he winced in response. He looked around to see if there were any witnesses and if the other clerk was still on the floor, which he was, apparently unconscious. The room seemed to spin and G was feeling a bit dizzy now, possibly from loss of blood or excitement, or a combination of both. He needed to get the hell out of there. He made a step toward the front door, but stopped himself and remembered the whole reason he had attempted this robbery. He then went into the back room and saw a pile of bills lying neatly on a desk next to a computer. He grabbed the bills, getting blood spatter on most of them and jamming the money in his pocket. It didn't look like much but it would have to do.

As he was about to turn toward the back door and make his escape, he realized something. On the desktop computer was an image of the store area. He could see on the monitor the two clerks lying on the floor. To his horror he realized that the whole robbery and shootout had been captured on video.

This was just too much for G. He felt a fit of frustration and rage began to well up inside of him. Nothing had gone as planned and now the police would find his picture when they came to investigate. He had to find the video and take it or destroy it immediately, since the cops would be coming soon. G began to search frantically for the tape machine. It wasn't around the desk area where the computer was, nor in another room, which served as the boiler and electrical room. The rage increased as his search for the tape machine was not producing any success. He shoved the .38 into his pocket and tucked the Colt into his belt to free his hands. G looked around for a blunt object. He wanted to smash the computer monitor thinking that since the image was on it, maybe the robbery incident was stored inside. He found a baseball bat in the corner of the darkened storeroom and began whaling on the monitor, smashing it with three angry blows, cussing with each swing.

He had to leave now before the police escort detail arrived on the front street. G dropped the bat, realizing, but not really caring at this point, that he was leaving behind his fingerprints on the bat and blood spatter all over the store room. He just wanted to get out of there and to find a safe place to lick his wounds. He pushed open the back doors that led to the alley behind the store, and peered outside. Not seeing anything suspicious, he exited the store and ran across the alley into a backyard then followed the predetermined route that would lead to George's apartment.

CHAPTER 9

"Well who is it going to be?" asked Tobias.

"Whaddaya talkin' about?" questioned Diaz.

"He is slyly asking who will volunteer to leave this warm car and stand in the rear of this house to watch for G to come out," Ruggerio answered in an exaggerated show of grammatical pizzazz. He was still feeling a little giddy with anticipation that things might finally be going his way in the nightmare that has been his life for the past several months.

They were now parked a few blocks north of where, unbeknownst to the three amigos, the liquor store holdup was taking place. They were sitting in Tobias's old Lumina, just down Monitor Ave from George's house, where G had been hiding out. The car blended in well with the other economy cars that belonged to the residents of this area, the owners of which were mostly Section 8 renters.

Section 8 was the state legislative act that enabled housing assistance for the state's poor population. This would be a boon to many landlords who would buy up older homes at low cost, then after minimal repairs, which made them marginally livable, they would rent them out to Section 8 recipients. It was a safe bet for the landlord since the rent check came without question each and every month from the government, eliminating the hassles of collecting rent from tenants.

However, these areas also seemed to produce high levels of drug and criminal activity. One reason would be from outwardly legitimate renters, permitting their residences to be used by drug dealers for a cut of the profits. Most often, this supposedly legitimate renter was a female who had children with the dealer. Since the woman usually didn't have an arrest record, she could qualify for Section 8 and thus provide a home base for her dealer boyfriend. This typical arrangement normally included several children that the girlfriend had to take care of, so the profits from the drug trade were a welcome stipend. Sadly, the fallout from this type of lifestyle had the obvious consequences one would expect for the children as they grew. The children, knowing only what they were exposed to as they matured, naturally turned into the next generation of drug traffickers. When they had children of their own, the cycle would perpetuate.

"Un-pucker your sphincter Toby. I'll go. I'm starting to sweat in this car anyway—I have so many layers of clothes on," stated Ruggerio.

"Wait," Diaz said abruptly. "What if I went around back? I would look more like I belong there. Besides, Guy, if you run into him how are you going to explain being here to the brass if the shit hits the fan?" he asked.

"At this point Tay, I am fighting for my life. Whatever they do to me for conducting an unauthorized investigation is nothing compared to spending time in the slam." He looked at his friend Taymond Diaz for a brief moment to let him absorb this thought, and then added with a smirk, "Capisce?"

"Capisce," answered Diaz.

Then Tobias remarked, "Besides, if you go out there Tay, two white guys sitting in a car in this neighborhood just screams PO-lice." He pronounced police in the vernacular of the street.

"Again, I stand corrected," Diaz said with a smile.

Ruggerio got out of the car and let Diaz climb into the front seat with Tobias. Ruggerio walked down to the end of the block and entered the alley that runs behind George and G's house, throwing his hoodie over his head so that his face was obscured. Inside his coat pocket, he placed his right hand on a Glock .9mm pistol that he had brought along. His duty weapon had been turned in upon his suspension, but he still had this .9mm at home for off-duty occasions. In a neighborhood like this, anything could surprise you, so he wanted to be ready just in case. Drug dealers, users, thieves, prostitutes, drunks, or just plain crazy people could appear from any hiding place and try to rob or assault a lone individual.

Abandoned houses were a common problem, especially in the winter when the downtrodden would use these places to keep warm. The greatest hazards were the fires that they would make in them for heat. Fire, he thought to himself. It was a fire that had given him the scars on his body that made him less desirable to this wife. He reached up with his left hand and touched the wrinkled flesh on the right side of his face, just as a reminder.

Ruggerio put his hand back in his pocket and told himself to concentrate on the task at hand and not to let his mind wander. He had to be ready in case he encountered the elusive and desperate G. He slogged through the alley toward the target house, half bent over in an effort to shield his face from the blowing snow. The ground had about one inch covering it now and tracks were clearly visible, so Ruggerio tried to stay on the edges of the alley where the pavement was still bare. He didn't want to advertise to anyone wandering into the alley that someone else was also there. A fresh set of shoeprints in the snow could scare G away if he happened to be on his way home and was walking in the same direction. G was running scared and an experienced cop like Ruggerio knew that a criminal in this circumstance can be paranoid and the slightest unusual observation can cause a change in routine for a fugitive.

Ruggerio saw that he was approaching the target house and began to look for a suitable surveillance point. He quickly saw a broken-down cinder block garage on the opposite side of the alley and about thirty yards south and west of the house where G was reportedly hiding out. The garage lay on the edge of the alley at an angle from the target house. Between the house and this garage was a large open lot that provided an unobstructed view for Ruggerio. If this turned out to be suitable, Ruggerio would have a perfect surveillance of the south and western sides of the house.

The roof of the garage was gone, having succumbed to the frailties of wood rot. This structure had seen better days. The crumbled debris could be seen still lying where it had probably fallen in on itself inside of the block structure. The alley side was still standing but the top portion of the south wall had fallen in with the roof. This was where the man door had been, and where Ruggerio could easily enter the decrepit structure. Gingerly stepping over snow covered and splintered wood from the caved in roof, he made his way to the observation point that he desired, a glassless window. Thankfully he reached the window without having impaled a foot on any rusty nails. He crouched down near the opening, and had a perfect vantage point to watch the rear and one side of the target location. Being cloaked in the darkness this position would completely camouflage him. He could see that one of the remaining intact walls of the structure cast a shadow where he could huddle within its darkness.

Cops learn very quickly, after working night shifts for awhile, how to conceal themselves in the shadows produced by both natural and artificial light. In this case, the light produced by the moon and the scattered luminance from the few working street lights, was enhanced by the ground covering of snow. This increased brightness also produced a more pronounced contrast between the light and dark areas. Just as if one were standing in the sunlight and looking into a heavily shaded area, the contrast made it more difficult to clearly see an object concealed by the shade. Ruggerio knew this and so chose this particular location for his surveillance.

He decided to call Tobias on his cell phone and let him know which areas of the house he could see, so that they could cover the opposite sides of the house. Ruggerio pressed the "push-to-talk" button and cringed at the chirping sound his phone made.
"Toby, I am on the southwest corner, can you cover the opposite side?" he reported, his voice in a whisper.

"CHIRP! CHIRP!" Ruggerio's phone announced as he held his hand over the speaker to muffle the anticipated sound of an incoming answer from Tobias.

"OK, let me get over there and see if I can find a good spot." Tobias said this in a loud voice, as if he believed that the phone wasn't capable of carrying his voice over the one hundred feet that separated the two cell phones. Ruggerio gritted his teeth and quickly covered the speaker with his hand again when he heard

Tobias' amplified voice. Then under his breath he said, "He always does that."

Even when Tobias talked over the police radio, he had a habit of shouting into the mic, unconvinced of the advanced quality of modern communications. Ruggerio lowered the volume level to mute the chirping sounds and the loud calls from Tobias, then pushed the "push-to-talk" button and said in a hushed tone, "Toby, try not to talk so loud. This alley is pretty quiet."

Tobias answered in the same loud voice, "OK, we found a good spot to see the northeast corner of the house. Let us know if you see anything."

"OK," he replied.

Ruggerio was still exposed to the elements since so much of this structure was gone, so he huddled into his body to conserve heat and waited. As was his habit in past stakeouts he began to go over in his mind different scenarios and how he would handle them if he saw G coming out of the house. The anticipation of witnessing and catching G, the last real hope for Ruggerio to save his career, was building up in him to a point that he needed to settle himself down.

Tobias and Diaz shifted in their seats as they settled into what they expected to be a long wait until G showed himself. Tobias killed the engine and the heater, although the car was still warm from the lingering heat.

"You think it was a good idea to let Guy in the back of this house alone?" Diaz asked. Before Tobias could answer, he felt he needed to qualify his question. "I mean he is so jumpy. You never know what he will do," he concluded.

"Do you think that either one of us could have stopped him?" Tobias said rhetorically. "Besides he is so keyed up that nothing as small as a cockroach will make it out of that house without Guy seeing it. So he is probably the best man for the job anyway."

"Yeah, I guess you're right," Diaz agreed.

The two officers became silent for a moment, staring at the house and watching for G to appear, each with his own thoughts and starting to feel the cold creep into the car as the residual heat began to disappear. Then Diaz broke the silence and revealed his thoughts. "Maybe now is a good time to ask. How did Guy get those scars on his face? I never had the guts to ask him personally."

"He never told you?" Tobias asked curiously.

"No. I didn't want to ask him because I thought it was a touchy subject or something," explained Diaz.

"Well, I suppose that it is, but I thought he had gotten over that a while ago. OK, here's the story. Guy was only on a few years, still full of piss and vinegar. On Thanksgiving Day we get a call for a house fire. I was working too in a nearby zone and I heard the call. Guy gets there first and some of the people that live in the house tell him that their baby is still inside. The place was engulfed in flames but he could still hear the baby crying. He must of dove into those flames like Evil Knievel and was able to grab the baby and bring him outside. But in doing so his uniform, which is made of nylon—one of the most flammable materials possible, caught fire and was burning the shit out of his upper body and his face. When I got there, he was rolling around in the grass of the house screaming in agony, trying to put the flames out. I took my coat off and jumped on top of him to snuff out the flames. It was crazy. The baby was lying on the ground screaming in pain and its skin was all black and smoking like a piece of charcoal. The mother and her other kids, who made it out of the house without a scratch, were crying and screaming their heads off for us to do something and save the baby."

"So, what happened?" Diaz asked in anticipation.

"The baby ended up dying from the severe burns. Guy was off for about six months. He almost died himself. His face mostly remained untouched by the fire, but his uniform had melted into his skin, a good part of his right side. What you see on his neck and part of this side of his face..." Tobias demonstrated the area of Ruggerio's face that was scarred from the fire by putting his right hand up to the angle of his jawbone under the ear. "...is only a fraction of his body that is scarred. Most of his torso and part of his right arm were severely burned. We weren't sure he would ever come back to work again, but he was determined and agonized through all the rehab. Finally he was able to make it back to full duty without much disability remaining," Tobias concluded.

"So why doesn't he talk about it now? Is he still broken up over the baby dying?" asked Diaz.

"That's part of it I think, even though he doesn't talk about it much. He did tell me once that he has dreams about the baby, seeing it crying in his arms while he is carrying him out of the house. Not that he feels that he did anything wrong or helped cause the baby's death, but there is a feeling of guilt..." Tobias stopped for a moment to search his mind for the right word or phrase to explain what he was thinking. "Or maybe he was experiencing frustration that he couldn't do more to help save that baby. Whatever it is, he just doesn't talk about it much and refuses to go for counseling, which has been offered to him many times."

"Why doesn't he go for help?" Diaz asked.

"Machismo, what else? That's how cops think. If we show weakness then somehow we aren't deserving of being a cop. What can I tell you? It's stupid but true," Tobias admitted.

"How did the department handle it? Did they try to help?"

"That was another thing. All the line officers were pushing for Guy to be honored with the Medal of Valor from the department, but someone decided that it would look bad to the public. Word came down from the commissioners that since the baby died, it would look more like the department would be recognizing a failure to protect the public instead of rewarding success, which is total bullshit. We formed a group and petitioned the commissioners to honor Guy for risking his life to try and save that baby. It didn't work. They simply ignored our petition and waited until the uproar from the officers petered out. The whole issue seemed to die, especially when Guy told me that he didn't want anything anyway. He said that he just wanted to forget the whole thing and that an award would just keep reminding him of the dead kid.

"I can't help but to think that Faust had something to do with the decision of the commissioners not to honor Guy. This happened shortly after their falling out and Faust was already a rising star in the department and had made some high level connections." Tobias continued. "Be that as it may, I think that it affected his marriage, too. He has never said anything but I noticed that he and his wife kind of grew apart after that. Whether it was how his body appeared or his mood from the guilt of the baby dying, I don't know. They stopped showing up at department functions and you hardly ever saw them together since that time. He seemed to get better as the years went by and rarely complained about his wife or said much about the fire. I thought that he made peace with himself over the situation," Tobias finished, and both officers resumed their vigil.

Diaz was thinking about Ruggerio and how he received the burn scars and the way Tobias described the department's treatment toward him afterwards. *Tormented,* he thought inwardly, practicing his word ritual again. Ruggerio is a *tormented soul,* Diaz concluded. As he watched the target house for any signs of the fugitive G, he couldn't help but to feel empathy for his friend.

G, who had safely returned to George's house before the cops could set up their surveillance, was in his bathroom drenching a bath towel with his own blood in an attempt to stanch the flow from his gunshot wound. He was huffing and puffing excessively after the escape from the liquor store and the intense pain he was beginning to feel from the wound. He watched the clearly visible bones of his rib cage rise up and down with each breath on his thin frame. How he craved a few hits from a rock right then and thought that it would help ease the pain. Maybe he could score some crack on his way to the bus station later, he thought.

G ran some water and wrung out the blood-soaked towel in the sink. Stripped to the waist so that he could tend to his wound, he watched as the dark red liquid swirled down the drain, wondering how he had gotten himself into this mess and how he was going to get out of it. G replaced the towel back on the wound and held it there for a while, taking a deep breath to calm down. While he stared at himself in the small but filthy shaving mirror above the sink, G began to contemplate his next move.

He probably should hold up at George's apartment until the early morning hours when the heat had calmed down a little from the robbery scene. The cops would be done investigating after a few hours, he thought. G had been a bystander in more than a few major crime scenes in Erie. He knew police practices and realized that they usually do not investigate a crime scene all night long. In G's estimation the cops get bored after a while and don't really care to solve any crimes anyway, so they simply leave and go home. He also knew that he had some time until they narrowed their search to him, since fingerprints and blood evidence takes a while to be processed and suspects identified. He had learned this while a prisoner at the state correctional institution. These facilities really are institutions of higher education for the criminal.

Just then in the mirror, he saw his eyebrows spike upward as a revelation struck in his mind... that little wino! He had been in the window during the robbery and seen what happened. He might be on his way to the cops right now. He knows who I am and might even know where I am staying, G thought. "Shit!" G said aloud.

He had to get out of there and get on the bus to Cleveland. He had to risk the possibility of being spotted on the street because if the cops found out where he was living, they could corner him in this house and that would be the end. It would be the true end, he thought, because G had already made up his mind that if he was cornered by the police he wasn't going back to jail. If they had him out gunned, he would take some of those dirty bastards to hell with him, he resolved. In a short time, these thoughts would turn out to be prophetic.

Faust was pulling out from the curb, craning his neck to make sure the way was clear to enter the travel lane, when the cell phone on his belt buzzed. He continued out onto the roadway as the cell phone buzzed again, all the while watching the Lumina that Tobias, Diaz, and Ruggerio were riding in. He steered the car with one hand and reached for the cell phone with the other, his mind focused on where these three soon-to-be ex-cops were heading now. The little wino must have just delivered a message to them and was running down the street toward the main drag, so he deduced that they must be headed to follow up on the information the wino had just given them. This is perfect timing, he thought. When the lieutenant arrives he will see all of them actively engaged in an investigation that has not been sanctioned by the department. All I have to do, Faust figured, is stay back from them so that his surveillance is not blown.

He flipped the phone open and answered the call. "Faust," he answered simply.

"Detective Faust, this is dispatch, you are needed at the state liquor store located on Main Street in North Zone. We have a report of a robbery homicide that just occurred. Units are on scene and they are interviewing witnesses. Can I relay an ETA?" the male dispatcher advised Faust of the robbery/homicide that had occurred only two blocks from where Faust was staking out the Lumina. Since Faust was in his personal car, the dispatcher couldn't reach him on his car radio, so he had used Faust's cell phone.

"Yeah, ok. Tell them I will be there in five minutes," he replied gruffly to the dispatcher.

"Thank you, Detective. Will do," the dispatch acknowledged professionally.

"Damn," he said aloud after closing his flip phone. He banged the steering wheel with the heel of his hand in frustration. At first he was taken slightly aback by the serious nature of the call, having just taken place a short distance away from his present location. Then just as quickly his personal motives overtook any sympathetic thought of the victim or victims of this violent homicide that had just taken place. His responsibility to be society's representative for justice was not nearly as important to him as was the opportunity to put the last nail in Ruggerio's professional coffin.

Regardless of his ulterior motives, he knew what he had to do. The homicide took priority. If he refused to go to the crime scene on the excuse that he wanted the lieutenant to witness departmental policy violations, he would be the one sitting before a review board answering questions about his conduct and not these three rogue cops. He just had to hope that the L.T. would take his observations into account and take disciplinary actions from his statement.

Two blocks north and west of the liquor store crime scene, Lonnie turned the corner onto the street that contained the house where G was staying. He was walking hurriedly with his hands deep in his pockets, keeping his head tucked down like a turtle into the frayed material of his coat collar. He was trying to keep warm and to conceal his face, just in case G might run into him before he reached Ruggerio and Tobias. Up ahead, he could see Tobias's Lumina parked along the curb among several other cars on this street. He felt a sense of relief, knowing that he was close to meeting with his protectors.

Tobias saw him coming up Monitor Ave. Even though it was dark he recognized him, from his slight frame and the way that Lonnie moved.

"Quick, lock your doors," Tobias said to Diaz.

Diaz did as instructed then asked, "What's up?"

"Lonnie is headed this way and I don't want him to climb back into my car. The stink from the last time he was in here is just starting to go away," Tobias explained.

Lonnie walked up to the passenger side where Diaz put his window down to talk with him.

Lonnie crouched down next to the window and Tobias asked him in a somewhat agitated tone, "What are you doing? You know that we are watching for G. He might see you."

"I know but I got to tell you somethin' impotent. G, he just robbed the liquor store and I heard shootin' inside," said Lonnie in between labored breaths, partly from his long walk and partly from fear.

"Did you see where he went?" Tobias asked.

"No way. Are you crazy? I got the hell out of there. I think he saw me witnessin' the crimes and he's gonna come after me. I just knows it. You got to protect me, Tobias," Lonnie implored.

Tobias thought for a moment about what to do with Lonnie. He desperately thought about how to avoid having Lonnie climb back into his personal car and re-introduce his bodily odor to the upholstery. At the same time, he wanted to protect Lonnie. Quickly and impressively, even to himself, he came up with a foolproof scenario that would protect Lonnie and his olfactory nerves at the same time.

Tobias knew that Lonnie was not really in much danger. At this point, G would be more interested in just lying low until the heat was off. The last thing G would be doing was roaming around out where he could easily be spotted by the cops, looking for Lonnie.

"OK, Lonnie. Here is what you do. You can't come with us because if we see G we are going to have to go after him and you would be in the way, right?" he asked Lonnie rhetorically.

"Yeah, I guess so," Lonnie agreed reluctantly.

"So what you can do is walk down to the corner so that you are out of sight from this house where G is living. Wait there for a patrol car and he can pick you up and take you to the station. Since you are a material witness to a robbery they can put you in a cell for your protection until we grab G. What do you think?"

Tobias reasoned that Lonnie would most likely refuse to go along with this plan, since being locked up in a holding cell for the night would mean that he would not have access to any liquor. He knew all too well that an alcoholic would rather risk death for the chance to have a drink than be subjected to an arrangement that removed all probability of scoring a bottle. He knew that Lonnie needed his whiskey, especially now.

Lonnie stammered at first from this unexpected proposal. He thought that Tobias would simply tell him to climb back into his warm car and he could ride out the night with them. He even held out a hope that Tobias might let him run into a bar along the way and let him use the money he had been given for a Black Velvet.

"Ah, well, no. That's OK. I think I'll jus' find a quiet place and hol' up for the night. Thanks anyway." Lonnie straightened up and was off in search of that elusive bottle he had been working so hard to acquire.

"Give Guy a call and let him know what Lonnie saw at the liquor store. I will call Quint and let him know that G just committed an armed robbery so he can pass the info on to the dicks," Tobias instructed, as Diaz quickly took out his cell and hit the "push-to-talk" function to call Ruggerio.

Since they had never gotten the chance to meet at the supermarket lot, Tobias called Quint and told him about Lonnie and his observations and clued him in on the Monitor Ave address as the probable location of the robbery suspect. Then Quint gave Tobias a little information of his own.

"I am actually at that location now, they called me here to use Max for a track from the store. Did your witness tell you that this is a robbery/homicide scene?" Quint asked.

"No he didn't. Who got whacked?" asked Tobias.

"One of the clerks. The other one survived and is giving a pretty good description of the actor. I think with your information the dicks can make a line-up and let the clerk pick out your man and crack this case tonight," Quint summarized.

"That sounds good. We are watching the house now. If the dicks can assemble a surveillance team and come over here then they can take over. Can you advise the primary that I got a tip from a snitch on this caper?"

"Only one problem, the primary is you know who, so I will leave out the part about you guys doing surveillance at the perp's house. If I were you, I would boogie on out of there before you get in more trouble," Quint warned Tobias.

"You're probably right, but we went this far and I am not giving this last hope any chance of getting away. I'll risk getting nabbed on this stake out in exchange for scooping up this G character for Ruggerio."

As Tobias was saying this, Diaz, who had already relayed the message about Lonnie to Ruggerio, was nodding his head in agreement and thinking that maybe "risk/reward" might be a good descriptor of how he and Tobias were summing up the situation.

"OK, I'll let them know about your informant's information. Be ready for a call from Mad Dog. He will probably want to grill you on this," he said.

"You know, Quint. Sometimes I have trouble with the signal on my cell... Oh, there it goes now. I'm losing you. Can you hear me? Hello, Quint. Hello!" Tobias said mockingly.

"OK wiseass, point taken. See ya," and Quint disconnected with a chuckle.

Just before Tobias and Diaz made their respective calls, G was preparing to embark on his run for freedom. After using some strips of bed sheets to bandage his wounds, he put his pea coat back on and made ready for his journey. First, he thought, look out the windows to see if there was any police already at the house. He drew back the old dingy curtains just enough to get a view out of the rear window. From this second floor apartment, the alley looked clear. G walked through the darkened apartment to a front facing window and preformed the same motion to peer out to the front street below, Monitor Ave.

"Shit!" he said aloud to himself. G could clearly see that the wino who had seen him during the robbery was standing next to a parked car across the street, talking to the occupants. He could also see that the driver was a white male. Probably cops and they were onto his trail already.

G began to panic. He could feel his breathing become increasingly labored and his wounded ribs throbbed with waves of excruciating pain. He cursed his bad luck because nothing seemed to be going right. In a fit of anger, G grabbed a half-full bottle of warm beer that was sitting on a chest of drawers and threw it against the wall, smashing it into pieces and spattering beer in a sunburst pattern on the plaster board.

Just then, G heard something in one of the bedrooms and quickly realized that George was home and must have been sleeping. The noise aroused him and he walked out of his room in his baggy boxers. George stood in the bedroom doorway that led to the room that G was in. George was shirtless, with his dark-skinned pot belly straining the elastic of his boxers, yawning and scratching his head at the same time.

"What's all the noise G?" he asked in mid-yawn.

G began to contemplate a plan and knew that he could use George to make good his escape. First, he had to convince George to help him distract the cops out front.

"George, I need you to help me out. I will make it worth your while," he said.

"What do ya need, G?"

"Come here and look out the window. Do you see that car parked across the street with the guys inside and the wino talking to them?"

"Yeah, what about 'em?" George asked, yawning again while rubbing his belly.

"It's the cops and they're after me. I need your help so I can get away from them," G said with trepidation.

"I don't know, G. I might get in trouble."

"No, you won't get in trouble. Just listen."

G took out some of the money that he'd stolen from the liquor store and held it up for George to see.

"See, if you help I will give you some of this and you can go get yourself a rock or two for tonight." G tempted George with the most enticing voice he could muster, despite the pain he still felt from his wound.

"G, where did you get that money? Did you rob somebody?" George inquired.

"That's right. That is why they are out there waiting for me to come out. Listen yo. You got to help me out here, dawg," he said, pleading.

"No G. I will get in trouble and lose my apartment. The counselor at the center said that if I gets in trouble I will lose my a-s-s-s-s-a-tance." (He had trouble saying the word.) "And I can't lives here anymore," George finished, flustered.

"Listen George. I can't go back to prison again. You hear me?" G said, grabbing George by the shoulders for emphasis.

"You know what it is like there? Do you?" he said, shaking George and feeling a stab of pain from his rib cage. George replied by simply shaking his head no.

"Well I will tell you." He let George go this time, turned away from him and gazed downward. "I spent some time in a lot of the state pens: Rockview, Huntingdon, Graterford. All hell holes, especially Grateford." He turned back and faced George. He saw that he had his attention now. George was silent and fixed on what G was saying.

"When you go to sleep at night you have to wait until you hear your celly snoring, before you can go to sleep, no matter how tired you are. If you don't and fall asleep before he does, he can rob you of your shit or if you got a fag celly he might try and feel you up while you're out. But that's not the most scary thing, dawg. What is worse is the yard. While you are out in the yard your head has to be on a swivel. Some nigga could creep up on you from any direction and stick a shank in your ass. And they will do it for any lame ass reason. One time I got cut up, because I didn't want to suck this fag's dick, so when he got his chance he stuck me while I wasn't payin' attention. Man, that's when I joined the crips, not because I wanted to but because I had to, for protection. They said that if I was a crip no one would come after me. Well, they was almost right. What they didn't tell me was that to be in the gang, I had to shank someone first. You know who I had to shank to get into the gang?"

"No," George answered.

"I had to cut up a member of a white supremacist group that the crips had a beef with. After that, I couldn't go out of my cell unless I had at least seven other crips around me for protection. Now since I been out I was supposed to meet up with other gangsters on the outside, it is part of the code. But since I didn't do that, if I go back inside they will carve me up like a Christmas ham for not living the thug life. So you see yo, you got to help me out here or I'm dead."

George put his head down and thought for a moment, then said, "What do I have to do?"

"That's my dawg," G said with a smile. Then as a gesture of thanks, he grabbed George's right hand with his own, thumbs interlocked with the fingers wrapped around the back of his hand, then pulled George in for a street hug, quickly retreating backward as is the custom.

CHAPTER 10

It was a wet snow, perfect for tracking, Quint reasoned. Not only were footprints visible, but in the areas where the footprints did not appear or were covered up by additional snowfall, Max had a good chance of maintaining the track. The moist air aided in holding the scent down at ground level, which made tracking by a dog much more efficient than in dry conditions. Quint was even more pleased when the first responding officers told him that they hadn't ventured out beyond the crime scene looking for the suspect. The first cops on scene had figured that the perp probably got into a get-away car, but this was before they interviewed the surviving clerk. After receiving the clerk's information, they called for the K-9.

Quint had first advised Faust and other detectives who were beginning to gather at the crime scene, of the information that Tobias had provided. He was puzzled by the lack of surprise that appeared on Faust's face when he gave him the information, like Faust expected it or something. But he quickly dismissed this feeling as he got Max out of the SUV and took him to the alley side of the store and began to prepare his partner to start the track.

After soliciting the assistance of two other officers, one with his sidearm, the other armed with a shotgun loaded with double 00 buck shot, to act as cover, Quint hooked up Max on his twenty-foot lead and they set off to track the killer. Since the surviving clerk had told the officers that the perp left the store via the back door, they knew where to begin the track. Even though the conditions were ripe for tracking, Quint was still surprised how Max took off on the proposed escape route. Max was so confident in the direction that the killer took that he was pulling Quint along by the end of the leather lead. Quint had to jog to keep pace.

The line that Max led the officers on, took them across the alley from the rear of the store and through a narrow passage between two houses, emerging onto the sidewalk in front of some homes. From there, Max went west, following the sidewalk, which was mostly bare of snow. Nose working hard, he took Quint across the street to the opposite sidewalk where there were more residential homes. Max pulled Quint along over the uneven slabs of pavement, many pushed upward by the roots of the massive oak trees that lined the street.

Max took a sharp right turn off the sidewalk in a northerly direction and up an embankment that led to an old wooden privacy fence, some of the slats of which were broken off at the top from rot. Max stopped at the fence and began to dig with his right paw at the snow at the base of the fence. Determined, he started to push at the joint between two wooden slats of fence with his nose. When that didn't work, he began to paw at the same point. Quint struggled up the snow-covered embankment and watched as Max tried to get through the fence. He knew that Max had the scent on the opposite side of the fence.

Quint grabbed at one of the wooden slats that Max was trying to work free. He noticed that the slat was loose, so when he grabbed the plank with both hands, it easily pulled away from the bottom cross member and he swung it to the side. Max immediately tried to get himself through the opening that Quint had just made, but he was too wide and was stopped.

"Hold on Max," Quint said, and then gave a Dutch command for him to heel.

Quint grabbed at the next plank in the row; it was also loose. After swinging this plank to the side, he released Max from his stay position and let him slide through the opening. Quint followed through and held the planks for the backup officers, so they could slip through the void. There were also fresh shoe prints in the snow, ostensibly confirming Max's scent trail of the killer.

On the inside they saw an open area next to a two-story house. From the appearance of the overgrown shrubbery, Quint thought the home was vacant. He didn't have much time to ponder this however, because Max was on the move, still heading north through the open area. The officers followed their K-9 guide and reached the end of the property, which was demarcated by another dilapidated fence, this time of the chain link variety. Max went along the fence, sniffing vigorously until he reached a section that had the links cut vertically about three feet upward along one of the support posts. The chain link was peeled back so that a hole was created in the fence line large enough for a person to fit through. The shoe prints led right to this opening. Max wanted to proceed through the opening into the alley beyond, but Quint stopped him.

They had to go around because the officers had a little too much girth to fit through such a small hole or jump over the top.

"Too much steak and potatoes for me to fit through that hole," said the officer with the shotgun in a hushed voice.

"Have to find another way around," Quint replied in a whisper.

The cops had to go back out the wooden fence and around to the alley. Max was on the trail again and took them east in the alley about one hundred feet. All the while, the backup officers, who were following about ten feet behind Quint in a wedge formation, scanned the edges of the alley for anything suspicious, guns at the ready position. The shotgun officer held his long gun with the stock tucked to his right shoulder and the barrel pointed downward. The second back-up officer was keeping pace with the shotgun cop, holding his Glock .40 caliber semi-automatic pistol with both hands, arms straight in a V configuration, with his barrel similarly pointed. Each officer was tasked with scanning his respective side of the alley for any threats and to taking action if one presented itself. The hiding places were too numerous to adequately check with the pace they were keeping.

Parked cars, garbage cans, telephone poles, heaps of trash bags, even a discarded couch and refrigerator were placed in the alley. All were perfect areas from which to launch an ambush on the officers. One thing that the officers had on their side was the faith that they had in Max. They were banking on him to give them a warning prior to any planned assault. They had worked with Max for a few years now and had seen him in action. They trusted him and Quint.

Near the end of the one-hundred-foot span, Max began to veer to the north, again angling toward the edge of the alley. Quint could see that Max was headed for a break in the line of buildings abutting the alley. It was another open field but this time, thankfully, it did not have a fence around the perimeter. Quint halted Max with a Dutch command and brought him backward into the alleyway. He wanted to confer with his backup officers before entering this open field, which could potentially be dangerous since there was no cover for the officers to hide behind in the event that gunfire erupted. In addition, Quint knew from speaking with Tobias that this was about the area where he and Ruggerio had been sitting and watching the house where G was supposedly hiding.

Quint gathered up Max and ordered him to stay and to be quiet; he started to whine a bit knowing that his prey was not far away. The group of three officers and Max huddled near what appeared to be a garage apartment combination. Above the garage was the apartment window with a light on inside, indicating that someone might be home. Since the garage apartment was on the north side of the alley, the same side as G's house, Quint wanted to be careful.

Ruggerio saw the group of officers and the dog coming at him but he wasn't sure when to try and signal that he was inside the garage. He figured the best way to alert them was to call out to Quint, reasoning that by using Quint's name it would quickly put the officers at ease. The real perp wouldn't know the names of the cops chasing him. Even though this tactic was a sound one, Ruggerio knew that the possibility of friendly fire was still present. So he took a deep breath and in a semi-soft voice said, "Quint, it's Guy."

Quint stopped dead in his tracks. Max turned toward Ruggerio and started to growl, but it wasn't his typical aggressive growl. It was more of a startled response to the voice that called Quint's name out from the darkness. Quint quickly recognized the voice and realized that Max recognized the voice too.

The shotgun officer wheeled toward Ruggerio's position and nearly leveled his weapon at him, but stopped abruptly when he realized that this person knew Quint's name.

"Guy?" Quint said.

"Yeah, I'm in here. Come around the back."

The officers crept around the back of the broken-down garage and met Ruggerio at the opening where he had originally entered the dilapidated shell of the building.

He was about to brief the officers on what was happening and work on forming a game plan when suddenly Tobias's voice came over the cell phone on the two-way frequency, shouting to Ruggerio, "He just ran out the front door east on Monitor!"

This direction was opposite from where Ruggerio and the searching officers were standing at that time. Ruggerio quickly assessed the situation and began barking orders to the officers before him as if he were in charge of this operation. He felt comfortable doing this with his career and possibly his life still on the line. He personally knew these officers and realized that they would back him up.

"Quint, stay here in case he doubles back. You two follow me," Ruggerio ordered and began to run eastward through the alley with the two search officers in tandem. With years of experience, police officers learn very quickly that a running suspect can go in any number of directions, thus bracketing a suspect as quickly as possible is standard procedure. The reason he advised Quint and Max to stay where they were was also standard procedure. The dog is only used to run down a suspect when all other officers are positioned to the rear of the animal so that the dog will not confuse running officers as the prey. In this case, with Tobias and Diaz sure to be going after the suspect, Ruggerio did not want Max confusing them for the perp and taking one of them down by mistake.

Ruggerio took off in the alley with his two new back-up officers trailing behind him, all the while holding his gun in his right hand and the cell phone in his left up next to his ear so he could monitor the direction of the suspect. He wanted to stay in the alley in case the perp cut between the buildings and headed in this direction. It was called "paralleling." He kept watch in the openings between the structures on his left hand side but didn't see any movement. As he neared the end of the block, he wondered why he hadn't heard from Tobias or Diaz again on the direction of travel, so he decided to call in and get an update.

Diaz had seen him first while Tobias was distracted putting in a fresh pinch of Copenhagen. Diaz was caught by surprise when he saw the door open and movement that made him bolt upright in the car seat, then exclaim to Tobias, "We got something. The door just opened."

They were a distance away and on the opposite side of the street from the house, with the Lumina facing back toward the target. Tobias had positioned the car so the two officers could watch the eastern side and the north sides of the house for any movement. When staking out a fugitive that may be inside a building, each point of escape has to be monitored. Every window, door, vent opening, chimney, from the inside to the outside has to be watched. Cops use a technique that limits the number of officers but still covers all sides of the location. The officers are simply deployed on opposite corners of a square or rectangular structure. If the officer positions himself correctly he or she can watch two sides at the same time while the officer positioned on the opposite corner can observe the other two sides. Tobias and Diaz were covering the front and east sides, while Ruggerio was watching the south and west sides of this house. What they didn't consider was that Mr. Holland, a.k.a. G, might have a few tricks up his sleeve, designed specifically to defeat this tactic.

As quickly as the front door opened, out stepped a male, which was all that Diaz could determine, because in the darkness a detailed description was impossible. The front area of the house was dark and there weren't any lights on, inside or out, to help identify the runner. As the figure quickly moved from the threshold of the front door to the sidewalk, then proceeded eastbound into some moonlight, Diaz could clearly see the telltale outline of a navy pea coat.

"That's him!" Diaz said, opening the door to jump out and run down the fugitive.

Tobias made the call to Ruggerio to alert him of the running fugitive then exited the vehicle to back up Diaz. Tobias figured that he didn't have time to start the car, turn it around and go after the perp, so he would have to try and keep up with Diaz as best he could.

The suspect started running as soon as his feet hit the pavement of the sidewalk. He didn't take any evasive moves, like duck between a couple houses or cut across the street. He just ran straight east on the sidewalk.

Diaz yelled, "Stop! Police!" Not because he actually thought the guy would stop, but because it was a legal requirement. Cops do this so the perp can't later claim in court that he didn't know it was the police chasing him. A defendant on trial will try to convince jurors that he thought the person chasing him was really a robber and not the police. Unbelievably, on occasion, this tactic works to the benefit of the defense.

While Diaz was running toward the suspect, he noticed that this guy wasn't running very fast and it looked like he would catch up to him very quickly, which is exactly what happened. Before the perp reached the end of the block, Diaz was on him and simply grabbed the guy by the back of his coat with both hands and pushed him forward onto the hood of a parked car. Tobias quickly followed up and helped to hold the suspect down, who wasn't resisting at all, and saying, "OK, I give up. I give up. Don't beat me. Please, don't beat me."

Diaz turned the perp over on his back while still on the hood of the car and looked at his face. He quickly realized this was not the same face that he had seen in the mug shot of G.

"This isn't him," was all he said to Tobias.

Realizing that they had just been duped, Tobias turned to head back toward the target house and quickly grabbed his cell to call Ruggerio.

Quint stayed in place across the open field from the target house and near the rear portion of the neighboring residence. He could hear Diaz shouting, "Stop! Police!" from where he was standing and it frustrated him that he could not participate in the chase, especially since he had Max, the fastest cop in the area, with him. Quint knelt down next to Max and rubbed him between his pointed ears. He did this to calm him down because Max, being a veteran police dog, was well aware that the game was afoot and he wanted to be a part of it.

Quint gave a few Dutch commands to help calm him down, "*Regel...* Max, *regel.*"

He then caught something out of the corner of his eye. He saw it before Max did, someone running west on the sidewalk in front of the target house. As the figure was halfway between the target house and the residence where Quint and Max were positioned, Max caught the runner in his sights too and took off from beside Quint.

Quint tried to maintain control of his K-9 as the twenty-foot lead rapidly stretched out to its maximum length as Max darted toward the new runner. At the same time, Max let out a loud and purposeful bark, followed by an intimidating growl. The runner looked in their direction and appeared to pick up his speed before disappearing behind the next structure and out of Quint's sight.

Quint gave Max a command to stop but it wasn't working, Max wanted this guy bad and wasn't going to be denied. His claws were scraping at the snow and the frozen ground beneath, while he strained against the collar around his neck and the leather lead Quint was holding.

Quint was slipping and sliding on the snow-covered ground, trying to keep up with Max and slow him down at the same time. His efforts were not succeeding and he knew, by the way he was losing his footing that he was going down soon. Just as this thought entered his mind, both of Quint's feet slipped out from under him and down he went, losing the grip on the lead that held Max from chasing the runner.

G watched from inside the front door after George, wearing G's navy pea coat, complete with bullet holes, took off running east on the sidewalk in front of the house. This was to make it appear to the cops as if it were G running down the street. He smiled with pride as he saw the cops bail out of their unmarked car and chase after George. He was a little disappointed though, when he saw the cops had caught up to him so quickly. G thought that the promise of an extra fifty dollars, which he had told George would be waiting for him inside the front door, would provide the proper incentive for George to run hard enough to make it to the next block. Since he got nabbed before reaching the first intersection he would not earn the money. G wasn't going to leave the fifty for him anyway.

The distraction was successful, apart from George's poor performance. G took a deep breath and bolted out the front door, heading west, the opposite direction from where George was stopped by the undercover cops. The first few yards were clear but soon he detected movement out of the corner of his left eye. Then he heard a familiar and terrifying deep and loud barking of a dog, followed by a distinctive growl making it quite clear that a large animal was coming at him from a darkened corner of the house on the opposite end of the open field next to George's house. He surmised quickly that it was probably a police dog. He had been chased by them before in Erie and did not want to feel those powerful jaws and sharp teeth ripping into him again.

G could see that it was a police dog, when he observed the cop trailing behind and holding on, or trying to hold on, to a long leash. G instinctively kicked his speed into high gear and zoomed past the front of the house next to where the dog and his handler were running, and crossed the street in an attempt to put more distance between him and the beast that was after him. He knew that he wasn't going to out-run the dog, so he weighed his options quickly. He couldn't return to George's house, nor did he see any other buildings that he could duck into quickly. The only other option was to put a bullet into the dog and kill him—and probably his cop handler also.

When Quint went down, he hit the ground hard. His backside hit so hard that his breath was taken out of him, briefly leaving him unable to shout the halt command to Max. Quint knew that the suspect was armed and he didn't want Max running at the perp for fear that he could be shot. Unable to stop his partner from running after the suspect, all he could do was look up to see Max churning up the snow-covered ground with his powerful strides, then turning the corner around the front house, chasing after his prey and still producing a low growl.

G crossed the street and took cover behind a parked car, having already taken out the Colt .380. As he wheeled around to face his four-legged pursuer, he took up a two-handed combat grip on the pistol and used the car hood to stabilize his aim. At that point he didn't see the dog yet, but could hear his claws clicking on the concrete sidewalk as he ran. He could also hear the low growl coming from the animal as it sensed that his prey was not far off.

Max followed the scent trail that G had left behind so he ran in front of the same house where he and Quint had been standing in back, and started to cross over the street toward the cars parked on the opposite side. The scent was strong, so he knew that the animal that he was chasing was close. As the strength of the scent increased, Max's growling amplified at the same rate. Now that the target was acquired, Max was preparing to pounce, with his teeth bared, saliva dripping from his mouth, growling in anticipation of sinking his teeth into his prey, and with the leather lead still dragging behind him.

Then suddenly, POP went the Colt in G's hands as he fired the first shot. The bullet missed Max, making an orange spark on the darkened pavement to the dog's left side. The round skipped off the pavement then traveled across the street and impacted the front street-side fender of another parked vehicle, creating a loud metallic sound, "DANK!"

G knew that he only had one chance at hitting the dog since he was moving so fast. When he saw that his shot had missed, he knew that the game was up. G tried to prepare himself for the mauling that he knew was about to happen. It was going to be painful since this dog was large and looked very powerful, he cursed himself for missing that shot.

Then, almost simultaneously as his round crashed into the fender of the car across the street, he witnessed a minor miracle. G saw the German shepherd that was chasing after him abruptly lurch backward. He watched closer and saw that the dog's leash had caught on something as it trailed behind him. The severe change in momentum jerked his head rearward, while inertia sent the rest of the animal's body forward. The violent backward pull forced the dog's body into the air for a moment then it came crashing down on the pavement of the street. He quickly regained his footing and G watched as the shepherd valiantly tried to go forward toward the direction of his prey, only to have the snagged leash deny his progress. The animal, quickly realizing that this tactic wasn't working, began to throw his head back and forth, trying in vain to work himself free, still growling and snorting with the same ferocity.

G couldn't believe his luck. Now that the animal was caught he had a second chance to take the dog out. But he wouldn't have very long because this beast was determined and wasn't going to stay snared long. He could see how the shepherd worked furiously to free himself and would eventually be successful in freeing up the leash.

The dog realized that he wasn't having any success; as he continued to pull forward, the end of the leash only seemed to wedge more firmly into whatever it was caught on. In the natural way that a dog tries to free his head from its collar the shepherd turned away from G and began to pull backward in an effort to pull his head through the collar opening, get free of the leash, and be able to seize his prey.

The dog's position gave G a perfect shot at the animal's hindquarters. He took careful aim and squeezed off a round that hit

Max on his right rear flank. Max let out a loud cry, simultaneously jumping forward away from the direction of the impact. He quickly limped back over to the side of the road and lay down between two parked cars, whimpering in pain.

G turned away after seeing that this threat was eliminated, and then ran northward away from the cops. With the shepherd beast down he felt more confident in his chances. Even though he was hurting from the wound in his side, he knew that he could still run fast and could probably out run any cops that would be chasing him. He had run from cops most of his life, even since his juvenile days.

Running from cops was seen as a sport where G grew up. He always knew that he had an advantage over the police since they were always weighed down by their equipment. The only times that G had been caught by the police were when he slipped and fell or when a cop got lucky and cut him off by anticipating his escape route. He didn't want that to happen tonight because it wasn't a sport this time, he was running to save his life.

After the realization that they had stopped the wrong man, Tobias stopped to notify Ruggerio and let him know that G might still be in the house.

"Guy we stopped a perp who ran out of the house, but it is not G. Are you still watching the rear side?" Tobias asked Ruggerio over the two-way.

"I am on my way back now," Ruggerio answered as he and his two backup officers began to run back toward the target house, hoping that G hadn't already run out the back door. They all knew, without saying it, that this had been a diversion and G would probably exit the rear of the house—if he had not already done so. The officers prepared themselves for a possible close quarters encounter. They spread out in a wedge type formation again, with Ruggerio leading the way. All weapons pointed forward in the direction from which they expected to see G emerge.

As Ruggerio and his backup were approaching the area where they had left Quint and Max in the alley, Tobias was on the front street and trying to decide what to do next. Meanwhile, Diaz was still holding George on the hood of a parked car, asking him repeatedly where G was and receiving the following contradictory answers: "I don't know," and "he told me it was just a joke," and "I never heard of G."

Suddenly they all halted what they were doing when they heard Max's barking. His bark echoed up and down the street and told the cops that he was after someone and that person was probably G. These are the moments in police work when events take place so quickly that the mind does not have time to fully comprehend and reason out all the potential consequences. These are also the times when veterans demonstrate, with quick decision-making, the benefits of experience.

Tobias summed up the situation rapidly. He had the benefit of seeing a second figure running westbound away from him on the sidewalk in front of the target house. He quickly realized that George, even though the wrong suspect, would still need to be debriefed for any information he might have on G's whereabouts and/or any knowledge or possible involvement in the liquor store robbery/murder. Tobias coupled this with the fact that Diaz was a hell of a lot faster than he was and could be of more help chasing the guy that was now running west on this street and who was most likely the prep they were after.

"Diaz!" Tobias bellowed, "I'll take him," referring to George. "You go help Guy," pointing in the direction of the running suspect and barking police dog.

Diaz had turned his head away from George when he heard the barking also, and had seen the second runner as well. He didn't need to reply to Tobias so he simply released George and jetted at full speed down the middle of the street toward the sound of the action. All the officers involved hoped that by the time they reached the scene where the action was now taking place, Max would have a mouth full of the perp's leg or arm and have him down on the ground screaming in pain.

Before Diaz or Ruggerio could reach the scene though, Quint who had just regained his feet and his breath from the fall, heard the shots that were fired at Max, including the one that found its mark on Max's hindquarters. When Quint heard Max's cry of pain, his heart shattered, similar to that of a parent who experiences his own child suffering from an injury or disease. Also like a parent, Quint's first reaction was to shout out Max's name.

"Maxy!" he called out, using the endearing name that he usually reserved for the privacy of home.

Quint turned the corner around the front of the house that he and Max had been stationed behind and instinctively had his weapon already drawn. Quint first saw Max limping toward the sidewalk nearest him and away from the shooter, trying to create some distance from the threat. Max looked up at Quint, who whimpered then collapsed on the sidewalk pavement, unable to keep his feet from the loss of blood.

When Quint saw this, he instantly became enraged at the would-be killer of his beloved partner. He could see G running away from him, about to turn the corner. He knew that it was a long shot but emotion overwhelmed him and he needed to seek out revenge.

Quint raised his Glock .40 semiautomatic pistol and rapidly squeezed off six rounds in the direction of the running perp. The first round was low and shattered a rear window of a nearby parked car. The second round was a little higher but was still low of the target and kicked up a tuft of snow before burying itself into the earth beneath, which was the front yard of a corner house.

G had wanted to cut the distance it would take him to make his turn from Monitor Ave to the intersecting street by cutting through this front yard. The yard was raised slightly from street level and on a higher plane than the parked car that was struck by the first round. This shot did however demonstrate that Quint's aim was improving, since it struck only a short distance behind the running feet of the suspect. But the third round was the closest to finding its mark. Quint had no way of knowing this but this bullet whizzed right by G's left ear and traveled through the air and over an interstate highway in the distance. The round traveled to the opposite side of a shallow valley, where it lodged into the side of a wooden fence bordering private property.

G on the other hand was well aware of how close this round was to his head. He heard the buzzing sound that the projectile made as it sliced through the cold night air and zipped by his ear. In reaction, G ducked his head down and away from the path of the bullet, which had already gone by and landed in the wood of the fence.

The fourth shot went even higher; it flew a few feet over and to the right of the running perp and struck square onto the aluminum standard of a street light. The impact created an ear deafening, "PINNNNGGG!" that seemed to reverberate a full three seconds after it struck. By the time the fifth and sixth rounds were fired, the recoil from Quint's Glock caused his aim to be so high that the rounds went off into the night air and landed in a wooded area beyond. These two rounds were just in frustration since G had already made the corner and was out of sight by then.

In a display of frustration, while firing at the fleeing felon, Quint was proclaiming his feelings by shouting several obscenities toward the actor, "I'll kill you, you mother-fucker!" and "You shot my dog, you son-of-a-bitch!" It was not professional and it didn't help one bit in apprehending the culprit, but it was a display of human emotion felt by an officer who had a loyal and trusted friend cut down in front of him by a criminal.

While running down the middle of the residential street packed with parked cars lined up on either side of him, Diaz watched Quint wildly shooting at the fleeing felon. He saw orange fire spit out of the front of Quint's barrel with each discharged round. He heard the glass shatter in the rear car window and the ping when the bullet hit the street light standard. He also saw the perp duck his head down and shrug his shoulders after one of the rounds nearly hit his head.

There were more sounds that Diaz took in as he approached the scene, Max whining and whimpering, Quint shouting his emotion-fueled remarks toward the running perp, all occurring in a matter of seconds.

It was surreal, he thought as he ran along chasing after this killer. The whole situation, which just a few minutes ago was virtually serene and calm, as he and Tobias were sitting nice and warm in a car, had quickly deteriorated into utter chaos. The feeling began to grow and fear started to rise inside him. As Diaz ran along, continuing toward the scene, he realized that he needed to suppress this fear to perform effectively. With that thought, the fear was gone just as quickly as it had been realized and unknowingly he was becoming a veteran in his own right.

As Diaz passed where Max had been shot and was now lying on the ground, he turned and saw Quint lower himself to his knees next to the body of his comrade. Diaz could hear Quint begin to whimper in despair before he turned his attention back toward the task at hand and kept running in the direction of the perp.

Diaz was still about thirty yards behind G when he saw the suspect disappear behind the corner house that had its front yard marred by one of Quint's bullets. He followed the same path that G took and effortlessly bounded over the small snow-covered hill in the corner yard of this residence. As he turned the corner, gun in hand, he saw that G was still running northbound on this intersecting street. He was increasing his lead now since it took Diaz time to make the corner. G was ahead by about forty yards now. Diaz, however, being the faster of the two and benefiting from the advantage of not having a bullet wound in his side was quickly closing the gap with the felon.

G knew he was being chased since he took a peek behind him. Sure enough he caught a look at Diaz flying around the corner onto the same street. G could see that this cop was fast and would surely catch up to him unless he did something to stop him. When he turned his attention back in the direction he was running, he could hear the foot falls of his pursuer getting louder and closer. G was getting more concerned and searched his mind on his next course of action; he didn't want to turn and shoot just yet, because if he missed then he would be a dead duck. He needed some time, so he decided to take evasive action to create some distance until he could find the right time to ambush the cop.

Diaz was sensing that he would catch up to the felon in a short time if he continued running straight ahead. He was also aware from having already participated in several foot pursuits, that fleeing suspects rarely continue on a straight path while being chased. But then a second thought popped into his mind; he might be justified in shooting this suspect in the back. Diaz had been trained at length on the Fleeing Felon Rule in the police academy. He felt fairly confident that the criteria of this situation fit this rule and therefore he would be justified in shooting this actor in the back as he ran.

The rule states that if the felon has just committed a violent felony, and is trying to escape, and requires that his capture be consummated immediately to protect society before he harms another person, and that all other means of capture would not be effective, and that the officer provide a verbal warning, i.e., "Stop! Police!" then the officer is permitted to use deadly force to stop the felon. Diaz amazed himself that he remembered all this from his academy days. He was again demonstrating that he was becoming a professional police officer.

The first step was to get the verbal warning out of the way; this part was especially important in this case since Diaz was not in uniform at this time. He needed to properly identify himself to the actor. However ridiculous it may sound, he still had to make the verbal warning. "Stop! Police!" He even made the statement in Spanish in case the actor made the claim that he didn't understand English. "*Policia! Alto!*"

He continued to chase the killer since the verbal warning failed to stop him. While still considering the option of shooting the suspect in the back, other visions began to flash in front of his mind's eye, the preverbal second guessing syndrome. Diaz saw how the courts, the police, the media, and the public had crucified Ruggerio, after his shooting. He didn't want to go through the same thing if there was a chance that shooting this guy would not be justified. He decided that he would not use lethal force just yet, so he continued to run, rapidly closing the gap.

At the same time that Diaz had made up his mind that he wasn't going to use lethal force to stop the fleeing felon, the fleeing felon decided that he would use lethal force to stop the chasing policeman. Not being constrained by court rulings or the ire of a biased public, G reversed his decision to take evasive action and simply decided to shoot the cop now. He could hear the footsteps almost on top of him now and knew that if he made any change in direction it would slow him to the point where the cop would be able to reach out and grab him.

G quickly wheeled around and snapped off a round from his .380 Colt in the direction of Diaz, who was about ten feet away at this point. The shot flew over Diaz's head, luckily, but caused him to dive quickly to his right side. He went down, onto the ground, off the sidewalk and rolled into the street since on his left were brick walls from bordering businesses, which didn't provide any cover. The street, which was bare of any parked vehicles, at least had a six-inch concrete curb that would give him something to get behind. After he rolled over, he slid his body in tight to the gutter and against the curb, gun hand out, pointing toward the direction of the last spot where he had seen the suspect. When he looked up again to pinpoint the felon, he saw his backside as he was running into another alley, back toward the direction that he had come from, east bound and two blocks north of Monitor Ave.

Diaz stood up and continued the chase, slightly winded now and not to mention a little nervous from nearly having his head blown off. He ran to the mouth of the alley but entered cautiously. One thing was for sure. All bets were off. There was no doubt in his mind now that lethal force was certain to be justified. Just as quickly as he thought of this he realized that he was not on regular duty at this time; he was still on suspension and legally not supposed to be engaged in police business. As these thoughts bounced around in his head like a pinball, he looked down the alley and saw the perp running straight again. Diaz took off in this direction while still contemplating what the ramifications would be when all this was over.

Then another legal phrase, citizen's arrest, entered his mind. Even though he was not working as a policeman at this time, he still had the same authority as a common citizen. Under that authority a citizen has the power, just like a policeman, to make an arrest for a violent felony. Diaz would therefore have a strong position to defend his actions even if he used lethal force. With his mind at ease, he decided it was time to stop this suspect before he had another opportunity to shoot at him.

G was about twenty-five yards away at that point and about to make another turn—this time between two garages that were side by side in the alley. He wanted to get out of the open and into some darkness where he could hide and wait for a chance to shoot the fleet footed cop chasing him. The opening that G was aiming for was still twenty feet away on his right side. Just before this passage was a telephone pole next to the corner of the nearest garage.

Diaz was well aware that eventually the felon would attempt to duck out of the alleyway to a spot conducive for an ambush, so he wanted to stop him before G made it to this dangerous position. While still running, his gun hand bouncing up and down, Diaz took aim as well as he could and fired his privately owned Glock .40, an identical firearm to his police-issued weapon. Unfortunately the round he fired sailed over G's head and into the telephone pole.

The effect of this shot was to convince G to change his plan and immediately get behind some cover before he got hit with the next round. The only cover available was the telephone pole and he held his breath hoping that he could make it before another shot found its mark in his back.

While still running, Diaz intended to take a second shot at the suspect, but before he could level his sights on him, the suspect grabbed onto the telephone pole to stop his forward momentum and then hunkered down behind it. Diaz suddenly stopped and moved toward the opposite edge of the alley and readied himself for the gunfight that he was sure was about to ensue. As he moved laterally, Diaz realized that he was in the open with no cover; his mind went back to the academy again. The firearms instructor told the recruits, *"If you have no cover in a gunfight, make your own cover with a wall of flying lead."*

And that is exactly what he did, with fifteen rounds of .40 caliber ammo left in his Glock, Diaz began to rapidly fire his weapon in G's direction.

"BOOM, BOOM, BOOM, BOOM, BOOM!"

All the while he was backing away a few steps with each shot creating distance. His firearms instructor had told him, *"Distance equals time."*

Even though none of the rounds found their target, they caused G to keep his head behind cover and prohibited him from returning fire. The wall of lead did the job and protected Diaz from hostile fire.

The incoming fire from Diaz had an even greater effect than simply keeping his adversary's head down; three of the five rounds fired at G had come so close to hitting him that two struck the pole he was behind and the third crashed into the concrete block wall of the garage building that he was next to. The impact of the bullet splashed a shower of sharp concrete fragments, like a shotgun round, into G's face, causing several small but painful lacerations in his skin. G cried out in pain and huddled down even lower, reaching up to his shredded face.

Diaz thought that he had hit the suspect and stopped firing. He also didn't want to expend all his rounds since he didn't have a back-up magazine for his weapon. He kept the Glock aimed in the direction of the suspect and waited for his next move, ready to commence firing again if needed.

Whimpering in pain, G still was contemplating his options. He couldn't get up and run again, because he would be shot in the back for sure. He didn't want to try and shoot back at the cop; he was afraid that if he showed any part of his body he would get hit again. The sting from the concrete fragments was burning as if his face was on fire. He was in so much pain now that he really didn't relish the thought of getting hit by another bullet.

Yet he couldn't give up. The cops were sure to execute him now since he had shot a police dog and now shot at a cop. They would never let him out alive. The only thing he could do was to reach around the pole with only his gun hand exposed and fire at the cop in the alley without taking aim and hope that he hits the target. So that is what he did.

"POP, POP, POP"

As G fired at Diaz, Diaz, who was now about twenty yards back, had found an aluminum garbage can to get behind and returned fire.

"BOOM, BOOM, BOOM, BOOM!"

The .40 caliber sound was much more intimidating than the weaker popping reports of the .380 Colt. In addition, unbeknownst to G, he had fewer rounds; in fact G only had two rounds left in his gun at this point.

G's three shots went harmlessly down the alley and wildly missed Diaz. On the other hand, Diaz's well-aimed shots struck the pole that G was hiding behind, resulting in three of the four rounds fired impacting the thick wooden pole, again causing G to recoil behind the pole for safety.

When Diaz stopped firing to conserve ammo, G saw a chance to renew his pointless assault. He squeezed the trigger again and fired the last two rounds.

"POP, POP…" then nothing. The slide on the Colt locked in the rear position, leaving the ammunition well opened and the gun empty.

Diaz didn't fire back at this point, feeling that it was only a waste of ammunition. He was pleased with his decision when he could see that his adversary had shot his gun dry. He decided to make another verbal challenge at this point. "Throw the gun out and come out with your hands up!"

G was overwrought with confusion; he didn't know what to do. He couldn't surrender because that would amount to a death sentence. He huddled behind the pole; his breathing was extremely labored and he could feel his heartbeat thumping in the fresh wounds on his face. The pain was so overwhelming he thought that he might pass out. The thought of what the cops would do to him urged him to stay focused. He had to keep fighting or die trying. Then he remembered that he still had the .38 revolver in his pocket. In all the confusion, he had forgotten that he had stuck the weapon in the pocket of George's oversized coat, which had been part of the original deception.

He quickly arrived at a plan that would give him a chance to trick the cop and make good an escape. G decided to feign surrender and lure the cop into coming closer; when the opportunity presented itself he could use the .38 and shoot him at close range. He knew that he only had a few shots left in the revolver so he needed to have the best chance possible to be assured of hitting his target.

"OK," G said to Diaz. "I'll give up," G stated, and threw the empty Colt out into the alley.

"Come out from behind the pole and let me see your hands," Diaz commanded.

"I can't. You got me so I can't stand up. I need an ambulance."

Diaz wasn't sure if he was lying or not. The perp did scream pretty bad after Diaz had fired his first volley and the guy was making a whimpering sound like he was severely injured. But he wasn't convinced just yet and was apprehensive about moving out in the open.

"Come on out where I can see you. Roll out in the alley if you have to," Diaz said sternly.

"I told you. I can't move. You done shot me bad, so's that I can't move. I'm bleedin' pretty bad. If you let me die it's on your head man." G said this as convincingly as possible.

Diaz decided to move in because it didn't appear as if this guy was going to get up from behind the pole, and he just might be hurt as badly as he said he was. In addition, his gun was on the ground and empty. There was the chance that he had a second gun, however. That was something else his instructors had told him, *"When you find one weapon on a perp always assume there is a second."* It was called the "plus one" rule.

This was the one piece of advice Diaz didn't follow on this night, and it would cost him.

While G was making his first attempt at shooting Diaz, Ruggerio and his two backup officers were making their way through the open field near George's house, moving cautiously and scanning all directions for possible threats. At this point, events were moving so fast that it was impossible for Quint to have radioed in real time what was occurring to the other units.

Therefore, Ruggerio and crew were not sure where the perp was or for that matter any of the officers in the area. They were however, already moving in the direction of Quint and Max since having heard the shots fired by G, then later by Quint. They were moving as fast as they could to find out what had just occurred, but to move too fast would be reckless, creating conditions under which a mistake could occur and cause one of the officers to shoot too quickly, resulting in a friendly fire tragedy. For these reasons, the three officers moved at a measured pace, checking all darkened areas with flashlights before moving forward.

The shotgun officer had a powerful light attached to his gun, located under the barrel, so wherever the light was pointing, the barrel was automatically pointed in the same direction. The other officer armed with his duty-issued Glock .40, was using his service light in a cross hand grip. While one hand holds the weapon, the other holds the flashlight. The flashlight hand crosses under the gun hand and the backs of each hand are pushed against each other, providing support. With this grip, the flashlight and the firearm can move in unison and will always be trained on the same target. The light is activated in short bursts to illuminate any darkened areas to check for threats. The officer quickly scans that area and shuts the light off when he is satisfied that no threats are present. This technique limits the time when the light is on, thus giving any potential assailants a smaller window of opportunity to use the officer's own light beam as an aiming point.

While the three officers were creeping through the open field, they heard the first shot that G had taken at Diaz. The three officers abandoned their cautious demeanor and quickened their pace; in moments they were standing at Quint's location, looking on as Quint Max cradled in his arms, gently stroking his muzzle.

"Hang in there, Maxy. You stay with me boy," Quint pleaded to his wounded companion, as his eyes began to well up.

Tobias arrived on scene also with George in tow, he had him handcuffed and told him to sit on the ground.

"What happened?" Ruggerio asked.

"That asshole shot my dog is what happened," Quint answered in a halting voice.

"I took a few shots at him while he ran. I don't think I hit him though," he continued.

Tobias knelt down with Quint and took out a handkerchief, which he held on Max's wound to slow the bleeding. He could see that Max was losing consciousness from loss of blood. The officers all knew Max well and considered him part of their number. Hearts were heavy as they looked on, feeling helpless to curb the dog's suffering.

"Diaz took off after him up the street," said Quint and pointed north in the direction where Diaz had run after G.

"OK," Ruggerio said, alerting everyone that he was about to give out instructions.

He pointed at the non-shotgun officer and said, "Stay with Quint in case the guy doubles back. We will go after Diaz."

After the officer acknowledged the new instructions, Ruggerio, Tobias, and the shotgun cop started off running in the direction Quint had indicated, where they had heard the last shot.

The officer who stayed back with Quint grabbed his shoulder microphone to his radio and notified other units what had taken place and where the perp had last been seen. He also requested that the shift sergeant respond to his location. This was standard procedure in officer-involved shootings.

As Ruggerio and crew turned the corner from Monitor Ave to the intersecting road, they heard the cavalcade of rounds that were exchanged between G and Diaz in the alley just one block away from where they were standing. With these new explosions, the officers turned their somewhat cautious jogging pace to an all-out sprint to assist their fellow officer.

While Ruggerio and the others were sprinting for the mouth of the alley where Diaz was, G was still lying on the ground behind the telephone pole, hand grasping his .38, waiting for the right moment. Just keep moaning and be patient, he thought to himself, hoping that this would lure the cop closer. He started to feel the wetness from the melted snow soaking through his pants to the skin of his backside. This sensation only briefly took his mind off the two wounds that he suffered and the pain that they were causing him.

Slicing the pie, Diaz thought, as he remembered from his academy days.

"Lean over the left hip with your arms extended forward and your weapon pointed at the target," his instructor had told the class. *"If no action is needed, straighten up and side step slightly. Repeat the process until you have a clear view of the threat."*

Diaz was reviewing the instructions in his mind as he was performing the technique called "slicing the pie," used when an officer needed to clear the area around a corner of a building—or in this case, the area behind a telephone pole. The officer stands a distance away from the corner and takes short side steps, which incrementally provide the officer with a safer way of peeking around a corner to see if the threat is viable or neutralized.

Diaz took a step to his left then put his feet together. While his feet were planted he leaned over his left hip with his weapon extended and caught a view of the perp from his feet up to his thighs; the upper part of his body was blocked by the pole. He took another step, then put his feet together, then leaned again.

He could see more of the guy's body, all the way up to his neck, but not his face. Due to the darkened conditions and the fact that the .38 revolver was black in color, Diaz did not see the weapon in the lap of the perp. It was a delay that gave the assailant the edge; the next thing that Diaz saw was an orange starburst shoot out the end of the barrel of the .38. Then something hitting the left side of his torso so hard it felt like someone swung a baseball bat and hit him on the hip bone. Diaz knew that he had been shot. In response he instinctively squeezed off two quick rounds. The impact of the bullet caused him to spin around to his left about twenty degrees, throwing his aim off and sending his two rounds into the outside wall of a building down the alleyway. Even though he missed his target, the fact that he was spun by the impact of the bullet was advantageous for Diaz because it caused G's second shot to miss him and go sailing through a basement window of a home behind Diaz. The round lodged harmlessly into the opposite wall of the basement.

The force of the bullet that hit Diaz caused him to crumple to the ground and lose sight of his assailant for a brief moment. The pain of the wound began to reach his brain at about the same time he turned back toward the perp's direction and fired off two more rounds—just as he saw him run through the opening between two buildings and disappear. Both rounds missed their intended target and crashed into the cement block of one of the buildings. He curled up into a fetal position, clutched his side and screamed in pain.

G smiled as he ran. It actually worked; the cop went down on the first shot, he thought, congratulating himself. He ran through the snow, slipping a little with each step while holding his left side and feeling the sting of his own bullet wound. It was dark running between these houses but he could see the street in front illuminated by the street lights. He figured he would cross the next street then find a secluded place in the back of one of the houses on the opposite side and hide out until it was safe to venture out again. The left side of his face pounded with pain each time his heart beat. When he reached up to touch the wounds caused by the concrete shrapnel, he felt warm blood oozing from the holes.

Emerging from the walkway between the houses onto the front sidewalk, he looked up and down, and to the rear, for any police. Seeing no one, he took off across the street and continued down the opposite sidewalk about fifty feet until he spied an opening between an old rundown one-story bungalow and a closed-up former pizza shop. This looked good, he thought. Maybe he could even break into one of these structures and hide out inside. That would be safer yet, he reasoned. To reach the rear of both buildings, he stayed on the pavement of the front walk to the bungalow, since there wasn't any snow accumulated there. When the pavement ran out all he had was natural ground to walk on so he was careful to make his footfalls on areas that the snow had not covered. Upon reaching the back of the house, he found that the back door had been busted open from a previous break-in and was not secured. The house was obviously abandoned, so he slipped inside and squatted in a dark corner of the first room he entered. The room was formerly the kitchen, which was evident from the battered linoleum floor and broken cabinetry.

The appliance fittings still sprouted from the floor and walls, which had supplied fuel for a gas stove and power to the refrigerator. What had once been someone's kitchen, where meals were prepared for a family, now gave shelter to junkies to shoot heroin, or light crack pipes to get high. Graffiti covered the walls, marking this territory for the wannabe gangs that roamed this portion of the city. The floor was littered with old newspaper, soda and beer cans, rotting remnants of food left on styrofoam take-out containers, cigarette lighters and scorch marks from where squatters lit fires to keep warm. This was one the realities of the urban poor and homeless—a portrait that is not often seen or cared about in middle- and upper-class America.

G tried to catch his breath while occasionally peering out of the side window to see if anyone had followed him. After a quick peek, he would slink back down into the corner again, each movement causing another stab of pain to emanate from the bullet wound on his left side. He thought about checking his .38 to see if he had any rounds left, so he broke open the cylinder and cursed when he saw all spent casings inside. G put the gun in his pocket for now; even though it was empty it could still be useful as a bluff; someone could easily believe that it contained live ammo. For now, he had to stay put for a while and wait until the searchers become bored and their numbers subsided to the point where it was safe to move again.

CHAPTER 11

Ruggerio, Tobias, and the shotgun cop made the corner of the alley where Diaz and the perp had exchanged gunfire and they witnessed the last two shots that Diaz fired at the fleeing felon. Ruggerio saw Diaz on the ground, curled up holding his side and writhing in pain. He knelt down beside his friend and partner and froze for a moment in shock when the realization set in that Diaz was seriously injured.

The previous computer-like efficiency of each of his thoughts and deductions up to this point immediately stopped and his mind became overwhelmed with thoughts of guilt and remorse for having involved his friend in this exercise to save his career. Now here was Diaz, a rookie, with his whole future still before him, lying in a dirty frozen alley, bleeding from a bullet hole, possibly ready to die... For what, so Ruggerio could get his precious job back and show his arch enemy Faust that he wasn't a screw up after all? Diaz should be home with his family taking care of his own business instead of out here helping Ruggerio in unauthorized police activity that could get the kid killed.

Tobias told the group that he would run back to the mouth of the alley to direct the ambulance to their location when it arrived. The shotgun cop knelt down beside Diaz on the opposite side of Ruggerio and asked, "OK, I'll get a medic on the way. Where did the guy go?"

Diaz pointed to the opening between the buildings where G had run and said with difficulty, "Through there. I think I hit him."

"Where you hit, Kid?"

"On my left side. A-H-H-H-H-H, damn it hurts," Diaz groaned.

Ruggerio couldn't think of anything to say except, "I'm sorry Tay, I... I can't tell you how sorry I am."

Between groans of agony Diaz replied, "You... don't... have anything... to be sorry about, Man."

Then after another groan, "You're not the one that shot me." He even conjured up a smile for emphasis.

It was exactly what Ruggerio needed. He came out of his funk and removed his ski cap and applied it to the wound to stop the bleeding.

"Stay with us, Kid. The meat wagon should be here any second now," Ruggerio said encouraging him. Then he saw the empty .380 that G had discarded in the alleyway.

"Where did that come from Tay?" he asked.

"The perp's, he shot it empty... He must have had a second gun. That's how he got me," he struggled to explain, then thought to himself about the proper word to describe his performance. *Stupid* was all he could come up with.

"It's OK, here comes the wagon," Ruggerio said as the ambulance's red rotating lights flashed into the alley and the blare of the siren was winding down from its crescendo.

After Diaz was safely loaded into the ambulance, he and Ruggerio said their goodbyes. The shotgun cop, who was standing near the area where Diaz had last seen the perp, was pointing the light attached to his gun between the two buildings where G had run.

"I got footprints over here Guy, and I think Diaz was right. He must of scored a hit 'cause there are drops of blood too," he said, looking in Ruggerio's direction with a grin on his face.

"Well, my bet is that since he is hurt and scared he probably ran to some dark corner and is holed up, waiting for the heat to die down," Ruggerio figured. He continued, "Smart thing now is to organize a search and get all the hardware we can."

"You're gonna need to get scarce then, because if they catch you out here workin' this thing your ass is toast," the shotgun cop reasoned.

"I am toast anyway. My only hope is to grab this creep and get all the info we can on what he knows about Bartlett Park. Anyway, now I owe it to Diaz." He paused, taking note of the sacrifice made by his friend, then simply stated, "It's the least I can do."

Just then the shotgun cop's radio summoned him to the previous location where Max had been hit. He was ordered to bring with him the "civilian" that he had with him, meaning Ruggerio.

"Looks like there is hell to pay now," he said to Ruggerio.

"Listen, and I don't want to hear an argument. I forced my way into this. You couldn't stop me from sticking my nose in. I already have gotten enough of my friends in trouble. Besides it's the truth anyway. How were you going to stop me from interfering in this chase? You would have had to shoot me, right?"

The shotgun officer knew he was right but didn't respond. It felt to him as if he was betraying Ruggerio. He knew that if he were in Ruggerio's shoes he would be doing the same thing. How could he blame a guy for trying to save his name, reputation and career—not to mention trying to avoid going to jail?

Ruggerio saw that he wasn't answering and he needed to make sure that the officer was not going to do something stupid and get himself in trouble. It wouldn't help Ruggerio anyway. So he repeated himself to emphasize that he did not want the officer to make any statements that he encouraged Ruggerio, Diaz or Tobias to help in the police activities in this incident.

"Right?" Ruggerio said, still getting no response.

"Listen, I appreciate your feelings but you're not going to help me out any by getting yourself in trouble. The best thing you can do for me is help catch this G character, OK?"

"OK, but we better stay here until another unit can relieve us. We would look pretty stupid if the dude doubles back right after we leave, right? We need to protect the evidence too," the shotgun cop remarked.

"Now you're thinking, Brother. Call a car up here," he concurred.

In a matter of minutes, several squads were in the alley along with detectives and the shift sergeant, a war-weary veteran of 29 years on the force. Sergeant Stanley Katowski, a stout man with hands the size of Christmas hams, the product of the quintessential Pittsburgh mill family. His grandfather, who emigrated from Poland, and his father toiled in the steel mills like thousands of other immigrants and sons of immigrants.

When first meeting Katowski, a person would automatically assume a typical blue-collar ancestry; his appearance and demeanor screamed mill-hunk. The term mill-hunk was first applied in the early 1900s to Hungarian immigrants working in the steel mills, but after time and the melding of the different ethnic groups the term came to refer to all laborers in the mills.

Katowski was known around the station house as a hardnosed boss. He demanded perfection in all facets of the police job. From the way an officer wore his uniform to the correct spelling and punctuation of his reports. This attitude, along with his flat-top crew cut, portrayed to the casual observer the former Marine that Katowski had been before joining the force. In fact, even though he never spoke about his experiences, word around the station house was that Katowski had done two tours of duty in Vietnam. The story goes that he was right in the middle of the heaviest fighting during the Tet Offensive. No one knew where or how severely, but they said he had been wounded during combat.

But even if he had never served a day in the service, the officers who worked for him both feared and respected Katowski. He was tough but fair and more than once stuck his neck out for a fellow officer when he thought the reasons were valid. Very soon he would lay his head on the chopping block again.

Ruggerio saw Katowski coming and from the way he was marching down the alley past the queue of parked squad cars with their reds and blues still rotating, he knew that he was about to receive an earful from the surly sarge. In tow with the sergeant was a crestfallen Tobias, walking with his head partially down and shoulders slumped; it was clear that he had already felt the wrath of the ex-marine. As he approached Ruggerio, the sarge in a typical mannerism that he displayed when upset, ran his beefy hand quickly over his flat-top from back to front then in a separate motion down his face in an effort to neutralize some of his anger.

As he approached, Katowski announced in his booming voice, "RUGGERIO, YOU DUMB DAGO, WHAT ARE YOU DOING HERE?"

Ruggerio held his hands out in front of him as if to try and stop a charging bull and said, "I know, Sarge, but I had to try. This guy was at Bartlett Park on the night of my shooting."

Still fuming but with some of the agitation replaced by curiosity he asked, "What do you mean, he saw the shooting?"

"I think so. Word is that he was in a house with a hooker at the time. We have to get him alive, Sarge, or he is no good to me," Ruggerio explained.

"Damn it Ruggerio… you know procedure. You give this info to the dicks and let them handle it," he replied, exasperated and then he did the hand thing over his crew cut and down his face again—but this time he turned away and walked a few paces, apparently trying to think of something.

When he turned back toward Ruggerio, he stated, "Listen, I can't cover for you. There is just no way. I have to report this. I mean, damn it, we got a shot cop and police dog here."

"I know, Sarge. I am not asking you to cover for me, and I am willing to take the heat. But if you could somehow ease the hit that Tobias and Diaz are going to take, they were just helping me out."

"We'll see. For now have a seat in one of the cars. I have to organize this search." As he turned away he snatched his shoulder mic from his epaulet and stated, "Where are the blood hounds?" into the microphone, abandoning protocol by not identifying himself first or for whom the transmission was intended.

"We are pulling into the alley now, Sarge, but it's blocked so we have to unload on the street," responded one of the K-9 officers just arriving for the search.

"Sarge, make sure no one disturbs the track," the K-9 officer continued, referring to the fact that if officers attempt to walk in the path the perp took, the mixed scent will confuse the dog and could cause a false trail for the dog to follow.

"Don't worry. We're staying back for now," Katowski replied. Then he switched gears to the other issues that he had to deal with. "7-10 to control. What is the status on the bird?" referring to the police helicopter that he requested.

"Air support reports that he is one minute out," the control operator reported.

"10-4," confirmed Katowski, and then continued his laundry list of resource checks. "How about the SWAT team. Are they close?" he asked into the mic.

After a short pause the dispatcher reported, "SWAT team reports that they are on-scene and forming up at the southwest corner of the perimeter."

Then the cops in the alley could hear the approach of the bird. First the thump, thump, thump of the helicopter was distant, then suddenly it came roaring overhead nearly at roof top level, its powerful spotlight shining down, briefly lighting up the officers fanned out in the alleyway where Diaz and G had their gunfight.

This was intentional on the pilot's part; it was meant to send a message of intimidation to the felon hoping to flush the fugitive out from hiding. It didn't often work, but it was worth a try. The pilot could also see by how the squad cars were positioned at opposite street corners. The officers had cordoned off a perimeter around the area where G had last been seen. The pilot knew that if the bad guy was inside this box, he wasn't getting out without being spotted. He knew that he really shouldn't be flying on a night like this. At times the snowfall was too heavy for safe flying. Luckily the snowfall had lightened up enough to permit sufficient visibility for him to participate in the search, but it was still risky. It was times such as these, when a cop is injured, that the familiar police adage, "brothers in blue," transcends from a laudable sentiment into real action.

First it was the wailing of approaching sirens, then the sound of barking dogs mixed with shouts from policemen and women in various directions, then to round out the cacophony of sounds was the ominous roar of the helicopter overhead. Increasingly with these observations G's heart rate went up, along with his respirations. This wasn't good for the wounds that he had sustained; not only was the pain getting worse but the blood was seeping out of each hole at a faster rate now, especially from the puncture wounds made by the cement shrapnel that pierced the left side of his face. He tried ripping some cloth from one of his T-shirts but couldn't do it. He decided just to take his coat off, then remove one of his shirts and apply it to the wounds on his face.

G stood up in the darkened room and looked out one of the windows to see what was happening outside. The window looked toward the back of the house into the alleyway. He couldn't see anyone in the area but he could see red and blue police lights bouncing off the surrounding walls of nearby buildings. He decided to move to the front of the old house and look out one of the front windows to survey this side. The searing pain in his side caused him to wince with each step. He finally reached the window and crouched down under it for a moment. He slowly rose up just high enough so that only his forehead and eyes were above the window ledge. As soon as he was able to look out the window, he just as quickly dropped back down out of sight.

The first thing he saw was a flashlight beam being fanned back and forth by a police officer walking down the middle of the street in front of the house, with a second officer trailing behind. He dropped down below the ledge of the window so abruptly and violently that when his bottom hit the floor the shock wave vibrated through his body, intensifying his wounds and nearly causing him to scream out in pain. G was able to move the T-shirt quickly from the side of his facial wounds to cover his mouth and muffle the scream. When he recovered from this wave of pain, he was able to take another look outside to see if the cops might have heard the noise. They apparently had not since they continued moving down the street in the same manner.

One thing was for sure; it was only a matter of time until the cops found his hiding spot. With blood oozing out of his wounds, which probably spattered onto the ground and the tracks he made in the snow, it wouldn't be long before the dogs located him in the house. Then he would be cornered and it would only be a matter of time until they stormed the place and killed him. He knew that he wasn't going to be taken alive, especially after he had shot one of their dogs and the cop. He had to make a move and right now while he still had the chance.

At about the same time that G was peering out the windows of the abandoned home, a PennDOT—short for Pennsylvania Department of Transportation—salt truck, spreading salt on the snow-covered roadways, approached the northeast corner of the police perimeter set up to hem in the fugitive. The driver of the fifteen-ton yellow Peterbilt was Jimmy, a.k.a. JJ Stokes. Jimmy was a good ole boy from outside of the city proper, who was relishing the overtime he was racking up in this snowstorm. JJ was clearly your prototypical redneck, with bulging gut, long brown hair, and the regulation tattoos. JJ's body art consisted of a ferocious panther's head on one arm and a voluptuous dark haired female in a bikini on the other. Similar designs could be found on the arms of his friends, with whom he hung out every evening at Jenner's Tavern, an old farmhouse converted into a bar. Also like his tavern pals, JJ had a perpetually unshaved face with an unruly goatee that was at least three days overdue for a trimming.

Topping off JJ's look was the requisite redneck mullet. Tonight, JJ had his dark brown mane gathered into a ponytail that protruded from under his baseball cap. The cap was part of the redneck uniform also, used for such activities as working, going out for the evening, or just relaxing at home in front of the TV while watching wrestling or auto racing. Of course it would also be used for the purpose for which it was originally intended: hunting wild turkey or whitetail deer. The redneck uniform demanded one more trinket—the ever-present fishing license.

In Pennsylvania, fishermen are issued a small square piece of paper that identifies the holder as licensed to fish within the state. Along with the license, the sportsman is given a clear plastic holder and an attached safety pin. The fisherman is to attach this sheath, with the license, onto an article of clothing while he or she engages in the sport of fishing. Most fishermen pin the licenses to their ball caps so that they are prominently displayed for any Fish and Game Wardens who might wander along the streams.

Many proudly wear these year-round, affixed to the standard-issue camo hat. JJ was wearing his fishing license attached to his hat on this particular evening. To complete the ensemble, JJ wore his red flannel shirt and blue jeans that hadn't been washed since Thanksgiving.

Even though it had slowed up a bit, the snow kept falling. JJ would have to go back over the ground that he had already covered and re-salt the roads, thus extending his overtime shift and fattening his next paycheck. But up to this point he still hadn't completed his first pass over his route. All PennDOT drivers worry that if any accidents occur before they are able to salt the roadways, it could mean severe consequences for the offending salt truck driver.

When JJ saw the cop car ahead, blocking the one-way road, he cringed and said out loud for no one in particular to hear, "Damn cops. What's going on now?"

He punched the button to roll down the window and spit out a saliva stream of tobacco juice.

After gearing down his rig in preparation to come to a stop for the roadblock, he grabbed the radio microphone from its cradle and called in to the dispatcher, "Truck 11-23 to base," he announced.

"Go ahead JJ," the male dispatcher said.

"I got a god-dern police roadblock here on the off ramp of I-279 South. I don't know how long I am going to be here and I am only halfway through with my circuit," JJ said into the mic with exasperation.

"OK, stand-by 11-23," replied the dispatcher.

JJ rolled the big rig to a stop. There were two other cars between him and the police car, which was parked diagonally across the street, its lights rotating. He couldn't see the officer and figured he must be inside the squad car. JJ was on an off-ramp from one of the interstates, approaching a one-way road that bordered a mixed business and residential district on the North side of Pittsburgh. To his left, a cement barrier separated the interstate highway and the elevated off-ramp. To JJ's right was a collection of one- and two-level business buildings. He needed to go through this section of the city in order to turn around and re-enter the interstate so that he could continue on his circuit. He quickly decided against turning into the one and only alley that connected to the ramp since his truck was too wide to pass through.

He could see from the headlights in his side view mirrors that cars were starting to line up behind him, so he couldn't back up all the way to the entrance of the ramp to avoid the roadblock. In frustration, he pounded on the steering wheel with the heel of his left hand and said, "It just had to happen now, just when I want to drive through here. Damn it!"

The dispatcher called him back, "JJ, I mean truck 11-23," he said, correcting himself.

"11-23," JJ answered.

"Get through any way you can because we are short trucks. 11-30 went down a little while ago with a radiator hose and he can't cover for you," the dispatcher reported.

"10-4," is all JJ could say. The dispatcher would later realize how ironic his relayed instructions of, "get through any way you can," would be.

On nights like this one these big rigs with their bright yellow paint jobs and rotating light beacons of the same color, were a pleasing sight for western Pennsylvanians. Drivers knew that Saint Christopher was watching out for them when they found themselves following behind one of these behemoths as it spewed out dicer and salt from the rear-mounted spreaders.

On the other hand, salt trucks could also be a point of agitation. After completing the back-breaking task of shoveling out a home driveway or parking spot, the last thing you wanted to hear was the unwelcome sound of a PennDOT rig's snowblade scraping the road.

The sound could be compared to what a soldier on the battlefield probably experiences when an enemy tank churns and shakes up the ground near his position. Since the drivers had so much territory to cover, they needed to clear as much roadway in as little time as possible. Speed also helped the snow blades work properly. Thus drivers had to press their rigs to over forty miles an hour, especially on highways, so the blades could throw the snow.

The blades mounted on the front of the trucks are designed to lift snow off the surface of the pavement and throw it to the side of the highway, sometimes up to thirty feet. Hence the cause of severe agitation for exhausted snow shovelers when one of these trucks comes rumbling along and buries his newly-cleaned area with snow tainted with road dirt, stones, and maybe even some previously-laid black dicer. Thus was the love/hate relationship between western Pennsylvanians and PennDOT. This infamous snow blade, which JJ had affixed to the front of his rig, would play a vital role in the events about to take place.

The only plan G could conjure up was to get out of this house and maybe happen upon a car he could steal or carjack, because going about on foot wasn't getting him anywhere. G moved to the back of the house into the kitchen again and looked out every window that he passed on the way to see if there was any activity surrounding the house. By the time he reached the back door he hadn't noticed any cops in the area. It was now or never, he figured.

He would take the alley behind the house toward the interstate only one block away. G knew where that was since it was the highway that led straight to Erie, and indirectly to Cleveland. If he ran into cops along the way he would have to bluff them with the empty .38 snubnose. If he could be convincing enough he might even coax one into handing over his piece, then he could have a fully loaded semi-auto to fight with. If he was lucky and could make the interstate without being detected he would have to wait for an opportunity to grab a vehicle and head north to Cleveland.

G cautiously leaned his head out of the threshold of the rear door and looked all around for movement or flashlights. Seeing nothing, he began to creep out into what had once been the back yard. Stepping over old tires, cans, boxes, and other debris, all snow-covered but still identifiable from their outlines, he made his way to yet another alleyway. G peeked out from behind one of the walls to the neighboring structure that was the former pizza shop. The building ran from the edge of the front street to the border of the alley, making a safe vantage point from which to observe.

Not seeing any movement, he turned toward the direction that led to the interstate and crept down the alley, staying close to the near side to be able to scurry through the closest opening between buildings and hide. The alley intersected with the street that doubled as an off ramp from the interstate and a local one-way roadway for the neighborhood. G was only about two hundred feet away and could plainly see cars lined up on the off ramp waiting, apparently for a traffic light or possibly a police roadblock. If he could make the street before being spotted he might be able to carjack one of the cars in the line without the cops seeing him. If he took the last car in line he might be able to have the driver back it up and re-enter the interstate from the off ramp. First he had to make the street then he would decide which car, if any, to take.

Just then, G heard the thump, thumping of the helicopter rotators coming closer. He pressed his body against the nearest building. Fortunately for him it was another old garage. This one was still intact and probably still in use since the area in front of the door was not lined with garbage or overgrown weeds. G flattened himself into the indent of the garage door, hoping that this would hide his body from the view of the pilots in the helicopter.

As the chopper flew overhead, its brilliant search light illuminated the alley; G's heart stopped for a moment as the light tracked just in front of his feet but never touched him as it went by. The sound of the chopper became a little less ominous as it flew off into the distance. G waited, figuring if the pilots had seen him they would circle to put the light back on the spot where they made the sighting. When the chopper kept getting further away he felt it was safe to continue down the alley.

Ruggerio was doing as Katowski told him and getting into the nearest squad car to be driven back to the command post. As Ruggerio sat in the passenger seat of the car, his mind wandered to moments earlier when he saw his friend lying in a cold wet alley bleeding from a gunshot wound. His mind's eye saw the pain on Taymond's face and still heard his screams of agony. Ruggerio had seen numerous gunshot victims in his career, and he realized that this wound was serious and it could possibly kill his friend and partner.

Every time it seemed like he was making progress in his cause to clear his name, something happened to squash his hopes. Now, not only was his career in jeopardy but his friend's life was also. When will it end, he thought, how much more can I take? Ruggerio silently pondered this while sitting alone in the squad car and anxiously wringing his hands. At this point, Ruggerio made up his mind to move over to the driver's side and take the squad car to pursue the fugitive.

At that same moment, the officer who was driving this squad appeared on the driver's side and quickly opened the door to get in. The officer was Shelisha Walker, a short wide-bodied black female whom Ruggerio knew very well and had worked with for years on the midnight shift.

Shelisha had the look of a wide load from behind. Her blue uniform trousers were so tight that her bottom threatened to burst the seam open at any moment. Of course this sight was the *butt* of many station house jokes, but she handled this issue with a fun-loving and self-deprecating sense of humor. When she was moving backward in the station house, she would make beeping noises like the warning signal that sounds when a piece of heavy construction equipment is being operated in reverse by the driver. One time when she was teasing Ruggerio about his short stature, Shelisha remarked with a hearty chuckle, "Honey, my butt is as wide as you are tall, you little Italian cutie."

But Shelisha's wide end was not her only remarkable feature. Her ample bust rivaled the generous proportions of her back end and acted as a counterweight to her buttocks. Shelisha would make comments about this part of her body also. "Come on in-between here darlin' and keep yourself warm," she would say on a cold night to one of her colleagues. Or, "I got my own airbags. I don't need to wear a seatbelt."

Along with her excessive body curves, Shelisha had the facial features of a cover model. The cops nicknamed Shelisha after another full-figured black woman with an attractive face; they called her Queen Shelisha, after the actress Queen Latifa. After a while, this was shortened to simply "Queeny." It became common to refer to her as Queeny Walker when two cops were talking about her out of her presence.

Irrespective of Queeny's physical qualities, Ruggerio had tremendous respect for her as a police officer. With her outgoing personality and her quick wit, she was excellent at soliciting street information on recent crimes and collecting intelligence information on gang activity. Whenever a serious crime took place, like a robbery or a homicide, the detectives always asked where Queeny Walker was to see if she had any information on the possible identity of the culprit. If Queeny didn't know the actor's name right off, she would hit the streets to talk with her sources and in short order she usually had a list of likely suspects who might be good for the caper.

When Queeny got her big behind into her seat, she looked over at Ruggerio sitting in the passenger side with a surprised look on her face and remarked to him in her typical style of witticism. "Good Lord. I ought a pray for a man more often," she said, cracking a smile on her smooth unblemished face. She then asked him, "What are you doin' here darlin'?"

"Katowski told me to sit in here. He wants you to take me to the command post for my ass chewing," Ruggerio said in deadpan fashion.

"Where is old sergeant flattop anyway?" Queeny asked.

At that moment they both heard a knock on the glass of Ruggerio's door window. It was Katowski wanting him to take his window down. When Ruggerio complied, Katowski leaned in through the opening to talk to Queeny.

"Queeny, take Ruggerio in to the command post, Lieutenant's orders," he said bluntly and was about to turn away when he felt a tug on his arm. It was Ruggerio stopping him from leaving and about to make another request of a fellow officer to go out on a limb for his benefit.

"Sarge let me go with Queeny after the perp, please," he pleaded.

"NO WAY. Are you crazy? If they catch you my ass is grass," the sergeant said forcefully then turned his gaze back to Queeny and repeated his orders, "Take him in. Go on."

But Ruggerio would not let go and implored with his sergeant to let him partake in the chase that was starting. "Sarge, what would you do if your job…" he paused for a second then continued. "Your life was on the line, like mine is now? I just can't sit back and not get involved. I'll go nuts. Come on, just turn your back and you didn't see me take off. I'll say that I forced Queeny to take me along with her," he begged with his eyes getting moist as he looked up at Katowski.

Queeny pretty much sealed the deal with Katowski by stating, "I'm game, what do you say, Curly?" her nickname for Katowski.

"I don't see anything. The last thing that I knew was that I told you to go in to the command post. Queeny, you're on your own, OK?" he said pointing at the female cop.

"Good enough, you are an old marshmallow. You know that Curly?" Queeny said with a big smile, showing off her brilliantly white teeth.

"Ah-h-h-h," was all Katowski said as he turned away and gave a dismissive half waving gesture to the two cops in the car.

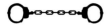

As he moved, all the while holding the T-shirt over his face wounds, he kept wondering what was going to greet him next. It seemed that every time he thought that he was in the clear some unexpected problem would pop up to smack him in the face; pun intended, he thought. First it was that damn liquor store clerk who tried to be a hero, and then it was the cop dog and then the undercover cop who tried to kill him. What next?

He saw cops behind every garbage can, and around every corner. He was starting to think that he wanted the cops just to come out and end it all right now. How much more could one person take anyway? Screw this, G thought. I am running the last one hundred feet and grabbing the first car I see.

As he started to jog in the direction of the off ramp ahead, he noticed a yellowish rotating light reflecting off of the hood and front windshield of one of the cars stopped in traffic on the off ramp. From the reflection of the yellow lights he could tell that it was stopped a short distance ahead of this car. He also realized that the vehicle with the yellow lights was a PennDOT truck, probably one of the big salt trucks that would be out on a night like tonight. Another plan began to germinate in G's head, involving this big rig.

Even though it wasn't the most inconspicuous mode of transportation, G figured that it would be big enough to smash through any roadblocks that the cops would have set up and get out of the immediate area. Once that was accomplished, he would abandon the truck and commandeer a less obvious vehicle to take him the rest of the way out of this city and on to Cleveland.

CHAPTER 12

JJ punched the power lock button to unlock the doors of his rig. He wanted to jump out and talk with the cop who had the road blocked to find out how long this was going to take. JJ jumped down from his cab and immediately dug his right index finger and thumb into his lower lip to extract the wad of tobacco from his mouth. JJ tossed the wet tobacco glob over the cement barrier to the interstate below, raining tobacco particles down on passing vehicles on the highway. He smiled as he thought about the jettisoned chew landing and smearing on someone's windshield. As he strutted past the two cars stopped in front of him, cowboy boots clicking on the pavement, he told the drivers that he would find out what the commotion was all about.

"I'll find out what's going on," JJ announced.

When he got to the police car, he found that his suspicions were correct. The lazy cop was sitting inside of his car where it was nice and warm. JJ thought to himself that this guy just wanted all the people sitting in their cars at the roadblock to guess at what the holdup was. Doesn't he know that people have places to go? He should be walking down the line of cars telling the drivers what is going on and how long the wait is going to be. They don't care, JJ said to himself as he approached the driver's window of the police car.

The cop put his window down and before JJ could utter a word started pointing his finger at the truck driver who dared approach his squad.

"Get back in your truck. We got a killer on the loose out here," the officer shouted at JJ.

"I...I was just wondering ..." JJ tried to explain, in vain.

"I don't care what you were. Get back into your truck and lock the doors or I'm gonna arrest you for interfering in a police investigation, you dumb hick," the cop ordered indignantly.

"OK, Officer. I just wanted a little information," JJ said as he started to turn to toward his rig. After a step or two, insulted and feeling as if he needed to defend his manhood from the tongue lashing that he had just received, JJ stopped and decided to try and even the score with this cop.

"Listen pal I need to advise my sup..." he abruptly stopped in the middle of the word supervisor when he saw the cop begin to exit his squad. JJ thought maybe he had over-played his hand a bit.

The cop shot out of the car and slammed the door shut. He wasn't real tall but had a meaty appearance—from too many donuts, JJ thought. His uniform collar was buttoned around a huge neck and double chin that resembled one of the black bears that JJ had killed while hunting. JJ towered over the cop and thought that if this was taking place at Jenner's this guy would be catching some knuckles in his chubby face about now.

Then the cop laid into JJ, leading with a pointed finger in his face,

"I don't care who you have to advise. If you don't get back in your truck you are going to jail," said the chubby officer, unzipping his leather jacket after making his threat.

JJ felt that he needed to reply just because he wasn't going to leave this encounter without getting in a few verbal jabs.

"I have a job to do just like you and if I don't get to my route soon we are going to have some accidents," JJ shouted at the officer, spit flying and steam rising from his mouth in the cold air.

The cop stepped back a few feet, reached inside his unzipped black leather police jacket, and pulled out the infamous taser. He pointed it at JJ and said, "You want tased just keep standing there and screaming at me!"

The taser has been around police work for decades, but has experienced a rebirth of sorts ever since a new, supposedly safer version was developed. The weapon delivers a tremendous amount of volts to the subject, rendering him or her incapable of attacking the officer. The effects are supposed to be temporary on the subject but this issue is up for debate since some deaths have taken place after its use.

At this point, JJ felt that retreat was the better part of valor. He had seen some guys get tased by cops during bar fights at Jenner's and he didn't want any part of that. Besides, he could see his job with PennDOT going down the drain if he got arrested tonight. It wouldn't matter to his boss that the cop was a jerk and all he wanted to do was get going and do his job.

Upon the presentation of the taser JJ immediately put his hands up in the surrender position and began backing away.

"OK, relax. I am going back," he said, still facing the cop while continuing to step backward. He didn't think the cop would shoot so he decided to deliver his own parting shot,

"If you didn't have that badge on, you would be spitting out teeth right now," he said in a calm but threatening manner, with a confident smile on his scruffy bearded face.

"Just keep walking hick," the chubby cop replied.

G was at the mouth of the alley at this time and saw the whole exchange between JJ and the chubby cop. He overheard the cop shouting to the big redneck, "Get back in your truck!"

Since the PennDOT truck was the only truck stopped in the line of traffic, it was logical to assume that the redneck was the driver. How lucky would he be, G thought, if the redneck left the doors unlocked while he was arguing with the pig? G decided to test his fortunes and sneak up to the passenger side of the rig and try the door. It was only about thirty feet away.

He left the veritable safety of the alley and leisurely walked down the sidewalk as if he were any other resident just wondering what was happening. He kept the bloody T-shirt down at his side and hoped that the passengers in the other vehicles did not notice the bloody and mangled side of his face as he passed them. G had placed the .38 inside the right pocket of George's oversized quilted coat. He kept his gaze straight ahead and fixed on the two clowns arguing in the street, ready to bolt toward the truck if either one of them noticed him and became alarmed.

G realized that if the door was unlocked as he figured it would be, with the driver outside and the engine still running, it would make a sound when he opened it and again when he closed it. If he was quiet, the loud Peterbilt engine should cover the noise of the door. The real worry was that one of the two morons arguing would turn suddenly and notice him climbing into the truck. His whole scheme was to get into the truck before the driver and surprise him when the redneck climbed back into the cab. G needed the driver since he didn't know how to drive a big rig like this. He hardly knew how to drive an automatic transmission car let alone a standard shift monster truck like this one.

G stepped off the sidewalk onto the roadway near the rear dump bed of the Peterbilt and went to the passenger door while the cop was pointing something in his hand at the redneck and shouting, "You want tased just keep standing there and screaming at me!"

G stepped up onto the footfall and boosted himself up to the door handle. He looked away from the two combatants to find the door handle. He gently pulled the handle out and the door clicked open. A quick peek toward the two men arguing, showed the redneck with his hands in the air as if the cop was about to shoot him. G thought to himself, just my luck the stupid redneck is going to get himself killed when I need the dumb honky to drive this rig.

G opened the door and eased himself inside the cab. He still hadn't been detected by either the cop or the truck driver. He slowly closed the door but did not secure it for fear the noise would be too loud. He simply held the door as close to the jamb as possible without completely closing it.

The warmth of the interior of the cab felt wonderful to G, who had been out in the cold for some time now. He just realized how cold he really was at that moment. With all the action he had been involved in, adrenalin had kept his body warm. He ducked his head down below the dashboard so when the driver returned to the truck he wouldn't see G sitting in the passenger seat—as long as he didn't get dusted by the cop. G figured the hick had a good chance of walking away since he was white and the cop was also. G removed the .38 from his pocket and waited, hoping that this honky didn't have his own gun like the liquor store clerk. G made a mental note to search the redneck at the first opportunity after he re-entered the truck cab.

JJ kept staring into the eyes of the chubby cop as he back peddled, because to turn his back on another man during an argument was like a dog tucking his tail and running away from a fight. It was the unspoken code of the male species. When he was a suitable distance away and felt that his manhood remained intact, JJ turned toward his truck and walked back passing the two cars stopped on the roadway.

The driver of the second car stuck his head out of the window and asked JJ,

"What the hell was that about?"

"That cop is nuts," JJ answered.

"What did he say the holdup was all about?" the driver asked.

"All he said was that they were looking for a killer. I think he was just making it up. That guy's got a screw loose," JJ expounded.

"Why did he get so mad at you?" inquired the driver.

"I guess you're not allowed to ask the police why they are blocking the road. If you're smart just stay inside your car or that nut job will shoot first and asked questions later. I guess they give anyone a badge these days," JJ surmised.

JJ turned and continued back to his truck, eager to get to his radio and report to his dispatcher that it might be a while until he returned to his circuit.

The chubby officer didn't want anyone leaving their vehicles to protect both the officers and the public. He had to wait until proper manpower was assembled to run an effective roadblock at his location. When sufficient officers became available, each vehicle in the queue could be searched for the fugitive. When the car was cleared, it could proceed through the roadblock. Until back-up arrived, all this lone cop could do was just keep the occupants of the vehicles inside their cars.

JJ reached up to open his driver's side door, still muttering to himself about the rudeness of the officer. "If I ever catch that son-of-a-bitch out of uniform I am gonna…"

Before he could finish his sentence the business end of a .38 caliber revolver was pointed at his nose. His head had been down to see the foot holds as he climbed up into the cab. When he had most of his body inside the cab and just getting ready to turn to put his butt in the seat, he saw the muzzle of the weapon and heard these words from the fugitive: "Get your ass inside here honky or I'll blow your brains out onto the interstate."

JJ just froze, trying to grasp what was happening. It only took a few seconds to put together the information the cop had just told him and realize that this guy was the killer. "I said get your redneck ass in here, now!" G said, with eyes narrowed and teeth clenched showing that he meant business.

JJ, by this time having fully come to grips with his situation, actually relaxed a bit and said to G with a sense of resignation in his voice, "This just isn't my night."

He closed the door behind him.

"No it is not, but if you listen to me you might just live to see tomorrow, OK?" said G.

"OK, what do you want?" JJ asked.

"I want you to get me out of here. Take this truck around the cop car and head out for the interstate. You got it?" "What? You know they're gonna shoot the shit out of this truck if I do that."

"Listen, it's either drive this truck where I want you to go or I pop your ass and I'll drive it myself. GOT IT!" said G, raising his voice at the end of the statement and pushing the gun into the ear canal of the defiant driver.

JJ cringed as he felt the cold steel muzzle pressed into his ear, "OK! OK! Whatever you say, man. Just don't pull that trigger!" JJ pleaded.

"Now pull out and run this roadblock," G demanded. JJ didn't move still not really believing what was happening.

Even though an armed criminal was pointing a gun at JJ's head, he still did not make a move to drive the truck through the roadblock. JJ figured that either way he was going to end up the loser in this deal, so he was frozen by indecision. G, becoming even more impatient, felt that the redneck needed some encouragement.

G took the gun out of JJ's ear and moved it down to his crotch area. In a calm and deliberate voice he said, "Go ahead, be a hero. You want to lose your balls?"

With this new incentive JJ saw the light and decided that he should do exactly as this crazy hoodlum wanted.

"OK, man. I'll do it. Just take it easy with that thing," JJ implored.

JJ raised his snow blade as high as he could, then put the Peterbilt into first gear and started cranking the steering wheel to the right to go around the passenger car in front of him. He knew that he was going to have to push the car directly ahead of him out of the way and hoped the snow blade would do the job. He hit his air horn a few times to warn the driver of the car, hoping that he might move a bit forward to give JJ more room to get around.

G wasn't pleased; he didn't want the cop to be alarmed until the last possible moment. When JJ hit the horn of the truck, the cop looked up from his position at the wheel of his squad to see what the commotion was.

"Just push that car out of the way!" G ordered.

JJ gently touched the back of the car's bumper. The driver of the car in front of JJ felt the force from behind and turned to look back. He waved his arms as if to communicate, "What the hell are you doing?"

This still didn't please G. He pressed the barrel of the Colt deeper into JJ's crotch and stated, "I said push it out of the way, NOW!"

JJ, feeling the pressure on his scrotum, pressed the accelerator to move the rig forward. The Peterbilt's snow blade pressed into the rear trunk lid of the car and, POP, the trunk lid came open. The car started to move sideways with the angle of overwhelming force exerted by the Peterbilt. The rear tires made a high-pitched screeching sound, the metal surrounding the trunk area wrinkling as the snow blade pushed into the right rear portion of the car. The rear brake light popped off and went flying to the side of the street. The front of the car was forced into the cement barrier on the left, which stopped its forward momentum. In a moment the blade came free of the back to the car and the truck was clear to proceed forward.

The chubby cop sat in his car for a moment stunned, his mouth hanging open in disbelief. After he collected himself he deduced that this PennDOT driver was off his rocker and was probably going to come after him because of the argument the two had just had. He exited his squad car and was starting to pull his Glock .40 from its holster when the truck began to roll right at him as he took a position behind his police car for protection. As the truck got closer the cop could see that there was a passenger sitting next to the hick driver in the cab. For the short few seconds that he could see the two he noticed that the passenger, who was a black male, was sitting rather close to the driver and shouting something in the hick's ear. The driver for his part looked as if he was scared to death of the black male, like he was being ordered to drive into the police car. In that instant, the cop realized that the fugitive they were looking for was the passenger in this rig.

JJ got his rig around the car and was headed for the police car. The way the cop had the car parked JJ either had to gun his engine and roll right over the front of the squad car or run square into a telephone pole that was situated next to the front of the police car, to get through this roadblock. JJ did not relish the thought of power lines falling on his truck because electrocution was a terrible way to go, so the best option was to run over the cop car. The latter meant that he might hurt or even kill the cop inside. This realization caused JJ to move tentatively toward the police car's front portion.

G, sensing that his driver needed another more convincing form of encouragement, shouted in JJ's ear, "Go over the top of the car!" and simultaneously drew back the hammer of the Colt. JJ took note of the metallic click, click.

JJ's mind was now made up for him, but he was worried that when he hit the squad, the force of the impact might cause the black guy to inadvertently pull the trigger, giving JJ an unwelcome vasectomy.

"OK, I'll ram it—but take that gun out of my balls first!"

G moved the snub nose a few inches back and yelled, "GO!"

With that last bit of incentive and seeing that the cop was out of the car and starting to move clear, JJ pushed the accelerator down to the floor to take the rig over the hood of the squad car.

BANG, the front of the Peterbilt violently popped upward as it made contact with the side of the squad car, like a power fullback hitting the line for a one-yard plunge into the end zone. The rear drive train kept the momentum moving forward on the rig and the front left wheel climbed up onto the top of the squad car's hood. The back half of the police car teetered upward as seven tons of metal crushed the front portion down. The Peterbilt rolled forward off the front bumper of the squad car and back down to the street surface, as the rear double axels climbed on top of the police car, turning the white paint black as the dark rubber ground and crushed the metal. Soon the truck was completely free of the vehicle and moving down the street toward the next roadblock two blocks away.

Officer Chubby's first reaction was to back away from the monster truck driving straight at him. When he went back as far as he could, right up to the concrete road barrier, he thought at first that it was far enough away and he felt rather safe. But when his squad car tires started to explode and the car windows began to pop, showering debris all over him, he wasn't so sure anymore.

At this point, all he could do was hunker down as low as he could and cover up until the truck rolled by. When he looked up, the truck was already past him. He made a futile gesture, pointing his Glock at the rear end of the Peterbilt, but soon realized that this was of no value. The only thing he could do was report the disaster to the command post via his portable radio so they were aware of what the racket was about and that the fugitive was onboard the PennDOT truck.

In the terrified tone of a man shaken by a scene right out of a Hollywood movie, the officer made his report, "7-45 to command post…I just had a PennDOT truck run over my squ-a-a-a-d!"

The officer's voice made it clear that he was unnerved.

"The homicide suspect is inside on the passenger side. It appears that he carjacked the truck, the PennDOT driver is still at the wheel!"

Officer chubby paused a moment as he let his thumb off the transmit button and collected himself. Then he stated the obvious in the general direction of the lumbering Peterbilt truck. "He is headed south. Look out, he isn't going to stop," like a line from any one of the Godzilla movies.

After making his obligatory report, the chubby officer, still lying on the pavement, looked up at his mangled police car. Taking in the scene of destruction, he saw his squad car mangled. The radiator was steaming into the air, both of the front tires were deflated, the driver's side front fender was popped off the body and lying on the street, the red and blue light bar was ripped off the roof and dangling over the driver's side. The lights were hanging by the thick electrical wire which miraculously still had power flowing to it and continued to rotate, flashing red and blue just as they had been before the incident.

Surveying the wreck of his squad car, he brought the radio shoulder mic back up to his mouth. "And send me a flatbed," he requested without emotion.

JJ looked in his driver's sideview mirror and smiled when he saw the chubby cop lying on the side of the road and his police car flattened like a pancake. A little pay–back, he thought to himself. He turned to look over at G to see what he was doing, relieved that all the jostling had not caused the gun to go off in his crotch. He could see G straightening up in his seat, attempting to recover from being bounced around in the cab after JJ took the Peterbilt over the cop car. He could also see that G still had the gun in his hand and any thoughts of slamming the brakes on and physically confronting this guy were out for the moment. The black guy was moaning though, as if he had been injured from being thrown around in the cab. JJ realized that Gs face was bleeding profusely. There was blood running down the collar of the quilted oversized coat that he was wearing. He also saw that this criminal was holding his left side with both the gun hand and the empty one, groaning in pain. JJ thought that the gunman may have slammed against the dashboard or some other hard object during the ramming of the police car.

After a moment G regrouped, then turned back toward JJ and saw his crooked smile. G said, "You liked that country boy, didn't you? OK you got more fun coming. Now gun the engine and run the next one too." As he spoke, he reached up with his non-gun hand and grabbed the seatbelt above his head. He had a little trouble locking himself in but was able to click the mechanism into place. After fastening it, he turned back toward JJ, pointed the Colt at his side, and said with intensity, "Come on, man. Let's go. Put the pedal to the floor!"

JJ turned his gaze back to the road and the next cop car blocking his path ahead. He was still on the one-way single-lane road. The next police car was across the road, but this time there wasn't any telephone pole in the way. However there was a brick building at the corner of this intersection. The one-way ended here and intersected with the main street of this part of town. This was where the surviving businesses were located for the neighborhood, and the same street that was the scene of the earlier robbery and homicide at the liquor store.

This main street on the North side of the city boasts a variety of small businesses that cater to the local clientele. These stores include necessary services for the public such as an urban fashion store, bars, music stores, shoe stores, a check-cashing business, a tax return business, and even the local magistrate's office. Unfortunately for this neighborhood, the public mostly includes people such as junkies, prostitutes, burglars, stickup men, and the most common resident—the drug dealer.

A tax return office was the building situated on the corner next to the police squad car that was blocking the one-way street. This was a "T" intersection that JJ was facing, so if he made his way through he would have to decide which way to go. JJ looked up ahead to see the cops scrambling around behind civilian cars parked on the right side of the one-way. They were aware of the imminent danger and moving out of the roadway to get clear of the on-coming truck.

He could also see them taking up stances that indicated to him that they were aiming weapons in his direction. The residual light of the street lamps on the main street allowed JJ to make out what the officers were doing. Some were taking stances that mimicked the position a person would take with a long gun, like a rifle or shotgun. Others were kneeling behind cars, mailboxes, and light poles with their arms extended out in front of them in the common stance taken when aiming a handgun.

Either way, JJ thought he was going to catch hell. He wasn't confident in the shooting ability of cops, especially when the bad guy was so close to him and they were both in a moving vehicle. This is when JJ made a necessary decision. Even though he wanted this common criminal, probably a gangbanger, to be caught and arrested, he first had to worry about his own survival. He didn't have a chance at this point to overpower this black guy so he had to buy some time. The only way he could do this was to obey the gangbanger and run this roadblock. Later he could find an opening and deal with his captor.

Having made up his mind, JJ surveyed the scene ahead of him, shifted the Peterbilt into fourth gear, and accelerated up to forty-five miles per hour. JJ had been to quite a few monster truck demonstration shows and demolition derbies, so he knew that the best part of a car to hit when trying to get it out of your way was the back portion. This was of course the lightest part of the car since the engine was in the front. But this was also where the gas tank was located and could possibly explode after a hard impact. JJ figured that he was going to have to take his chances with the gas tank because if he didn't make it through this roadblock he would be a sitting duck for the crowd of cops who, he was sure, would unload their weapons upon the cab of his truck.

He also knew that the snow blade on the front of his truck would act as a scoop and would literally pick up the back of the police car and toss it out of the way as it did with the snow, if he hit the car right and at the proper speed.

JJ lowered the snow blade to a few inches above street-level and fixed his eyes on the center portion of the trunk area of the car that was parked broadside. Then he pushed the accelerator to the floor, bracing himself for the collision. The Peterbilt's powerful engine roared with the injection of additional diesel fuel into the turbine. JJ hit the air horn, hoping that it would warn the cops to scatter so he didn't run any of them over. It appeared to work when he saw the officers behind the blocking squad car rise up from their kneeling positions and run to opposite sides of the roadway.

SMASH!

The monster Peterbilt PennDOT salt truck impacted the Metro squad car and bull-rushed it aside. The back end of the police car vaulted violently into the air and pivoted out into the middle of the intersecting street as the tires screeched along the pavement upon coming back to earth. The overhead light bar flew off, crashing to the street. Windshield glass shattered and showered into the air, while the rear driver's side fender came free and slid down the middle of the main street, throwing up sparks as it went along.

Some cops were cowered behind cars parked on the opposite side of the main street from the collision. Others in the same area opened fire on the Peterbilt but did so on impulse and without authorization. This was a hostage situation and due care was to be taken to protect the life of the hostage. Unfortunately, the order that officers should restrain from firing could not be relayed in time due to the speed in which events were taking place.

When the Peterbilt made contact with the car, the sudden impact caused the big truck to shudder for a moment and briefly halt its forward progress. This is when the firing started. Officers opened up on subjective targets of opportunity. Some cops across the street behind the parked cars felt that they should try to hit the hostage taker sitting in the passenger seat, so they aimed for this part of the cab area. Other officers positioned to the right of the rig felt that they could best help stop the rig from proceeding much farther by shooting for the tires of the truck, so they directed their fire to these areas.

A few of the officers who were in front of the truck and shooting at the cab area managed to score a few hits on the windshield but did not hit either occupant. One bullet smashed through the center of the front windshield and sailed right between G and JJ and then passed through the rear window and flattened out on the steel body of the dump bed. Another bullet zipped just over the top of the snow blade, crashed through the lower part of the cab windshield on G's side, and buried itself into the dashboard just in front of where G was sitting. If this shot had been a few inches higher the bullet would have found its mark and the incident would have abruptly ended.

Most of the shots fired from officers in this forward position sparked, ricocheted, and made pinging sounds off of the front of the sturdy metal snow blade. An objective observer would have heard a variety of sounds produced by these bullet strikes, which created kind of a melodic rhythm.

"DINK, dank, P-I-N-G-G-G-G, dunk, dunk, dunk, DANK."

A similar scenario played out on the right side of the truck. A few officers found their target and hit the tires, but firing low muzzle velocity .40 caliber rounds and impacting the hard rubber of a huge truck tire caused the rounds to bounce off without impeding the vehicle from continuing on its way.

After the PennDOT truck recovered from the initial impact, it regained forward momentum and the driver turned the rig east to proceed away from most of the officers and continue on the main street of the neighborhood. As the Peterbilt drove away from the firing squad of police, several officers continued to crack off rounds at the truck even though their only target was the back end of the dump. The ill-advised shooters were trying to hit a small portion of the rear tires, barely visible below the mud flaps. Several bullets sparked and ricocheted off the pavement and several more sparked and pinged on the metal tailgate of the truck. Before any innocent bystanders or building occupants were hit by an errant shot, one of the commanders at the scene radioed an urgent call to the officers, "CEASE FIRE! ALL UNITS, CEASE FIRE!"

Shortly after this call, the shooting quickly petered out until finally all guns were quiet. What followed was a madcap dash by all cops in the area to their respective squad cars so they could pursue the fleeing PennDOT truck. Cops were banging into one another in their haste to reach a vehicle so they could chase down the fugitive. Hats came off, flashlights clattered to the street, officers tripped and fell to the ground, so pressing was the desire to be the first after the escaped killer.

Part of what instigated this emotional and reckless display was the recognition that a cop and a police dog had been shot by this perp. Another reason was the bruising of their collective pride for having permitted this killer to break out of the trap they had set up. If that wasn't enough, there was the fact that this guy committed murder and demonstrated quite clearly that he was willing and able to do it again if not caught as soon as possible.

CHAPTER 13

Even though the impact into the second police squad car jarred him so hard that he thought he would pass out again, G still enjoyed the sight of the snow blade tossing the car aside like a rag doll. The scene of all the scrambling cops brought a smile to his face and even inspired him to hoot out loud, "Woo-wee..." G exclaimed, then realized that he sounded a bit like a honky redneck himself, so he finished off his cheer with more of an urban, "DAMN, look at those pigs run!"

"OK country," as he had begun to call JJ, "Take the ramp to the interstate!" G pointed the .38 again at his driver, but this time only at his side and without making contact.

To reach the entrance ramp to I-279 north, JJ had to travel down this main street through the business district for about three quarters of a mile, then make a right turn to the ramp. The ramp itself was a one-way elevated single lane that curved around one hundred and eighty degrees before a gradual downward gradient onto the freeway.

The main thoroughfare was a two-lane street with curbside parking on either side. G and JJ were now traveling on the same street but in the opposite direction from the scene of the liquor store robbery and homicide. More precisely, they were two blocks east of the crime scene. The officers who were working this scene heard the commotion and witnessed the PennDOT truck crashing through the roadblock and then fleeing eastbound. The crime scene officers all looked at each other in disbelief until one of them broke the silence with a simple, "What the fuck?"

Faust witnessed the breakthrough of the roadblock also. When he heard on the radio that G was probably inside the PennDOT truck, he ran for his car to follow up on the pursuit. The scuttlebutt had reached Faust that this perp was a possible witness to the Ruggerio shooting. He wanted to be there when this guy was cornered, if possible to ensure that G didn't live to tell what he saw at Bartlett Park. Faust reasoned that he had come this far in securing the fate of Ruggerio, so there was no turning back at this point.

Queeny put the squad into drive then accelerated in the direction of the one-way street where the PennDOT truck had last been seen. At about the same time, Ruggerio flipped the toggle to activate the overhead lights; he reached for the knob and activated the siren just as Queeny wheeled the car onto the one-way ramp in the direction of the main street. The chase was on.

Queeny and Ruggerio were not the first squad behind the suspect vehicle. At this point in the pursuit there were four other units ahead of them. Since the pursued vehicle was a huge PennDOT salt truck, the task of keeping up with the suspect vehicle was not a difficult one—at least for now.

G looked into the passenger sideview mirror and saw the flashing lights of the pursuing police cars. He realized that his hastily designed plan to escape was severely flawed. He hadn't foreseen that after breaking out of the roadblocks using the PennDOT truck that backup units would be so quickly all over them and could easily follow the slow-moving rig.

G put the window down and peeked out of the passenger side to gauge how many cop cars were following. With so many lights flashing and cars jockeying for position he could only settle on a whole mess. Not only were he and JJ being chased by cops in squad cars but all of a sudden a brilliant white light illuminated the truck from above, followed by the sound of the thumping rotors from the police chopper.

G put his head back in the cab of the truck and with a tone of defeatism in his voice simply stated, "Son-of-a-bitch."

Then he looked over at JJ and urgently inquired, "Can't you make this thing go any faster?"

"This is it. I still have almost a full load of salt in the bed," JJ reported, having to shout over the mixture of police sirens, helicopter blades, and the Peterbilt's own engine noises.

This statement gave G an idea and again he amazed himself with his quick thinking.

"Dump your load," he said to JJ.

"What?" JJ replied.

"Dump your load of salt on the road," G shouted at JJ.

"What is that going to do?" JJ asked.

"Just do it man. Raise the bed and dump the load, now!" G commanded.

"OK, whatever you say," JJ answered and he pulled the floor lever to raise the bed of the truck. A motor in the undercarriage of the rig kicked on and the huge bed began to rise up in the air. G looked back to his side view mirror to watch if this new plan was going to work. They were still on the main street heading for the interstate ramp about twenty yards ahead. While surveying the dimensions of this main thoroughfare in the mirror, he began to realize that this road was too wide for his plan to be effective.

His plan hinged on the large amount of road salt in the bed. He hoped that the jettisoned mound of salt would create an obstacle that could block the cop cars from continuing their pursuit of the truck. But if the salt were dumped on this street with its two lanes of travel the pursuing cops would be able to use the opposite lane, swerve around the pile of salt, and continue the chase. Even though he hadn't thought it out thoroughly, luck— along with the light beam from the chopper—would again shine on this determined felon.

G's gratuitous timing couldn't have been any better. As it would turn out, the truck arrived at the optimum location to cause a perfect roadblock. If the bed had elevated any faster, the salt would have been dumped while the police were still on the two-lane street. Fortunately for G, just as the truck made the right turn onto the single-lane ramp leading to the interstate, the bed height reached the point where all the salt came pouring out, with the exact effect that G was hoping for.

Ruggerio and Queeny were trailing the other units following the yellow monster as it barreled down the main avenue of this business district. Ruggerio shut down the siren since some of the other units already had theirs sounding. To leave it going would have been redundant. He could see one of the lead squads maneuver to ride next to the Peterbilt on the driver's side, possibly to shoot out a tire. When Ruggerio saw the passenger side officer stick his arm and head out of the window, gun in hand, his suspicions were confirmed. When the officer fired, he hit the tire, but forty-caliber ammo is no match for heavy rubber and an over-inflated truck tire. The bullet bounced off the tire then ricocheted off the metal of the truck bed, angling the bullet path right back at the officer who had fired the shot.

Fortunately for him, the driver of his squad instinctively slowed the unit down when he heard the discharge of his partner's service pistol. This lifesaving change of speed altered the intended angle for this projectile from his partner's skull to the front A-pillar of the passenger door. When the round impacted into the door frame, both cops looked at each other and silently communicated, "Holy shit!"

Taking the hint, the driver decelerated his car, permitting several units to pass so that he and his partner slid back to the number eight spot in the queue of squads trailing the suspect vehicle. This seemed far enough away from the action that the two officers, especially the passenger, could collect themselves after their near-death experience.

When they passed his squad car, Ruggerio and Queeny looked over at the passenger officer who fired the shot to see if he had been hit. They were relieved to see that he was okay, save for the look of fright still on his face.

They pressed on, following the caravan of vehicles rolling down the avenue, colored emergency lights reflecting off the glass storefronts on either side of the street. He watched the ominous overhead beam of light shine down from the chopper like the ascent of some heavenly being, reflecting off the slick black pavement. Interwoven with this impressive light show were the blare of police sirens, the pounding of chopper blades, the roar of vehicle engines, and the occasional squeal of car tires on pavement.

Observing this show of police power, Ruggerio began to feel confident that G would not have much of a chance to elude the forces committed to his capture. He reasoned that the situation would eventually revert to a hostage incident when G finally realized that he couldn't outrun the overwhelming forces chasing him. At that point it would be a matter of negotiating to get him to release the truck driver....

This last thought restored his anxiety as he imagined seeing a sharpshooter fixing his telescopic sight on G's forehead and blasting his brains out with a .308 rifle round. If G didn't respond to negotiations then this type of force might be used to end a hostage standoff. In that event, any knowledge that G might have concerning the Bartlett Park shooting would be lost forever.

He saw something curious happening with the PennDOT truck; the driver was raising the bed of the truck. Ruggerio quickly realized the motive. He tried relaying this message via the radio but by that time it was too late; the scene deteriorated with stunning speed. Fortunately he was able to convey his suspicions to Queeny.

"Queeny, slow down. He is going to dump the salt load on the street!" he warned.

Queeny had recognized the danger herself, "I see it darlin'."

Queeny slowly reduced the speed of the squad and moved the car over to the opposite side of the street, in the lane that opposing traffic would have used if there had been any. She kept cautious pace with the others, not wanting to fall too far back because it was still uncertain what was going to happen. As other units passed by, some still with their sirens going, they watched as the PennDOT truck made the turn onto the ramp, and as the dump bed continued to rise nearly to its apex. As her squad got closer to the ramp entrance, Queeny stopped the car in the opposite lane and they both waited, while rushing police cars whizzed by them, earnestly pursuing the truck.

Ruggerio and Queeny continued watching as the Peterbilt entered the curved area on the ramp then disappeared behind a concrete pillar that supported a separate bridge deck above the interstate on-ramp. While it had been visible to Ruggerio and Queeny the truck still had not emptied its load of salt, but their suspense would be short-lived.

This location was a cloverleaf of elevated roads and bridges connecting the interstate to the local streets and to the road network city-wide. From the air, it looked as if someone had plunked down strands of cooked spaghetti on a table top. This was the area of the city where a newcomer could easily get lost. The street signs were tucked under the overpasses, so missing a sign while driving wasn't unheard of. By making one wrong turn a traveler could easily end up on the wrong side of town from his intended destination.

The type of frustration from the metro-Pittsburgh roadway system that was about to befall JJ and G along with some pursuing police officers, wasn't being on the wrong ramp and wishing that they were on the bridge deck above, but instead wishing the overpass ahead of them was not there at all.

Just as JJ negotiated the Peterbilt around the ramped curve, he could feel the speed of his rig slow down quite a bit. He realized that it was from the truck bed being raised in the air, which acted like the sail on a boat catching the wind. Only in this case, it was traveling against the wind instead of along with it. The reduction in speed actually helped him maintain control around this curve since the deck surface was very icy.

G was still checking out the pursuing cops in the side view mirror and impatiently waiting for the salt to come tumbling out to block the road. He turned back toward JJ and accused him of purposely stopping the load from dumping out of the bed.

"Where is the salt, country? I don't see it yet. Did you stop it from coming out?" he implied, again pointing the gun at JJ for emphasis.

"No, I don't know why it hasn't spilled from the bed. It could be that the salt got wet from the snow and the moisture packed the salt together in the bed," JJ explained.

G wasn't sure whether to believe him or not, but it sounded credible. "So how do you get the shit out?" G asked, shouting over the engine noise of the truck.

"It will eventually loosen from the road vibration," JJ answered.

G simply nodded his head and turned back to look in the side view mirror to see what the cops were doing.

When the driver of the first squad, directly behind the PennDOT truck, saw the bed rising, he instinctively backed off and maneuvered his vehicle off angle from the rear of the rig. Seeing only some loose salt pellets fall from the elevated dump, he sped up closer to get a better look at what the driver was trying to do. He kept his squad close to the left side concrete road barrier of the ramp as he edged closer to the truck. At this point, gravity won the tug-of-war and sufficiently loosened the salt. Just when the PennDOT truck was traveling through the sharpest angle of the curve, a large portion of the salt load poured out of the tailgate and onto the road deck.

The suddenness of the load dropping out of the bed surprised the cop in the first car. His first thought was to brake hard but since he had gotten so close to the truck and since the road surface was iced up he realized that hitting the brakes was futile. Therefore, his only course of action was to keep up with the Peterbilt and hope that he could manage somehow to squeeze past this waterfall of salt. His chances improved dramatically when he saw a section of packed-in salt still hanging up inside the bed of the truck. This large chunk of salt was positioned on the same side as his police car and was holding back about one quarter of the salt load from spilling out onto the roadway. If this section of packed material could hold back the salt long enough and he kept his car on the same side of the road between the shoulder barrier and the spilling salt, his squad just might fit through without getting buried. He changed his thinking from braking to accelerating and hoped he could thread the needle.

He realized that his space calculation was a bit off when a fraction of the packed in salt started pouring out. Luckily it wasn't enough to stop him. Salt chunks banged off the top of the car's hood, leaving large dents in the metal but then sliding harmlessly off the side of the vehicle. Some of these larger pieces of coagulated salt bounced straight up the front of his car and impacted the windscreen, cracking the glass but not breaking through. Naturally, he flinched when he saw this impact, not knowing whether this icy chunk of salt would come through the glass, but at the same time he knew that he had to keep his squad from veering toward the middle of the road and into the heavier stream of debris pouring onto the road. The combination of this thought and the instinct of closing his eyes during the impact of the solid chunk on the windshield subconsciously caused him to drift left toward the concrete road barrier until the car impacted into the wall with significant force— so much so that his driver's side front wheel began to climb the barrier, lifting this side of the police car off the road surface.

The driver's heart stopped for a moment at the thought that the vehicle might roll over, then a vision flashed through his mind of the other pursuing police vehicles crashing into his overturned squad. This moment of terror quickly passed when he noticed that the act of taking the car up onto the barrier actually helped him squeeze the squad through the small space that was left between the jersey barrier and the salt that was now completely expelled from the bed of the truck. As he jerked the wheel back toward the right and the middle of the travel lane, he found himself on the opposite side of the salt pile, still following the PennDOT truck. When he looked in his rearview mirror to see what happened to his backup, he noticed that the other officers had not been as fortunate.

What made it difficult to stop their vehicles was the slick road surface. The infamous western Pennsylvania "black ice" was neutralizing the police cars' stopping power. Since this was an elevated ramp, the deck surface could freeze very quickly. Since the asphalt is black, the ice that forms on top of it also looks black—hence the name.

The police units that found themselves on the wrong side of the makeshift roadblock helplessly slid on this ice and into the four-foot high pile of road salt that effectively stopped all forward movement. It was like a James Bond film when the secret agent, using his specially designed spy mobile, would expel some super slick substance out of the back of his car causing his pursuers to slip and slide, crashing into each other. But this was not a James Bond movie and the scene being played out would prove once again that real life was truly stranger than fiction.

The proverbial domino effect took place; since each trailing unit was following close behind the other they started to bang into each other like they were in a bumper car ride at an amusement park. If they had been driving on dry pavement, the later squads would have been able to stop at a safe distance.

The officers were not only victims of the black ice, but also another common police syndrome during vehicle pursuits: adrenalin dump. The increase of adrenalin in the system can cause a decrease in clear reasoning ability in the midst of highly charged events like this one. If not for the officers' single mindedness in staying as close as possible to the fleeing felon, they would have immediately recognized that this road surface was ice-covered and dangerous and would have exercised more caution.

Queeny and Ruggerio did not directly observe this pile-up of squad cars on their side of the road salt barrier, but they heard the sound of banging metal and shattering glass. They silently looked at each other and each hoped that none of their friends had been injured in what was obviously a serious collision.

Still on the business district boulevard, Queeny wanted to get a better look at what had just occurred on the interstate entrance ramp; she moved the squad forward about fifty feet where she and Ruggerio could get a view from the opposite side of the concrete overpass pillar. Their first sight was of the Peterbilt proceeding nonchalantly on its way around the curve of the single lane ramp, the bed still fully elevated and the yellow beacon continuing to rotate—as if it were just salting the highways of Pennsylvania without a smoking battered pile of Metro police cars just a few yards behind it.

`The second sight they caught was the first squad in the pursuit, which had managed to squeeze through the obstacle thrown down by the perp and was still in the chase, following about two car lengths behind the truck. Just as this sight provided some degree of encouragement to the two cops, their hopes were snatched away just as quickly.

In another unparalleled scene never witnessed before by any Pittsburgh Metro cop, this PennDOT truck, commandeered by the commonest of criminals again evaded its pursuers by a stroke of pure luck.

While G was watching in his sideview mirror with great satisfaction the positive result of his scheme to dump the road salt, he failed to notice what was coming next. Neither did JJ–or he would have lowered the bed of the truck immediately after the load of salt broke free and released from the cargo area. Even though JJ was not a fleeing criminal, he still had a strange fascination with seeing the police out-done by his own handiwork. The chewing out that he received by the fat cop earlier hadn't improved his opinion of the police.

JJ's realization that he had made a terrible mistake came with a sudden and violent jolt when the highest point of the raised dump bed impacted with a steel support girder of the overpass deck of a separate roadway above the interstate ramp. The truck shuddered and jumped upward and the front two tires came off the surface of the pavement for a moment. JJ instinctively applied his brakes, but the wheels simply locked up on the icy conditions and the big rig started to slide out of control.

With the combination of the speed that the Peterbilt was traveling and the strength of the object that it impacted with, the forward portion of the truck bed tore free of its mounting frame, which was attached closest to the cab area. The swivel end, positioned over the rear tires, was still holding and acted as a fulcrum while the truck bed began to somersault over the rear of the truck. The two-ton steel truck bed swung completely over and was about to come crashing down on the road immediately behind the Peterbilt.

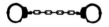

Ruggerio and Queeny watched in horror as the truck bed came down directly onto the police car that was trailing the PennDOT truck. The motion of the huge metal shell rotating backward then down on the front portion of the police car, coupled with a loud metallic screech, sounded to Ruggerio like some prehistoric beast chomping down on its prey. The weight of the bed smashing down on the hood area of the squad car caused a deafening sound of metal on metal, mixed with glass shattering and the explosion of airbags inside the passenger compartment. The impact on the squad halted it immediately at the point of the collision in the roadway and Ruggerio could see from his body position in the car that the driver appeared to be unconscious—or possibly dead.

Queeny and Ruggerio also saw that the PennDOT truck went spiraling out of control, spinning around like a huge top, after the bed shell broke free of the truck frame. The Peterbilt bounced hard off the concrete barriers on both sides of the ramp roadway, taking large chunks of concrete off the cement barricades with each impact. Finally after a complete three hundred and sixty degree revolution the monster truck slammed against the right side barrier and came to rest facing in the same direction where it had started out before the bed shell was torn off.

Inside the truck, G was screaming uncontrollably, both from fright and from the excruciating pain that was coursing through his body like a lightning bolt. At first he didn't realize what was happening. All he could understand at the onset of this terrifying ride was that something on the truck had smashed into a solid object. He felt as if he was going to vomit and possibly pass out. Somehow, he managed to stay conscious and keep his cookies down at the same time. Finally, the right side of the truck hit into the wall on the side of the ramp and the spinning stopped.

G looked over at JJ and saw that he was bleeding from his nose and appeared to be unconscious. JJ was sitting back in his seat with his head slumped over to the right side; his hat had come off and his unruly hair was draped over most of his face. Blood was dripping onto the floor of the cab from JJ's nose, which had probably smashed into the steering wheel. "Lucky I put my seat belt on when I did," G thought to himself, then realized that he better check on his pursuers.

He snapped around in his seat to survey the cop situation. He was astonished to see that the truck bed was gone. He noticed the steaming wreckage of the squad that had been devoured by the Peterbilt bed shell in the middle of the road. There was not one police car still in the pursuit. He needed to collect himself and get out of the truck and to find another form of transportation as quickly as he could. Just then, the brilliant light of the helicopter shone down on the wrecked Peterbilt truck; not all the cops were out of the chase.

"Lord Jesus," was all Queeny could say at the scene of chaos.

"I'm gonna go over there. He is still inside the rig," Ruggerio stated as he began to open the passenger door.

"You don't have a portable," Queeny warned him, meaning that he did not have a mobile radio from which to maintain contact with other police units.

"Do you have your cell on you?" he asked, knowing that he had her number on speed dial in his phone.

"Yeah, but I don't think you should go over there Guy," she warned him again, knowing that it was probably futile.

"I'll keep you informed and let the others know I'll be out here." He jumped out of the car and ran toward the ramp that would lead him to the crashed PennDOT truck.

Queeny lowered the passenger side power window and shouted to him as he ran away. "I will circle around. You call me, you hear!"

Queeny immediately removed her car radio mic from the cradle and notified all units that a plainclothes off-duty armed officer would be out at the scene of the PennDOT truck crash. She included a description of his clothing so that he could be easily identifiable to the uniform cops. This procedure may sound academic to the layperson but it doesn't always work; the problem was that some cops simply lose focus in these situations. Occasionally, patrol officers, between the radio transmission of the plain clothes officer's description and the encounter with the undercover officer, forget that he is a police officer acting in the line of duty and mistake him or her for a suspect. Fortunately, in this instance most of the cops on this assignment knew Ruggerio personally and were already aware that he was actively pursuing this suspect.

Ruggerio found the footing difficult, slipping and sliding with each step on the frozen pavement. When he reached the elevated ramp deck, both feet went airborne and he crashed down hard on his butt. The adrenalin was pumping so fast that he didn't feel anything. As he ran, he kept his eyes on the truck, watching for any movement. Since he couldn't detect any movement inside, his first thought was that G might have been knocked unconscious in the crash.

After rising up from his fall, he was on the opposite side of the concrete pillar in the middle of the curving interstate entrance ramp, the one that had earlier blocked his sight of the truck for a few moments. He moved more cautiously, not wanting to fall again on the icy surface. Ruggerio gasped as he moved among the wreckage that had been caused by the dumped salt pile.

Officers were climbing out of battered squad cars, some bleeding from injuries, sustained mostly from flying glass. Steam was rising from the engine compartments of some of the wrecked cars and the sweet smell of radiator fluid was thick in the air—a familiar odor to the veteran officers, something they routinely experienced at serious car accidents.

Ruggerio maneuvered through the jumble of cars and dazed police officers who were walking around the scene, aimlessly trying to figure out what had just happened. He decided to go right over the top of the salt pile, thinking that he should have sure footing on this part of the ramp. As Ruggerio climbed on top of the salt, he could see that the passenger door of the PennDOT truck was opening.

"Damn!" he said to himself, wondering if he would ever catch up to this elusive criminal.

The chopper pilot saw this movement also and put his light right on G as he climbed down from the truck cab onto the top of the cement barrier that the vehicle was resting against. As he stood on the barrier, G looked up into the beam of light and squinted from the brightness, momentarily holding his right hand up in front of his eyes as a shield. G closed the door to the cab and, still holding onto the outside handrail of the truck, looked down over the edge of the ramp deck into a void of space. Below was an auto salvage yard with rows of wrecked cars lined up in either direction. There was a chain link fence bordering the yard with V-shaped barbed wire attached at the top to keep intruders out.

Since there was no place to climb down onto the road deck where the truck had crashed, he needed to climb over the front of the cab area of the Peterbilt to find an area where he could descend to the road surface. G gingerly began to climb toward the front right fender of the Peterbilt, cautiously moving so as not to slip on the truck body made slick by the falling snow. One misstep or loss of a handhold and he would be falling into the salvage yard about fifty feet below.

Ruggerio, moving closer to the PennDOT truck and observing G's movements, grabbed his cell phone to call Queeny. He wanted to let her know that the perp was still active and was exiting the truck cab. He wasn't sure what was over the ramp deck, so in case G took off running, he wanted to have Queeny on the line to inform her as best he could where the perp was headed. Ruggerio hit the designated number on his touch pad, which automatically dialed her cell. He kept moving toward the felon as he put the cell phone up to his ear to listen for Queeny's answer. Simultaneously with his right hand, he removed his weapon and kept the barrel pointed down at the ground in a ready position. The perp was climbing over the front of the truck to get down to the roadway and it looked like he was taking his time about it. Ruggerio recognized that this slow progress gave him the opportunity to cover the distance remaining to the wrecked truck before the perp could climb off.

As he moved closer, he walked around the wreckage of the squad that had been crushed by the overturned bed shell. Ruggerio was relieved when he noticed that the officer inside had regained consciousness. He could hear the cop coughing from the dust particles that are expelled when the airbags were deployed. Ruggerio couldn't stop to render any aid, but he gave him a few words of reassurance as he passed. "Help is on the way, pal. Just sit tight."

Ruggerio never took his focus off the perpetrator still climbing over the Peterbilt body. He could hear Queeny's phone ringing on his handset but she hadn't picked up yet. While listening for her voice, he moved over toward the left side of the ramp onto the narrow shoulder area where gravel collects after being kicked to the side from the weight of passing car tires. He felt that his footing would be better there and he could move faster.

He was at the back end of the truck when he noticed the perp was just beginning to step off the fender area and was looking down to find a foothold on the front bumper. Ruggerio kept moving past the driver's side and still Queeny had not picked up. As he closed in on his prey, he became fixated on the perp and without thinking about it placed his still-open flip-style phone inside his jacket pocket to free up his other hand for action. Queeny's phone went to voice-mail and acted as an audio recorder to the events that were about to take place.

The chopper was orbiting above, its search light fixed on the felon climbing down from the Peterbilt. The combination of the bright light beam and the chopper blades thump, thump, thumping, made for an intimidating effect on the fleeing suspect. He knew that wherever he tried to run his movements would be tracked and that ground units would be hot on his trail. When G climbed down from the body of the truck, he simply stood in the road as if he didn't know where to go. The pilot saw Ruggerio stealthily maneuvering along the opposite side of the truck to surprise the perp. He told his co-pilot, who radioed the ground units that the plain-clothes off-duty officer was about to encounter the suspect at the crash site. The pilot could see that a swarm of backup officers was converging on the ramp. Their progress was slow due to the icy road conditions and the injured officers still waiting for treatment.

G was concentrating on not slipping and falling from the truck body instead of noticing Ruggerio. He carefully reached with his foot down from the bumper of the Peterbilt onto the road surface and instantly felt relieved that the danger of falling had passed. With the helicopter light still focused on him, he turned to run down the ramp toward the interstate where he would attempt to commandeer another vehicle to continue his escape. Suddenly, he noticed Ruggerio standing in front of him.

"Don't move Mr. Holland. I have a weapon pointed directly at you. You are under arrest for homicide," Ruggerio stated calmly and professionally, as if he were still on duty. He knew that this action was going to be strenuously scrutinized later since he was officially under suspension from the department. Like Diaz earlier, he was acting as a civilian, but his actions could still remain within the law if he conducted himself properly. Ruggerio knew that a civilian could make a legal arrest of a criminal if he has probable cause to believe that the perpetrator committed a felony, and this particular case certainly qualified. A civilian can use deadly force if he has probable cause to believe that the perpetrator has the ability and intention to use lethal force himself; this suspect had shown a high probability for violence. Ruggerio felt very confident in his words and actions, stating clearly that he was arresting G for a felony homicide and that he was using lethal force to make the arrest.

G turned toward the voice he had just heard, looked into the face of the plain-clothes cop, and immediately recognized him from the Bartlett Park shooting. His eyes widened in disbelief at seeing the very same officer who had actually placed him in this precarious position. Quickly, his look of bewilderment changed to anger when he contemplated the thought that this very same cop was about to dust off his second black man in a few short months. G quickly thought to himself that the white cop standing in front of him probably couldn't wait to squeeze the trigger on his weapon and send another nigga to hell.

"You gonna have to pull that trigger, man, 'cause I ain't goin' to your jails no mo'," G said defiantly, spitting on the pavement in the universal street gesture of disrespect toward the police.

"Listen, you do have an out whether you know it or not. That night at Bartlett Park. You were there. You saw what happened. If you testify, it can help you in your case," Ruggerio said with sincerity.

"What? I wasn't at no Bartlett Park. I don't know what you're talkin' about man." He replied as he moved back over to the truck to lean against it, feeling a bit weak from his wounds and pain.

"It can really help you out, believe me. That clerk died at the liquor store. You don't think they are going to ask for the death penalty? If you testify to what you saw at the park, you might be able to get them to drop it to life in prison, maybe with parole." Ruggerio was stretching the truth and G knew it; they might drop the death penalty but they would never let G out of jail again.

"I didn't shoot no liquor store clerk and I don't know what Bartlett Park you are talkin' about. Just shoot me and get it over with, you honky punk!" Leaning on the snow blade of the truck and slightly slumped over with pain, G's breathing was visibly labored.

"Just come with me and I'll get you fixed up. We can talk about it later. Come on, Holland." He waited for a reply but G wasn't answering. He looked like he might fall over at any moment. Then to Ruggerio's surprise he made an astonishing statement.

"I should have shot you instead of aiming in the air that night." G said, as calmly as if shooting another human being was the equivalent to making a selection about which meal to eat in a restaurant.

"So you were there," Ruggerio said more to himself than to G, putting to rest any doubts that this was a legitimate chase.

G looked up at Ruggerio with narrowed eyes, a look manufactured out of a life of poverty, prejudice, and hopelessness, and stated, "You're the murderer. You killed that boy, cold blooded just 'cause he was black!"

"No, you're wrong. I thought he had a gun and was going to shoot my partner. If you hadn't fired at me, I would not have shot that boy," he pleaded.

"You wanted to shoot him. All you cops are the same. The only reason you ain't shot me already is 'cause you want me to save your ass," G said unequivocally.

"It will save your ass too. Come on with me. We can get you medical attention for your wounds," Ruggerio said coaxingly, but received no response from G.

The back-up officers were starting to arrive, some SWAT members and other road officers. They made a semi-circle around the suspect as he was propped against the snow blade, unresponsive to the commands being shouted at him from the gathering of police around him.

"Don't move!"

"Let me see your hands!"

"You're under arrest!"

"Get on the ground you piece of shit!"

With the divergent orders shouted at him, typical in a scenario like this one, the suspect often becomes confused.

Ruggerio felt compelled to issue a warning to his fellow officers at this point. "Don't shoot him. He saw what happened at Bartlett Park. I need him to testify." He would have had no idea that this was probably the worst thing he could have said. Because when G heard this, his hatred for the police, along with his desire to never go back to the hell that was state prison, settled in his mind what his next action would be.

With the chopper still keeping its vigil above, thump, thump, thump, and the snow gently falling on the asphalt and buildings of the city, G made up his mind that this was where his miserable life would end.

Damn if he would help out this killer cop and go back to jail again, he confirmed in his own mind. He took one more look up at the bright light of the chopper and thought about something he had only contemplated a few other times in his life—whether there is a God and whether he would be seeing him soon. All the while the officers' commands were being repeated again and again since the perp wasn't complying.

G decided that he wanted to face death standing up, not cowering on the front of this truck. He stood up as erect as he could with the pain in his side and faced the firing squad of officers in front of him. All manner of weaponry was pointed at him: several Glock .40s, one shotgun, and one AR-15 rifle, more than enough to do the job. The commands continued but since G straightened himself from his slouching position as if he were about to do something their voices had a touch of nervousness.

"Don't move!"

"Put your hands up!"

"Turn away from me!"

"Get down on the ground!"

And Ruggerio's repeated pleas not to shoot his crucial witness, "Don't kill him. We have to take him alive!"

Ruggerio was taken by the arm by Katowski, who had just arrived on scene. "Guy, come on. Let the guys handle this," the sergeant requested gently.

A second officer took Ruggerio's free arm and began to walk him away. He resisted, wanting to capture the suspect without violence.

"No. They are going to shoot him. I need this guy!" he pleaded with the two officers.

They took a stronger hold of Ruggerio's arms. Katowski clamped his arm around and under Ruggerio's like a vise.

"Come on, Guy. We have to get you out of here before you get in more trouble than you are already in," Katowski said, strain in his voice as he struggled to pull the resisting Ruggerio away from the scene.

G turned and looked directly into Ruggerio's eyes, and gave him a defiant smile as if to say, "Checkmate." With his back now toward the cement barrier, he reached his right hand into his pocket where the .38 was, just as calmly and as innocently as if he were reaching for his cigarette lighter. The chorus of officers anxiously picked up their tempo of commands.

"STOP, DON'T MOVE!"

"TAKE YOUR HAND OUT OF YOUR POCKET!"

"LET ME SEE YOUR HAND!"

Undeterred, still projecting the eerie smile, and still looking into Ruggerio's eyes, G calmly stated, "That's right, bitch."

Then he pulled the empty .38 Colt from his pocket and began to raise it up, but before he could even point the harmless revolver at the officers, a salvo of weapons opened up on the felon. Nearly every officer pointing a weapon at him fired, one officer standing approximately twenty feet from G fired his .12 gauge 00 shotgun directly into the suspect's chest. The force of this blow, along with the fire from five other cops, sent G's lifeless body toppling over the four-foot-high barrier and freefalling into the salvage yard below. Along with it went Ruggerio's hope of redeeming himself.

Ruggerio broke free of Katowski's grip, ran over to the edge of the road barrier, and peered over the side, with a faint hope that his only witness might still be alive. His hope was dashed when he observed, with the assistance of the strong search light of the helicopter, that G was obviously dead. His lifeless body was positioned face up, his arms spread crucifixion-style on the roof of a junked car.

CHAPTER 14

When Tobias was brought to the scene where G had met his demise, he found Ruggerio sitting in Queeny's car, the female officer trying to console him. Queeny had worked her way around to the crash site and Katowski told her to deal with the despondent ex-cop. She arrived just after the shooting took place and witnessed the beginnings of a man going through a nervous breakdown.

When Tobias approached her car, he could see that it wasn't going very well. Queeny had the interior light on and he could see Ruggerio's face was still fixed in a trance-like expression. Queeny put the window down on the passenger side so Tobias could talk with Ruggerio.

"So we got the bastard," Tobias said as he grabbed Ruggerio's shoulder and shook it in a congratulatory fashion.

"Yeah, we got him. Full of about five pounds of lead," Ruggerio remarked dejectedly and looked back down at the floor of the car.

Tobias changed his demeanor from upbeat to consoling. "It couldn't be helped, Guy. This perp just wasn't coming in alive. It was suicide-by-cop." He realized too late that he had put his foot in his mouth but he couldn't take it back—and he couldn't change the reality of what happened either.

All Ruggerio answered was, "Yeah, a lot of that going around."

Joe Massimo came to join them. He had been called to the scene by the brass at the command post. He was assigned to handle the liaison duties for the investigation between the Metro force and the County District Attorney investigators who would be reviewing the police actions that took place after the liquor store robbery/homicide. He put his meaty paw on Tobias's shoulder as he bent over slightly to speak to Ruggerio. "Sorry we couldn't get this guy alive *cuom*," he said, using the Italian slang word for friend. "Listen, this isn't over. We got a lot more to do. You keep your chin up and don't call it quits yet, OK?"

"Whatever you say, Joe. And thanks for all your help. I really appreciated it," Ruggerio said, looking up at him and Tobias in a way that projected a sense of finality to the statement.

"Sure, kid. You just hang in there. We are going to break this thing. You'll see, *capisce?*" Massimo told him, slapping him on the shoulder again.

Ruggerio didn't respond. He just looked straight out the front windshield. Massimo turned away when he was summoned by Lt. Marks, who had just arrived on-scene. Then turned back to Ruggerio to give one more word of encouragement, "I have to go. I'm working this part of the incident with the DA guys. I'll be back." He turned to confer with Marks.

As Massimo was making his way over the ramp deck to reach the lieutenant, he caught Faust standing a distance away with his hands in his pockets, looking toward Tobias and Ruggerio. Massimo looked over in Faust's direction and saw him smiling widely and even chuckling quietly to himself. He made a mental note of this as he greeted the lieutenant.

"OK, Joe. You will be working with Detective Lewis from the DA's office on this part of the incident. From when the perp made his escape from the safe house to this point where he was shot by our guys, OK?" the LT said succinctly.

"Fine. I've worked with Lewis before. Where is he?"

"Back at the safe house working that side of it. Maybe you can start here then meet up with him later to compare notes. The County Forensics Unit will be here soon to collect the evidence," he concluded, then turned away to deal with the myriad of other issues that he was going to have to resolve that come with an incident of this magnitude.

Now, Massimo thought it was time to deal with Faust. When he saw the arrogant smirk on Faust's face at the expense of the misery that Ruggerio was experiencing he just couldn't let it pass without responding. He was now over his fear of political repercussions that may result from a show of defiance toward the well connected Faust. Massimo was not built like that, this guy had to be dealt with or he will just go on and destroy other good officers in the future.

As he approached Faust, who was still thoroughly enjoying himself, observing the misery of his nemesis from afar, Massimo met Faust's eyes as he stopped within two feet of the heavy-set detective.

"What do you want?" Faust asked, with a touch of disdain.

"Just wanted to let you know that I will be working the officer involved end of this thing. Anything you need for your half of the investigation, go through Lewis with the DA's office, OK?" Massimo said, clearly projecting his contempt for his colleague.

"Uh huh, fine. Anything else?" Faust replied.

"Yeah, just one more thing…" Massimo edged closer, nose to nose now, internally wanting to strike the evil detective. "You ever want to meet sometime after work, just let me know. I would really enjoy that," he concluded, looking into his opponent's eyes and seeing fear in response to his challenge.

When Faust didn't respond, but actually looked away from Massimo's intimidating gaze, he turned and walked away to find Lewis and start his investigation.

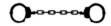

Tobias and Queeny privately discussed involuntarily committing Ruggerio to the hospital for mental evaluation since they were afraid that he might want to hurt himself in the state he was currently in. They went over to speak with Lt. Marks about this possibility. He agreed and told Queeny to take Ruggerio to the station and start the paperwork for the commitment. He then turned to Tobias and told him to go to the station house also and wait there until Marks was through at the scene. He wanted to talk with him about what had taken place. Tobias knew that he was about to be suspended and wasn't surprised; he had been well aware of this possibility when he engaged in this adventure to clear Ruggerio's name. He was willing to accept the consequences with a clear conscience, but anxious about what his future could hold.

Tobias went to the squad car that was assigned to transport him to the station. He got inside with the officer operating the vehicle. Just as they were about to pull out, Queeny waved at them to stop. "He's gone. Guy is gone!" she told Tobias as he sat in the squad. "When I went over to my squad he was gone," she restated.

"Shit!" was all Tobias could say.

Queeny reported her discovery to Lt. Marks and a half-hearted search was conducted for the missing Ruggerio, but to no avail. Marks's statement was that all the manpower was exhausted working the two enormous crime scenes that were still many hours from being declared secure. For his part, Tobias was ordered to go to the station and not participate in the search. He tried Guy's cell but did not receive an answer and left several messages on his voice mail but did not receive a return call.

After waiting a few hours, Tobias saw Marks return to the station and was given the inevitable news. He was under suspension without pay until a disciplinary hearing could be held to decide his fate. He handed over his badge and gun, then without comment left the station house to look for Ruggerio on his own.

He checked Ruggerio's house but did not find any trace that he had been there since they had picked him up earlier in the evening. He even went to Bartlett Park to see if Ruggerio might have gone there out of some emotional need to be at the place where this whole mess had started, but he wasn't there either. After aimlessly searching the streets for hours, without any luck, he decided to go to the hospital and see how Diaz was doing.

When he got there, the sun was coming up in a virtually cloudless sky; the snow had stopped a few hours before dawn. Tobias was glad to see the sun. It seemed to wake him up a bit as he had been awake for over twenty-four hours. He walked through the automatic sliding doors of the emergency room and asked the admitting nurse about Diaz.

She told him that Diaz was in surgery now and would be there for about another hour. Since she was familiar with Tobias, having seen him many times in the past bringing in injured arrestees to the ER, she told him in confidence that Diaz should come out of this just fine. The bullet had not hit any vital organs, but there was one complication. The bullet had nicked his large intestine and was leaking waste fluid into his system. This fluid was infectious and if it was allowed to spread throughout his body it could kill him. Diaz had to be placed in a comatose state so his body could remain motionless for an extended time to reduce the chance that the infectious cells will spread. This would give the antibiotics a chance to fight the infection to the point where his body could take over and complete the removal of these detrimental cells.

Therefore, when Diaz came out of surgery he would not be able to speak with Tobias. The comatose state could take up to one full month until Diaz could be allowed to regain consciousness, she concluded. Tobias thanked the helpful nurse and left to continue his search for Ruggerio, at least until the exhaustion got the best of him and he would have to rest.

Massimo and Lewis worked their end of the case the remainder of the night and well into the morning after the sun rose on another cold December day. Massimo had worked with Lewis before and the two detectives seemed to go together well. Jefferson Lewis was a black cop who stood about five foot ten with an average build, not too fit but not completely out of shape either. He was forty-nine years old—a few years older than Massimo—but he wasn't showing any gray in his nearly-buzzed hair or on his neatly-trimmed beard. He had high cheekbones that at first glance gave his face a boyish quality, but this youthful appearance was marred by the presence of dark brown skin tags that peppered each cheek.

Massimo often thought that it must be difficult to shave without slicing some of the tags off and causing quite a bloody mess. Maybe he uses an electric razor, Massimo concluded as he watched the crime scene guys photograph G's dead body lying frozen on the roof of an old junked car." Man, they really pumped a lot of lead into this poor bastard," Lewis said to Massimo.

"Yeah, they killed him a couples times over," Massimo replied.

The medical examiner wanted to know if it was alright to move the body. Lewis told him that they were finished and his crew could bag up the remains. The two detectives had coordinated a search of the scene and completed preliminary interviews of the officers that were involved in the shooting. They had found the .38 that G used to kill the liquor store clerk and to shoot Diaz. The gun was discovered in some snow that had collected inside the circle of a discarded old tire found lying in the salvage yard. They planned on tracing the owner of the gun to find out how G had gotten his hands on this weapon. This was of particular interest to the detectives since G was a felon and therefore prohibited from owning a firearm. They were anxious to find out who had provided this criminal with the instrumentality to wreak all this destruction that had just taken place.

Now they were about to head back to the station house to conduct more in depth interviews of the officers involved who had been ordered to stand by at the office until the detectives could return. This also provided time for the officers to obtain legal counsel from the police union, which was standard procedure in cases like this. After this was accomplished, the two detectives agreed that they would call it quits for a while and go home to get a few hours of much-needed sleep before meeting up later and continuing the investigation.

There would be much more information to compile before they could declare this shooting justified and complete. For example, a wealth of information was contained in the tapes and transcripts of the officers' radio transmissions. This data would be compared against the officer statements to see if the two sources of information corroborated one another. Then the detectives would spend hours, if not days, comparing the ballistic reports with the autopsy results to see if this data coincided with the officer statements. This is why the original officer statement – usually placed in report form – is such a crucial source of information to the investigators, and the reason officers involved in shootings request legal advice before providing this statement.

Before they could leave the crime scene however, another source of information that would dramatically change the emphasis of this investigation was about to be presented to the two detectives. As Massimo and Lewis were walking back to their respective unmarked police vehicles, they were halted by the familiar voice of Queeny Walker calling out to them from a distance. "JOE! Wait up! I have something for y'all."

When Massimo and Lewis turned back they saw the chunky female cop with one of her arms raised in the air, waving to them to wait. Queeny was moving as quickly as her body would allow. Her arms bent and heaving similar to a competitive speed walker. Only in Queeny's case—well it just didn't look quite as graceful. Since her thighs were so large, her uniform pants rubbed together with every stride, creating a sound, "Vip, vip, vip."

The way Queeny was walking, it was apparent to the detectives that she had something important for them. She approached them with her cell phone held out in front of her and stated, "Wait 'til you hear what's on my phone."

"What is it, Queeny?" Massimo asked.

"Vip, vip, vip...." She stopped near the two detectives, brought her cell in front of her face and started punching buttons on the touch pad. "Just listen to this. Guy must have left his phone activated when he called me. I missed his call and it went to my voice mail," she explained.

Queeny put the phone back up to her ear and listened for a moment, then handed it to Massimo. He started to listen, his facial expressions showing that he was intently absorbing the recording. He didn't say a word except for the occasional, "Holy shit!"

Lewis was watching, anxious to find out what the recording was about. After Massimo removed the phone from his ear, he handed it to Queeny and said, "Make sure you save this and we need to get this dubbed right away."

"What is it?" Lewis asked impatiently.

"Only the proof that will clear Ruggerio and Diaz from the Bartlett Park shooting, that's all. This Holland guy admits to being at Bartlett Park and witnessing the shooting. He said to Ruggerio that he should have shot Guy instead of shooting up into the air. This fucker was there and witnessed the shooting. He must have fired a shot into the air to scare the cops or something. That is what Ruggerio and Diaz heard that made them think the perp they were after fired a gun."

Lewis simply replied, "I'll be damned," then turned to Queeny and asked, "Could I listen to that real quick?"

Queeny reset her voice mail and handed the phone to Lewis. After he finished and handed the phone back to Queeny, he said, "I have a mini-recorder in my car. We have to preserve that right away." Lewis turned to retrieve his recorder.

Massimo added a second thought, which made Lewis stop and turn back. "Yeah, and someone needs to find Ruggerio."

Nothing further needed to be expressed. Both Queeny and Lewis knew what he meant and both nodded their heads simultaneously in agreement.

After Lewis made the recording of the voice mail he asked, in a diplomatic manner, if he could please have Queeny's phone as evidence. The district attorney's office would want the original recording since the tape recording would not be admissible in court. Even though it was an inconvenience, she understood and handed the phone to them, after demonstrating how to retrieve the voice mail. She also added that she would go straight home and bring back the charger for the phone, since it would eventually go dead and need to be recharged. She said, "When we find that runaway dago he owes me a cell phone."

"I think he will gladly replace your phone," Massimo replied.

He jumped into Lewis's car for the ride to the district attorney's office. The interviews with the cops that were involved in the shooting would have to wait. Priority dictated that this development was more urgent, taking into account that Ruggerio was in a bad way and would probably need the reassurance of the DA that his case could be reopened.

After he called the DA and advised him that they had vital information in regard to the Bartlett Park shooting, Massimo called Tobias and told him the same thing. He also inquired as to the progress in finding Ruggerio. Tobias reported, "I can't reach him on his cell and he is not at home. I'm worried, Joe. I don't know what he will do."

"I know. Keep looking. I'll let you know what the DA says," Massimo answered and disconnected the call.

Lewis wheeled the car around a corner, squealing the tires and zipping through some early morning traffic, showing his urgency in getting to the DA with this new information. He looked over at Massimo and stated something that both detectives had been thinking but were too afraid to say out loud. "Joe?"

"Yeah," Massimo acknowledged.

"What chances do you think that this voice mail will make the DA drop the charges against Ruggerio?" he asked gently.

"Not much. We need to find something to corroborate this recording. With this guy G dead, we sure can't get him to testify and the courts probably won't accept this tape without being able to cross-examine the contributor of the information. As you know this tape will be viewed as less than credible. A judge will simply say that G could have made the whole thing up for the shock value during the standoff on the ramp," he concluded.

"Sorry, Man. I just wanted to see if we were on the same page," Lewis replied.

"I know, but I do think that we can persuade the DA to reopen the case and maybe with more resources we can come up with something that will support this tape," Massimo said.

Lewis, in a tone indicating that he thought that it was not very possible, answered, "Yeah, like if we find a spent round in the Park that matches this .38 the perp was carrying."

"You may have something there …" Massimo turned and looked at Lewis, then stated, "It won't hurt to look, will it?"

After their impromptu meeting with the DA, both detectives emerged from the courthouse building onto the sun-bathed sidewalk headed back to their car. The rare winter sunlight would have started to melt the snow that had fallen over night if the temperature wasn't so cold. Lewis held his hand up to shield his eyes from the sting of the brightness. Not having slept for several hours and just coming out from the near windowless building made him sensitive to the brightness. Massimo had the same reaction and saw his case partner's reflex to the light. "I know, it reminds me of when I pulled double shifts, midnight-daylight, remember?" he said to Lewis.

"Do I. When you start getting a little older double shifts are more painful than a root canal," Lewis replied and both detectives chuckled at the accuracy of his observation.

"Yeah, but it's all for a good cause. At least we were able to persuade the DA to reopen Ruggerio's case. Now if we can just find him he can hear the good news," Massimo said.

"What if we try to triangulate his cell?" Lewis asked.

"Good idea. I'll call my guy that works computer crimes. He does it all the time. He can obtain an exigent circumstance warrant and track Guy's cell phone. Only problem is Tobias said that he couldn't reach him on the cell. If Guy has it turned off, the track won't work—but it is still worth doing in case he turns it back on at some point."

Massimo removed his own cell from his belt and called the computer crimes tech to start the paperwork on the warrant for Ruggerio's cell phone. Both detectives continued their walk along the busy morning sidewalk in front of the courthouse, Massimo dodging courthouse workers hustling to get to their jobs as he spoke on his cell to the computer tech.

After he disconnected he looked at Lewis and said, "OK, he said that he'll drop what he is doing and apply for the warrant. Now if you are not too tired I have an idea on locating that round from the .38 in the park."

"Let me stop for some go-go juice and I'll catch my second wind," Lewis answered as they both got into their unmarked car. "What's your idea?" he asked.

"I'm going to call Tobias back and have him meet us at the park. He will know exactly where Ruggerio and the perp that he shot were standing at the time the shooting took place. If we can come up with a likely location of where G was when the shots went off, we might be able to figure the angle that his round traveled. Then maybe we'll have a general area to search for the spent round—unless of course it was fired into the air. Then we are on a wild goose chase," Massimo replied, ending on a flat note.

Lewis, realizing that it was a worthy exercise, remarked, "Like you said, it's for a good cause. Let's give it a try."

Tobias didn't want to meet Massimo at the park. He was too concerned with finding Ruggerio at this point, but was willing to verbally explain where all the actors had been positioned at the time of the shooting. He told Massimo that he had gone over the scenario with Ruggerio and Diaz so many times that he knew the chain of events as well as they both did. He suggested that Massimo call him back when he and Lewis got to the park. This way, Tobias could help orient the two detectives to the specific area of the shooting scene. Massimo thought this was a good plan and promised to call back.

He also told Tobias that he would call the state police to assist in the search for Ruggerio. Tobias told him not to bother—that this had already been done. By now Ruggerio's picture and description was in every police station and state police barracks in Western Pennsylvania. Also, the media had been alerted and included this story on their morning television broadcasts. Everything possible was being done to find the distraught ex-cop, Tobias explained. He told Massimo that both the Metro and State Police choppers were searching the immediate area around the incident site from last night. They had even called out the local National Guard to lend manpower to conduct a grid search in the area.

Tobias ended by saying, "Everything is being done that can be." He sounded exhausted to Massimo.

"Then there is nothing that you can do. Why don't you hit the sack for a while? I'll call you if anything comes up," he reassured Tobias.

"I will after we find Guy, but thanks anyway." He disconnected the call.

Lewis and Massimo parked a short distance away from the shooting scene at the park and wanted to approach the area in the same direction that Ruggerio and Diaz had on that night. They started at the very end of the Bartlett Street where the two uniformed cops had been on that night and walked along the street up to the dumpster near where they had parked their squad. At this point, Massimo called Tobias back and started describing the scene around him.

Tobias went through all the movements that Ruggerio, Diaz and the perp had taken up to the moment that the shooting had taken place. He knew the sequence verbatim. He explained that Ruggerio told Diaz to flank around the suspect, to find a large tree to use as cover, and to keep in mind the cross-fire possibility. He explained how Ruggerio quietly crept along the parked cars until he got within approximately twenty feet of the actor, about six parked cars from the next cross street on the lane that he was on. The suspect was standing near the second or third parked car from the intersecting street. Then he saw the perp point something at Diaz. At the time he hadn't been sure what it was, but when he heard the shot and saw a flash from the object in the perp's hand, he thought it was a gun and he fired. Later, of course, he found out that the object was probably a cell phone and the flash was the light inside the phone that activates when a call is received.

Tobias stated that after the shooting Ruggerio told him that it seemed upon reflection that the shot fired sounded like it had come from somewhere behind him. Massimo thanked him for his information and told Tobias that he and Lewis were going to look around a bit and he would call back if they found anything.

Massimo had placed Tobias's voice on the speaker so Lewis, who didn't work the Bartlett Park shooting case either, could listen to the details. Massimo carefully depressed the speaker button with a gloved finger to disable this function and closed the lid of his flip phone to disconnect the call. The sun was now behind a large cloud mass and probably wouldn't show itself the rest of the day. The two detectives were both dressed in their three-quarter length woolen winter coats that ended at about mid-calf. This was a necessity since the temperature was now in the twenties. But their professional clothing looked out of place for this neighborhood and they were well aware that many eyes were on them.

Both detectives walked up past the dumpster to the area where they thought that Ruggerio had been standing at the time of the shooting, as described by Tobias. Massimo mimicked the shooting stance that Ruggerio would have taken at the time that he fired his shot at the suspect. As he remained in this position, he directed Lewis to the positions of the other actors who were there on that night. Then the two detectives switched roles and Lewis took the role of Ruggerio and Massimo moved to each position that Dickson and Diaz had been in at the time of the fatal shot. The exercise was to simply get a feel for what the scene looked like on that night.

The hope was that something might strike either man as a lead on where the errant round fired by G might be located. Unfortunately, when the two investigators huddled together after their role-playing experiment, nothing of consequence was observed.

The next course of action was to conduct a cursory search of the grounds and the surrounding buildings and vehicles for the .38 bullet. Both officers knew this was another long shot but they also conceded that it would not be the first time that a crucial item of evidence was located on a follow-up search of a crime scene.

The search would be limited to what could be seen at ground level. If G had pointed the snub nose up into the air, the round might be lodged into a tree, which would take bringing a ladder out to the scene or maybe a truck with a lift on it. Or, what if G had fired the shot on a downward trajectory? The round may have buried itself into the grassy earth of the park grounds. This would take the use of a metal detector. Both search options would have to wait for another day; for now they would do what they could and conduct a search of the area by foot. At least they knew that the shot came from an area to Ruggerio's rear at the time of the shooting. From this area, general angles of trajectory could be extrapolated then searched.

Lewis told Massimo that he would check out each tree that could have been the path of a round fired at shoulder height. He explained that he appeared to be the same or close to the same height as G, and this would help in checking the correct height of the tree trunks. Massimo would check the car bodies, buildings and any other objects that could still contain a spent .38 round fired three months ago. It was unlikely but they both thought it was worth a try. As they started, Massimo's cell buzzed on his hip. It was the computer crimes tech.

"Joe, we have the warrant and made the first ping of Ruggerio's phone," he began.

"Anything?" Massimo asked with expectation.

"Nothing. He still has it off. But we will keep trying. The phone company will ping the cell every fifteen minutes to see if he reactivates," explained the tech.

"OK, thanks. Let me know," Massimo replied, and went back to his search for the spent round.

Lewis walked over to Massimo, who told him what the tech had said. As Lewis nodded acknowledgment he said, "OK, before I start tramping through the snow, I have to get rid of the coffee we just had. I'm going in the alley behind these row houses for a quick whiz."

"Don't dangle too long. There are some hungry stray cats in that alley," Massimo remarked with a grin.

"Not to worry. As cold as it is the shrinkage factor will protect me." Both cops chuckled.

Lewis saw a walkway between the last row house at the end of the line and the two-story dwelling beside it. He decided that he would take this walkway to reach the alley behind the row houses to relieve himself. Upon reaching the alley, having walked through a few inches of snow that had not been removed from the walkway, he noticed an area where he could semi-privately take care of his bodily needs. Toward the last few row homes was another garbage dumpster in the alley and a telephone pole positioned next to it. He could squeeze between the two for some privacy, which he did. He quickly began to urinate into some snow that was lying on the ground, turning it a bright yellow, like lemon Italian ice. How ironic, he thought to himself. He looked up at the back wall of the row house that he was standing next to and noticed that it was probably vacant, evident from the boarded up window that he saw just above his head.

Then his cop's spidey sense began to tingle, like a wild animal that uses instinct to hunt or protect itself from predators. Most bystanders would view this same scene he was standing by and not think anything about it, but to an experienced investigator this all meant something when pieced together logically. He looked down again at the ground and saw a heavy plastic bucket that was turned upside down on the opposite side of the telephone pole. The base of the bucket was absent any accumulation of snow, which was odd. If this bucket had been sitting here all night there should be snow piled up on this flat surface. He noticed fresh shoeprints in the snow next to the pole and dumpster.

As he continued to empty his bladder, melting the snow in his stream of hot liquid, he looked up at the plywood covering the window on the house. He saw that it was slightly askew and he tried to move it but couldn't get his fingers between the wood and the recessed brick work around the window frame. He finished his nature call and zipped up. Then he looked around the border of the wood and saw a small area that had been chipped away near the top of the plywood section. He hit the rectangular piece of wood with the palm of his hand and noticed that it was loose. His suspicions were confirmed. It was a crack house probably for addicts to go and smoke up their rocks, or maybe take shelter from the cold.

They use the overturned bucket as a step to get up on the dumpster, then the chipped out area of the plywood is a finger slot to pry the wood section out from the recessed brick. This could be another location from which G had seen what was taking place when the shooting happened. He took note that this house was the third one in from the walkway that he had taken to reach the alley and then he quickly went to tell his case partner of this discovery.

He knew exactly where he was going and what he was going to do when he got there but how he was going to get there was the question. He had to travel probably two to three miles away, and if he tried to make it on foot he would be discovered before too long. His head start would not be a significant one. They were sure to notice that he was missing very soon.

Ruggerio needed a ride to get out of the area and to his intended destination. Luckily, Queeny had left him alone in the squad so he could slip away undetected, for the time being. He made his way down the entrance ramp onto the interstate and crossed the median to the opposite side, which were the south bound lanes that headed into the city. Next, he tried hitch-hiking to catch a ride but there were no takers. His shoddy appearance, meant to help him blend into the crime-ridden streets, was working against him, until a lone car pulled from the freeway to the side of the road ahead of him and stopped. The driver waited there until Ruggerio jogged up to the passenger side.

The vehicle was an old run-down Chevrolet Caprice, the kind of car the cops used to drive in the early '90s. It was white but the paint job had faded drastically to gray, and rust spots had developed on the rear quarter panel on the passenger side. Ruggerio opened the door and was about to get in when the driver, a older-looking black male, stopped him. "Hold it, Man. I'll give you a ride if you got some money. This ain't a free lift," he said curtly.

The interior dome light showed that he was very thin, skeleton-like with dark skin that showed deep crevices around his mouth. His skin tone contrasted with the graying facial hair, which appeared to be a several–days' growth. When he spoke, Ruggerio caught a glimpse of his tarnished teeth. He also noticed that he couldn't say more than a few words without having to make a lip smacking sound. Ruggerio could see that his lips were severely chapped, with telltale flakes of white crusty skin. He quickly surmised that the driver was a crack head and that this was a jitney car.

The metro area was full of these drivers. They undercut the commercial taxis by charging reduced fares so they could earn some money to support their crack habits. They were unlicensed and illegal but this didn't stop them from operating, they filled a service that was in demand for the drug addicts and occasionally for drug dealers. Since they had vehicles, usually in their own names, and voracious crack addictions, drug dealers could get cheap transportation from one point to another in exchange for a few rocks of crack cocaine.

Ruggerio saw a good opportunity. "I got some money. Can you take me to the overlook?"

The driver didn't answer immediately. He just looked over the prospective fare standing in front of him and continued to smack his crusty lips together making a motion with his mouth that closely imitated that of a horse eating grain. Ruggerio deduced that he was inspecting him to see if he was a cop or not.

Then the driver finally said something,

"How'd you get that burn …*smack, smack?*" he asked Ruggerio, pointing to his own neck and mimicking where Ruggerio's burn mark was.

"An accident," was all that he replied.

Then the driver stated, "Did your stem blow up on you… *smack, smack?*" He chuckled at his own humor, showing the browned teeth in his mouth. This statement meant that he now believed that Ruggerio was a crack user and safe to give him a ride. This was due not only to the burn mark on Ruggerio's neck, but to the unhealthy sunken appearance of his features, which was the result of a disregard for his health over the last few months.

Then the driver quickly got back to business, "Let me see your cash. I'll need ten bucks to take you to the Overlook… *smack, smack.*"

Ruggerio took out a ten-dollar bill and held it out for the driver to see.

"OK, get in," he said, then took the bill from Ruggerio.

Ruggerio slid into the passenger seat and was quickly overcome by the stench of the interior of the vehicle. It was the familiar smell of cat piss that cops routinely experience upon answering calls in low-income homes, where cleaning a house is as foreign as planning a family vacation to the beach.

Ruggerio didn't care about the odor. He just needed a ride to the Overlook and this was his only means of getting there. As the jitney driver pulled back onto the freeway, Ruggerio began to replay the events of the past three months in his mind and came to accept finally that his fate was assured. He was not going to clear his name and was sure to be convicted of the charges against him. This meant that he would certainly go to jail and be humiliated. His whole family would have the indelible stigma of shame cast over them for their entire lives.

Everything he had worked for—his career, his dream of being a successful police officer, held in high regard by the community and his fellow officers, was now destroyed with no hope of ever recovering his integrity. The ultimate injustice of the whole affair was that the evil Faust was going to prevail. He just couldn't live in a world where this kind of person could freely and easily destroy someone's life and that of his family. He needed to make the situation right, if not for himself then for his family's sake.

"*Smack*...what you want to go to the Overlook for, *smack, smack*...there ain't no dope up there, *smack, smack*," the driver inquired, interrupting his thoughts.

"That's where I live," Ruggerio lied.

"I don't take too many people to the Overlook... *smack, smack*." The driver looked over at Ruggerio quickly and remarked, "*Smack*... Man you don't look so good...*smack, smack*."

"I'm OK," Ruggerio answered, staring straight ahead into the cracked vinyl of the dashboard.

"*Smack, smack*...we all got troubles Man, *smack, smack*..." the driver said. He continued, "You see this jalopy I drive, *smack*... this is where I sleep. I got no place except this here junk car...*smack, smack,* so you think you got troubles." He took the interstate exit with the road sign indicating it was the route for the Overlook section of the city.

"No, Man. I said I was OK," Ruggerio replied in a detached manner.

"*Smack, smack*...I ain't had a house for three years now, livin' out my car, squattin' in vacant buildings...*smack, smack*... gettin' robbed by these low life crooks out here and stopped by the PO-lice all the time, *smack, smack*... It ain't easy," the driver stated.

"Why don't you quit using?" Ruggerio asked.

The driver burst out in an uproarious chuckle underscored by a rasping that came up from his smoke-damaged lungs, "Yeah, just quit, just like that, *smack, smack...*" he said, amused. "Why don't you...*smack?*"

Ruggerio didn't reply. He just turned back toward the cracked dashboard.

"*Smack, smack...*that's right, you can't. You know it and I know it, *smack, smack...* This is our disteny," he mispronounced the word. "We are always going to be crack fiends and that is a fact, *smack, smack...* You may as well learn to live with it, Man," he proclaimed, as if he was imparting some valuable wisdom to a younger protégé.

But to Ruggerio his words did have some meaning. His destiny was set and he knew what he had to do now. There was no other choice. Just like the old jitney driver, he was trapped in an uncontrollable addiction and there was no recourse but to simply play it out until his heart stopped beating. Then maybe he would find peace in the afterlife, if there was one.

His religion told him that there was, but there were also requirements upon entering this world and suicide was one sin that kept the gates to heaven closed for the departed. Maybe there was an alternate existence alongside heaven for someone who had circumstances on earth that forced his hand into committing suicide?

God had to recognize that he was now in a position that was untenable and he could remain here on earth no longer. How could anyone withstand the terrible fate that was waiting for him and his loved ones in the near future? There was no possible alternative. He couldn't live through the agony and shame that would devour him and his family. God had to know this.

It was just like the old man said. Just learn to accept it. It was your fate, Ruggerio concluded as the jitney stopped at the Overlook for him to exit. He said, "Thanks."

The old man replied, *"Smack, smack…no, thank you,"* as he held up the ten dollar bill. He brought the folded bill up to his crusty lips and kissed the money, then said, "With this I can buy myself paradise for twenty minutes…*smack, smack.*"

Ruggerio exited the Caprice and closed the creaking old door behind him. As the car drove away, Ruggerio walked over to the parking lot, a place he liked to visit occasionally while on patrol and where he had taken Diaz on their first night together. He wanted to gaze out over the city one final time. He stood near the edge of the parking lot where the overgrown hillside began and looked down on the city of his birth.

The buildings were shining brightly as the lights from the tall buildings refracted off the freshly fallen snow. The glow from the lights seemed to hang just above the tops of the buildings, creating the illusion of a transparent dome covering the downtown area. Adding to the illusion was the darkness of the rivers surrounding the city center. This contrast in brightness highlighted the city's beauty.

He stood there for a long while, simply staring down at the scene and contemplating what he was about to do. Ruggerio was suffering from several physical and emotional factors at this time. His body was reacting to a lack of sleep over several days, as well as very little to eat. These symptoms would be coupled with the enormous effect of the crushing stress that he had been under for several months. When his last best hope had been snatched from right before his eyes, the will to carry on was exhausted.

Soon he began to cry, and as the tears ran down his cheeks and into his mouth, he could taste the salty liquid. He thought about his wife Sally and his friends on the force and how they were going to take his death. His father had passed away several years earlier and his elderly mother, who was experiencing severe dementia, wouldn't understand what was happening anyway. He rationalized that their suffering would be never ending if they were forced to endure the shame created by the inevitability of the trial, conviction, then a long prison term. The publicity of these events would shine the light of humiliation on them to such an extent that they could never live a normal life again. He also reasoned that after this stain became permanently attached to his name, there could be nothing he could do to remove it.

In contrast, the suffering he would cause them by his untimely death would diminish after a while. The memory of him would fade with time and eventually they would all return to a somewhat normal life again. It was the least he could do to make his last human act one that would hold some redeeming value.

He turned away from the city lights and walked back through the parking area toward the hillside across the street. It was tree grown and ascended upward approximately two hundred yards. At the top was a community of upscale homes and condos where the fortunate population of the metro area lived. The view of the city came with a price and only the wealthiest could afford this real estate.

Ruggerio began to climb a cement set of stairs that had been cut into the hillside almost a century ago when this land was not so prized by the well-to-do and when Pittsburgh was known as the smoky city. The name had been applied when the steel mills were at their peak and created tons of smog from the twenty-four hour production schedules. This smog floated into the air and hung over the town like a large black cloud. During the day, the street lights would have remained illuminated so people could find their way around. This part of town would get the worst of the smog since it was elevated, so at that time the property value was subprime.

This neighborhood had been populated by the working-class steel hunks who purchased homes in this area. Since cars were not a commodity for the blue-collar family at that time, the workers walked to their jobs if they lived close enough to the mills. Workers in this neighborhood would descend down this hillside to cut the distance that they needed to walk to their respective mills. With the factories running around the clock at full capacity, the workers climbing up and trudging down this hillside created a well-worn path. Over time, a cement stairway was constructed to ease the journey the workers had to make.

Since the demise of this industry, the stairway had fallen into disrepair and had been closed off from pedestrian traffic due to safety concerns. But it would serve the purpose for Ruggerio's mission. He was headed for a certain spot on the hillside that he had visited only a few times before, another relic from a simpler time.

It was a monument that had been erected off the stairway in the middle of the hillside. The immigrant workers who toiled in the mills were from a background that had deep roots in European Catholic religious practice. Some of the wives of the laborers had placed a monument to the Virgin Mary at this spot on the hill overlooking the mills. They would come here on a daily basis and pray for their husbands down below working in the factories. At that time, the production procedures for making steel held little regard for the safety of the laborers. Therefore, the death of a steel worker was not an uncommon occurrence, hence the reason for the women to appeal for divine protection to bring their loved ones home after their work day.

Ruggerio was headed to this monument that was still maintained by some of the descendants of steel workers who remained in this part of town. As he climbed the stairway, clutching the rusted metal handrail to keep from slipping on the snow-covered steps, the sun began to peek over the city and the three rivers that lay below. The grade was steep and the monument was situated high on the hillside, so exhaustion started to slow his climb. Ruggerio stopped once in the middle of his ascent and caught his breath for a moment, looking down on his city briefly then continuing his upward trek.

When he reached the place on the stairway where an offshoot footpath leads to the monument, he climbed over the rusted handrail. He nearly fell off when he felt the handrail quiver as his weight shifted the framework at its supporting sections. The steel tubes that held up the metal handrail were also rusted and loosened at their base by erosion of the concrete that once held them firmly in place. After jumping to the ground from the shaky handrail, he started to make his way along the footpath toward the monument. The ground was frozen hard and snow covered. No footprints were visible, indicating to him that no one had come to visit the statute recently. Ruggerio struggled to walk on the slanting and snow-covered terrain toward the statue.

Upon finally reaching the spot, he turned to face the monument that was carved into the hillside. The monument constructors, immigrants of several European nationalities, had dug out the hillside and created a level area where the statute was positioned. The leveled off portion was then covered with large flat Pennsylvania flagstone, which created a small area suitable for two or three people to stand or kneel. Against the hillside, a wall was constructed by stacking the stones on top of each other to a height of about six feet. In the center and about four feet above the ground was a concave area, where the Madonna statute was placed. The builders fashioned a shelf area for the statute, approximately two feet high by one and one half feet wide, with an arch at the top.

Ruggerio could see the remnants of hundreds of melted wax candles that had been lit over the years. Attempts were made to keep the wax cleaned but as fewer interested parties remained to maintain the monument, the wax had been left there to collect into thick mounds of red and white colored trails running down the stone wall. Along with the rivers of frozen wax were numerous trinkets of reverence left by worshipers over time: rosary beads, saint cards, pictures of deceased loved ones, dead flowers, and slips of paper with messages written on them stuffed into the spaces between the stones of the wall.

Ruggerio began to think of his own mother and the worries that she had for her husband, the same worries of the women had who worshiped at this site. Her husband had been a mill laborer like his predecessors who had erected this relic. Even though they had immigrated to this country in 1972, the Ruggerios still felt a bond with those early immigrants.

These thoughts instigated Ruggerio to reflect on an old memory. It was 1984, when he was only ten years old. He was in his family's kitchen, sitting at the table while his mother was stirring a large pot of red sauce at the stove. The memory was so vivid that he could almost detect the sweet aroma of the tomato sauce that would permeate the house when his mother cooked.

His mother placed a plate of polenta covered with red sauce in front of him, then sprinkled some grated parmesan cheese over the steaming mound. He didn't like polenta then and refused to eat the bland corn meal concoction.

"Gaetano, mangia la polenta, ti fa bene" ("Gaetano, eat your polenta, it is good for you"), his mother implored in Italian, throwing her hands up for emphasis.

"Non mi piace la polenta, voglio braciola" ("I don't like polenta, I want braciola"), the little boy said, looking up at his mother with chubby cheeks and dark brown eyes.

"Non c'abbiamo la braciola oggi." ("We don't have any braciola today.")

"Mamma, parlano inglese" ("Mama, speak English"), the little boy asked.

"Mangia" ("Eat"), she ignored the request. She was still learning the language and didn't feel confident speaking it.

"Mamma dov'è papà?" ("Mama, where is poppa?")

"Sta ancora fuori cercando lavoro, è da quando ha chiuso la fabbrica che cerca." ("He is out looking for work since the mill closed down.")

"Avremo la braciola domani?" ("Will we have braciola tomorrow?"), he asked.

"Non avremo la braciola per un po', la carne è costosa e tua padre non lavora in questo momento" ("No we won't be having braciola for sometime. Meat is expensive and your father isn't working right now"), she explained to her son. *"Siam venuti a questo paese in cerca di una vita migliore, ma ora viviamo come in Italia"* ("We came to this country for a better life and now we end up living like we were in Italy"), his mother said, and began to weep as she sat down at the table.

The little boy got up from his chair and placed his tiny hand on her shoulder to try and ease his mother's anxiety.

The memory faded and he was back on the frozen hillside. Ruggerio felt a warm tear run down his cheek and brushed it from his face. He turned toward the Madonna and knelt down to pray. He prayed for forgiveness for what he was about to do. He prayed for the protection of his friends and family from the evil of certain people in the world. He prayed that his soul would be accepted into heaven. He was so deep in his prayerful trance that he didn't notice that night had turned to day. Several hours had gone by and he was suddenly shaken from his state of meditation when a barge sounded its horn on the river.

After he prayed for a while longer, he decided that he needed to leave a message for his friends and family to find after he was gone. He took out his cell phone, called his home, and left his final message—which in effect was his final will and testament—on his voice recorder. After disconnecting the call but failing to power down, he put the phone down on the stone façade of the monument and removed the Glock from his jacket pocket.

CHAPTER 15

When Lewis re-emerged from the alleyway, he saw Massimo diligently inspecting the parked cars along the curb of the street where Ruggerio's shooting had taken place. A heavyset black woman wearing a low-cut yellow pullover top exposing deep cleavage, poked her head out of the front door of one of the row houses and shouted to Massimo. "What you want with my car?" she inquired with agitation.

In this neighborhood plain-clothes police officers were spotted with ease; this woman knew exactly who Massimo was and was not afraid to challenge his authority.

"We are investigating a shooting," he replied.

"What shooting? We got one every night up in here," she answered with a sarcastic snicker.

Massimo, seeing an opportunity, started to walk over to get closer to the woman. "This happened about three months ago…" He paused, not wanting to reveal any further information until he was close enough to speak with the woman without the worry of anyone overhearing that the shooting had involved an officer.

He knew that folks living in this neighborhood were looked upon as being distrustful, or snitches, if they cooperated with the police. If someone were to assist the authorities in helping to absolve an officer in a shooting of a black male, that person would most assuredly have the label of snitch attached to him or her. With this in mind, Massimo still needed to ask the woman if she knew anything; he realized that keeping the subject of his questioning as discreet as possible would increase the chances of this woman speaking freely.

As he reached the porch area of the woman's house he began to explain to her who he was, then he told her about the police shooting that had taken place on the street just outside her home. Lewis returned from his bladder break and joined Massimo at the front of the woman's house.

"Wasn't that the little 'Eye'-talian cop that shot that boy?" the woman asked.

"Yes it was, Ruggerio," Massimo stated.

"Yeah, I know him. He was the nice one. I never believed that he shot that boy on purpose like the paper said. What you all doin', tryin' to prove that the cop was right?" she asked curiously.

"Well in a way, yes ma'am. We have information that there was possibly another person out here that could have fired at or near the officer, making him think that the boy had fired a shot," Lewis explained.

"That don't seem very likely," the woman deduced.

"Well we have to follow up on the information. Would you have heard anything that night?" Massimo asked.

"Those other detectives already asked me back when it happened. I'll tell you what I told them. I didn't see anything," she replied. At the same time she did and said something unexpected. "But if I were y'all, I'd look into this place next door." While she was talking, her eyes darted over to her right side two times in rapid secession and she even gave a little corresponding head jerk at the same time.

Both detectives looked in the direction that the woman was indicating with her eyes, but neither one could see anything remarkable. Lewis wanted to buy some more time with the woman so they could possibly get her to explain what she was gesturing about, so he asked, "Where were you on that night, ma'am? Were you home?"

"No," the woman said. "I told you I didn't see anything. I have to go." Abruptly she retreated back into her home and closed the door.

Both detectives turned to walk away, keeping up the charade that the woman had no pertinent information just in case they were being observed. In fact, they were being watched and had been since they arrived to inspect this shooting scene. The woman had attempted to alert the detectives to the observer with her subtle gestures.

They walked a away to a point where they both felt would help protect the woman's integrity to the other neighbors and stopped to make it appear as if they were conferring about something else. What they were really doing was trying to figure out what the woman was trying to indicate to them by her actions. Lewis stood facing in the direction of the woman's house and toward the area she indicated, while Massimo stood facing his partner, making it appear as if they were engaged in a conversation. They did not have to play act, they were beginning a conversation about the woman they just had spoken with and about the vacant row house where Lewis took a whiz.

"You see anything?" Massimo asked.

"Nothing. Maybe she was just screwing with us?" he suggested then continued to explain his other observations from the alley. "While I am trying to look for something that I don't know exactly what I am looking for, let me tell you about what I saw in the alley during my piss stop," Lewis said, trying to vary the direction of his gaze so it didn't look obvious that he was looking for something in the area of the row houses.

Massimo was doing the same thing, shuffling around with his feet looking into the park area then turning toward the row houses to catch the scene quickly then back to Lewis to continue their conversation. "OK, go ahead," Massimo prodded.

"There is a row house a few houses back from this lady's house that we just talked with. It is vacant and I think it is being used by squatters. The back window is boarded up with plywood. But when I tried to move the board it was real loose like someone placed it back into the window opening to make it look like it was secured." Lewis turned in the direction of the abandoned row house then said to Massimo, "Right there." He didn't need to go into to detail on the house description. It was obvious from the boarded front windows that this building was not being lived in at the time.

"If this place was vacant at the time of the shooting, it is in the right location to fit the information G gave Ruggerio," Lewis inferred.

Massimo turned to look at the structure that Lewis was talking about and concluded, "Yeah, it's possible. And there was mention that G and New Ho were inside a house when the shooting went down. But that place is in the opposite direction from where the lady was indicating with her eyes. Like you said, she might have been trying to jack us off. It wouldn't be the first time."

Both detectives continued their little dance, stamping their feet occasionally to knock off the frozen white snow from their shoes and at the same time trying to determine what they were looking for that could help their investigation. Nothing was obvious enough to strike either officer as being relevant to the case. The scene was one of a typical neighborhood in the low income area of the city.

There were vehicles parked all along the front curb, many of which a person would expect to see in this area: low-cost economy cars that would fit the lifestyle of people with a humble budget. Then the class of vehicle changed drastically as they looked down the line of parked automobiles. A huge white Cadillac Escalade, all tricked out with oversized stainless steel rims and grill work over the front and rear lighting units. This was also typical of the urban underclass neighborhood. Each street most likely had a car like this, or several, parked on the street. The obvious conclusion would be that the user of this vehicle was a drug dealer. How else could someone living in such humble surroundings afford such a high-end vehicle? Both detectives looked at each other and were thinking basically the same thing.

"Maybe she was trying to tell us that she has a drug dealer living next to her," Massimo said.

"Could be that she may be legit. She either wanted us to know about the drug dealing or that house has something to do with the shooting," Lewis theorized.

Massimo concurred, "Yeah, she was just too sincere with the way she made her gestures. I think she was genuinely trying to tell us something."

The proverbial hunch—that mysterious skill that many police officers develop from years of experience dealing with people from all walks of life, a skill that has been part of criminal investigation since the days of the Roman Vigiles. Officers have varied degrees of ability. Some can pick out a liar after a few minutes of conversation but others couldn't tell if someone was lying if the subject's nose started to grow during the interview.

The good ones are usually the officers who aggressively investigate their cases and over the years have encountered people from every stratum of society. Having this day-to-day exposure to people and learning how each person reacts and responds to police interaction, gives this type of officer the benefit of learning how to read people. Even though it is more art than science, it can be a valuable investigative tool.

"I thought the same thing. She looked truthful to me. She said that she knew Ruggerio too, and seemed as if she liked him. I think she was trying to help him out. Why else would she stick her neck out?" Lewis deduced.

"Yeah. She doesn't know us. We could have walked right over to that drug dealer's house and said to the guy that the lady next door just told us that you know something about the Bartlett Park shooting. That would have brought a lot of misery down on her," Massimo remarked.

The officers stood facing the row houses, silent with their own thoughts, then turned toward one another and Massimo said, "We better go back to the station house and research both these houses and try to find out more about them."

"That sounds right," Lewis agreed.

The sun was shining through the naked tree branches directly on the statute of the Virgin Mary, illuminating her downcast face. Ruggerio interpreted her look as a message, telling him that it was alright, you have suffered enough, come and find peace. It comforted him to realize that he did not need to worry any longer about his problems. At that moment he was cognizant that anything he had been afraid of was irrelevant now. All the anxieties that had plagued him for these past several months were gone.

He looked up into the sunrays that were streaking through the trees and he put his hand up to shield his eyes, but the warmth felt wonderful. He thought about how long it had been since he had felt so relaxed. No one could touch him now. No more humiliation or smearing of his name and reputation. No more evil men who could destroy a young police officer's life with a simple snap of the fingers, just because they feel threatened. No more...

With that final thought, he raised the Glock .9mm, pointed it at his temple, and squeezed the trigger. The human will can only withstand so much pressure and Ruggerio had reached his breaking point. Another victim had fallen in this insane drama that was playing out simply because one highly-connected, mentally disturbed police detective could not let go of his jealousy of a colleague.

As the detectives were driving back toward Lewis's headquarters to begin their research on the two properties they uncovered, Massimo's cell phone erupted with a sudden vibration indicating an incoming call. Massimo flipped open his phone connecting the call.

"Massimo?" It was the computer crimes tech that Massimo had called earlier to have Ruggerio's cell phone signal triangulated.

Lewis, half distracted by driving, intermittently looked over to Massimo out of the corner of his eye to catch what the call was about. He heard Massimo say excitedly,

"Really? Where?" Then a short pause and Massimo remarked back to the caller, "Did you call anyone else? OK I will send a unit over there right now." He took the phone from his ear and held it in front of him looking at the display screen. While trying to find the disconnect button he explained to Lewis the content of the call. "They found Ruggerio's cell phone signal. It's on the West End near the overlook. I'll call for a squad to run over there. We better go ourselves. I don't know what condition he is in right now. He could be suicidal."

Lewis nodded in agreement and without comment pushed the accelerator down on the Crown Victoria. He knew the unpredictable nature of an emotionally distraught person. A suicidal individual is obviously not thinking rationally. Sometimes the subject may be considering that he needs to carry out the fatal act before his friends and family arrive so he will not be talked out of his intentions. Thus he may commit suicide when it appears that his hand is forced and this might happen upon the arrival of the first police unit. As a result, many police officers have experienced this scenario played out right before their eyes, as Lewis had. He knew how crucial it was to reach Ruggerio to give him the new information on his case before another cop unfamiliar with the situation beat them to the scene.

Tobias was in the process of rechecking all the locations he could think of where Ruggerio might have gone to seek refuge. He was just leaving the convenience store with the Middle Eastern owners where Ruggerio often used to stop while on duty. While re-entering his Lumina he felt a buzzing of the cell phone in his pocket. It was Massimo calling to tell him the good news that Ruggerio's phone had been reactivated and they had a fix on its location. They ended the call telling each other that they would meet at the West End Overlook.

While in route to the Overlook at near breakneck speed, Tobias repeatedly called Ruggerio's phone, murmuring to himself, "Come on, come on," willing Ruggerio to answer but every time receiving voice mail. Nearing the Overlook, Tobias raced through a red light at the base of the hill that led to the site. As cut-off drivers sounded their car horns in protest at Tobias's aggressive driving, he pushed the Lumina's engine, willing it to go faster as he climbed the steep grade toward the summit of the hill. Coming to the top, he noticed a squad car already on-scene, the driver waiting outside of his car. The cop probably had arrived shortly before Tobias and was awaiting further instructions on what he was dealing with.

Tobias recognized the cop and exited the Lumina to go over and speak with him to explain the situation. As both officers acknowledged each other with perfunctory waves, Tobias stopped dead in his tracks while walking over to the officer. He had a sudden realization why Ruggerio had come to this location. It hadn't occurred to him until he had actually arrived at the site. Tobias knew about the Virgin Mary monument on the side of the hill. He also was aware that Ruggerio occasionally visited this area while on duty and now realized that they would probably find him at this shrine.

He motioned for the officer to follow him and he ran across the empty parking lot where their cars were parked to the base of the hill. They began to scale the hillside using the old stairway that led to the top. The trailing uniform cop called out to Tobias, "What's up, where are we going?"

"Just follow me," was all Tobias said, not caring if the officer continued up the hill or stayed at the bottom. His only goal was to find Ruggerio alive and make sure he stayed that way. He thought he had a good chance of doing this, especially with the new information that the DA agreed to reopen the Bartlett Park shooting case. Tobias thought this new development should lift his spirits and give him hope for redemption.

Tobias pulled on the handrail as he climbed the snowy cement stairs. Not caring about the treacherous footing, he was taking the steps two at a time in the beginning of the climb. With the incentive of desperation fueling his body Tobias quickly outpaced the backup officer by a good twenty-five yards as they moved upward on the stairway. Frosty plumes of breath exhaled from the cops' mouths as they struggled up the steep incline.

"Guy!" he called up the hill, but received no response.

"Guy, we have new evidence. Don't do anything stupid!" he shouted, his voice echoing against the hillside and then into the valley below. Again, no reply.

As the two officers continued the climb, Tobias, now slowing and only taking one step at a time, looked upward and could barely see the monument coming into view but did not see Ruggerio yet. In the background, he could hear the screeching tires of police cars arriving at the base of the hill. Pulling on the surviving sections of handrail to assist his climb, he felt his lungs burning as fatigue and the fear of what he might find began to take over his body—but he kept going through the discomfort. He reached the level of the hill where the foot path to the monument intersected with the stairway; he paused to catch his breath for a moment and to prepare himself for what he feared that he might find.

Ducking under the handrail he began to make his way along the path, slipping and sliding as he went, grabbing tree limbs to stay upright. Once he even lost traction and nearly stumbled to the ground, only to catch himself by an outstretched stiff arm against the hillside. Looking down into the snow he could see fresh footprints that only led in toward the monument and not back out to the stairway. He never noticed the prints that had been left by Ruggerio on the cement steps, distracted by his haste to climb the hill. He felt a pang of anxiety stab against the lining of his stomach because the prints had to be Ruggerio. Why wasn't he answering his calls? Tobias asked himself, not wanting to know the answer.

"Guy?" he said tentatively as he continued to make his way toward the monument.

The first part of Ruggerio's body that he saw was the soles of his boots, duty boots that the officers wore in the winter. He was lying on his side with his back toward Tobias, motionless. Tobias didn't need to go any further; he knew what had happened. Tobias froze right there on the path about twenty feet from Ruggerio's body; he didn't want to go any closer.

Shock ran through him and he felt his legs go weak, so weak he had to drop to his knees to keep from falling and tumbling down the hillside. Tobias turned his back to the hill and dropped down on his backside, knees bent and feet facing down the slope. Exhausted, dejected, and feeling helpless, all he could do was let his head fall into his hands. He couldn't say or feel anything; it was like he was in his own dream and was powerless to do anything.

The trailing officer finally made it to where Tobias was sitting and maneuvered around him to reach Ruggerio's body, to render any aid that he could. Tobias never moved; he just sat there on the path looking down into the snow in front of him, his eyes fixed into a trance. The cop knelt over the body to check for a pulse, then quickly grabbed his shoulder mic and called for an ambulance, but he knew—as Tobias did—that it was futile.

One week and a half passed before Ruggerio's funeral. It turned out to be a scantily attended affair with only a few family members and some of his friends from the force. Of course Ruggerio's mother was there, his wife and her parents, some cousins, and a few aunts and uncles that were still living. Members of the Metro Department were even fewer in number, which is unusual for a cop funeral. But this was an unusual case, since Ruggerio was officially an ex-cop and had committed suicide. This circumstance meant the department was not obligated to recognize his death. Therefore, no emissaries were sent from the Pittsburgh Metro PD to honor this ex-officer or to comfort his widow and family members. The only members of the police community that attended were Tobias, Massimo, Lewis, and Queeny. Out of their deep respect for Ruggerio they all came in uniform, except for Tobias who dressed in a suit. He was still on suspension and forbidden to wear his uniform. Diaz of course was still in the hospital unconscious from the induced coma and unaware to this point of his friend's suicide. Katowski was scheduled to work that day; his request for a day off was denied, but he promised to drive by if he was able.

When the Catholic priest gave the final blessing, the small group of mourners slowly began to file out of the tiny cemetery chapel. Tobias gently passed his hand over the coffin lid as he walked by, as a final goodbye gesture. Queeny followed suit right behind him, then Massimo, also a devout Catholic, paused at the side of Ruggerio's coffin and made the sign of the cross, kissing the metal crucifix attached to the rosary beads that he held in his hand.

Once outside, the small group of officers all replaced their "class A" police hats and re-grouped next to the queue of parked mourners' cars, hands dug deep into their pockets for protection from the chilly air. They all stood on the cemetery road in a semi-circle for a few moments as if there should be something more to this ceremony. There was a common feeling among the officers that the funeral somehow was not complete; something was missing and they all knew what it was. Ruggerio deserved better. Even though he took his own life and was not officially a member of the Metro force when he died, the department should have done something for him. But they also knew the political reality of the situation. The department did not want to appear to show any kind of support to Ruggerio since he was still considered a criminal in the eyes of the public.

The officers said goodbye to the family and escorted them to their cars, then watched as the last of the mourners drove off the cemetery grounds. On cue Massimo reached into his vehicle and pulled out a full bottle of Sambuca, a clear syrupy licorice-flavored liquor, common to the Italian dinner table, drunk at the end of the meal as a *digestivo*. He passed around paper cups and poured a shot into each one before placing the bottle down on the asphalt cemetery roadway. As they all raised their cups, Tobias gave a memorial toast, "To our friend Guy, a dedicated cop and loyal friend. We will not forget you."

Then they all said in unison, "To Guy," and each officer gulped down the liquor.

"Mmm, that was good, how about another one?" Queeny asked Massimo while licking the remnants from her lips.

Massimo knelt down and grabbed the bottle and began re-filling all the cups. As he was pouring the liquid into Lewis's cup, Massimo broke the silence.

"Well one good thing that came out of this, if you can consider anything good about this situation, the DA officially closed the case against Guy. So that means he was never convicted of any crime."

Lewis replied, "What did the dead kid's family have to say about that? I bet they were not very pleased. What was his name…? Dickson right?"

"Yeah. No they weren't happy at all, but the DA said that you can't prosecute a corpse.

"The Dickson family will still make some serious coin with a wrongful death suit," Queeny added, and all the officers nodded their heads in agreement.

Massimo was beginning to refill the cups again when Lewis remarked, "How about Ruggerio's wife? She is out of luck, right?"

"That's right. Since Guy was fired, he and his wife lost his partial pension and life insurance benefits," Tobias replied.

"That's a damned shame," Lewis commented.

"To make matters even worse, Guy's wife just told me that she is pregnant," Tobias said.

"*Madonna!*" Massimo said.

Queeny interjected next, "We are starting a benefit fund for her and the baby, without the support of the department or the union of course."

Massimo quickly retorted, "It won't be enough. What we have to do is clear his name and then the department has to do right by Guy's wife and child. Toby and Diaz can have their records cleaned up too," he said with determination in his voice.

"OK, what do we do?" Tobias asked.

"We keep doing what we were doing. We investigate the hooker's death and at the same time we keep digging into the Bartlett Park shooting. That's if everyone is on-board here, because this would be considered an unofficial investigation and against department policy. We could all be reprimanded and suspended if they find out," Massimo said, then scanned the faces of the others for a reaction.

"I don't have anything to lose. I'm as good as fired now," Tobias replied.

"You just tell me what you need darlin'," Queeny said with conviction.

"I'm in too," Lewis said. "I didn't know Ruggerio like you all did, but I have this unfinished feeling that I need to resolve. I just can't walk away without trying to help Guy's wife and baby to be, and still sleep at night," he finished sincerely.

"I was hoping that you would say that. I could really use your help, Jeff," Massimo said as he gestured with his cup of Sambuca for him and Lewis to tap their paper drinking cups together in acknowledgement.

After they all drained their cups, Massimo doled out the assignments.

"OK, Jeff and I will work the homicide part and you guys can look into the drug dealer's house in Bartlett Park to see if there is anything of value there. Queeny this is where we can use your talents in finding informants," he commented, leaning in toward Queeny's direction.

One hour after this strategy meeting in the cemetery between the officers committed to clearing Ruggerio's name and re-instating Tobias and Diaz back to full duty, Faust walked into Lt. Marks's office and plopped down several photos in front of the bewildered lieutenant.

"What's this?" asked Marks.

"They just can't get enough. Look at these assholes drinking while in uniform," Faust answered, with a touch of pleasure in his voice.

Faust had been hiding in a concealed part of the cemetery with a camera, hoping for just such an incident so that he could start on his next target, now that Ruggerio was out of the way. Ever since he and Massimo had the encounter at the scene of G's shooting death, he made it his next mission to take him down, too. Faust's manhood had been bruised by Massimo, and the inner defects of his personality could not let this slight pass without rectifying the situation and restoring his machismo.

Just as in the issues that made Ruggerio an undesirable to Faust, Massimo was cut of the same cloth, all righteous and uncompromising. The last thing that guys like Ruggerio and Massimo consider was protecting their fellow officers. Faust felt that it was his self proclaimed duty to protect the integrity of the force so he set to work on taking down another subversive in his crusade to cleanse the police department. As luck would have it, he was able to get Tobias and the others too as they partook in this illicit cemetery party.

"What is that they are drinking?" the lieutenant asked as he perused the still photos.

"Some dago drink. Sambuca I think it's called," he replied.

Marks thought this was strange that Faust was familiar with this drink, but dismissed it and continued. "Well, what they are doing is against policy, but they were attending a fellow officer's funeral." Marks began to waffle a bit.

"Ex-officer, under homicide charges and they drove away under the influence," Faust cajoled subtly.

"I tell you what I'll do. Since you were on the mark with the Ruggerio business, I'll send this on to IA for them to deal with it, OK?"

"That's fine, boss. I got to get back to my paperwork on the liquor store mess." Faust got up from the seat and walked out of Marks's office with a vague smirk on his face, content with the job he had done this day. As he made his way down the hall and turned the corner to enter the detectives' office, he was shocked to see Massimo sitting at his desk, still in his class "A" uniform, pecking away at the computer.

Massimo looked up briefly from his work and the two cops gazed at each other, neither saying anything. Massimo quickly put his head back down and concentrated on his computer monitor and returned to typing. Faust turned around, doing a one hundred and eighty degree turn, and went back into the hallway. Since the detectives' desks were all collected into a common room and there were no other detectives in the squad room except for Massimo,

Faust did not want to sit in there with just the two of them. He made his way to the second floor break room, plugged four quarters into the pop machine, and waited for a Coke to drop out. He grabbed the ice-cold can and sat down at the wooden table in the center of the room.

He had the liquor store shooting case folder under his arm so he opened it up to make it appear to any casual observers that he was reviewing his notes from the case. In actuality the sudden and unexpected sight of Massimo had triggered a flashback to his childhood.

It was 1975. The scene playing out in Faust's mind had taken place when he was 12 years old and he was just walking in the door of his house after coming home from school. His father, a muscular steel worker, was sitting at the kitchen table wearing a white undershirt which today would be called a wife beater, his bulging biceps apparent and a scantily clad female tattooed on one arm. In front of him, a half drunken bottle of whiskey sat on the table. Faust's father appeared to be in a trance, hunched over staring down at the table top, one meaty hand around a half-full glass of whiskey. When Faust entered the room, his father slowly turned his head toward his young son then without saying a word, returned his gaze to the table top and drained the glass of its contents in one quick gulp.

Faust had seen this before and knew not to say anything to his father when he was in this condition. Better to go to his room and wait until he passed out. As he turned to exit the room and head to his bedroom his worst fears were realized when his father abruptly asked, "Where are you goin'?"

Faust tentatively turned around and said, "To my room."

"Get back here," his father commanded and the twelve-year-old dutifully obeyed, wondering if his mother had been smacked around again today. He hoped not. The brightest part of his life was his mother; she usually protected him in situations like this one and he was wandering where she was.

"Listen," he told his son, pouring himself another drink. Faust could tell that he had been drinking for awhile. His father's eyes were drippy and blood shot; the lower part of his mouth seemed to hang slack jawed and he was breathing heavily as if he had just climbed ten flights of stairs. Faust wondered if this had anything to do with the big argument his mother and father had the previous night. His father continued slurring his words. "Your mother is gone. I threw the bitch out." He replaced the bottle on the table having filled his glass.

"Don't you try talking to her either or I'll break your scrawny little neck. You got it?" he ordered, pointing a thick finger at the boy for emphasis.

Faust was standing in front of his father, terrified, thinking that any minute he was going to get a back hand from this man, as he had experienced before. To try and move before being told was inviting a swat from the old man, so he just had to stay put and hope for the best.

He stood there staring at his father for a long silent moment as he watched him return his gaze back to the table top. His thoughts appeared to drift away from the son standing in front of him to another place. Feeling uncertain about what to do, not sure if his father even realized he was still standing there, Faust decided to break the silence and ask a question about his mother. "Why...?" was all he was able to say.

His father quickly and violently snapped out of his meditation, grabbed the boy by the shirt and drew him up close to his face. "Don't even say a word about her, you hear me?" his father growled at him, the boozy smell of alcohol attacking the frightened boy's nose, and spittle showering his face with each word.

"OK, Dad, OK I won't. Don't hit me," he pleaded with his father.

Faust's father maintained his stare into the boy's face as if he were the source of all this strife to the family. Then he shoved the boy away and turned back to his drinking. Not wasting a moment, Faust took off running down the hall toward his room. When he was safely inside he closed and locked the door, hoping that his old man would pass out soon so he could sneak out and call his mother. She always went to Grandma's house in these situations and Faust knew he could call her there.

Later that night, with his father on the living room couch snoring loudly in front of a flickering television screen, Faust tiptoed out of the house and ran to his usual pay phone to call his mother. After he talked briefly to his grandmother, Faust's mother got on the phone and in a weeping voice told her son, "It wasn't supposed to happen this way."

"What wasn't, Mom? What happened?" the boy asked.

"He found out that I was leaving him and he got angry and threw me out," she explained between sobs.

"You better go home before your dad finds out that you left. I will call you soon. OK, Mommy loves you."

"Why do you want to leave?" he asked, trying to comprehend in his 12-year-old mind what all this really meant.

"Curt, you see how he beats me and you. I couldn't take it anymore. I had it all arranged. I just needed a little more time, but he found out. Now get home now before he realizes that you left. You know what will happen if he finds out you are gone. I will talk to you very soon. Don't worry. We will be together real soon. Now go!" She hung the phone up and Faust could still hear her crying just before the phone went dead.

The pop machine in the break room made a loud thump as another detective reached down to take his soda can from the tray. The noise broke Faust from his trance and he looked up at the detective who was turning to face him.

"I said, how you doing with that liquor store mess?" the thin sandy-haired detective repeated.

"Sorry," said Faust, flustered. "I was deep in thought. It is going OK. I just need to sit down for about a month and type, that's all."

"You need any help, let me know," the sandy-haired detective said as he turned and walked out of the break room back toward the detectives' squad room.

Faust thought it was time to get up and start typing his report. Since the other detective was in the squad room, he would not be alone with Massimo. Faust collected his papers and put them into the case folder; with the other hand he took his half-finished Coke and walked into the squad room.

Massimo was still at his desk engrossed in his computer screen—or so it appeared. What Faust didn't realize was that Massimo was completely interested in the Coke that Faust was drinking, more specifically the can from which he was drinking. Massimo had taken the day off to attend Ruggerio's funeral but he decided to stop in at the office to catch up on some paperwork before heading home.

Having accomplished the work he intended, he was about to leave but decided to stay when he saw Faust drinking the Coke.

All he had to do was look busy until Faust finished the Coke and dropped the can in the garbage. At that point it was abandoned property and subject to seizure. It would make a perfect specimen to send to the DNA lab to compare against the blood found on New Ho's clothing. It took about twenty minutes until Faust rose up from his desk and walked out of the detectives' squad room, dumping his empty pop can in the trash on the way.

"Thank you very much, dumbass," Massimo said under his breath as he scooped the Coke can out of the waste basket and slid it into a paper bag. As luck would have it, there were no witnesses in the room who could have told Faust what Massimo did. Not that it was illegal, but now was not the time to show his hand, Massimo reasoned.

CHAPTER 16

One week after the Ruggerio funeral, as the crusader cops were still digging around for information that would help clear the names of the officers involved in the Ruggerio affair, Tobias and his crew finally received some good news. The doctors at the hospital were going to permit Diaz to come out of his coma. Tobias had received a call from Diaz's father, who explained that since his son was so young and in such good physical condition—and according to Mr. Diaz in good graces with the Lord—he had responded very quickly to the antibiotics and the infection was cleared up. Mr. Diaz wanted Tobias to know and invited him to come to the hospital the next day when Taymond was scheduled to be released. Tobias quickly accepted and they arranged to meet at the hospital in the morning to take Tay home to finish his recovery.

Mr. Diaz explained that there was another reason he wanted Tobias there when Taymond was released from the hospital. He said that no one had told Tay about Ruggerio as yet and the hospital had orders not to mention it to him until his family was consulted first. Mr. Diaz asked Tobias if he would be the one to break the news to Taymond; since they were all such good friends it might soften the blow a little. Also Tobias was more equipped to answer the inevitable flurry of questions that Taymond was sure to ask after receiving such bad news. Tobias agreed to this request; he thought it was very considerate of Mr. Diaz to suggest this method of telling his son about the death of his friend and mentor.

The next day when Tobias met with Mr. and Mrs. Diaz, they had a brief meeting in the lobby of the hospital to plan the best way to tell Tay about Ruggerio. After the short strategy session, they all went up to Diaz's floor and entered his private room, where they found him sitting up in bed eating a breakfast of toast, grapefruit and coffee. They had made sure that the television would not be on so that Diaz could not inadvertently catch a follow-up story on the Ruggerio affair on the news.

The three visitors exchanged hugs, handshakes, and in the case of Mrs. Diaz, numerous kisses on Tay's forehead and cheek. A wide smile on his face, which was minus the goatee now, showed his happiness to see his parents and Tobias. They all expressed how pleased they were to see Taymond doing so well and that he was going home. His father said that he had a room set up for him and that Taymond's landlord was holding his apartment for him rent-free until he could move back in after his recovery. They all talked very fast, as agreed upon in the lobby, not giving Diaz a chance to ask about Ruggerio. After a few more minutes, Mr. and Mrs. Diaz excused themselves and explained that they needed to ask the doctor something about Taymond's recovery and that they would come right back. Tobias had also arranged that Diaz's mother and father would walk out into the hallway and wait by the door. After Tobias broke the news about Ruggerio to Diaz, they could be summoned by Tobias very quickly if Taymond did not take the news well.

After Diaz's parents left the room, Diaz inquired of his friend, "Where is Guy? Is he OK?"

"Tay, I gotta tell you that Guy didn't make it. I'm sorry but he took his own life that night. His funeral was a week ago," Tobias said as gently as possible, and then waited to see how he would react.

"Jesus ...why?" he asked Tobias, seemingly still trying to understand what he had just been told.

Tobias explained how G had been shot and killed, leaving Ruggerio with the impression that his last hope for redemption was gone. That he found his way up to the Overlook and shot himself in front of the Madonna statute. He continued and told Diaz about the voice-mail recording of G claiming to have witnessed the Bartlett Park shooting, which justified Ruggerio's actions and confirmed Diaz's account of what happened. Tobias then cautioned Diaz from getting too excited—even though the criminal case into the Bartlett Park shooting had been dropped, the internal investigation against himself and Diaz continued. He explained that more information was needed to corroborate the G voice-mail recording in order to clear their names and that of Ruggerio's. He finished with the efforts being taken by Massimo, Lewis, and Queeny and assured him that if there was anything to be found out, they would dig it up.

Tobias reasoned that Diaz had heard enough for one day and called in his parents. Mr. and Mrs. Diaz entered and his father stood next to his bedside, while Mrs. Diaz held Taymond's hand on the opposite side. Without preamble, Mr. Diaz announced to the room, "Let us pray."

All put their heads down, including Tobias and listened as Mr. Diaz gave thanks for his son's quick recovery and asked for blessings for the tormented soul of Gaetano Ruggerio, even pronouncing his name in perfect Italian. Being Spanish speaking, Mr. Diaz's diction was similar. They all made the sign of the cross; Tobias, being Jewish, performed the religious gesture backward.

Soon afterward, the discharge nurse came in and processed Diaz through the requisite paperwork. Then they all escorted Diaz out to the parking lot, where he was loaded into his father's car. Tobias, leaning into Diaz's open car door, told him he would be over to see him soon. The Diaz family drove out of the hospital lot and took their son home to recuperate.

The next night following Diaz's discharge from the hospital, Queeny was on patrol at about three a.m., navigating through the streets of her patrol zone on a busy Friday night in Pittsburgh. It was a cold wintry night and she had the car heater cranked up high since she always seemed to feel cold, even in the summer time. While stopped at a red light, Queeny looked out the driver's window onto a street scene of bumper to bumper traffic. Random groups of bar goers belting out drunken cat calls at girls in cars, street walkers bundled up to fend off the icy winter air, and a small group of drug dealers wearing their requisite puffy coats, as they call them, hanging out near a jammed twenty-four hour stop and rob.

The light changed and Queeny moved the squad through the intersection then aimlessly wheeled onto a side residential street as she listened to the steady drone of the police radio. She sang along to a song on her car radio when she heard the electronic beep from her onboard computer signaling an incoming e-mail. Queeny, still quietly singing along with the song, reached over to her computer keyboard and, using the glow from the monitor screen, found the proper key to accept the e-mail message. Stopping the squad at a stop sign, she was able to read the message. It was from her sergeant, Katowski, telling her to head over to the after-hours club in her zone and keep an eye on the parking lot.

"...The place is really hopping tonight and that means trouble," Katowski wrote, adding that he was sending one other car over with her, along with his own, hoping that the police presence would prevent any possible violence.

She replied in typical Queeny fashion with the following acknowledgement, "Aye, aye, skipper. If any trouble breaks, we can always call in an air strike from the USS Polack," a friendly reference to Katowski's flat-top hair style and his ethnicity.

"OK, smartass. You won't be making fun of my hair when you need a battering ram will ya? Make sure you have your Taser ready, OK?" Katowski answered, always the concerned father figure with his reminder for Queeny to check her Taser in case she needed it at the club. For this reason the officers truly loved Katowski; his first thoughts were always about the well-being of his troops. The officers reasoned that he had probably been like this in Vietnam. It was a big deal with Katowski that he attended every regimental reunion with his old Marine outfit. This told the officers in the department that he was just as close with his Marines as he was with them.

Before Queeny accelerated her squad away from the stop sign, she did just as Katowski requested. Without having to see in the dark, she reached down to her waist and found her Taser in its holster attached to her gun belt. The battery pack was engaged and ready for action; it was one less thing that she would have to worry about if trouble broke out.

Making the turn onto a cross street in the direction of the club, Queeny went over in her mind the information that had been given to her by Massimo and Lewis on the "Ruggerio Affair" as it was being called around the station house. They had researched the row house near Bartlett Park that the semi-cooperative woman was trying to alert the detectives about during their re-dux investigation at the scene of the shooting. Lewis had dug up the property information from the county recorder of deeds website, which showed the entire block of fifteen row houses was owned by one entity, the "Renew Real Estate Company." They had owned this property for five years and rented the houses to low-income residents who had most of their rent paid through the Pennsylvania Section 8 program. Through Section 8 the company has a significant portion of the rent guaranteed, with the state sending the company an automatic check each month for that portion covered by the program. The remainder of the rent, a small percentage, was the responsibility of the renter.

The company hired a property manager who lived rent-free in one of the houses to collect the balance of the rent that wasn't covered by the program. Lewis called the real estate company and asked about house number four, the one that the quasi-witness had indicated to him and Massimo with her eye movements. He was told that it had been rented for five months by a woman named Latoya Drexler. Lewis was given all of Drexler's personal information so that he could do a background check on her later. He also asked about house number six, the one that G had used on the night of the shooting. The rep told him that this property had been vacant for about one year. She explained to Lewis that even though the company would like all the properties to be rented out, they were still making a tidy profit with the current number of residents. They don't really push the property manager for one hundred percent occupancy, as long as the properties were maintained. Having the dilapidated vacant house number six in mind, Lewis asked when was the last time the company had sent a representative out to check the condition of the properties. The company representative on the phone could not answer that question.

He was told that the manager was listed as Marcel Tompkins, who lived in house number one, the first row house on the corner. The representative didn't know anything about Mr. Tompkins— only that there hadn't been any complaints from the residents for about five months since he had been hired. Lewis thought this might be a strange coincidence since this was the exact time frame in which house number four had been rented by the Drexler girl. Lewis told Queeny that either Marcel Tompkins was the greatest property manger in the history of rental management or there was something else going on. People always complained about rental properties and having seen the condition of some of those houses himself, Lewis was suspicious about why there hadn't been any complaints filed recently.

Queeny agreed since she knew Mr. Tompkins very well. She told Lewis that the type of *'aholic* she knew Tompkins to be, would not be categorized as the *workaholic* type. In her opinion, the lack of resident complaints was probably not due to the untiring work ethic of Mr. Tompkins but to another reason.

Queeny told Lewis that Tompkins was not in her estimation a hardcore alcoholic, but he did like his whiskey. Queeny knew him from a neighboring patrol zone she used to work. Tompkins was an older black guy with an ample beer belly and a pigment condition that turned his skin color white on large sections of this body. He would work odd jobs around the neighborhood to keep himself in whiskey money and to satisfy his other desire - girls. Tompkins liked his prostitutes and at any given time he would have at least one of them living with him, sometimes two or three. It was a good deal for all parties involved; Tompkins got his rocks off occasionally and in exchange he would provide the girls a safe place to live. As an added bonus to the girls, Tompkins also could be relied upon in a pinch when one of the girls needed a quick twenty-dollar rock to satisfy her crack habit.

Queeny took a moment and pondered this in the solitude of her darkened patrol car, how these chemical substances could create the oddest social arrangements between people, each one hedonistically using the other to satisfy his or her own desires, neither one however contributing even the slightest amount toward a constructive life or the betterment of society. On the contrary, their life styles served only toward the detriment of the community. It was just interesting to contemplate during the idle times while on patrol, she thought to herself.

Queeny knew Latoya Drexler too. After Lewis told her that he could not find any criminal history for her, only her driver's license information, she told him all she knew about this girl. She was a well-known girlfriend to the drug dealers. Passed around from dealer to dealer, she had two children to two different fathers, neither of whom had anything to do with his children. Drexler lived off the proceeds of whatever drug peddler she happened to be with at the time.

Lewis and Queeny surmised that she had the perfect profile to rent an apartment and to provide other services for this type of man. She had no criminal background, and therefore she was eligible for the Section 8 funds. She had a driver's license, while most drug dealers do not possess valid driver's licenses.

The license status of the drug dealer is usually suspended or revoked as a result of having been stopped and cited by the police on numerous occasions. Since she had a good license, all the cars that were needed for the drug trade could be rented or purchased in her name, keeping her paramour's identity off any official documents. Also, she could drive her man around without fear of being stopped by the police on the pretext of driving without a valid license. Of course the cops could always think of another pretext, but at least this one could not be used. Last but not least, Drexler and women like her could provide the drug entrepreneur with a safe house from which he could base his operations.

The safe house is where the drug dealer does a number of things that are vital to his business enterprise. The safe house is where the dealer stores his dope, money, guns, and records of his suppliers, distributors and customers—what they have paid or how much they owe him. The smart drug merchant does not keep all these items in one place. He or she usually has more than one of these houses for the simple reason that drug dealers, although criminals themselves, can become victims of crime also. It has become very popular to storm a drug dealer's safe house with several armed men and take all the valuables, i.e. money, drugs, guns - the proverbial *home invasion* that is heard on the news so regularly. These types of crimes are almost never perpetrated on a purely innocent victim. When a cop hears in the news about a home invasion that has occurred, in his or her mind there is a 99.9% chance that the victim was a drug dealer.

The safe house is usually where another necessary drug dealer activity takes place and that is the packaging process for his product. Cocaine comes to the local drug dealer in a white powder form. To get every dollar possible out of his product, the dealer will add into the raw cocaine a filler substance that looks like and feels like powder cocaine, the result being an increase to the quantity of the product but a decrease in its purity. The common filler, or "cut" as it is called, could be substances like powdered milk, baking soda, or a number of white powder nutritional supplements that are commonly found in the health food store.

The next step is the cooking process, which turns the powder coke into crack. The dealer simply adds some water to the powder and then heats the concoction by placing the mixture into a microwave oven. When heat is introduced to the solution, it causes a chemical reaction that increases the intensity of the narcotic, making the end product a highly addictive substance.

Drug peddlers exploited this powerful new form of cocaine, back when it was new in the late 1980s, with clever marketing ploys to expand their customer bases. Many dealers would simply give out the first rock for free. Since crack is so addictive, especially with first-time users, this first taste would usually create lifelong addictions to the substance, thus creating new customers. In effect, dealers transformed regular people into criminals who would rob, steal or even kill to obtain the money they needed for another fix.

With the recent influx of heroin and methamphetamine into the drug culture, the same marketing techniques are used with much more dire consequences. Whereas the continual use of crack cocaine over several years will usually not kill a person, heroin and methamphetamine have much higher rates of mortality and health problems. With their intense addictive qualities, these two substances also make their users more desperate for the drug than crack users, thus more violent. To Queeny's pleasant surprise, she was about to find out that a safe house was exactly how row house number four was being used.

As Queeny wheeled her squad into the parking lot of a small playground, which sat across the street from the after-hours club, she saw Katowski and a third officer already parked next to each other there. Their cars faced in opposite directions so they could converse driver's window to driver's window. Queeny eased her cruiser toward the cop cars and nestled next to Katowski's passenger side. She slid the gearshift into park and punched the window control button to lower her driver's window while Katowski did the same to his passenger side.

"This doesn't look good. That lot is full," Queeny observed, looking across the street to the club parking lot, which was overflowing with cars, several parked in the travel aisle of the lot, blocking the vehicles that were parked faced into their spaces.

"There are probably enough guns in those cars to supply the Mujahedeen," Katowski remarked, referring to the ubiquitous presence of vehicles in the lot that were obviously dealer mobiles. Since the club security *wanded*—meaning used handheld metal detector--all customers for weapons before they entered the club, the drug dealers left their guns in their cars parked in the lot.

The after-hours club was completely illegal, what used to be termed and was still referred to as a "speakeasy" in this part of the country. The club was situated in the back part of a restaurant named "The Rib Tickler," a hastily established rib joint that was just a front for the real business of the speakeasy club in the backroom. The cops all knew about it but had not been able to successfully infiltrate the club to shut it down as of yet because only known members were permitted to enter. To combat the problem, the officers relied upon the standard operating procedure for this situation, which was to introduce such strict enforcement on all patrons of the club that it became a hassle to go there, thus encouraging people to move on to another location.

"Hey Queeny," the third cop bellowed through Katowski's two open car windows.

"Yeah."

"You think Katowski is ever going to retire?" he mused.

"Shit, you and I are gonna have to carry his dead white Polack ass out of here before he retires, right Curly?" Queeny replied.

Then Katowski rebutted, "I can't retire. You guys couldn't lace up your own boots without me around. It's more a moral obligation than me wanting to stay on. I couldn't live with myself if I retired and left yunz on your own."

As the other two officers chuckled Queeny replied sarcastically, "Yeah, that's the reason."

Just then a white Cadillac Escalade with chrome spinner rims jerked to an abrupt stop in front of the rib joint/speakeasy. The pimped out vehicle screamed dealer mobile.

"Look at this," Queeny said.

A black female exited the vehicle without turning the engine off or the lights. She was wearing a tight black mini-skirt with a waist-length white fur coat over top. Her long black hair was immaculately styled, and her wrists were adorned with several layers of yellow gold bracelets that the officers could hear clinking together as she moved. She was young and shapely and showed all the signs of a drug dealer girlfriend.

There was no doubt that she was upset about something by the way she jumped out of the SUV, slammed the door closed and marched toward the front door of the rib joint her high heels clicking on the pavement with every angry step. In her rage-fueled state she either didn't care or did not notice the police cars parked and idling only fifty feet away.

"Well, it shouldn't be long now," Katowski said, picking up his squad radio microphone and calling for two more units to respond as backup. Then he turned to Queeny and requested, "Queeny, why don't you drive over there and run that plate."

Queeny did as requested and pulled in behind the Escalade. She punched in the PA plate number of the Escalade on her in-car computer. Within seconds, the registration information came back. Queeny's eyes lit up as bright as her computer screen when she saw the name, Latoya Drexler as the owner of the vehicle. She reported this to Katowski on the radio and added, "…When she comes out, let me handle her, Sarge. I know her."

"10-4," Katowski answered.

Katowski and the third officer moved into more suitable positions for covering each other and waited for the inevitable eruption to hit. It didn't take long before the cops saw the frosted glass door to the rib joint come flying open. Next a large black man came out of the restaurant, stepping backward. From his body position, it appeared as if he was dragging something out of the building. The back of his shirt read, "SECURITY," in large white letters. In short order the officers saw what he was dragging. To no one's surprise it was the Drexler girl, driver of the Escalade, being forcefully removed from the establishment.

Even though he was a big man, he was having a tough time with the petite Latoya Drexler. She was kicking and thrashing around in the muscular arms of the security guard and shouting angrily back toward the inside of the restaurant, mostly inaudible statements except for some of the profanities. Queeny and the other two cops exited their cars and made their way over to the action. The guard had Drexler out onto the sidewalk now, but she was still flailing about all high heels and clanging jewelry, pieces of which were breaking off and flying around like shrapnel. Queeny could hear during the girl's tirade that she was cursing her boyfriend, Marquis. She walked over to Katowski and quickly told him, "Act as if you want to arrest her."

"No problem," he said. He knew that Queeny wanted to try and get some information out of this girl, because they had played this game before.

Drexler was still out of control, jumping up and down kicking her feet in the air and launching her high heels out into space while the guard struggled to hold on to her.

"Marquis you run around with that ho don't think you gonna touch me again. That bitch has herpes. I hope your dick falls off!"

Just then several black males emerged from the restaurant and a few females also, one of whom came bolting out the door toward Drexler, but before she could get to her one of the black males from the club grabbed hold of her and held her back. Obviously this was the girl that Marquis was cheating with and the cops knew that it was time for them to step in.

As the officers approached, both girls were shouting profanity laced threats and insults toward each other.

"You nasty ass ho. I'll smack that pound of makeup right off your trashy face," proclaimed Drexler.

"Go ahead, Bitch. I got more class in my little toe. Marquis wants more of a woman these days," retorted Marquis's mistress.

"Take your herpes laced ass and get on out of here, Bitch," Drexler rebutted.

"If I have herpes it's from you givin' it to Marquis first, you ho!" shouted Marquis's date.

As both females continued their verbal jousting and trying to break free from the restraining holds of their inhibitors, Marquis finally made himself known by stating to Drexler, "Listen, Baby. You knew I was steppin' out on you, why you so surprised?" he professed while helping the others hold back the other woman. Queeny thought she heard a hint of an accent but he hadn't said enough for her to be sure.

About twenty-nine years old, Marquis was a well built young man, which was evident even though he was wearing a loose-fitting long-sleeve pullover sweat top that said "Nike Air Force One" on the front. The top was part of the drug dealer uniform. To complete the outfit he was also wearing several gold dangling necklaces, one of them with a crucifix—there was always a crucifix—and loose-fit black jeans with bright-colored blue sneakers.

"You said that you weren't gonna do that anymore. Now I find out you with this ho bitch!" Drexler replied.

At this point the three officers on scene interjected themselves into the situation and pulled the combating parties apart, at the same time the reinforcements that Katowski had called for were arriving. Marquis quickly disappeared back into the restaurant, not wanting any contact with the police. Katowski and Queeny took Drexler a distance away, back toward Queeny's squad car while the other officers dealt with the crowd and the "other" woman.

Katowski had a hold of the upper part of Drexler's left arm and with his other hand controlled her wrist on the same side.

With this hold he was keeping her from advancing toward her boyfriend's mistress.

"Settle down lady. Settle down or you're going to jail!" Katowski threatened.

"*That* no good bitch is gonna die!" Drexler exclaimed.

"Listen, I'm not gonna warn you again. You better just settle down or I'm puttin' you in cuffs," Katowski said, pulling on her arm to keep her in place.

That was the cue for Queeny to make her presence known to Latoya Drexler.

"Sarge, let me talk with her. I know this girl. Maybe put her in my car so she can't get at the other woman?" Queeny requested.

"OK, whatever you say—but if you can't control her I'm gonna throw her ass in jail for the night!" Katowski proclaimed and gently pushed Drexler toward the rear passenger door of Queeny's squad. Queeny did a quick pat down of the woman just to make sure she wasn't carrying any weapons before she was placed into the car. They hadn't handcuffed her though, since the back doors of squad cars do not open from the inside, both cops knew she would be secure in the back seat.

Queeny re-entered her squad and sat in the driver's seat. Looking through the rear view mirror at Latoya, she could see a scowl on her face and her shoulders heaving up and down with labored breathing; she was visibly agitated and winded from her tumultuous behavior. Queen watched her looking out the side window and heard her mumbling,

"That bastard, that no good bastard."

Queeny, seeing an opening decided to go with this theme and eased into the discourse that she wanted to have with her.

"Men, if not for that thing between their legs what would we need 'em for, right?" Queeny asked, hoping to get the conversation rolling.

"Ain't it the truth," Drexler replied, still looking out the side window.

"That's why I don't keep me one in my house, just date once in awhile," Queeny remarked, deliberately leaving the interior dome light off. From experience, she knew that informants feel more at ease when they are cloaked in darkness in the back of a police car. Queeny would always remind them that any outside observers could not hear their conversation, so how would anyone know that the person was giving criminal intelligence information. Even though this fact is obvious, it sometimes helps to relax an informant so he or she can speak freely.

"You know it, Girl. No mo' hustlers for me. They just use you 'til they don't need you no mo'," Drexler said defiantly.

"He's in there right now, probably doin' his thing on that other one," Queeny proffered.

"And she is dumb enough to fall for it," Drexler deduced.

Queeny thought it might be the right time to reveal how she knew Drexler from a few years earlier, when Queeny had worked in another part of the city. At that time, Drexler was having trouble with yet another man. He was beating on her but she was too afraid to file formal charges against him. Queeny had answered several calls at their residence but Drexler would never go through with the complaint. Queeny set out to arrest the abuser on other charges just to get him out of Drexler's house.

After several nights of staking their house out, Queeny had finally seen her chance. As was typical, the man didn't have a driver's license and was using Drexler to drive him around. Queeny knew that eventually he would get into a car and drive himself, and on this night she was finally right.

Upon pulling the abuser over, she saw in plain view the butt of a firearm sticking out from under the driver's seat. When she got the man out of the car he found an opportunity and ran from the scene. In a case of the perp getting his just desserts, good old "Max" the German Sheppard got hold of the fleeing felon and kept him there until the good guys arrived.

Queeny had checked the criminal background of this actor before the traffic stop and knew that he was prohibited from carrying a firearm due to his record. Violating this section of the criminal code made him a felon and fleeing from this type of violation made him liable to be seized by a police dog, with which Max and Quint had gladly obliged.

Queeny made sure that Drexler knew she was the officer that made this arrest and freed her from her abuser. Queeny thought that someday this debt could be cashed in, and today was the day.

"It's a damn shame that he gets away with using girls like that," Queeny said, then looked up into the rear view again and with her best actor's voice exclaimed, "Don't I know you? Yeah, from the Hill right, you had that boyfriend that used to hit you, remember?" Queeny turned in her seat so Drexler could see her face.

"Is that you, Queeny? Damn, how you been?" Drexler said.

"Good girl, what you doin' messin' with another one of those hustlers?" Queeny said.

"Girl, I got to get away from this one. He is gonna ruin me with his drugs and all."

"You know I could work with you and get this one out the way, same as that last one. We could make it so he won't do the same to you or anyone else again. What do you think?" Queeny waited and held her breath, hoping to get the right response.

"What you mean?"

That was better than a flat negative, Queeny thought.

"Girl, you do just a little somethin' somethin' and we can lock him up for twenty years no sweat."

"If you know what I know, you all would take him and throw away the key," Drexler said, simultaneously sweeping her right hand across her face and shaking her head.

"All you got to do is tell me and it stays between you and me. No names, just information," Queeny stated.

"No names?" she asked, seeking reassurance.

"No names I guarantee," Queeny said encouragingly.

"What do you want to know?" Drexler asked, and Queeny knew that she had hit pay dirt.

Drexler went on to tell Queeny as much as she knew about her boyfriend and his drug operation. Marquis Belford was his full name, a.k.a. "Ease." He had earned the street name by the calm demeanor he displayed most of the time, but he could turn violent when provoked, Drexler explained. She said that Ease was one of the "Jersey Boyz," a crew of drug dealers who came to Pittsburgh from the northern New Jersey area. That was the accent that Queeny had heard in his voice, she now realized.

This type of crew is officially termed a "criminal group." Not highly organized, and not officially a gang, but a loosely connected group of people working toward a common criminal goal of distributing narcotics. The most common reason these groups migrate from their home territory and infiltrate a different city, is the pressure applied by local law enforcement. With the mobility of today's society, it is just easier to pick up and move out to another city where the heat is not as intense.

This phenomenon is occurring all over the country with "criminal groups" moving in and out of cities everywhere. In any particular city in the United States, the local police agency could be battling several different criminal groups that have originated from various parts of the country. To combat these groups, the police will expend huge amounts of time, money, and manpower to disrupt their activities. This process will most likely take years to accomplish and all the while the members of this group are reaping the rewards of a profitable drug enterprise.

Drexler also told Queeny that row house number four was one of Ease's safe houses. He stored a portion of his dope there, crack and some heroin, along with several guns, and a bullet proof vest that he occasionally wore. The balance of his dope she assumed was spread among several other safe houses throughout the city, the locations of which he did not confide to her. She also surmised that he stored his large sums of cash in the other safe houses.

Drexler reported that Ease owned a couple of small convenience stores that sold very little legitimate merchandise, but were valuable to him for laundering his drug profits. The amount of income that he reported to the government was reported as profit from his convenience stores.

Queeny wanted to know more about row house number four, so she asked Drexler to describe the interior of the house and where Ease had his dope and other illegal property. Drexler said that he hid the dope under the floor boards of a second floor bedroom under the bed. He had a huge Pit Bull in the house to protect his property while he was not there.

He didn't stop with just these security features however. Ease also used a camera system to protect his valuables. Drexler explained that Ease had all parts of the house, inside and outside, covered by cameras that were all hooked up to his computer system. She finished by saying that Ease had been watching a few weeks ago when the white and black detectives were outside investigating something.

The camera system is another common drug dealer practice, utilized by the more sophisticated dealers. Due to the nature of his business the dealer is well advised to have a system like this in place for several reasons.

First, for self-defense purposes, it is of enormous advantage to be able to see who is at the front door before you open it. The people on the other side could be any of several different adversaries that a drug hustler develops just by the very nature of his craft. They could be members of a rival drug group sent to kill or rob him, they could be the police preparing to hit the house with a search or arrest warrant, or they could be people that the dealer does not know. Why expose his identity to enemies, police or potential informants?

Secondly, the camera system can keep a watchful eye on his house and property while all the residents are gone. In the case of a burglary, the camera system can possibly record the perpetrators in the act. If he can identify the parties that burglarized his safe house and took his dope stash, then it is that much easier to mete out revenge and possibly retrieve his valuables.

Queeny stopped Drexler and asked a question when she heard about the camera system. "Do one of them cameras cover the street in front of the house?"

"I think so," Drexler replied.

"Does Ease keep these recordings somehow?"

"Some of 'em, he puts them on CD," she explained, mistakenly using the acronym CD instead of DVD.

Before Queeny could ask her if Ease's camera had recorded the Bartlett Park shooting, Drexler beat her to the punch.

"As a matter of fact, Ease has a CD with that shooting, where the cop shot that boy on the street in front of my house."

Queeny could not believe her ears. This could be the break that they were all hoping for--a video of the shooting could exonerate Ruggerio and the others.

"Oh yeah?" Queeny said, trying not to be overly anxious, and then asked, "Where does he have this CD?"

"I don't know for sure. He said that he was gonna save it for when he needs it, whatever that means," Drexler commented.

"Do you know where he keeps the other CDs that he copies?"

"Some are at my house and he keeps others somewheres else." Drexler was starting to sound as if she were tiring of the snitch role. She made her feelings very clear when she added, "Can I go now? I just want to go home. Fuck Ease. He can have that ho and her nasty diseases."

Queeny realized that Drexler had quickly lost her extreme anger at Belford. If she follows the profile, Queeny thought, Drexler is starting to realize that she was forgetting the most important reason to keep up her relationship with Ease—the money! Where else could she live the way she did if not for Ease and his drug money? Queeny had seen this before. The jilted girlfriend gets all fired up at the moment that her boyfriend is caught in the act. But very soon after the blowout, she realizes that the relationship of using each other is a two-way street.

When she has her mind cleared of this blind rage at her boyfriend's cheating ways, the drug dealer girlfriend starts to imagine how drastically her life style will change if she completely breaks ties with him. Without his drug money, no more fine clothes, new cars, almost daily trips to the beauty salon, big screen plasma television sets, clothes and toys for the kids, et cetera, et cetera. Queeny knew when the scorned drug dealer girlfriend began to contemplate life without her man, the cheating didn't seem so egregious. She also knew that when this realization finally sank in, the girlfriend's cooperation with the police would immediately halt.

"Hey Queeny, this has been nice and all but I should be gettin' back to my kids. Can I go?" Drexler said pleadingly.

"Yeah sure, Girl. Here is my card. If you want to talk again let me know, OK?" Queeny offered, even though she knew that there was more chance of her fitting into a size four bikini when summer came.

Diaz sat in his parents' living room in his father's recliner, staring mindlessly at the flickering television screen in front of him, his thoughts reviewing all the events that had taken place over one month ago. Since he had recently awakened from the drug-induced coma, his wounding at the hands of a career criminal seemed as if it had just occurred the other night. He could still see the muzzle flash of G's gun and feel the shock of the bullet that had wounded him and nearly ended his life. Reliving the shooting incident caused him to remember the intense pain he experienced that night. He remembered thinking, while curled up writhing in agony on the pavement of the alley, how could anyone survive the overwhelming waves of pain caused by a bullet wound? The memory brought with it a sharp stabbing sensation coming from the area of the now-healed injury. Diaz thought to himself that he had gained a new appreciation for how wounded combat soldiers must feel on the battlefield.

He was shaken from his thoughts by the mid-afternoon game show playing on the television set. A contestant had just won a Caribbean cruise and she began to jump up and down, screaming loudly. Adding to the noise were the dings and dongs of digitally mastered bells and sirens celebrating the prizewinner. Diaz shifted in his seat to try and find a more comfortable position, which he quickly realized was not possible. He hadn't felt comfortable since they woke him up at the hospital. There was relief only when he took his pain medication. This was problematic, because the medication made his head foggy, so he only took the pills when he could not stand the pain any longer. He usually popped a few when he came back from rehab. After stretching and flexing for an hour, his insides felt like he had swallowed a handful of broken glass. The doc said it wouldn't be much longer, another week or so and he could start walking without the cane—or try to anyway.

As had often happened over the last week when he had been recuperating at home, Diaz's thoughts went back to his friend Guy Ruggerio. Why? he thought to himself for the thousandth time. He surely knew that we weren't going to give up on clearing his name, Diaz said in his mind. Then a second contestant lost in one of the game shows on TV. He was having a tough time imagining what amount of desperation could cause a person to commit suicide, especially someone like Guy, who was a role model for

Diaz. The qualities of dedication, strength, and loyalty that Diaz saw in Guy made the suicide a dumbfounding act.

Just then the doorbell rang and he heard his mother walk over and open the front door. He could hear Tobias's voice and immediately his spirits were lifted.

"Come in please. He is in the living room. Go right inside," Mrs. Diaz said, then offered Tobias something to drink.

"No thank you," Tobias answered.

Being a typical mother, Mrs. Diaz didn't hear that response.

"I'll bring in some coffee and cookies. You make yourself at home," she commanded.

"Yes Ma'am, thank you very much," Tobias said, then switched to Taymond's recovery. "How's the patient? Giving you any trouble?"

"So needy. Get me this, get me that, you'd think somebody shot him or something," Mrs. Diaz quipped, and they both chuckled.

"OK Mom, good one," Diaz called out from the other room. Playing along, he said, "Can I have another pillow? This one is too hard."

Tobias walked into the living room and reached out to shake Diaz's hand. "How's it goin', you feeling any better?"

"Every day I get a little closer to 100 percent. It won't be long. Next week I get rid of the cane," Diaz said encouragingly.

"Good, that's good news. You'll be off the injured reserve list in no time," Tobias said cheerily.

"OK, now that we got that out of the way. What the hell is going on? You guys haven't called for a few days," Diaz said sardonically.

Tobias was about to fill him in on the new developments, but he could hear Mrs. Diaz coming into the living room with the refreshments. She entered the room and set down a huge tray with a thermal coffee urn, mugs, sugar, cream, and four different kinds of cookies.

As she backed away, she stated, "You boys talk as long as you want. I have to go out for a bit. Taymond, I have the cell phone. You call if you need anything. I think you are in good hands with Toby here." As she said his name, she put a hand on Toby's shoulder and gave him a gentle squeeze. It was a gesture of thanks for Toby being such a good friend to her son. Mrs. Diaz knew that they were going to talk about the Ruggerio suicide and was aware that it was a conversation that should be unfettered by a third party. So she conveniently excused herself to let them discuss what had happened. It would be good therapy for Taymond, she reasoned.

"I'll watch out for him, Mrs. Diaz," Tobias said, and she smiled and turned to walk out of the room.

Over the next half hour, Tobias began to fill him in on all the news. First, he went over the painful situation of Diaz's work status. He told Diaz that he was probably looking at dismissal from the force, since he was still a probationary officer. Having this status meant that Diaz did not have union protection and could be fired for a much lesser infraction than a tenured officer. Tobias explained that the department didn't want to reveal this to Diaz just yet since it had only been one week since he had been released from the hospital. However, Tobias said with enthusiasm, "You may be saved, because Queeny has come up with something very interesting."

He explained the new developments that Queeny discovered and the hope that an actual video recording may exist of the shooting incident. Diaz was astounded at their luck but was curious about how they planned on retrieving this recording. "This guy, Ease—he isn't going to just hand it over to us. How are you going to get the video from him?" Diaz asked.

"We had a sit down: me, Queeny, Massimo, and Lewis. We are going to work on getting enough probable cause to get an arrest and search warrant for Ease and his row house. We figure when he is locked up on drug charges he will have to turn over the DVD of the shooting to save his ass," Tobias stated.

"How are you going to get the warrants?" Diaz questioned.

"That's the tough part. Massimo and Lewis called every agency on this side of the state and in Jersey to see if they had any leads on this guy but they came up with nothing," he said, putting a dip of Copenhagen in his lip.

"So we are back to square one," Diaz said dejectedly.

"Keep your head up, kid. We are working on it. Eventually this mope is going to screw up, and when he does old Tobias will be there," he said, picking up his coffee mug and taking a swig.

Diaz smiled and mimicked Tobias by sipping from his mug also, and then he delicately broached the subject of the Ruggerio suicide.

"Toby, I have to ask you, why do you think Guy did it? I mean, I know he was under pressure and everything, but he didn't seem like the suicide type."

"I know, and I have gone over this in my mind a thousand times. Think about it this way, Guy was very hard on himself. Did you ever notice that?"

"Yeah, I guess."

"I think part of it goes back to his upbringing. You know, his parents weren't born here. They came over from Italy. Even though there are a lot of Italians that live here, they are either third or fourth generation or inner mixed with other nationalities. Guy was second generation. His parents didn't speak English when they first came here. One hundred years ago they would have thousands of other Italian immigrants to connect with, but when they got here everyone was Americanized.

"Guy spoke English as a second language and it probably caused him to feel a little self-conscious. He had to translate for his parents their whole lives. Being an immigrant in Pittsburgh is not like other areas. We don't have much population moving in and out like other cities. Hell, our numbers have been going down for twenty years now. So if you speak in another language or with an accent, you tend to stick out more here than in other places."

"He never mentioned that to me. We had something in common and I didn't even know it," Diaz commented.

"That's right, your dad came here from Puerto Rico. I'm sure that meant something to Guy when he met you," Tobias said, and added, "Then there was the thing about being so short. Let's face it when you are as short as Guy was, some people just don't have as much respect for you—especially as a cop."

"That's true, and then you add on his problem with Faust," Diaz replied.

"Right, with Faust criticizing every move Guy made it just added to his desire to be perfect at his job," Tobias remarked and after a pause added, "Hey, aren't you the psychology major? You should be doing this analysis."

They both snickered and Diaz finished the profile they were compiling on Ruggerio. "On top of all that, when G was cut down he must have felt that there was no hope left. Being from a proud immigrant background and seeing nothing but humiliation down the road, he must have thought that suicide was the only answer.

Also it is rather symbolic as far as where he chose to commit the act, right in front of a religious shrine—an obvious appeal of forgiveness for the sin of suicide." Diaz was not looking at Tobias any longer but straight ahead over the top of the television screen and beyond to the living room wall. Tobias could see that he was coming to a realization about Ruggerio's death, something that Diaz had never seen before in his dead friend and training officer.

"He must have been really torn up inside, all those conflicting forces pulling in opposite directions. I mean, his religious background telling him that suicide is a sin and a one-way ticket to hell. Then he was inundated by the influence of his immigrant parents telling him that he must be respectable and without flaw, to show others that they are good people. Not to mention the possibility of going to jail on this shooting and losing his family and the job he loved. Sometimes I feel that way too, I mean about the immigrant parents and fitting in," Diaz said mournfully.

"I think when Guy saw you lying there on the street with a bullet wound in you, he may have thought he was responsible for putting you in that situation. He may have had that on his mind also," Tobias reasoned.

They both sat in Diaz's living room quietly for a moment and in the background the game show noise of dinging and donging erupted again from the television set. Then Diaz looked over at Tobias and said with a fervent expression, "Tell me what I can do to help."

CHAPTER 17

The steady *"THUMP, thump...THUMP, thump..."* of the windshield wipers broke the silence inside the vehicle. She hadn't really heard the other two cops say much since they left the drug enforcement office. It was snowing again, she thought, and the snowfall from the previous night had just melted away during the sunlit day. Now in the darkness of early evening a heavy wet snow was covering the ground again. For Pittsburgh, even though the winters were cold, having snow on the ground for more than a few days was considered unusual.

The darkness of the van's interior made the task of setting up the wire kit difficult for her. For lighting the work area she used a modified book light that was affixed to the kit body. The light resembled a reptilian creature. With its long narrow shaft extended upward, then bent over to cast the light down on the controls, it looked like a cobra ready to strike. The bumping and jostling, as the van traversed the potholed city streets, didn't help either as the drug officer tried plugging in the numerous electrical connections on the kit's receiving unit.

The wire kit, officially known as the "Electronic Interception Unit," was composed of two main parts: the transmitter and the receiver. The transmitter was a thin rectangular box-like object with an attached twelve-inch wire that had the microphone at the end. This piece of equipment is the part that is seen on television crime shows being taped by the cops under the clothes and to the body of a police informant before he or she meets with the bad guys.

The other main component is the receiver, the unit that receives and records the relevant conversation between the informant and the target of the investigation. This unit is built into a suitcase-like container so it can be portable. Its power coming from a vehicle adaptor plugged into the cigarette lighter. As she knelt on the floor of the rolling van, she tested the audio level and the digital recorder on the receiver. She thought about all the complicated circuitry and electrical connections that comprised the kit, the kind of complex things that cops neither understand nor want to. Only the knowledge of how to use it is necessary.

Detective Sergeant Celeste Parker, 'Lest for short, had been in the narcotics unit for five years now and had been promoted to sergeant in command of five other narc officers almost two months ago. She loved her work and knew that her promotion was merit based. But she was cognizant that being a black female did not hurt her selection either. She was nervous at first, being in command of five male narc officers. But she was starting to feel more at ease being in charge, largely due to her colleagues. During her five years in the unit she had worked with all of them and they observed firsthand the long hours Parker had put in on her investigations. In their minds it was unanimous that she should be the next supervisor.

Celeste Parker was a relatively tall woman, six feet with an athlete's physique and short cropped black hair. She owed her athletic build to her time at the University of Pittsburgh, where she had starred as a forward for the basketball team before graduating with a degree in sports management. The sports career did not evolve, so when she heard of the police department openings she took the plunge. After joining the Metro force she discovered that it was her true calling, especially the drug work. Even though it had cost her one marriage, she was too dedicated to the job to settle down at this point in her life.

When Parker received the call from Massimo she knew this was going to be a big deal. She had worked with Massimo in the past on several cases. In fact, she had worked with almost all the homicide dicks in the last five years. This was not unusual since most homicides are drug-related anyway; the narcotics unit would be a valuable resource in identifying suspects. She and Massimo had gotten along famously due to the common work ethic that they shared and the thrill of the hunt that they both enjoyed. Hence, the reason Massimo asked for her specifically; he knew 'Lest would dig into this case with a vengeance.

He explained to her on the phone that he needed a personal favor. She could turn it down if she wanted and he would not hold anything against her. He told her that it had to do with the Bartlett Park shooting case and that he and other officers had developed information that contradicted the official investigation and media reports. Massimo told her the information that Queeny had received on Ease and about the DVD that he possibly possessed, which could break the case wide open.

419

Parker told Massimo that she had heard of Ease recently, but he was able to stay off the Drug Unit's radar for the year plus that he has been in town. He was part of the Jersey Boyz clique, not a formal gang but as close as a group of drug dealers could get to being a gang. She explained that she really didn't have much intelligence on him but was told that he was one of the more important members of this criminal group. In fact, until Massimo had told her, she hadn't even known Ease's real name.

Massimo said that the other officers assisting him were Queeny Walker and Toby Tobias and if Parker wanted to, he could arrange a meeting between her and these two officers so they could provide her with more detail. He explained that he was jammed up with a double shooting investigation that had just occurred and the other investigator Jeff Lewis was assigned to a time-consuming voter fraud case. Regrettably, Massimo could not attend the meeting but promised to actively take part when he cleared up his shooting.

"What do you think?" he asked, crossing his fingers on the other end of the phone.

"Isn't Tobias one of the officers suspended in the whole Ruggerio mess?" she asked.

"Yeah, I don't want to pull any punches 'Lest, this could hurt you career wise. I don't want you to feel obligated and I wouldn't blame you if you said no. But, damn, wouldn't it be something to clear Ruggerio's name and get back his benies for his wife and kid, not to mention clearing the internals on Tobias and Diaz?" Massimo proposed in his best salesman routine.

"You had me when you mentioned the Jersey Boyz connection. You sharp-tongued devil," Parker replied and heard a relieved sigh on the other end of the phone.

At the meeting with Queeny and Tobias, Queeny showed Parker a biographical background check that she had done on Marquis Belford, a.k.a. Ease. This was a suggestion from Katowski just after the incident with Drexler outside of the speakeasy. Katowski suggested that Queeny run Belford's name through the PaCIC center to obtain more information on him.

PaCIC, pronounced PAYSICK, which stands for "Pennsylvania Criminal Intelligence Center," is a new service that emerged from the fallout of the 9/11 attacks. This service was the State of Pennsylvania's effort to increase their intelligence capabilities to thwart any possible terrorist activity. In addition to the terrorist component, PaCIC also provides intelligence on street crime. Administered by the Pennsylvania State Police, PaCIC collects data from numerous sources and provides intelligence information to local police agencies throughout the state.

As Katowski explained to Queeny, "Before you can fight your enemy you have to get to know everything you can about them," an obvious lesson from his Vietnam days.

That night Queeny called the twenty-four hour PaCIC hotline and explained her situation to the intelligence analyst in Harrisburg. He told her that she should receive an e-mail the following day with a full bio-profile on Belford. The next night, when Queeny came to work she downloaded a thirty-page background on Marquis Dequan Belford. As Queeny flipped through the printed out version of the bio-profile, she was impressed by the breadth of background categories that PaCIC researched on Belford. She read off categories of information that detailed practically any and all official or government-generated documents relating to the name Marquis Dequan Belford. These areas included: postal addresses, real estate ownership, vehicles registered, any civil court actions, job history, driver's licenses, names of neighbors, etc. But what would turn out to be the nugget of information that helped the cops the most was the category listed "Associates."

During their sit-down with Parker, Queeny and Tobias laid out all the information that they knew on the Ruggerio shooting case. Part of the meeting included Queeny handing over the PaCIC bio-profile on Ease. Parker leafed through the document while Queeny was recounting her conversation with Drexler. Then suddenly Parker stopped turning pages and pointed to one of the names under the "Associates" category and said, "I might know her."

"Who?" asked Tobias.

"Sequita Brooks. We had an informant by that name about one year ago. If this is the same person we may be in luck," Parker remarked.

"How does she know Belford?" Queeny inquired.

"She is listed under associates in the profile, so she might be one of his girlfriends or she may have worked for him running drugs in the past, and/or present," Parker added.

"You think she will work for us again?" Tobias asked.

"I don't know. Let me check it out and I will get back to you."

After the meeting was adjourned for the evening, they went their separate ways until a few days later, when Parker called Queeny.

"We caught a break. Meet me at the Drug Enforcement Office tonight at 6:30. Bring Tobias and wear plain clothes. We are doing a controlled buy on Drexler at the row house," Parker told Queeny succinctly.

Parker had to be brief with Queeny on the phone since she had a lot of paperwork to finish before the controlled buy that evening. What she explained to Queeny and Tobias later, when they met up at the Drug Enforcement Office, was that Sequita Brooks was in fact the same informant her office had used in the past. She said that another narc used her and she worked out fine. Brooks had been on the hook for a PWID "Possession with Intent to Deliver Controlled Substance" charge and didn't want to go to jail, so she had agreed to cooperate. She made a controlled purchase of one ounce of crack cocaine from one of the Jersey Boyz which resulted in his conviction and sentencing to five years in state prison.

Parker explained that Brooks cooperated by introducing an undercover officer to the suspected drug dealer. The undercover officer actually made the controlled purchase of crack. Therefore, the undercover officer testified in the court case instead of Brooks, thus keeping her anonymity from the Jersey Boyz. This meant that she could still be of use as an informant if she wanted to cooperate again. This led to Parker explaining how she was able to convince Brooks to provide her services again.

She said that Brooks had received probation instead of a prison sentence on her drug charges, in exchange for her cooperation in the drug buy of the Jersey Boy. However, while she was on probation Brooks provided her probation officer with a hot urine sample, meaning that she had marijuana in her system. The probation department told Parker that Brooks had also missed a few meetings that she was required to attend; therefore an arrest warrant was issued and still outstanding for Sequita Brooks.

Parker saw to it that this warrant was duly executed and within one hour she was sitting in an interrogation room with Sequita Brooks. She nearly beat Parker to the point of the meeting by stating that she would do anything to stay out of jail. She was afraid that her previous involvement with the police would be revealed while incarcerated and her life put in jeopardy. She asked Parker what she could do for her.

Parker brought up Belford's name to Brooks. Brooks stated that she could not deal with him because they used to date and they were on bad terms.

"But I can do his baby's momma," Brooks told Parker.

"Latoya Drexler?" Parker asked, hoping for the right response.

"Yeah, I can buy a quarter from Toy," meaning a quarter of an ounce of crack cocaine. She continued, "I can say that I need to make some money and that I will sell the quarter for a profit."

"You can make the buy at her house, right?" asked Parker.

"She trusts me; it's no thing," said Brooks.

"How about wearing a wire?" Parker asked.

"I can do that. I got to take care of my kids. I can't go to jail."

After completing the paperwork for the "consent to interception" forms, Parker drove Brooks over to the district attorney's office and had Brooks interviewed by one of the assistant DAs. This was required by law to ensure that the subject was willingly and voluntarily consenting to have her voice recorded by the police.

For a recorded conversation between individuals, whether it's over the phone or face to face, all that is legally required is that one of the parties consent to the interception. This level of interception only requires the approval from a DA, which Parker satisfied.

The rules change dramatically, however if the interception would be made inside the target's home. This type of recorded conversation is considered a much higher level of invasion into an individual's privacy. Therefore, in this case an affidavit of probable cause was required and had to be signed by a Common Pleas Court judge. The level of probable cause did not exist in this situation to enable Parker to apply for this type of interception.

Parker explained all this to Brooks and cautioned her not to go inside the house when she went to Drexler's residence. Brooks promised that she could make the buy of crack while staying on the front porch of the row house. She told Parker that she would tell Drexler that a prospective buyer for the crack was waiting in Brooks's car so she was in a hurry and couldn't come inside her house. Parker agreed that this should work, but if she would happen to go into the house they would not be able to use the portion of the conversation that takes place inside the residence in court. Brooks stated that she understood and the two females parted ways until the evening meet.

With all the red tape completed, Parker called two of her narc unit partners and arranged to meet up in the evening for the controlled drug buy operation. She explained that she would have two additional plain-clothes cops along as back-up. Then she gave Massimo a call also, thinking that he would be interested in this latest development. He told Parker that he was familiar with the meeting place she had picked and that he might see them there later.

After Parker briefed Tobias and Queeny at the drug enforcement office on the developments that had taken place during the day, she walked the two plain clothes officers to the parking lot and over to the undercover surveillance van that they were going to use for the operation. It was a large customized van with Venetian blinds over the windows to aid in concealing the passengers. The body was a dark blue color with horizontal beige stripes down the sides. Parker pulled open the side door and slid it back on its runners, revealing an interior that looked like a Radio Shack on wheels to Queeny and Tobias. Having worked in patrol their entire careers up to this point, neither one of them had ever seen a police vehicle like this one.

There was a lap top computer attached to a mounting assembly, a stack of electronic components that resembled a home stereo system, head phones, cassette tapes, VHS tapes; DVDs, and digital cameras—one for still photography and a second for digital motion photography. The other noticeable feature of the interior of the van was the familiar look of overuse that most police vehicles take on shortly after being put into service. Both Queeny and Tobias were accustomed to this appearance in police vehicles, owing to the fact that most police units are used by a vast array of officers, none of whom take full responsibility for maintaining the vehicle. Hence, very quickly the unit takes the look, and sometimes the aroma, of a college frat house. File folders, used notebooks, and report forms were scattered haphazardly about the interior, some with dirty shoeprints visible on them. Candy wrappers, pop cans, and partially-empty food containers completed the décor.

Parker let out a curse at the sight of the mess, then grabbed a large Rubbermaid receptacle and started shoveling the heap of garbage into the trash can. Tobias and Queeny lent a hand and they quickly made room to enter the van and take a seat. Parker instructed Tobias to take the wheel for two reasons; first a van such as this looks more convincing as a non-police setup with a white guy driving than a black female, and second she had to get the wire kit ready before they arrived at the location to meet the informant.

Pulling out of the station lot onto the street, Tobias engaged the windshield wipers to clear the screen of the almost steady downfall of snowflakes.

426

"We're headed to the old U.S. Steel Plant off of 28. It's a tool and die shop now, McGregor Industries," she told Tobias.

"I know where it is," he answered.

Then Queeny asked, "Why are we meeting there?"

"These druggies have look-outs watching the enforcement office so we can't meet up with CIs (short for confidential informants) there," Parker responded. She remembered something. "Toby keep an eye out for anyone following us. They have been known to do that, too."

Toby nodded his head and said, "You bet, Sarge."

Parker put her head down and flicked on the book light to set up the wire kit as Queeny looked on in fascination.

The van turned onto a yellow-bricked entrance road that went down the side of the old steel plant building. The structure was built of red brick up to a certain height. Then the construction turned into poured cement, which capped the top. Framed in the cement were rows of old windows, their metal parts rusted from years of neglect. This building, like most steel plants, had been positioned next to the river—in this case, the Allegheny River. The legitimate rationale was so the plant was accessible to river barges carrying the coal and other materials necessary for steel production. The illegitimate motive for the positioning of the plant next to a river was to dump the plant's waste product into it, thus saving on disposal costs. This of course polluted the rivers and killed off scores of aquatic species—some to the point of extinction. In addition, it can only be speculative as to what affect this pollution may have caused humans who drew their drinking water from the rivers.

With the demise of the steel industry in Western Pennsylvania over several decades, the river system has made a dramatic comeback. Biologists have even cleared some species of fish for human consumption. Fishing in the Three Rivers became so popular that the "Bass Master's Championship" was held in Pittsburgh for the first time in 2005. Recreational boating has become all the rage, so much so that the PA Fish and Game Commission reported that this type of river traffic had outnumbered commercial traffic for the first time in the history of the region.

The van bucked and bounced over the old bricked road, splashing through water-filled potholes as they passed by the towering wall of the plant building.

"Follow the yellow brick road," Parker jokingly told Tobias.

"Just imagine twenty or thirty years ago, this plant had thousands of workers walking into it every day. Now how many work here for the tool and die company, thirty or so?" Tobias asked rhetorically.

"Those was the good ol' days and they ain't comin' back," Queeny said flatly.

When Tobias wheeled the van around the rear corner of the building, the headlight beams swept across the two vehicles parked there and the three cops standing outside of them. Snowfall had partially covered them and all three had their hands dug deep into their coat pockets. They stood with their shoulders shrugged high to fend off the wind coming off the river.

The cops standing there were the two other narc officers that Parker had called and Massimo. There was no sign of the CI, Brooks. She was late. This made Parker's heart sink a bit with the possibility of Brooks ditching the operation, an occurrence that is all too common in drug investigations. It reminded her of the axiom that narcs like to recite, "for every CI that works to the favor of the police, there are ten more that bomb out." Parker was hoping that Brooks fell into the former category. Besides she had more to lose by not cooperating with the police than by helping in this investigation, Parker rationalized.

Tobias parked and killed the engine and they all three unloaded from the van. Parker, the operation leader in this case, made all the introductions. The two narcs from Parker's unit were Detective Tom Simon, who was white and Detective Al Jones, who was black. Parker said to the others that the unit members referred to these two as "Alias Simon and Jones," a reference taken from an old television series from the 1970s that was set in the Wild West and was called "Alias Smith and Jones." She explained that they have a little bit of the cowboy in them, hence the moniker.

"Yippee-yo-ki-ay motherfucker," said Simon to the group.

"How original. You're gonna make this homicide detective think you're a dork," quipped Jones. "Young, dumb, and full of cum," said Massimo in jest, then reached for a styrofoam cup that he had resting on his dark blue Ford Crown Victoria. Steam rose from the peel back tab opening on the plastic lid as he took a sip of hot coffee, relishing the hot liquid but more importantly needing the caffeine. He was still wearing his sport coat and tie under a long beige woolen winter coat.

"You working some long hours on those shootings, Joe?" Parker asked.

"That is where I'm headed in a bit. I have an interview with one of my vic's relatives. This was on the way so I thought I would stop to hear the details of this girl's info," he explained.

Parker then went into all the information that was supplied by Brooks, which had already been explained to Tobias and Queeny, but the two narcs and Massimo had not heard the details as yet.

"This could turn into a big one, those Jersey Boyz are movin' in a lot of shit," Jones stated.

"What do they deal in mostly, crack?" Tobias asked, knowing that this was the most commonly sold and used narcotic in this region.

"Mostly, but they are also bringing in a lot of heroin, pure stuff, nasty," remarked Simon.

"And they're all armed, every last one," said Jones.

"They got the heavy artillery too, assault rifles, Uzis, sawed off shotguns..." Simon stated.

"They some bad dudes," said Jones.

Just then they all heard a vehicle approaching on the brick access road they had all used. They could hear the telltale sound of water being splashed from the vehicle's tires as the car bounced in and out of the potholes. Instinctively, the officers moved to positions that would be the most advantageous in the event that this approaching vehicle turned out to be loaded with hostiles. They all knew that it was more than likely the CI approaching, but a cop can't afford to take anything for granted.

As the car got closer they could see the headlights shining down the brick road and bouncing up and down with the road surface. The vehicle stopped short of the corner that led to the rear of the building, a car door opened and a female voice said, "Hello?"

Parker recognized the voice as that of Brooks, so she peered out from around the building and called out to Brooks, "You alone?"

"Yeah."

"Bring your car back here," Parker requested.

Brooks did as asked and parked her car out of sight from the main road, a beat-looking, cream-colored, early '90s Toyota Corolla.

Parker brought Brooks over to the other officers and introduced her only as Sequita. She did not give Brooks the officers' last names either. Narcs all know not to trust CIs; today they may be helping the police, but tomorrow they could be supplying their drug dealer friends with information about the cops. At this point, Massimo announced that he had to leave and wished everyone good luck. Parker promised to call him later with their results.

Parker told Simon to search Brooks's car and then she took Brooks into the van with Queeny and closed the sliding door behind them. The other three officers climbed into one of the two undercover cars that the narcs drove to the operation and fired up the engine to keep warm.

Inside the van, Parker explained that Brooks had to be searched, along with her vehicle, to make sure she was not carrying any dope, money or any other illegal items. This was to counter any future claims by a defense attorney that the CI brought her own dope to the scene and simply pretended it was purchased from the target. It sounds ridiculous but this claim has been made before and successfully sold to jurors. To avoid this tactic, it was just easier to search the CI before the deal went down.

Parker also had to hold any money that Brooks had on her. This was done to ensure that she would only use bills that were supplied to her by Parker, the serial numbers for which had been recorded earlier by the narc supervisor. If and when a search warrant was executed on the row house, the officers could compare any currency found against Parker's recorded serial numbers. If there were any matches, this would be damning evidence to provide in court.

Parker counted out $275, the going price in this area for a quarter ounce of crack cocaine. She then had Brooks sign a form indicating that she had just received this amount in funds from Parker. Then she had Brooks raise her shirt so that she could attach the transmitter to Brooks's body. The unit was placed inside a pocket specially made for this item. The pocket was part of an ace bandage type wrap that had Velcro on it so that the bandage could be wrapped around the wearer's torso. The wrap was elastic so the unit held close to the skin, keeping the profile of the transmitter to a minimum from any observers. The microphone cord was fed between Brooks's breasts and taped just above the left breast bra cup. This was an attempt by Parker to place the microphone in the best position to record the conversation and at the same time to keep this component out of sight. Parker was always glad to use this type of interception unit in the winter time, because the heavy clothing made concealing these components much easier.

Parker then moved some dials on the receiver unit and opened the sliding van door. She walked Brooks outside and around the corner of the old steel plant building, leaving Queeny inside the van with instructions to listen to the receiver to confirm that the transmitter was working. Parker reached under Brooks's Baby Phat coat and the two layers of undershirts and hit the on switch to the transmitter.

"Test, test, one, two three," she said, about two feet in front of Brooks. Then she walked around the corner and Queeny gave the thumbs up to Parker.

"Turn on the recorders," Parker requested of Queeny. She had demonstrated to Queeny earlier how the recorder was to be turned on. There was also a back-up tape recorder that Queeny was to activate just in case the digital recorder malfunctioned.

Queeny hit the appropriate buttons and gave the thumbs up sign again.

Parker walked back over to Brooks and began speaking in the direction of the microphone. "This is Detective Sergeant Parker of the Pittsburgh Metro PD, the date is 16 January 2009 the time is 1905 hours, my A-Tech certification number is A-55223, this operation is a controlled purchase of one quarter ounce of crack cocaine for $275 from Latoya Drexler from the front porch of her residence at number four Bartlett Street, Pittsburgh, PA by a cooperating witness." Called a preamble, Parker had recited this speech a hundred times in the last five years and then she continued by directing a question to Brooks. "Do I have your permission to record your voice on this device?"

"Yes," said Brooks.

"Did you arrange to purchase one quarter ounce of crack cocaine from Latoya Drexler on this date?" Parker asked into the hidden microphone.

"Yes."

"At what price and at what time is this purchase to take place?"

"For $275 at 7:30," Brooks answered.

"The device will be deactivated now and reactivated when needed," Parker finished and walked around the corner, giving Queeny the finger across the throat sign meaning to kill the recorders, which she did. Parker then asked Brooks, "OK, if something goes wrong and you are in danger we need to work out a signal. A word that you can say that will alert us that you are in trouble. Do you have any suggestions?"

"Ah, how about 'my kids are sick I need to go'?" Brooks suggested.

"That's fine," Parker approved. Then she turned to the other officers and gave some last-second instructions to all of them. When she did not receive any questions, Parker simply stated, "Let's roll."

Alias Simon and Jones left first; they were to take up surveillance positions in the front and rear of the row of houses on Bartlett Street; Jones in the front, Simon in the rear. They did this first because it might look suspicious if all four of the vehicles that were going in on this operation arrived at the same time and in the same general area. In addition, the two narc officers could scout out to see if anything was suspicious or out of the ordinary at row house number four. They were to keep in touch with Parker via Nextel cell phone, using the two-way radio function.

After Alias Simon and Jones reported back to Parker that they were in position and that all looked normal in the neighborhood, Parker was ready to tell Brooks to move out. But she first explained to her that the van had to follow her, to and from the scene, so that it could be testified to later in court that Brooks didn't stop anywhere and pick up a stash of dope to use as the substance purchased from the target. Brooks acknowledged the instructions. Parker then reactivated the body wire and gave her the go sign. Brooks fired up the Corolla and pulled away with Tobias, Queeny, and Parker following in the van.

It took just five minutes to reach the area of Bartlett Park and Tobias found a parking place about fifty yards from row house number four, which offered a clear view of the area. He killed the engine and the lights, then slid his driver's seat rearward in an attempt to make himself less visible to outside observers. Parker looked out the front windshield and saw Brooks exiting her parked Toyota and walking up toward Drexler's residence.

"Good thing the snow tapered off so we don't have to have the wipers going to see," she said to the other two cops.

Parker had turned on the recorders before leaving the old steel plant, so all the audio was now being recorded for use in court later. The three officers sat back in the van and listened live as the scene developed. They could hear the rustling of the fabric of Brooks's undershirt against the microphone. They could detect her footfalls on the pavement of the sidewalk and then how the sound changed when she began climbing the stairs of the wooden front porch to Drexler's residence. Then the sharp rapping on the front door to the house as Brooks summoned the occupants to the door.

Parker put up to her eyes a pair of field glasses to watch and get a better look at what was taking place on the porch. She wanted to physically see the deal if possible and to positively identify Drexler as she sold the dope to the CI. She watched and heard the door open and Drexler appear from behind it, saying, "Hey girl, come on in."

"I can't, my kids are sick...shit!" Brooks said, inadvertently giving the code words for help.

Parker knew not to move in, because it was a common occurrence with CIs to let the code words slip out. They have the phrase in their mind and being under some tension the words are mistakenly blurted out before they are aware. She could see and hear that Brooks wasn't in any trouble and that she had just made a mistake, so they all sat tight for the time being.

"What's wrong?" Drexler asked.

"Nothing. I just forgot something; I have to pick up some medicine for the kids," Brooks covered nicely.

"Come inside girl, out this cold," Drexler offered.

"I can't. I got to pick up that medicine before the store closes. You have my stuff?" Brooks inquired.

"We got to wait on Ease. He is comin' with a load from Jersey. He should be here soon. Now come on, you're lettin' in the cold air," coaxed Drexler.

Brooks had no choice. She knew that the conversation inside was not going to be admissible but she had to enter or call the deal off. She wanted this over with tonight, so she accepted the offer to go into the house. The cops would have to just deal with it, she reasoned.

"Damn!" Parker said and killed the recording devices as per legal requirements. She left the receiver on and still listened to what was transpiring inside the house. This was completely legal, with the justification being to ensure the safety of the confidential informant. However any incriminating statements heard by the officers in this situation were inadmissible in court.

The officers could hear the rustling of the microphone against Brooks's shirt as she walked inside, then the door closing behind her. Drexler told her to sit down and offered a drink; Brooks declined. The cops heard a metallic jingling sound and then a bark from a dog.

"When did you get the pit?" Brooks asked.

"Ease got him about a month ago. Said that he could protect his stash when we weren't home. But I can't stand him and I'm afraid for my kids," Drexler complained.

The cops then could hear two small children playing in the background. An occasional shout or laughing and the banging of a toy on the floor could be detected. Also in the background a television set was blaring the sounds of an up-to-date action movie.

Except for the intermittent explosions from the movie track, the cops could hear most of the conversation between the two women.

Drexler did most of the talking while Brooks sat quietly and listened. Parker was pleased with this informant so far. She was doing exactly what she had to under the circumstances. Drexler droned on about her problems with Ease and his womanizing.

"Men," was all that Brooks answered, concurring with Drexler.

Then she went into how he was using her not only to sleep with but as a safe house for his *stash,* as she called it. Parker and the other two perked up to listen. "He's bringing in a half kilo from Jersey tonight," she told Brooks. Then the cops could hear Drexler walk across the room.

"Look at this here," they could hear a door open.

"Damn!" Brooks answered. "Where did he get all those guns?" she asked Drexler.

"Hell, I don't know, but if I am caught with this shit it's my ass not his. What does he give me—a thousand a week? It ain't enough for the risk I am taking and the cash he makes," Drexler stated angrily.

"Can we call him? I really have to get going. I got to get to the store, remember?" Brooks requested.

"Yeah, I'll call him. Where is that fool?" Drexler asked no one in particular.

They could hear some movement amongst the noise of the television set and the kids still playing.

"It's me. Where are you?" Drexler said, presumably into the phone.

"What?"

"Well when you comin'?"

"I needs some money that's why," Drexler said to Ease on the other end. Without even a goodbye, she disconnected the call. Then to Brooks she stated, "He ain't comin'. He got tied up in Jersey. He'll be here tomorrow if you want to come back."

"OK, should I call you?" Brooks answered.

"No, I'll call you after he drops the stuff at my house," Drexler replied.

The next thing they heard was Brooks ask, "What's the matter?"

"That damn thing is on again," said Drexler.

"What?"

"This monitor that he put in. It's supposed to pick up if someone comes in here with a wire on, but it goes off all the time," Drexler explained to Brooks in a disturbed voice.

"Shit!" Parker said to the other two.

"Should we go in?" Queeny asked.

"No. She said that it goes off all the time. Maybe she will think it's a false alarm," Parker explained, then picked up her Nextel. "Be advised there is a RFI inside the house. We don't think our hero has been compromised. Sit tight," she reported to Alias Simon and Jones, using the cop slang "hero" to refer to the CI.

Both narc cops acknowledged their Sergeant by simply stating, "OK."

RFI was short for "Radio Frequency Indicator." The more sophisticated drug dealers would use them to indicate the presence of body transmitters in the room, just like in this case. Fortunately this monitor appeared to be faulty and did not seem to alarm Drexler that it was indicating the presence of a transmitter. This unit plugged into a simple wall socket and had two small LEDs on the face; one was to show that the component was powered on and the other would light up when the frequency of a transmitter was detected. Drexler and Brooks saw both lights activated. Brooks hurriedly moved toward the door, not wanting Drexler to think into this warning device too deeply until she was out the door and safely driving away in her car to meet up with the cops outside.

"OK, I'll call you tomorrow," Brooks said and could be heard walking across the room again. The dog barked and the rattle of its tags could be heard. Then the door opened and Brooks reappeared on the front porch.

Then Drexler called out from the front door to Brooks as she walked to the street and her car, "I'll call you when it gets here." Then she closed the door.

CHAPTER 18

Back at the Drug Enforcement Office the cops sat down with Brooks to totally debrief her on what had been said and exactly what she had seen inside row house number four. Brooks was sitting on a creaky wooden chair that the cops used for CIs and other non-police personnel. It was partly an interrogation thing but mainly the cops wanted the comfortable chairs for themselves and would rather not sit on the same chair as the suspects they dealt with. She was sitting in the middle of a room that was full of detective desks. The typical government-issue desks constructed of drab gray industrial metal, some dating back to the '70s.

The cops surrounded her, all sitting on the cushioned office seats, leaning forward trying to catch every word. Except for Alias Simon and Jones, they were sitting on separate desk tops, one cheek on the desk and the other leg on the floor. Simon was playing with a rubber band while Jones was doodling in a notebook.

Parker had a digital voice recorder going as she led the questioning of the CI. "What did the guns look like?" she asked Brooks.

"There were about five of them and they were all with long barrels and they were all black."

"Were some of the barrels wider than the others?" asked Parker.

"I think so, but most looked about the same. Some were longer than the others," expounded Brooks.

"Were there any handguns?"

"I didn't see any."

"How about any dope in plain sight?"

"No I didn't see that either," said Brooks.

"Did you see a computer anywhere?" Queeny chimed in.

"Yeah, I did. It was in the living room on a desk top, a big black one," Brooks answered, sounding pleased with herself now that she had apparently given a response that the cops wanted to hear, judging from how their demeanors changed.

They all sat quietly for a moment, the cops trying to figure if there were any more questions they needed to ask the CI. Brooks was wondering when she could leave. She was nervous being in there even though she had been driven into the station concealed in the undercover van. Jones broke the silence, "Whadaya think, Sarge?"

"Well she has the known and reliable status so it might be enough for a search warrant," speculated Parker.

"What does that mean?" Brooks asked.

"It means since you cooperated with the police in the past and as a result that person was convicted of a crime, in the eyes of the courts you have demonstrated that you can be a reliable witness for the police. When you have that status, anything you observe that is of an illegal nature, like drugs or guns, is as good as having the actual evidence in our hands. So the conversation that you had with Drexler about the dope coming in and the guns that you saw in the closet can possibly be used for us to apply for a search warrant for the house and an arrest warrant for Drexler and Belford," explained Parker.

"But you are not sure?" Tobias asked.

Parker looked at Tobias and answered his question by saying, "Let me call the on-duty DA."

Parker walked into her office, which she shared with the other Drug Enforcement supervisor. The outside of the office door had the words Drug Enforcement Supervisor stenciled on the window glass. The other cops leaned back in their chairs to wait for Parker's return. Tobias pinched a fresh chew while Queeny continued questioning Brooks on her observations inside the row house. Alias Simon and Jones began a heated debate on which was the most valuable Pittsburgh Steelers football player, James Harrison or Ben Roethlisberger.

"Roethlisberger is only as good as his line," Simon proclaimed.

"You show me one other QB in the league that has the size of Big Ben and can move in the pocket the way he does," Jones countered.

"Donavan McNabb, smart ass. That's one."

"McNabb isn't as big as Roethlisberger and you know it. Give me another one," challenged Jones.

"I can't think of any right now but my point is that the Steelers' defense is number one in the league and Harrison deserves most of the credit. The offense is just mediocre so Harrison is more valuable than Roethlisberger, case closed." stated Simon.

"Case closed my ass. You don't know football. You can barely throw a spiral," Jones said as Parker re-entered the room from her office.

All discussion stopped to listen to what Parker had found out from the on-call DA. Simon took the chance to shoot his rubber band at Jones, hitting him in the side of the face.

"You're gonna regret that," Jones threatened.

"We have to do another buy," Parker said flatly.

"What!" all the cops in the room said in unison, along with Brooks.

"He said that we don't have enough. The judges have been very strict lately on CI information and they probably won't sign the warrants on what we have, so we have to do this all over again tomorrow," explained Parker. "I know it sucks but what can we do? This time you have to go in without the wire since they have that RFI. Try the same thing to make the buy on the porch so we can watch you. Do not go inside for any reason, OK?" she asked Brooks.

"I don't know. What if they think I'm a snitch since they have that radio thing?"

"Drexler didn't think anything of the RFI tripping while you were inside so I think you are alright," deduced Parker.

"If she is suspicious of you she just won't make the deal—that's all. She will make some excuse why she can't sell to you, like telling you that the shipment didn't come in," stated Jones, having experienced a similar situation several times before.

"OK, I'll do it," Brooks replied.

Massimo kicked the snow off his shoes on the cement stoop at the base of the full-length glass entry way to the station house. He had finished his interview and was very pleased with the progress of his double shooting case. The relative of one of the victims that he had just interviewed gave him the final piece of information that would lead to charges against the actor.

The relative who was a male cousin of one of the victims told Massimo that he was with the victim just prior to his demise by a hail of bullets on 34th Street and Littleton Way. The relative said that his cousin received a call from Slade, a street name that Massimo was familiar with and belonging to his prime suspect. His cousin had stated that he was going to meet Slade at the corner of 34th and Littleton for a drug deal. The witness continued by reciting Slade's cell number to Massimo. This was confirmed when Massimo pulled out his case file which contain Slade's cell phone records for the date in question, and the numbers matched. Massimo asked his wit about the second victim that was also shot and killed. The witness said that his cousin had planned on taking this second victim along with him for his meeting with Slade. Thank you very much, Massimo thought and went off to the station to complete his report of the interview while the information was fresh in his mind.

As he climbed the stairs to the second floor to the detectives' squad room, he was hoping that he would get home before midnight. The wife had been chewing him a new one ever since he started this case, having to work several late nights. Then he began to wonder why Parker hadn't called him back yet. That wasn't a good sign, he reasoned. When he entered the squad room, he saw Jerry Aultman, one of the afternoon dicks, working at his computer. Sitting at a parallel desk was the infamous Faust. This caught Massimo off guard since Faust was a daylight dick and was rarely seen working this late. Massimo said hello to Jerry but ignored Faust and sat down at his own desk to start on his report.

Massimo's work station was three desks away from Faust's but the two desks faced each other. Fortunately, their respective computer screens blocked a direct view of one another, Massimo thought. He began to take out his case file and notebook that contained the notes from the interview he had just conducted when Faust opened up his big mouth. "Hey Jerry!"

"Yeah," Altman answered.

"How's that stabbing case going that you have?"

"OK, why?" Jerry replied incredulously.

Massimo knew why Jerry answered this way, because Faust never asked how anyone was doing on his or her cases; he was strictly concerned for himself and no one else.

"Just asking. You getting all your interviews done?"

"Almost. I have a few more to do," Altman responded, as if he were waiting for a punch line to a joke.

"All those people to interview; that can be very time consuming, but vital to a good case. I hope all our dicks do good interviews and cover all the bases. You know wasting time on frivolous things or investigations that could be considered unauthorized would be a serious failure to do one's duty, don't you think?" said Faust like he had been practicing this speech a while.

Jerry, along with Massimo, now recognized what was taking place. Altman realized that this directed at Massimo, about exactly what he didn't know, nor did he care. He had seen Faust do the same thing to other officers and tonight he just wasn't in the mood to play along, so he simply answered, "Yeah, whatever."

"No, I mean if you spend time working a shit case that is already DEAD, the cases you should be working, are going to go into the crapper. I hate to be that guy," said Faust sarcastically.

Altman just shook his head in disbelief and went back to his own work.

Massimo decided that he just couldn't let this one go, even though his better judgment told him to stay silent and wait for the outcome of Parker's drug investigation.

"You know Jerry, there is one thing that Faust said that is right on the mark." Massimo didn't wait to see if Jerry would acknowledge him; he just plowed ahead and finished his thought. "If Faust is an expert on anything, it's shit, because he is full of it."

Altman shook his head again and giggled silently to himself then returned to his computer screen.

Faust didn't say a word but continued to smile in Massimo's direction for a moment in defiance. Massimo narrowed his coal black eyes right back at Faust and locked his gaze directly into those of his enemy. Faust began to waver and looked over to his computer screen. His grin disappeared for a moment but then returned to his face.

What Massimo didn't know was that Faust was looking at a video that he had shot that very evening on his own digital recorder. He had followed Massimo to the meeting point at the old U.S. Steel plant and recorded all the cars that went in and out from behind the plant building. He was intending to show this video to Lt. Marks in the morning and was sure that it would give Massimo a reprimand or a suspension. With this bit of comfort to rely on, he looked down at his keyboard and hit a key that saved the video to his hard drive. He popped the DVD out of the tray and then turned off his computer. As he rose from his desk he stated, "Another case solved. I'm goin' home."

All the time Massimo's determined stare followed him out of the room, Faust was careful to divert his gaze as he left. Massimo could see that Faust was a coward and so could Altman. Jerry was watching the whole exchange and after Faust left the room he simply snickered again to himself and said, "What a tool."

The next evening, they were all in the same positions as the previous night. This time however the snowfall that took place during the day had accumulated to four inches, so the ground was covered in a carpet of white. Though the snow had abated, the bone chilling cold remained. The thermometer dropped to ten degrees Fahrenheit; factoring in the wind chill, the mercury was nearing zero.

Tobias had used the time in the day to visit Diaz again and bring him up to speed on the latest events. Diaz in turn reported to Tobias that his recovery was just about complete; as proof he showed Tobias how he was walking without the cane any longer. When the cops all gathered at the Drug Enforcement Office earlier that evening, he relayed the good news about Diaz to the other officers, which did not include Massimo this time. Tobias figured he was still dogged down with his double shooting investigation.

Parker, who was sitting in the back passenger area of the van, put the field glasses up to her eyes and spied Brooks at the front door to row house number four. She reported the time that Brooks had reached this location so that Queeny could write it down on a notepad. All the relevant times were to be recorded in Parker's report on this drug buy. The door opened and Drexler appeared from behind it; so far so good, she thought. Parker was confident that the buy would go tonight. Earlier, Brooks had reported to her that she spoke to Drexler and was told that Ease had arrived from Jersey and dropped the new supply of dope at the row house—then left again to attend to some other business matters.

"Come on," Drexler said to Brooks and turned back toward the inside of the house, leaving the door ajar so Brooks could enter.

"I can't. My kids again. Do you have the stuff ready? Just bring it out so I can get on out of here," Brooks encouraged.

"It's upstairs. I have to get it. Get on in here girl. You're chillin' the whole place down with that door open," Drexler insisted.

Brooks simply saw no other choice, so she walked inside and closed the door behind her.

"Damn! That bitch did it again!" complained Parker, then she grabbed her Nextel and called Simon.

"Tom?" Parker said into the mic of the Nextel after the electronic chirp.

"Go ahead," Simon acknowledged.

"The hero went inside again. Can you get close enough to catch what is going on in there?" Parker requested.

"I think so. It's getting so you can't find good CIs anymore," joked Simon.

Then Jones had to add his remarks, "Simon. Let me know if they strip down to have a pillow fight."

To which Simon answered, "Yeah, like I would tell you."

Simon killed the engine on his undercover car. He was parked in an alley that ran perpendicular to the one that led behind the row houses on Bartlett Street making a T. Simon was able to watch the back door of row house number four from this position without being noticed and while sitting comfortably in his car with the heat running. He now grudgingly stepped out into the icy cold air and raised up his hoodie to cover as much of his face as possible—to fend off the cold wind and for concealment. Simon walked down the alley toward the rear of the row house, hands dug deep into his hoodie pockets. His left was on the Nextel, his right on his Glock, just in case.

He sidled up next to a telephone pole at the mouth of the perpendicular alleyway. He stood leaning against the pole as if he were waiting to meet someone and peered through the back window of the row house. He couldn't see much because the room behind this window was dark. Beyond this room Simon could see through an entryway to a second one; fortunately for him this room was lit. In the area that was visible to him, none of the occupants were in view. He couldn't hear anything from this distance but on the other hand he didn't want to get any closer at this point, remembering the camera system that had been described to him.

Then he saw Drexler walk over to a dark leather chair in the lighted room; he figured it was the living room, and she plopped down in the seat. She lit a cigarette and from the way she was gesturing with her hands it appeared that she was talking to someone, probably Brooks, on the opposite side of the room. He couldn't see for sure due to a partial wall that separated the darkened and lighted rooms. Simon was viewing Drexler through the entryway connecting these two areas of the house. Everything looked relaxed and causal to Simon so he withdrew the Nextel from his pocket and hit the preprogrammed button on the touch pad for Parker's phone.

He reported his observations to her and Parker stated in response that she would call Brooks on her cell and make sure that she was OK.

In the van Parker hit the numbered button that she had programmed in for Brooks's cell and after a few rings Brooks answered.

"Everything OK?" Parker asked simply.

"Yeah I'm aw-ight," she answered in street lingo.

"Is Ease in there?" Parker whispered, not wanting the sound from Brooks's cell to reach Drexler's ears.

"No, I'll be home in a minute," Brooks play-acted.

"OK, but the minute something seems wrong you come out or we are coming in," commanded Parker.

"No problem. I'll get it," Brooks replied then she heard Parker's phone disconnect.

Brooks, who was sitting on a couch against the opposite wall from Drexler, took a drag from her own cigarette and looked up at Drexler across the room, feeling as if she had to explain the phone call she had just received.

"That was my neighbor. She is watching my kids. I better get goin'. Can I get that stuff?"

"Yeah, it's upstairs. I'll be right back," Drexler said then rose from the chair and walked slowly up the stairs to the second floor.

The television was blaring again, this time with one of those reality shows in which people always seem to be screaming at each other about the most trivial issues. Maybe it is like reality? Brooks thought. She could hear the kids upstairs stomping around in one of the rooms and laughing occasionally at things unknown to her. The Pit Bull came down the steps and walked into the room with Brooks, the dog's tags jingling with each step. He stopped and looked at her when he entered the living room, then gave a low growl.

"Shut up and lay down, you nasty-ass beast," Brooks ordered and to her surprise the dog complied.

Outside Parker and the other two cops in the van saw a car pull up in front of the row house and stop double parked in the street. The door on the passenger side opened and a black male exited. Parker spied him with the binoculars and informed her partners, "It's him. Ease."

She quickly snatched up her Nextel and told Alias Simon and Jones, who had just arrived at the row house and advised them to stand by in their positions. She instructed Simon to get as close as possible and see if he could listen to what was going on inside. Simon acknowledged the new instructions and saw another telephone pole he could stand next to, near the rear of the row house. He crossed the alley that made the top of the T intersection, nestled up next to the rear window of the house, and waited to see what, if anything, he could detect from the inside.

Parker watched as Ease jogged up the front steps of the row house then opened the door and went inside. He was wearing a red New Jersey Devils hockey team hoodie, which stood out against the white backdrop of snow like lights on a Christmas tree. The car that Ease had just gotten out of was all blacked out, from its paint job to the dark tinted windows, a mid '80 s era Chevrolet Monte Carlo SS, which remained idling in front of the row house.

Drexler had stomped back down the stairs with the cigarette hanging from her lips and upon reaching the bottom raised up the clear plastic baggy in her hand to show Brooks the white irregular ball of rock cocaine that was inside. Brooks smiled, thinking finally I can get out of here. Just as Brooks was reaching into her pocket to retract the pre-recorded $275, she turned at the sound of the front door opening and in walked Ease.

Brooks quickly pulled her hand out of her pocket without the money; at the same time Drexler shoved the quarter ounce ball of crack into the front pocket of her tight-fitting jeans. She didn't realize it, but the tail of the baggy was protruding out of her pocket. If Ease discovered that she was slinging dope from his safe house she knew that he would get angry and possibly cut off her source of cash. He had been very adamant about this with her, stating that he didn't want the heat on the house where he kept his stash.

Ease could see from the expressions on their faces that he had interrupted something.

"What's going on?" he asked.

"Nothing. What are you doin' here?" Drexler asked him, then sat in the leather recliner.

"I gots to get me somethin'," he replied and walked deeper into the living room. The Pit had gone over to him and sniffed around his bright white, blue-trimmed Jordan Air Force One sneakers. Ease kicked at the dog to shoo him away.

Ease looked at Brooks sitting on the couch. Since she was an old girlfriend of his and her presence was a bit unusual, he asked, "What you doin' here?"

"Just visitin' Toy," Brooks used the abbreviation of Drexler's first name.

Ease, still suspicious, looked over at Drexler who was snuffing out her cigarette in a glass ashtray on the recliner's armrest. He quickly saw the portion of the baggy sticking out of her pants pocket and he slowly walked over to her and in his calm and controlled manner asked Drexler, "How about a square?" street slang for a cigarette.

As Drexler reached for the pack of Newports on the same armrest as the ashtray, Ease quickly snatched the baggy out of her pocket and held up the ball of crack.

"Damn you bitch!" he said in a voice somewhat louder than usual for Ease. "I told you not to do this. What if she is working for the PO-lice?" he questioned, pointing at Brooks.

"She is OK, Ease. Don't worry. She was here last night too and nothing happened," Drexler pleaded, not sure what this fact really meant to her case. But it did remind her of the RFI that had activated while Brooks had been in the house last evening. She quickly looked over at the RFI unit and was relieved when it showed no indication of a transmitter present. She thought if she reported this to Ease it would calm his fears. She could not have been more mistaken.

"See the unit is not on. It turned on last night but now it's off. She isn't wired or anything."

Ease quickly deciphered what Drexler had just said and remarked, "When she was here the unit went off?"

"Yeah, but it wasn't working right," she replied.

Brooks was getting very nervous and began to rise up to leave because she knew where this was going.

Ease, seeing her move, pushed her back down onto the couch and said, "You aren't goin' anywhere, Bitch."

Ease did a quick pat-down of Brooks's body, searching for an electronic transmitting unit. Not finding one, he straightened upright. Then he turned back toward Drexler and tossed the quarter ounce of crack back into her lap and walked over to the closet where the long guns were kept and opened the door.

"They are probably outside right now, you dumb-ass ho." As he said this, he grabbed an Uzi submachine gun from the closet and slammed a magazine home into the receiver of the weapon. Then racking the bolt to put the first round into the chamber he looked down at Brooks and said, "You're lucky I don't kill you right here."

The words came out monotone, and to Brooks this made the statement even more chilling. But the content of the threat also told her that he wasn't going to do anything to her at that time. Probably because he realized that the police were right outside and any shooting inside would not end well for him. Then Ease went over to his computer and hit a button on the keyboard. The screen lit up and displayed live images of several different camera views from the outside and inside of the row house. Ease's eye caught some movement on the camera near the rear door. He could see a figure standing there next to the row house back window.

"See, they're out there now," he said to both women, pointing at the computer monitor.

Ease scooped up another magazine for the Uzi and turned to leave. As he moved, he looked over at Drexler and said, "You're on your own now." Then he tucked the Uzi inside his coat and bolted out the door.

Earlier on the same day Massimo arrived at work around 10:00 a.m., two hours later than usual since he worked such a late shift the night before. When he sat down at his work station there was a yellow sticky note pasted to the middle of his desk that read, "Joe, see me when you get in. LT. Marks."

Massimo had the reaction that most cops initially do when seeing such a note. He scanned his mind about anything he may have done wrong lately that would rate being called in by the lieutenant. Not coming up with anything, he didn't know what to expect from this request. But having been around long enough, he knew this could turn out to be a shit storm, especially since the LT and Faust were A-hole buddies; he braced himself to be ready for anything.

Seeing Marks in the hallway just outside of his office, the lieutenant waved Massimo inside then said, "Close the door," not a good sign.

"What's up?" he asked the LT.

"Something has come to my attention and we need to nip this thing now before we have another Ruggerio type situation," said Marks.

"OK, what would that be?" Massimo replied, expecting to receive another salvo from Faust.

"Have you been working with the Drug Enforcement people?"

"As a matter of fact I have, why?" Being a trained and experienced investigator, Massimo knew how to draw out information from people—even another cop. By answering his questions with another question he might be able to elicit the nature of this meeting. He had to play it close to the vest since exposing the possible existence of the Ruggerio video at this point could be dangerous. Marks could squash the whole effort he and the others were mounting to try and obtain this video.

"Well, I have heard that you were working with them on something. What is it?"

"I received information that a Jersey Boy by the name of Belford was operating in town and moving heavy weight so I gave it to the narcs. They are doing the leg work on it," Massimo said, defending himself.

"Why were you meeting the narcs behind the U.S. Steel plant off of 28 last night?" Marks inquired bluntly.

"Oh, OK," he answered with an inflection that related, "now I get it." "This is coming from Faust," Massimo stated starting to fume. He continued, "So he is following me around. I should have expected as much. Yes, I met them there just to see if they needed anything before they went off to do a controlled buy on the perp. After I met with them for about ten minutes I left and did an interview on my double shooting case," Massimo said defiantly.

Marks sensed the edge in his voice and took issue with Massimo's attitude.

"Well Joe, you don't need to stick your nose into drug business. You gave them the info and you should have let them run with it. Showing up there with an unmarked police car could have blown their cover and I don't need to have the Drug Enforcement commander giving me any static. I am going to have to give you a verbal reprimand on this, which of course will go in your file for six months. It will be removed if there aren't any more violations."

"Is that all?" Massimo asked, gaining his composure back and realizing that any further debate would be futile.

"Yeah that's it," was all Marks said.

As Massimo went back to his desk, he began to contemplate that he was experiencing a taste of what Ruggerio had been taking from this obviously unbalanced detective for all those years.

Simon had listened to the whole conversation that took place between the three parties inside of the house. He couldn't believe how transparent the walls of this row house were, even though they were constructed with brick and mortar. Then he noticed why he was able to hear so well, because the window he was standing next to had a wood frame that was completely rotted. Probably the original window hadn't been re-painted or caulked in years. He could see openings between the frame of the window and the brick work, right to the interior. Simon even considered himself fortunate that the window didn't suddenly fall out of its frame and right onto his head.

His first instinct was to call Parker and let her know what he had just heard, so he moved away from the window along the rear of the row houses approximately thirty feet, to give himself some distance for privacy. He knew that this was the evidence they needed to arrest Ease and secure a search warrant for his house. Simon crouched behind a metal dumpster in the alley, took out his Nextel, and made his report to Parker.

Jones, hearing Simon's transmission to Parker, took his Glock .40 from its holster and placed it on his lap while he watched the blacked-out Monte Carlo idling in the middle of Bartlett Street and facing in his direction. Jones was looking through his driver's side and rearview mirrors to monitor the car and to wait for Ease to reappear. To Jones, that seemed to be what the driver of the Monte Carlo was waiting for. Idling outside until his boss picked something up or to conduct a brief exchange of business at number four, then get back in the car. This was confirmed with Simon's new information that he had heard right from Ease's mouth. Incredible, he thought, that schmoe actually got close enough to hear what they were saying inside. Even though Jones didn't know what Parker wanted him to do when Ease re-emerged, he needed to be ready for anything.

He was parked next to the curb with his engine idling. At first it was to keep warm but with the arrival of the Monte Carlo it could be to follow the vehicle to its next destination. He thought about calling Parker on the Nextel and asking what he should do when Ease got back into the Monte Carlo, but knew that these instructions would be forthcoming. Parker usually didn't miss a trick.

"RAP! RAP! RAP!" Jones jumped in his seat and turned to look at what the hell that noise was that just took five years off his life. He looked over to the passenger side of his car and saw an old black man knocking on his side window with his left hand and holding a bottle of Jim Beam in his right. He was shabbily dressed in a dark blue sweatshirt, light-gray cotton jogging pants and black snow boots. He had apparently been working on the bottle for a while, evidenced by the quarter of its contents that remained and the unsteady stance that he displayed. Then he said through the window glass in an angry voice, "What the fuck you doin', boy?"

Jones didn't know it, but the old man was Marcel Tompkins, the super of the row house complex. Tompkins had been watching the undercover car idling outside his house for about fifteen minutes. As he watched he would take a pull from his Jim Beam bottle occasionally. He was waiting for one of his new hoes to show up; she was moving into his house and she would need the parking space that this car was sitting in. Becoming increasingly impatient and drunk as time went by, Tompkins decided to go out and get this intruder moving so his girl could have the space available when she arrived.

Jones quickly transitioned from fright to anger and didn't have time to explain to this old rummy that he was a cop and on a case. So he did the only thing he could think of to quickly get this old drunk away from a scene that could involve shooting in a short while. He raised the Glock .40 from his lap and pointed the weapon at the guy's face through the window glass and said in his most commanding voice, "GET YOUR RAGGEDY OLD ASS OFF THE STREET BEFORE YOU GET HURT, OLD MAN!"

Not expecting this response, the old man unconsciously released his grip on the Jim Beam bottle, which fell to the sidewalk, breaking upon impact. Then with an expression of disbelief on his face, he looked down at his crotch area. Jones could see a rapidly-growing dark spot develop on those gray jogging pants and he knew that the old man had just wet himself. Then without saying a word, the old man turned and scampered back inside row house number one. Jones couldn't help but chuckle a little at the old man's distress. With this distraction out of the way, he turned his attention back to the street where the Monte Carlo was still idling.

Then, just as Jones expected, *"Chirp, chirp,"* announced his Nextel, indicating an incoming message.

"Al, when Ease gets back in that Monte Carlo, block the road. We need to take him down," Parker instructed.

"You got it, Sarge," Jones replied.

Parker called the dispatch center and was arranging for back-up to assist when she was cut short with the reappearance of Ease on the front porch. He didn't take his time either. He shot out of the house and into the car as quickly as he could. The Monte Carlo lurched forward and pulled out from its place in front of number four. At the same time, Jones rammed the gear shift into reverse and backed his car out onto Bartlett Street and into the path of the Monte Carlo, completely blocking the road.

The Monte Carlo screeched to a stop just inches away from the rear bumper of the undercover car that Jones was driving. Jones was already bailing out of the car, trying desperately to put distance between him and the undercover vehicle in anticipation of a collision. Not hearing one, he took cover behind the driver's side front wheel of his car. Jones trained his Glock on the passenger side of the Monte Carlo then commanded, "Police. Get out of the car and put your hands up!"

In one quick and stunning motion, the passenger side door to the Monte Carlo flung open and Ease popped his head over top of the blacked out door. Immediately, Jones saw a bright orange flame exploding out from the barrel of the Uzi in his direction. While bullets sprayed out from the Uzi and peppered Jones's car, a rainfall of expended shell casings arched into the air then clinked off the asphalt street surface next to the shooter. Jones quickly realized that he was out-gunned by this assailant, his automatic weapon spewing out ten rounds with one pull of the trigger. Luckily, none found their intended target.

Jones, hearing the bullets impacting the metal of his vehicle, dropped down and hugged the pavement, waiting for the fusillade to end. Just as with the old rummy that had shocked him a few moments earlier, he had quickly regained his composure and was entering the anger phase that cops experience when being fired upon.

"Mother fucker!" he said to the pavement, then angrily pushed his body off the street surface and rolled back toward the center portion of his vehicle; his back struck the driver's door, which he had left open, so hard that it slammed shut. At this point he didn't hear any follow-up gunfire from Ease, so Jones stood up and threw his arms out and over the roof of his car, training his Glock in Ease's direction. Using point shooting, Jones snapped off two quick shots at Ease, one hitting the upper part of the door frame Ease was standing behind, the other passing within an inch over his head, so close that Ease heard the bullet whistle past him.

Ease took the hint and bolted rearward on Bartlett Street in the opposite direction of the cop who had nearly creased his skull, running with the Uzi still in his right hand.

When Tobias saw Ease jump into the Monte Carlo, he jerked the van into drive and zoomed down the street. He made a left turn onto Bartlett and was approaching the location where Jones had the Monte Carlo stopped, then he saw Ease running right at him in the middle of the street. Tobias thought about waffling him with the van but realized that they still needed this guy alive to get the DVD of Ruggerio's shooting incident so he hit the brakes and brought the van to a stop. Ease veered left, jumped onto the sidewalk, ran right past Tobias's van, and continued down Bartlett Street.

Parker grabbed the inside handle of the sliding side door to the van and pulled the door open. At the same time she shouted to Queeny to follow her. Then she yelled to Tobias, "Toby! Go after that son-of-a-bitch!"

Parker and Queeny jumped from the van, leaving the door open, and ran down the street toward the stopped Monte Carlo. Parker went to the driver's side and Queeny ran to the passenger side, which still had the door hanging open. When they reached the car, Parker quickly pulled open the driver's door while Queeny pointed her Glock and the beam of her flashlight into the interior of the car toward the driver.

Parker, holding her Glock .40 in her right hand, whipped the car door open with her left then reached for the driver's shirt collar. She grabbed the driver, apparently terror-stricken since he wasn't moving, and yanked him out of his seat and onto the pavement of the street face first. Parker followed this up by jamming her right knee into the middle of the driver's back and pointing the barrel of her Glock at the base of his head.

The driver, a twenty-something black male, was frozen with fear from what he had just experienced. He had never been in a shootout before, not like Ease, who had at least one body to his name back in Jersey. This poor kid was so scared that if the cops told him to stand on his head and quack like a duck he would have done it to keep from getting shot. So when Parker told the driver, "Don't move," in a low but determined voice. The driver simply responded, "Yes ma'am."

Queeny ran over to Parker's side of the car and stated, "The car is clear," meaning there were no further occupants inside and Parker didn't have to worry about another threat. Queeny quickly holstered up and produced her handcuffs, snapping them on the driver while Parker stood upright.

Jones had been covering both the female cops as they arrested the driver. After seeing that the suspect was secured and there were no further threats, he jumped back into his car and pulled out to assist in chasing down Ease.

Parker, still thinking clearly, told Queeny to get inside the row house and make sure that the CI was OK and to arrest Drexler. Queeny gave a quick, "OK," and ran toward the house.

As she approached the front porch, Queeny remembered that there was a Pit Bull inside this house. She drew her Glock and shifted it to her left hand, then retrieved her Taser from its holster with her right. The door was slightly ajar so Queeny kicked it inward and shouted, "POLICE!"

As she expected, here came "Fight-o," snarling and frothing at the mouth, running at Queeny. While holding her service pistol down at her left side, she carefully took aim at the charging beast with the Taser. When the animal got within approximately ten feet, Queeny pulled the trigger. Two metal barbs attached to thin electrical wires shot out of the Taser unit and struck home into the dog's chest and left leg. The barbs buried themselves into the canine's skin and delivered a jolt of electricity to the animal, causing him to yelp in pain and tumble onto the floor, incapacitated. She had made sure her Taser unit was ready for duty earlier at the station. Silently, she thanked Curly, her grisly sergeant, for instilling in her the habit of checking her equipment before going out on a detail.

After confirming that the dog was out of action, Queeny entered through the threshold of the door, raised the Glock with her left hand, and pointed it at the two females. She found both of them still inside, looking out the front window at the action outside. She ordered both of them to get down on the floor and stay there while she held them both at gunpoint until additional units could arrive.

Tobias rammed the gear shift into reverse to follow after Ease, then punched the accelerator causing the rear tires to screech and smoke on the pavement of the street. The van shot backward causing the side sliding door that Queeny and Parker had left open to whiz on its runners and slam shut. To see where he was going

Tobias had to look through the side view mirrors since the blinds in the van covered all the windows, including the two rear windows that were on the back double doors. Tobias didn't slow up at all but tried to keep the van straight as he sped backward and hoped he wouldn't hit anything.

He zipped past Ease as he ran on the sidewalk, then Tobias quickly made it to the street that he had just come from. While still moving rearward he snapped the wheel to the left and maneuvered the van onto this intersecting road; he was now facing in the direction where Ease was running. He watched as Ease made it to the end of the block of row houses and made a left turn away from Tobias. He jammed the van into drive and went after him, following as Ease made another left turn into the alley that ran behind the row houses and in the direction of where Simon was staked out.

Simon, after hearing the commotion coming from the front street, stayed where he was behind a dumpster. This was the same dumpster that Lewis had found next to the rear of row house number six, the house G had used. Simon figured this would be good cover just in case Ease should burst out of that back door of his residence. He was really operating blind because none of his fellow officers had a chance to get on their Nextels and keep him informed of what was happening. So he was left to simply prepare himself for anything.

As he crouched there, gun at the ready, he detected tires screeching toward the opposite end of the alley from his position. Simon turned to look in this direction and suddenly picked up a form running toward him. He quickly moved from the end of the metal dumpster that exposed his back to this unidentified runner and moved to the other side, which offered protection from this possible threat. He watched and waited with his firearm aimed at the runner as he got closer. Simon spied the downward cast of a street light that shone onto the alleyway, making a circular form on the pavement. He knew that when the runner reached this lighted circle he would be able to identify him. The foot falls got closer and Simon readied himself to make a verbal challenge.

Just as the runner was into the beam of the street light, the headlights of Tobias's van jerked around the corner, shone down the alley toward Simon, and backlit the runner. Simon was able make out the outline of an automatic submachine gun and knew this had to be Ease coming at him.

"STOP! POLICE!" he shouted.

The answer was a quick burst of machine gun fire in his direction.

A few rounds dinked and danked off the metal body of the dumpster, the rest impacted above Simon's head into the brick surface of the wall to the row houses. The debris showered down onto Simon as he ducked behind the dumpster for protection.

He did a quick peek around the side of the dumpster to see where Ease was running and to see if he could get a shot at the bastard who had just tried to kill him. The van's headlights still barreling down the alley showed Ease turning away from Simon and to his right, darting between two buildings. Simon jumped out from his place of concealment and waved at Tobias to stop, then shouted, "Go back and parallel him."

Tobias did as requested and reversed the van to head for the street that would be on the perp's right-hand side.

At about the same time, Simon heard a car approaching from his rear position. When he turned to look he noticed that it was Jones coming to back him up. He quickly waved at Jones to proceed up the second alley, which made the post of the T intersection. With Tobias on the right and Jones on the left side, Ease would be kept in the middle between them. Simon could then follow in Ease's tracks in the snow and possibly flush him out from between the buildings. If he was still in there, Simon hoped.

Jones, recognizing what Simon wanted, turned up the perpendicular alleyway then sped up to the end of the block, passing Simon's parked undercover vehicle at midblock. Simon reached for his Nextel and advised his backup that he had last seen the perp run between two buildings across from his position. He told them that he was going to follow his trail from where he was now.

Jones got on the Nextel and told Simon, "Wait for backup Tom."

"I just want to get a better read on where he went," Simon answered.

Then he took out his small but powerful Mag light from its belt holster and cautiously moved over to the location where Ease entered between the buildings. Once at the corner of one of the buildings, he shined his light in the last direction that he saw the perp running. Simon could see his shoe prints in the snow leading between the structures. The front building appeared to be some type of business. The outbuilding, which he was standing behind, was a storage structure for the business, he figured. The tracks ended at a wooden stockade-type fence that divided the first property from the next one in line. Simon shined his light above this fence in the direction of where Ease had run, but he could not see beyond the fence. However, he did hear movement coming from the reverse side of this fence. Simon stayed put behind the corner of the storage building. Since it was made of brick also, he thought it was a safe position for the moment.

He could hear sirens coming, so backup wasn't far away. He could either sit tight until they arrived or he could move in on the perp's likely position behind this fence. As he debated what to do, he looked up and saw a metal fire escape to the business building. He decided that he didn't want to wait for backup to arrive but instead he wanted this guy himself. This jerk had the audacity to shoot at him and Simon wasn't going to leave it at that.

As quietly as he could, he began to climb the ladder to the fire escape, which had been left down for anyone to climb onto from the ground. While he was climbing the ladder, little did he know but Jones was thinking the same way as his cowboy-up partner. Instead of waiting next to his car to see if the perp popped out from the concealment of the buildings, Jones began a search of the spaces between the structures to find the shooter. With his gun and flashlight leading the way, Jones was just as determined as Simon to find this SOB.

When Simon reached the first landing, he heard most of the sirens shut down, followed by several car doors slamming closed. He carefully peered over into the ground area on the opposite side of the stockade fence but did not see anything due to the darkness. He didn't use his light, thinking that it would make him an easy target. But then as his eyes adjusted, he could see the faint reddish color of Ease's New Jersey Devils hoodie as he lay next to the rear of the second building that fronted the street side.

Just then, he saw Jones creeping along the alleyway approaching the area where the perp was hiding and lying in wait. Simon, thinking that Jones could be walking into an ambush if the perp saw him, had to make a quick decision. Simon knew that he couldn't let his partner walk right into this death trap, so he readied himself to make a challenge and possibly shoot down at the perp.

He flicked on his light and pointed it and his Glock downward into the void that lay beneath him. Luckily, his light blinded the perp, hitting him right in the face with the beam as he looked upward. Jones had caught him completely by surprise.

Ease had found a two-foot high cement block wall that was attached and jutted out from this building. The short wall was at ground level and extended out from the rear exterior wall of the building, making an L shape. It was perfect cover from any threats made toward him at this level but offered no protection from above.

"Peek-a-boo mother fucker," said Simon.

Jones, hearing his partner's voice and seeing where his light was shining, moved in quickly, while Ease was still looking upward at the light. He aggressively bounced on Ease and stuck his Glock in the suspect's mouth. "Go ahead, shoot your mouth off. I've always wanted to say that," Jones said with a wide grin on his face.

CHAPTER 19

Two days later, Parker was walking up the footpath to a two-story Victorian-style house, thinking to herself that whoever made these bricks back in the day must have been a millionaire. Everything from that era was made of brick. This house, like most of the others in this neighborhood, probably dated back to the '30s and was well maintained. The landscaping was immaculate, so much so that even at this time of year when many perennials were dormant the plant life around the residence was still complimentary. Massimo's wife must have good taste, she thought. As she was about to press the doorbell, the front door suddenly opened.

A youthful-looking middle-aged woman with long dark hair appeared, wearing a friendly smile. She was very attractive, sporting a Pittsburgh Steelers long-sleeved jersey that was tight enough to show her well-proportioned bust line.

"You must be Celeste?" the woman said, then invited Parker inside.

Parker was also wearing a Pittsburgh Steelers team jersey. She had on number 86, Hines Ward's number. It was all part of the masquerade that Massimo devised to circumvent Lt. Marks's prohibition of his collaborating with the Drug Enforcement unit. He took advantage of the playoff game that the Pittsburgh Steelers were playing on that Sunday against the Baltimore Ravens to assemble all the officers working to clear Ruggerio's name. Massimo figured that he couldn't be disciplined for having friends over to his home for a Steelers party, no matter what division they worked in or their employment status at the time.

"Nice to meet you Mrs. Massimo," Parker said.

"Please call me Mia," she told Parker.

"Like Mamma Mia," Massimo interjected as he appeared from the kitchen holding the handle to a ceramic bowl with one hand and a huge tray full of several different types of vegetables, meats, cheeses, and broken pieces of bread in the other.

"Let's go, girls. The game is about to start," he told the woman and they followed him down to the basement. Upon reaching the basement, Parker saw Diaz, Tobias, and Lewis all sitting on bar stools next to a bar that had been constructed of T-111 paneling with a white laminate bar top. Queeny couldn't make the meeting; she had to work a day shift today but she had been promised a call if anything important developed.

"Welcome to my man cave," Massimo said then introduced Parker to Diaz and Lewis.

"What's that smell?" Tobias asked Massimo as his wife Mia filled a glass with red wine for Parker.

"*Bagna Cauda*, it means "hot bath." It's made of anchovies, butter, garlic, and olive oil. It's a dip for the veggies and bread. Big surprise, we are eating Italian today," Massimo said, putting the tray down on the bar and the dip over a fondue flame.

Mia, the perfect hostess, corrected her husband. "I have a bread bowl with a cheese and beer dip in it if you prefer that instead," she said, pointing to the other hors d'oeuvre on the bar top.

"OK, does everyone have a drink?" Massimo looked around at his guests and saw that they all had full glasses, the girls with wine and the guys with beer.

"I suggest we raise our glasses, and drink a toast to the purpose of this meeting," Massimo purposed.

To which Diaz saw an opening to make a joke. "To watch the Steelers lose to the Ravens."

They all chuckled and Lewis remarked, "We are going to convert you yet."

Diaz was the only one there not wearing a Steelers-themed jersey but he was wearing a solid black button-up shirt, which was half of the team colors of black and gold. Then Massimo started his toast, "Raise them up… here is to Ruggerio, Tobias, and Diaz. Let's make things right and clear their names… ah, salute."

They all responded together, "AH, SALUTE!" and clinked glasses.

Then Mia told everyone to help themselves, "Please make a plate and sit down."

"Yes, *mangia, mangia*," said Massimo.

The television erupted with the crowd noise from Heinz Field as the opening kickoff took place.

"OK, let's get down to business. Were you able to get the file, Celeste?" Massimo asked.

"Here it is," Parker said as she pulled the file from under her Hines Ward jersey.

She handed the file folder to Massimo and he laid it down on the bar top, then stated, "Before we get to the file 'Leste why don't you get all of us up to speed on the latest developments?"

Parker began to explain all the findings from the drug operation from row house number four. She told the group that Ease had been brought into the drug enforcement office and questioned immediately after his arrest. Being the streetwise criminal that he was, Ease's response to questioning was the expected, "I wanna talk to my lawyer first."

Of course Ease's lawyer was the highest profile attorney in the region and the highest priced also. While Parker sent people out to contact Ease's attorney, she and her team executed a search warrant at row house number four. They found a treasure trove of evidence against Ease for drug trafficking. Right where Drexler had told Queeny that night at the speakeasy, under the floorboards in the bedroom they found the half kilo of crack cocaine. Parker said that Ease must have cooked up the powder in Jersey before transporting it back to the 'burgh. They also seized numerous firearms and a large amount of cash. That was the good news, Parker stated.

The bad news was that the computer forensic analyst that Massimo connected Parker with didn't find any videos on Ease's hard drive that showed the Bartlett Park shooting. Along with Ease's drug business records, all he found were a collection of raunchy porno movies saved on the computer. They did find several DVDs in the house that were videos burned from the surveillance cameras. All of the DVDs were dated but none contained the date of the shooting. Parker had a civilian police employee begin to watch the content of each DVD, in case Ease had mistakenly put the wrong date on the DVD that contained the footage of the shooting. So far the employee hasn't found the disc they are looking for.

"Now for the even worse news," Parker announced.

"Wait, let me get another drink. I think I'm gonna need it," Tobias replied.

Parker reported to the group that the DA called her and advised that he did some research on the CI, Brooks. It turns out that the previous case, in which Brooks had assisted the police, had recently been challenged in appeals court. The defendant's attorney found a technicality and was appealing the case. So the DA was not sure if Brooks was still going to maintain her "known and reliable" status for the case against Ease. If Brooks's reliability was put into question, then the whole case could be tainted by what lawyers call "the fruit of the poisonous tree" doctrine. This means that if the probable cause police used to seize evidence was based on a fatal error, then all the seized evidence would be deemed inadmissible and not available for court.

Then Lewis chimed in an opinion. "What about the CI's observations inside the row house corroborated by Alias Simon's testimony from outside? What did the DA say about that?"

Parker answered, "He has a good feeling that this will save the case, even without Brooks's reliable status, but that isn't the problem. The problem for right now is, since there is a doubt about the case, the DA is obligated to tell the defense the issue. When this happens on Monday then the defense attorney will move to have Ease's bond reduced and he will mostly likely make that bond and be released from jail. Then who knows where he will go from there. We may never find him again and that means no DVD of the Bartlett Park shooting."

As Parker was talking, Diaz was flipping through the case file on Ease. He was curious to see what Ease looked like and what type of criminal history he had compiled during his young life. He noticed several drug and weapons charges but they all seemed to have the status of "withdrawn" or "dismissed." High priced lawyers, Diaz thought to himself. He reasoned with the right amount of money, a person can practically get out of anything; OJ proved that.

Then Tobias asked Lewis, "Did you guys get anything from house number six?"

On the same date as Parker's search of house number four, Lewis and Massimo had conducted their own search of row house number six, the location where they suspected that G had fired the warning shot in the Ruggerio shooting. The two detectives had agreed to wait on this search until the conclusion of the drug investigation that was in progress on house number four. They didn't want to tip off Ease before Parker had finished with her CI.

"Nothing. Just a lot of drug paraphernalia," answered Lewis.

As the group lamented over these set-backs, Mia moved to the opposite side of the bar where her husband was standing.

"Every time we seem to take one step forward we slide two steps back," said Tobias.

Then from out of nowhere while all the cops in the room were taxing their brains over what the next move should be, Mia provided an interesting opinion. "He probably has that DVD in a safe somewhere."

"Yeah!" Lewis said and continued, "A safety deposit box. He knew how valuable it would be to him if he ever got hemmed up by the police. He couldn't risk just leaving it lying around in one of his houses."

But as quickly as they saw hope, Parker brought them back down to reality. "We checked that, we didn't find any safe deposit keys in his house. If we had, the search warrant covers searching any safe deposit boxes that Ease may have access to. Without having a key or knowing which bank he uses, there is no way of knowing where to search."

As they talked, Diaz found the copy of Ease's inmate log-in sheet. Just as a matter of interest, he looked at the section marked, "Inmate Property." "Hey! He was booked with a set of keys on him. It says here on his log-in sheet," reported Diaz with excitement.

"We should check that out," Tobias said.

"Already doing that," Parker replied and at the same time started dialing a number on her Nextel.

The television set in the background came alive with the home crowd cheering a Pittsburgh Steelers score. Massimo grabbed his wife's hand and gave her a kiss on the cheek for her astute suggestion.

Hearing the crowd on the TV, Lewis turned toward the screen and solemnly said, "They just scored. I hope that is a good sign."

Parker was able to contact one of her friends who worked as a supervisor at the county jail where Ease was being housed and where his personal property was in storage. Her friend told Parker that they would check out Ease's belongings and call her back in a few minutes.

During the interim, the group sat largely in silence and stared at the television screen, watching the game, their thoughts not really concerned with the ebb and flow of the football contest but silently willing Parker's cell phone to ring. After about twenty excruciating minutes Parker's phone vibrated indicating an incoming call. "Yes!"

she answered. "OK describe it to me," she asked her jail friend. "Right, right. Is it about two inches long? Does it have a number engraved on it? That's it; hold on to it. I'll be right there!" Parker said with excitement then disconnected the call.

"It is definitely a safe deposit key," she explained to the group.

"How will you know where the box is?" asked Diaz.

"We can run the number on the key and find the bank and the box from that," she answered.

"Now let's hope that DVD is in that box," Massimo stated as the crowd noise on the TV indicated that the Pittsburgh Steelers had just scored another touchdown.

By midmorning on Monday, Massimo was on the verge of suffering a nervous breakdown anticipating the call from Parker that still hadn't arrived. Slightly calming his anxiety was his knowledge of such exercises from his own investigations. When he was required to interact with private entities like banks, delays and red tape were the norm. The problem comes in from the ubiquitous fear of liability that affects these organizations to the point of virtual paralysis. No matter what degree of reassurance the police investigator provides to the organization's representative through the legal protection of the court order, a decision to release the information may still be delayed. Typically, this decision is not forthcoming until the representative receives an almighty blessing from the proverbial "legal department," then the company rep will finally release the material that is being sought by the police.

This is why, when Massimo had executed these types of court orders in the past, he first contacted the company's legal department ahead of arriving at the business location. He found this to be a great time-saver for a job that rewards one who recognizes the value of efficiency. He was hoping that Parker had learned this lesson as well.

The sound of the phone on his desk startled him at first. "Massimo."

"We got it. Get your ass down here," Parker said with excitement in her voice.

"Did you watch it yet?" he asked.

"Not yet but it has the correct date written on it. We found a shit load of money in the box too. I called the DA and he is going to hold up the bond hearing on Belford for now with this new discovery," she explained.

"I'll be right there," Massimo stated and hung up the phone.

Before leaving, he called Tobias and Diaz and invited them to see the video at Parker's office. They were entitled to see it too, he thought. He was pleased to hear that they were waiting for this call together at Diaz's house and said that they would meet him at the Drug Enforcement Office.

When Massimo arrived, he walked into Parker's shared supervisor's office and found Diaz and Tobias already inside waiting with Parker.

"What took you so long?" Tobias said jokingly.

"OK, here we go," stated Parker, already having the DVD in the tray ready to play.

The four cops crowded in close together in front of Parker's computer screen as the video began to play. It showed the numerous camera views of Ease's system; front and rear of the row house, the inside living room and the upstairs bedroom where he hid his dope under the bed beneath the loosened floor boards. There was also, very conveniently, a date and time stamp on the screen, making the viewer's chore of searching for the time of interest on the video much more efficient. The screen time displayed was several hours prior to the actual time of the shooting. First, Parker was able to isolate the front porch and street camera view from the other camera views. When she clicked on this camera selection, the display of this view enlarged to full screen viewing.

Then Parker clicked on the fast forward command and the screen went into fast motion. Within a few minutes, seeing that the screen time was nearing the shooting, Parker slowed the motion speed halfway between normal play and fast forward. The scene displayed the street in front of the row house. They first saw a person enter from the left side of the camera view.

"That's him, Dickson," said Diaz identifying the figure on the screen.

Parker stopped the fast forward and let the video play at normal viewing speed. Within a short time the cops recognized Ruggerio on the video, creeping along the rear of a parked car. They could hear audio also and the cops listened to the angry and chemically-impaired taunts of Dickson to the unseen officer that would have been Diaz but he was out of the viewing frame. Then very clearly, they could see Dickson extend his hand while holding an object in the direction of where he had been shouting the taunts. After a few seconds, they heard the shot that G fired from the empty row house, followed immediately with Ruggerio firing the fatal shot that killed Dickson. The group witnessed the obvious flame discharge, making it evident that this was the only shot that Ruggerio fired at the suspect.

They were all silent in the office as the video played on, portraying the urgent shouts of Ruggerio calling for an ambulance and Diaz telling his partner that everything would be alright and not to worry. Very quickly more officers appeared at the scene and Ruggerio left the camera view with Diaz.

Diaz, while watching these events come alive, began to experience the same feelings that he had on that fateful night. He could feel his eyes begin to well up with tears at the thought of his friend having to go through such torture when it all could have been avoided.

Massimo was the first to speak. "That son-of-a-bitch Belford, he could have prevented one hell of a lot of misery if he would have produced this video rather than horde it for himself."

"There's a special place in hell for him," Parker remarked.

"For the time being there is going to be a special place in the state pen for him," proclaimed Tobias.

"Wait look!" Diaz said, pointing at the computer screen.

It was Faust crouching down between two parked cars in the immediate area of where Dickson had gone down. They couldn't see what he did between the cars but when he stood up it appeared as if he had placed something inside the inner breast pocket of his sport coat.

"Three guesses what he just did?" Massimo offered.

"That's where the mysterious cell phone disappeared to," Tobias remarked.

"That guy is pure evil. I don't know which one is worse Belford or Faust?" Diaz pondered.

"Faust in my book. You would expect what Belford did, but one cop trying to set up another one in this way is just beyond comprehension," Massimo concluded.

Then Massimo began to walk toward the office door and stated, "I have to make some phone calls. Can I use one of the phones in the squad room?"

"Go ahead," replied Parker.

"We better make a copy of that video before something happens to the original," requested Massimo.

"I'll put a copy on my hard drive then burn another DVD from that," Parker offered.

After Massimo left the office, Diaz and Tobias shook hands, congratulating each other on finally discovering the proof that would clear their names with the department. Then they both turned toward Parker, still sitting at her desk clicking the computer mouse, feverishly working on making the copies that she had told Massimo she would handle. She paused from her work for a moment, feeling the stares of the two off-duty officers in front of her. She looked up at them and asked, "What?"

Tobias and Diaz both moved in unison to go behind her desk where she was seated, then Tobias said, "Come here." One at a time they both hugged the dedicated narc cop who saved their careers and cleared Ruggerio's name, freeing up his benefits for his widow. It was a tremendous feeling of relief that the two affected cops were experiencing and they had to show their appreciation.

Massimo came back into the office and upon seeing the scene was spurred to comment, "Did I interrupt something?" He said, "Listen, you are not going to believe this one."

"Now what? I can't take much more of this!" Tobias complained.

"NO! It's good news. I had a message from the crime lab on my voice mail. I called them back; guess whose DNA was matched to the blood found on the dead hooker that was fished out of the Allegheny a few months back?"

They all said it together, "FAUST!"

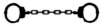

At about mid-day Faust was driving around aimlessly in his unmarked squad, contemplating the meaning of the Narc activity that had been taking place over the past two days near Bartlett Park. He had no tangible reason to think that it could affect him but he couldn't shake the feeling that somehow it had something to do with the Ruggerio shooting. He had asked all his contacts at the Narc office and all of them to a man said that it was a straight-up drug search warrant on a guy named Ease. Parker had been successful at keeping the Ruggerio officers' involvement in the investigation of Ease from becoming public knowledge, for the time being anyway.

Stopped for a red light at a downtown intersection, Faust let his mind wander as he watched the cross-street traffic passing in front of him. He relived the events that took place on the night of the Ruggerio shooting, looking for a loose end that he hadn't addressed to this point. There was nothing apparent that he could come up with, so what were they looking for at Bartlett Park? he wondered. He tried to reassure himself by considering that the drug case at the row house near the park could be just that—a simple drug case that had nothing to do with the Ruggerio shooting. But as the light changed to green and he proceeded through the intersection, the uneasy feeling was still there nagging at his thoughts.

Instigated by this imagery, his mind's eye conjured up the picture of Ruggerio's face to which he shook his head, trying to clear this vision from his thoughts. Attempting to stay focused, he reviewed the scene of finding the cell phone under the car where Dickson had dropped it, then when he concealed the phone in his breast pocket of his blazer. He didn't think anyone other than that hooker could have seen him, but maybe there was another witness?

Then Ruggerio's face came back into his mind. His conscience was playing with him. But abruptly Ruggerio's face was replaced by the face of his stepfather, the man that his mother married after she left Faust's biological father. There were similarities in the facial features of Ruggerio and Faust's stepfather, probably because they were both of the same ethnic background, Faust reasoned. Then Massimo's image appeared and Faust shook his head again and said aloud to himself, with disgust, "All wops."

Then, as the human brain will work at times, this series of thoughts logically linked to his long-term memories and his own father's face appeared to him. As different memories of his father whirled through his brain, Faust latched on to one of those scenes and the memory played out in his head.

He was eighteen years old and his father had just committed suicide by hanging himself with a belt strung over a thick metal natural gas line in the basement of the family's old house. Faust's uncle, his father's brother, had called him over to the house to claim some of his father's belongings. For the past six years, ever since his mother had left her abusive husband, Faust had been living with her and her new husband. His name was Dominic Vitali and Faust hated him, placing all the blame of his family's break-up on this man.

Vitali had come over on the boat and spoke with a heavy accent. He was a bricklayer by trade and worked hard to support his family. Faust's mother would continually reinforce how Vitali made their lives so much better, an escape from the constant abuse of his natural father. Vitali wanted to forge a strong relationship with Faust and he worked hard at getting along with his step-son. He took Faust to ball games and bought him presents, even taking him out to his worksites on occasion. But all the efforts of Faust's mother and Vitali were rejected by the boy who just couldn't reconcile the fact that his biological family was torn apart and the blame lay with Vitali.

A few months after his father's suicide, Faust gathered some of his possession and left home, first setting fire to Vitali's work truck for a little pay-back. In Faust's mind he considered the dago brick layer a murderer; Vitali may as well have placed that belt around his father's neck himself. He lamented the memory of how his father must have suffered seeing this dumb immigrant come to this country and take advantage of people in this way. The arrogance of this foreigner to steal a man's family was too much to bear for Faust, and obviously for his father.

Faust came to despise all people of the Italian persuasion seeing in each one of their swarthy complexions the face of Vitali, his father's de facto murderer. This was the image that he saw every time Ruggerio had been around him also. It was the same image he saw when he saw Massimo and it had to stop. Just as Vitali tore apart his family, these two dagos were also trying to destroy his life. He had already taken care of one. Now he needed to deal with the second.

Just then, as he was still navigating through the city streets, his cell phone vibrated on his belt. He answered the phone. It was Marks. The nagging feeling of doom that he hadn't been able to shake since the row house drug investigation, was about to be realized.

CHAPTER 20

Joe Massimo was in his mid forties but still in good shape thanks to the daily walks that he and his wife Mia shared every morning before they went to work. He added to this a regular weight lifting session in his home gym each evening, a habit formed back in high school when he wrestled on the school's team. Partly due to his genetics and also from his weight-training habit, Massimo's most distinctive feature was his barrel-like chest, presenting an image of a man who possessed great physical power. Reinforcing this image was his massive Popeye forearms, which he largely owed to his pedigree. Along with these genetics came traits like thick black hair on his beefy arms and legs. He kept his hair in the trendy cop-cut, nearly a crew cut, and since it was receding he figured why try to hide it? His dark skin and cleft chin only added to his rugged good looks and clearly announced his Sicilian decent.

Growing up in rural Western Pennsylvania, the youngest of five children and to second-generation Sicilian parents, Massimo's upbringing was very humble. His father was a forty-year coal miner, as his father had been before him back in Sicily, only he mined salt not coal. Massimo's father, Pasquale, or Patsy as he was called, died at an early age of black lung. But the fruits of his labor sent all his children through college, all of them going on to have successful careers in various professional arenas. The exception was Joe, his legal name being Giuseppe. Joe was charted to become a lawyer, having graduated from college with a pre-law degree. He was even enrolled in law school and in the midst of his first year discovered that his heart just wasn't suited for this career. Whether it was some dormant internal connection to his laborer ancestors or his slow-paced rural background, he didn't quite know. But he craved excitement and a career that allowed tangible results from work that could change lives for the better. He found that police work was the job that best fit his desires.

Having a sharp intellect and a dedicated work ethic, Massimo quickly rose through the ranks to the position of detective sergeant in the homicide unit, one of the most coveted positions on the force. Homicide dicks were revered by the uniformed cops, owing to the presumption that intellectual powers were more important than brawn to accomplish the job. This image still remains, even though in contemporary policing all officers from patrol up the line can choose to be challenged in their work. A sharp patrol officer with the proper legal knowledge and honed street skills can turn a mere traffic stop into a huge seizure of drugs hidden inside false compartments of a vehicle, for example. As every police administrator knows, the patrol function is the backbone of every police force. Numerous cases are solved by detectives, that never would have been, if it were not for the efforts of dedicated and intelligent patrol officers. Still, the way the media glorifies the job of the homicide detective, the perception is that there is no more important or challenging role in police work.

When Massimo was still in college, debating his life's work, he noticed a dark-haired olive-skinned beauty walking through the mall area one sunny autumn day. It was on his way to one of his classes across campus, a class that was scheduled on Mondays, Wednesdays, and Fridays. He began to notice her routinely on these same days of the week in this same area. As the weeks passed, he found himself anxiously anticipating that walk through the mall to see this pretty girl. One day he just couldn't take not knowing her any longer and he managed to get up the nerve to talk with her. As the relationship evolved, he found out that Mia, his future wife, had had the same feelings about seeing him walk through the mall area. In fact, Mia confessed that on that first day in the fall when they saw each other, she had taken the wrong direction on her way to class. But since seeing Massimo on that day, she decided that the detour through the mall was the way she would routinely walk to get to her class, just so she wouldn't miss seeing him.

Massimo found out that she was a music and art major and had always wanted to be a singer. Also that she was half Italian and half Slovak. Although he was pleased, he hadn't been specifically seeking a mate who shared his ethnicity. However, he couldn't help thinking that subconsciously Mia's Mediterranean appearance was what attracted him to her. Having a beautiful operatic voice, Mia performed in the college show choir and sang several solos during the group's concerts. Massimo never missed a performance and still always seemed to find time to break away, no matter how deep he was in work duties, to catch her singing in the city civic theater shows. Even though her dream of stardom as a singer never materialized, Mia had a rewarding career as a high school music teacher and voice instructor. The couple had two daughters, both away at college, giving them their two-story Victorian house all to themselves. As they said to each other numerous times, it felt like they were back in college again.

It was about five-thirty in the evening when Massimo wheeled the unmarked blue Crown Victoria into the asphalt driveway at this residence. He had a very contented feeling after the day's events began to sink into his consciousness. As an experienced investigator, he had seen this happen before and it was always a great feeling when a case was broken wide open. The proverb *"a weight is taken off my shoulders"* perfectly described how this type of result affected the morale of an investigator. Even more appropriate in this case was Massimo being so close to the individuals adversely affected by the crimes committed. This was also one of those instances when an officer reminds himself, *"this is one of the reasons I became a cop!"*

With this relaxed and satisfied mind-set, he approached the front door of his house, anxious to spend a quiet and, if he was lucky, romantic evening with his wife. During the long debriefing he had undergone that day with the district attorney investigators giving them new information on the Bartlett Park shooting and the New Ho homicide, his mind had kept projecting forward to this time in the evening when he would come home and see Mia. His body was exhausted from the arduous investigations that he had just completed, but along with this feeling was the relief that he had accomplished what he set out to do. The evidence was ironclad and Faust's days were numbered. He would sleep tonight knowing that a dirty cop had been exposed and could hurt no one else any longer. Or so he thought.

Massimo reached the front door and turned his key in the lock. The door swung open. As he walked inside, he peered into the living room and saw Mia sleeping on the couch. Not an unusual occurrence since sometimes after coming home from an unusually hectic day she would take a nap on the living room sofa before preparing dinner. Massimo thought that on this particular evening he would give her a break and call for takeout. He walked into the living room and bent down to kiss her on the cheek, hoping not to disturb her—but he just couldn't resist the temptation. As he bent over, he felt a presence in the room but before he could turn around to see what may be causing this strange sensation he felt a hard jab in his side and then heard the chilling voice of Curt Faust.

"Welcome home, Honey. Had a hard day?"

"What the fuck are you doing?" Massimo said with surprise.

"I'm here to read the meter and you're over budget. We're gonna have to do something to rectify that," he said with a sinister smirk.

"What do you want Faust, and what did you do to my wife you piece of shit?!"

Massimo knelt down to Mia's face and placed his hand over her mouth to feel if she was still breathing, silently praying that he would detect air moving in and out of her mouth and nose. Thankfully he did, then just to be certain he placed his fingers on her carotid artery and felt a strong pulse.

"Don't worry pisan, she's OK. I just gave her some tranquilizers. Boy was she surprised to see me though, when she came in through the back door," Faust said sardonically.

"I'm gonna tear your head off you dirty bastard," Massimo said, feeling fire burning in his veins as he stepped forward, nearly forgetting that Faust's Glock .40 was trained on his torso.

Faust took a few steps backward in response to Massimo's advance, then stated, "Wooo... that's tough talk for a guy with a .40 cal pointed at him. But that's enough small talk, drop your piece on the floor jack-off and use your left hand," he commanded brusquely.

Massimo, having no other choice, decided he had to comply but thought to himself that he would make a move at the first available opening.

"Now the cell phone. We wouldn't want you sending out the bat signal before we have our fun, now would we?"

Massimo again complied and dropped his cell phone on the carpeted floor, the phone landing next to his service pistol.

"Kick them both under the couch."

Massimo again did as he was told, trying to keep both his gun and phone as close to the edge of the sofa as possible. Why, he didn't quite know but he just thought it made sense.

"OK, now let us take a walk downstairs to your basement, shall we? Less chance of any nosey neighbors catching a glimpse through the windows," he explained.

He pointed Massimo in the direction of the stairs and stepped back again to put some space between himself and his hostage, in case Massimo made a grab for his gun. Massimo walked slowly and considered his options, waiting for an opportunity to make a move to disarm this lunatic. He thought to himself that he needed to get as close as possible to Faust's gun before he reacted if he was to be successful. While he walked down the stairs to his basement bar, he took a chance and glanced rearward to gauge how far the distance was between himself and Faust. Faust caught this and kicked Massimo in the back with his foot, saying, "Get your ass moving! Don't think I'm stupid enough to give you a chance at my piece."

Massimo stumbled forward down the last few steps and went down on his knees on the floor of his basement, catching himself with his arms extended to keep from smacking his face on the floor. The disrespectful nature of this kick into Massimo's backside made his blood boil and ignited his Sicilian temper, something he usually can keep in check. But this situation, with a maniac breaking into his home, drugging his wife and now pulling a gun on him, then kicking him to the ground was all that he could stand. Without really considering all the consequences, Massimo threw caution to the wind and sprung up from his kneeling position then turned to punch Faust. Unfortunately, Faust had anticipated this move and he remained standing in the middle of the stairs and out of direct reach for Massimo to strike him. Massimo was committed however, to this rash maneuver and kept advancing toward Faust in a desperate attempt to disarm his captor. Faust having ample time, took aim at one of Massimo's huge thighs and cracked off one round, "POW!"

The .40 caliber bullet slammed into his left thigh, spinning Massimo around and knocking him back down to the basement floor. He cursed in pain, "FUCK! YOU MOTHER FUCKER!"

"Not yet, you greasy WOP. We are just starting to have fun," Faust said in a sinister monotone. "Now crawl your fat ass over to the bar rail and hook yourself up to it with your cuffs," he ordered. When he wasn't moving fast enough, Faust kicked Massimo again and shouted, "NOW!"

With no other recourse, Massimo did as ordered, writhing in pain the whole time, blood pouring out onto his beige carpet, leaving a trail of dark red as he slid across the floor.

"Hook up one hand then put the chain around the bar and hook up the other."

Massimo snapped one cuff on his left hand then wrapped the connecting chain and empty cuff around the foot rail that he had screwed into the base of his home bar. Then as ordered he snapped the empty cuff onto his right hand. Now he was attached to the footrest and could not move to defend himself. He figured that his only chances were either someone outside heard the shot that Faust fired or that Mia awakened and called for help without Faust being aware.

"Now we can relax and just take our time," Faust said confidently then walked behind the bar and poured himself a shot of Jamison Whiskey.

"Oh, where are my manners? Would you like one?" Faust asked sarcastically then leaned over the bar top and poured some of the whiskey from the bottle onto Massimo's head.

Massimo shook his head and tried mopping up the burning wet liquid that had run into his eyes on the sleeve of his sport coat.

"Faust, what are you accomplishing by doing this?" Massimo thought that he better get him talking to stretch time and hope for a miracle. He didn't want to mention all the new evidence that had just come to light against him, because he wasn't sure if Faust was aware of these new developments yet. But he had a sneaking suspicion that Faust was aware. Why else would he be here about to commit murder? This was probably his attempt to go out with a bang, take out as many as possible until he finally gets his, Massimo figured.

His leg felt like it was on fire and it was still bleeding steadily. He put his finger in the hole as far as he could without passing out from the pain, to stop the bleeding.

Faust took down the whole shot of booze and slammed the empty glass on the bar top. "AHH! Now that is good whiskey, " he said contentedly, then placed the gun down on the bar top, confident that Massimo was unable to react offensively any longer.

Faust then placed his elbows on the bar and crossed his forearms, leaning over to have a better angle of sight at Massimo on the floor below. "What do I expect to accomplish? To get even, what do you think? When Marks told me about your new evidence- well you forced my hand," he said, answering Massimo's question and clearing up how he had found out about the new evidence.

That damn Marks, Massimo thought to himself. Why couldn't he just leave this to the DA's investigators to handle?

Faust turned around and saw the family photographs that Massimo had hung on the wall and placed on either side of a large mirror that was also attached to the wall behind the bar.

"Nice family, dago," he commented, looking at a picture of Massimo with his wife and two daughters. It was graduation day from high school for his oldest daughter. From the photograph he could see that it was a sunny day and the family had been standing in front of a fully leafed out maple tree, all smiles on a happy family occasion. "Yeah, you got the life here, nice house, nice family, the American Dream...right?" Faust said, leading up to some yet-to-be revealed conclusion.

It made Faust think about his own graduation day. His make-believe stepfather, the grease ball himself, acting like he belonged there instead of his real father. By this time in Faust's life, his father had already committed suicide. How he hated that whole day, the fake smiles and pretend congratulations; it was embarrassing. He told his mother not to let the wop come but she insisted; she wanted Faust to get along with him. Faust refused to appease his mother. In his mind, this man had caused his father's death and ruined what family life he had as he grew up.

Faust rediscovered that family feeling again when he joined the Metro force. On the department there was structure and at least in theory, no one was treated any differently. It was clear who the bad guys were and who were the good ones. They all wore the same clothes, for goodness sake.

It was clear until these types of people, meaning Ruggerio and Massimo, came along and blurred that line between the good guys and bad ones. These self-righteous know-it-alls thought that they were better than the rest of us. They just walk right in and shove other guys aside, good guys—the ones that break a few skulls when they have to on the street—and then they step right over top of them like they are the masters. This is wrong. It muddies the water and turns officers against one another. Just like the wop that broke up my family. Well now it's time for another one of these do-gooders to pay!

Tobias refilled Diaz's glass with more beer from the half-drunk pitcher on the table between them. The bar crowd came in early that night and everyone seemed to be in a relaxed and jovial mood. It being the Monday after a Steelers victory didn't hurt either. Even though it wasn't possible, it seemed to Tobias and

Diaz that everyone in Pittsburgh was celebrating the resolution of the Ruggerio shooting and the soon-to-be reinstatement of the two officers back on the Metro force.

"That's the last one. I'm driving you know? How would that look, we are about to be reinstated and I get stopped for DUI?" Diaz explained to Tobias, who was knocking back the alcohol at a steady pace. "Maybe you oughta slow down?" Diaz cautioned.

"Don't worry. I can handle my liquor. Besides, like you said, you're driving," Tobias reasoned, and dug a pinch of Copenhagen from his can and squeezed the black grit into his lower lip.

They both had been interviewed by the DA's investigators and the internal affairs cops earlier. They received the unofficial word from the IA lieutenant that they were as good as gold to be reinstated. When they were released from the interviews, Tobias wanted to celebrate, so he suggested that they stop for, "a drink or two."

They called Massimo and asked him if he wanted to join in but he thanked them and explained that his wife was waiting for him at home. He told them that he would have them both over to his home for the Super Bowl. The Steelers had won all their playoff games and were playing the Arizona Cardinals for the championship. He told them to bring their wives or girlfriends this time because there would be no shop talk at this party.

"I'm a little worried about Joe," Diaz said.

"Why?"

"Faust is still on the loose. I think he may want to even the score with him. Faust seems to have a real hard-on for him," said Diaz with concern.

"Let me tell you something. Joe Massimo can take care of himself. Shit, his forearms are as round as a leg of proscuit," Tobias said, starting to show the signs of drunkenness.

"What's that?" Diaz asked.

"Oh yeah, you haven't been around here long enough. That's Italian ham. When you live around so many dagos you tend to learn these things. Ruggerio used to eat it all the time. It's actually pretty good, *hiccup!*" Tobias proclaimed, then continued on the subject of Faust.

"Anyway, you think Faust is going to stay around here? He is probably long gone by now," he said, flipping his hand in the air apathetically.

"Toby, we better get going. My side is starting to act up on me," Diaz lied, hoping to get Tobias on his way home before he got too drunk.

"OK, OK I hear you Nancy," he answered, then gulped down the remainder of his glass of beer.

When they were on the road, Diaz was driving Tobias home and realized that he was not far from where Massimo lived. He looked over at Tobias in the passenger seat and saw that he was getting close to passing out. He was slouched down in his seat with his head tilted back on the head rest, uncontrollably rocking back and forth with the movement of the car.

"Toby, did you take that chew out of your mouth?" he asked, concerned.

"Yes Mother," Tobias answered.

Diaz pulled up to a stop light and noticed that the late rush hour traffic was heavier than usual. It was just starting to get dark and the temperature was a tolerable thirty-nine degrees. Along with the warm temperatures, another reason the partiers are out so early, the city must be priming itself for the Super Bowl, he figured. He looked to his left down the intersecting street while waiting for the light to change and realized that he was just two blocks away from Massimo's house. He was still concerned about Faust possibly wanting to seek revenge. Hell, even he and Tobias should be worried, he thought.

Then he took out his cell phone and pressed the number on his touch pad that was programmed to dial Massimo's cell number. The phone rang as he accelerated through the intersection after his light had changed. After four rings it went to his voice mail, then he heard Massimo's recorded message, *"This is Detective Massimo please leave a message and I will call you ba…"*

Before the word "back" was completed, someone picked up the phone but Diaz did not hear anyone on the other end.

"Hello…Hello, is anyone there?" he asked expectantly.

Diaz faintly heard breathing from the other end and a groan.

"Hello, Joe is that you? Are you OK?" he implored.

Still hearing the breathing but nothing further, he was convinced that he better check this out. Diaz left the phone connected but placed it in his lap as he performed a U-turn in the middle of the street, instigating a chorus of angry horn blowers. His tires screeched as he negotiated the turn and sped back in the direction of Massimo's house.

What Diaz could not have known at that time was that the breathing and groaning noises he had heard over the phone were coming from Mia. She had regained partial consciousness from her drug-induced sleep and heard the vibrating cell phone. Since Massimo had intentionally left the phone partially under the sofa she was lying on, she was close enough to detect the incoming call.

Mia was well aware that this home intruder was the infamous Faust that her husband had been talking about for several months. She also knew he was there to hurt or possibly kill her husband. This knowledge, concerning the safety of a loved one, provided Mia with an internal will to fight through the chemical effects of the tranquilizers and regain a scrap of awareness. Long enough to recognize the vibrating cell phone on the floor and that she needed to answer this phone and try to summon assistance.

Mia, still barely able to move her body, but fueled by her desire to help her husband, found the inner strength to reach down and open the two halves of Massimo's flip phone. As hard as she tried however, she could not get her mouth to form words to ask for help. The most she could muster was a few grunts and groans before the adrenaline that helped her awaken and answer the phone tapered off and she fell back into unconsciousness.

Diaz was dealing with his own sleeping patient, now that Tobias had fallen into a drunken and snoring stupor in his passenger seat. Diaz just hoped that if Tobias needed to throw up that he would be able to wake up and project it outside the car. He made the turn onto Massimo's street, then killed the lights, acting the same as if he were responding to a prowler call while on duty. The only problem was that he didn't have his gun or the rest of his gear as he would have if in uniform. As he parked the car approximately three houses away from Massimo's, again staying in patrol mode, he thought briefly about calling 911 and having the "real cops" check this out. He decided against it until he could come up with more evidence indicating there really was trouble at the Massimo residence.

Diaz put Tobias's window down; in the event he decided to hurl, at least he had an open window to stick his head out of. The cold air would do him good anyway, he decided. He then crept up along the front sidewalk toward Massimo's house; trying to stay in the darkened areas, he sidled up next to a window on the north side of the residence. He took a quick peek inside through the window and could see Mrs. Massimo lying on the living room sofa. The top part of her head and her right arm, which was dangling off of the sofa, were visible. The scene didn't look as if anyone was in danger. But he saw Joe's unmarked police car parked in the driveway. Where was he?

He decided that the best thing to do was to knock at the front door and talk to Joe personally just to be safe. Besides if he remained where he was, looking through a window at a sleeping woman inside a house, he could easily be mistaken for a "weenie whacker." Now wouldn't that look good on the same day that his name was cleared from the IA files?

Diaz walked around the front of the house and approached the front door. He was about to knock when he saw Massimo's cell phone lying on the floor in front of Mrs. Massimo with the top portion still open. That was weird, he thought. Diaz cupped his hands around his eyes and pressed them up to the glass of the front door's sidelight windows to get a better look. Yeah, he thought, that *is* an open cell phone on the floor. Then he heard a voice very faintly coming from inside. He waited…listened… nothing. Was he hearing things? Was it background noise that he heard from some surrounding location that appeared as if it came from inside the house?

Wait! There it is again. I know that voice! he thought. THAT'S FAUST! HOLY FUCK! Diaz said in his mind.

He looked down at his cell phone and called 911. When the operator answered the phone, as silently as he could, he whispered his name, the address, and that there was an intruder in the residence, possibly armed. The operator then asked for Diaz's home address and telephone number. But before he could provide this information, he heard shouting coming from inside the Massimo house. It was definitely Faust shouting and from what he could tell it was coming from the basement bar area where they had gathered for the last Steelers football game. The sound of his voice sounded angry and maniacal. Diaz was worried. By the time the cops get there it could be too late.

He could hear the 911 operator asking, "Sir? Sir are you there?"

Diaz thought for a moment then decided that he should try and get closer to hear exactly what was happening inside. He put his cell phone down, still connected to the 911 center, thinking that if he should get into something with Faust before the cops get there, at least 911 can triangulate his phone to its exact location for the responding officers to follow. He reached for the front door knob and was surprised when he found that it was unlocked. Luckily, Massimo did not lock the door behind him when he arrived home from work earlier.

As quietly as he could, he turned the knob on the door and slowly pushed it open. He could now hear Faust talking from the basement area, he wasn't shouting any longer.

"You and your kind have screwed with me and my family all my life. Now you take my job away. You and your *goomba* Ruggerio couldn't mind your own business; you just had to fuck with me. Well now who has the upper hand?"

While he listened, Diaz analyzed Faust's voice, using his background in psychology as a reference. Faust's voice had dramatically changed from loud and maniacal to low and deliberate. This indicated that he had just made a decision about something. Diaz was afraid that he knew what that something was.

He crept closer, now at the top of the stairway that led to the lower level of the house. Should he try going down the steps, would they creak and alert Faust that he was there? Faust's next statement answered that question for him.

"Now it is retribution time, grease ball," Faust said in the same low and deliberate tone.

Then Massimo, sensing the same urgency as Diaz, said,

"Faust you can kill me, but what about my wife? She hasn't harmed anybody."

As Massimo said this, his volume was more amplified than Faust's. Diaz used this louder voice to cover any noise he made while creeping down the four steps it took to reach the lower level. He arrived at the bottom landing and was relieved that Faust apparently hadn't detected him.

"I don't want to be remembered as a mass murder Massimo. I'm not going to hurt your precious wife. Besides, after you're gone she can remarry a decent guy the next time around." Faust chuckled at his own humor.

Diaz used the conversation to make his move. He darted into the entertainment room where the two were located and lowered his shoulder as he raced at Faust. Faust, sensing something to his rear, began to turn in Diaz's direction, but he was too late. Diaz slammed his left shoulder into Faust's side and drove him flying into the far corner of the room. Faust's gun hand hit a heavy wooden end table during the fall. The impact caused his grip on the gun to loosen, enough so that the Glock flew out of his hand and went bounding against the wall, then clattered to the floor about three feet away from where Diaz and Faust were now grappling.

Faust tried to rise up and move where the gun had fallen but Diaz prevented this by applying a wrestler's move. He slid his left arm under Faust's left arm then across his chest up to the right side of his neck. While positioned behind Faust, Diaz used his right hand to complete a sleeper hold, grabbed his own left wrist, and squeezed Faust into a headlock. This immobilized him temporarily and gave Diaz time to think of his next move.

Massimo used the time also. He slid himself and the cuffs along the foot rail to the extreme end nearest where the gun was lying. He tried to reach it with his non-wounded leg; it was painful but he fought through it to try to retrieve the gun. It was too far for his reach.

Unable to reach the gun on the floor, he looked down at the handcuffs securing him to the foot rail and quickly decided what he should do to help Diaz. He took both hands and grabbed onto the rail, then began to jerk on the fitting that was screwed into the wood of the bar front. If he could pull out the three screws that fastened this end of the footrest to the bar, he could pull his handcuffed hands out from behind the rail.

The first pull loosened the fittings slightly, so he saw a bit of hope in this method. He pulled again and the screws were starting to protrude from the wood they had been driven into. Massimo knew this wasn't going to be easy because he had attached this rail himself. He remembered that he wanted this footrest to be secure so he had used three-inch wood screws. He swung his legs around so he could push off the bar façade with the leg muscles of his unaffected side to give himself more power.

Diaz was squeezing with all his power, thinking that maybe if he had his left forearm in the right spot he could cut off Faust's blood flow to his brain and choke him into unconsciousness. Unfortunately, due to his long layoff of inactivity from the bullet wound he had suffered, Diaz had lost some of his former strength. So the effects on Faust were not immediate. This gave Faust the opportunity to dig his chin downward, placing Diaz's left forearm in front of Faust's mouth. Faust clamped down with his teeth on Diaz's arm, inflicting severe pain. As a result, Diaz released his grip for a moment.

Faust, seeing a chance, tried again to rise up and move toward the firearm but Diaz, fighting through the pain, grabbed Faust by the collar with his right hand and pulled him backward away from the gun. When Faust saw that he could not reach the gun, he decided to reach out for a slender brass lamp and use it as a weapon. The lamp was lying on top of the wooden end table that had jarred the gun loose from his grip earlier. In the scuffle the lamp had fallen over but stayed on top of the table.

He took the lamp and spun around and got himself on top of Diaz, who was now in a precarious position, a position that all cops dread in a fight; he was on his back. Faust used the lamp to jab Diaz in the stomach. This brought his hands downward with the natural reaction to protect his abdomen, leaving his face and neck unprotected. Faust quickly moved the lamp in a cross checking position and brought the length of the lamp down on Diaz's neck. Now it was Faust who was attempting to choke Diaz.

Massimo saw this and knew that with Faust's weight, Diaz would not last long under the pressure. He knew that he had to break free of his ensnarement quickly or his friend would be dead, along with himself and possibly his wife. Even though Faust said that he would spare Mia, Massimo knew not to trust what this killer had told him.

With these thoughts processing through his mind, the adrenalin fired in his body and exploded into his veins, feeding the muscles in his unaffected leg and both his arms. With a force that would have snapped metal, he pushed off of the bar façade with his right foot and at the same time pulled hard with his hands on the foot rail, letting out a primal scream that would have even frightened Iron Mike Tyson. The three three-inch screws exploded out of the wood of the bar, splinters showering over Massimo. One of the screws that was particularly determined to stay attached, pulled out with it a whole plank of wood from the bar structure. The plank cracked in half at the point where this screw had been driven into it and the jagged edge stuck out from the bar at a downward angle. Massimo still on the floor and on his side, then lifted his handcuffed hands out from behind the railing and was free to assist Diaz.

Faust, hearing the piercing sound of Massimo's scream and the splintering wood, turned to see that his prey was freeing himself. He began to let up on the pressure he was applying to Diaz's neck and decided that he better go for the gun before Massimo was completely free.

Massimo noticed this and saw Faust's eyes move in the direction of the gun. Massimo quickly calculated this distance equation. Who had the better chance to get to the gun first, he asked himself? Then in a millisecond he determined that the best maneuver was to go for Faust before he could get to the gun. Massimo got to his knees without feeling any pain from his bullet wound, the adrenalin masking the pain.

Like a starving animal freed from a lengthy captivity, he growled with pleasure as he lunged at Faust. His Sicilian blood coursing through his veins fueled his anger and his lust for vengeance - vengeance against this man who had brought evil into his home.

Massimo clasped his two handcuffed hands together and extended his arms outward. Then he coiled his upper torso backward and quickly released his shoulders and upper body, swinging his arms at Faust's head. With tremendous force, the back of his right hand impacted the left side of Faust's temple, snapping his head backward and sending his body crumbling into the opposite corner from where Diaz was lying. He lay there on the floor, unconscious and motionless, Massimo staring down at him and thinking about finishing the job.

He heard Diaz coughing and choking and went to help him stand up. As he got Diaz to his feet, he heard the front door open and the first arriving officers, "POLICE. Anyone in here?"

CHAPTER 21

A gentle April wind blew across the open ground of the cemetery, giving a bit of pleasant relief to the officers decked out in their Class A dress uniforms. The cold and winter snow was finally gone, giving way to the rebirth of the green landscape familiar to this region. The sun shone brilliantly down on the throng of mourners on this glorious Easter Monday.

Massimo figured that the number of cops who were attending probably counted over one thousand. Officers came in from all over the Western Pennsylvania region and some from different parts of the country. It was a touching demonstration of the deep respect officers don't always show but most truly feel for each other. This notable participation at this memorial ceremony was appropriate, underpinning the fact that this occasion was to mark the beginning of a new philosophy taking hold in American policing.

Massimo, also wearing his Class A uniform, stood in the formation of officers, a double line approximately fifteen feet apart to show reverence to the surviving officer's family. Still requiring the use of a cane for his wounded left leg, he turned to admire the throng of cops all spit-shined and crisp. He looked down the line and felt a pang of emotion when he saw the officers who were involved in the "Ruggerio Affair." Standing at attention in the gauntlet with him were: Taymond Diaz wearing his Medal of Valor awarded for bravery in action; Toby Tobias; Quinton O'Neal and Max his K-9, who had recovered from his wounding, sitting regally at his side sporting his own medal for his service to his human partners; Jefferson Lewis; Shelisha "Queeny" Walker; Stanley Katowski; Celeste Parker; and even Tom Simon and Al Jones, a.k.a Alias Simon and Jones, dressed up for the event.

Massimo reviewed in his mind the outcome of the investigation that had cleared the names of Ruggerio, Tobias, and Diaz. Ruggerio was posthumously re-instated as a police officer and his record was reconciled to reflect that all criminal and internal charges had been dropped for lack of evidence. This resulted in the automatic eligibility of Sally Ruggerio to her husband's pension and other benefits as if he had resigned from the force in good standing. Tobias and Diaz were also re-instated to the force with retroactive pay covering the period when they were under suspension. Both of their records were reconciled in the same way as Ruggerio's. Massimo's reprimand letter was destroyed and his personnel file was returned to its former condition.

Lieutenant Marks was fired from the force, for his handling of the Bartlett Park shooting investigation and the manner in which he had coddled Faust and unjustly disciplined the other officers of his station. Also, in his charging document it was remarked that he was dismissed for releasing the details of a criminal investigation to the target of the probe before authorized to do so, the result of which placed the lives of several officers and civilians in danger of serious bodily injury and/or death.

Even Thomas Wilkes did not elude the net cast over the heads of the evildoers involved in the "Ruggerio Affair." Thomas, having successfully severed the relationship between his daughter and Jamar Dickson, still felt that Lauren needed to be taught a lesson. He decided to forgo the purchase of Lauren's new Mercedes for the time being as reminder of who was in charge between the two of them. This infuriated Lauren to such an extent that she used some information against her father that he unwittingly let slip out to her. Thomas, since Jamar was dead and gone, thought it would not hurt to tell Lauren about the private detective he had following her and monitoring her phone calls. He wanted to reinforce to her the power that he held and to prevent any further attempts she might want to make of engaging in another relationship that was beneath her status.

This strategy backfired horribly on Thomas; unfortunately for him, this passion for superiority had been passed down to his daughter. Upon learning of the "Ruggerio Affair" through the media reports, Lauren saw the chance to get even with dear old dad by calling the Pittsburgh Metro Homicide Unit and reporting the possible existence of phone recordings that may assist in the investigation. Massimo and Lewis quickly obtained a search warrant for the office of the private detective that Thomas Wilkes used and they found the recorded phone calls between Jamar Dickson and Lauren Wilkes. These tapes corroborated the other information concerning Jamar Dickson's suicidal state of mind just before the Bartlett Park shooting, making the "suicide-by-cop" motive crystal clear to the DA.

The discovery of these tapes placed Thomas Wilkes and his private detective under charges of "obstruction of justice" for withholding valuable evidence from the district attorney's office. This wasn't all for the lawyer-turned-defendant, Thomas Wilkes; there was one more surprise waiting.

As his trial date was nearing, there was one particularly frustrated golfer/judge who pulled some well-orchestrated strings to insure that the toughest and most honest judge in the county presided over the criminal trial of Thomas Wilkes. Judge Holmes was going to even the score for all those weekend golf rounds in which he lost a sizable amount of money to his cheating opponent. In the end, Thomas Wilkes committed what might be termed a "suicide-by-lawyer."

Finally, Faust was placed under suspension from the department until final deposition of his criminal trial for the following charges filed by the DA's office: criminal homicide of Constance Lebeau, attempted homicide of Massimo and Diaz, burglary of Massimo's home, tampering with evidence for illegally taking the cell phone at the Bartlett Park shooting scene, false swearing for submitting a bogus police report on the Bartlett Park shooting, and obstruction of justice for the reasons contained in the previous charges. He was looking at a sentence of life in prison with no possibility for parole and was currently being held at the county prison pending his trial.

In the months since the details of the "Ruggerio Affair" came to light, a groundswell of pundits surfaced, expressing concern about some key issues of police work that have never really been spoken about openly before. Experts debated on nationally-televised cable news programs about the effects of interpersonal relations between officers. Both the beneficial aspects of these relationships and the detrimental points were highlighted. The national discussion also led to the matter of stress in police work. The fact that policing ranks near the top among all other professions in regard to the amount of stress experienced in the workplace was exposed.

Then finally, the revelation, shocking to the populace and to some cops too, that police suicide vastly outnumbers the incidents of officer deaths due to felonious assault and on-duty fatal accidents combined. Since this topic is the police world's dirty little secret, no system of tracking the number of police officer suicides exists. Some respected police experts put the police suicide numbers into the four hundreds each year compared to the average of about one hundred deaths from criminal attacks and accidents. This stunning revelation brought about cries for more discussion on the matter and research into the problem to determine what is causing this epidemic.

The city and the Metro force saw the importance of the subject and recognized the slight that was delivered to the memory of Ruggerio, so this memorial ceremony was organized in his honor. Dignitaries from the city, state, and the federal government were in attendance, along with some of those police experts who were calling for reform in police management and stress treatment. There was even a representative from the "National Police Officer's Memorial Foundation" in attendance who later in the ceremony gave a surprise announcement to the crowd.

Then with the command, "ATTENTION!" given by Sergeant Katowski, the moment arrived that all the officers, especially the ones in the procession line who had given their time, talents, and in some cases their actual blood to clear Ruggerio's name, were there for: the arrival of Mrs. Ruggerio. She entered the memorial procession with an honor guard preceding her. She walked by the officers, looking dignified in a black dress, blonde hair flowing down her shoulders tears streaming down her cheeks but still maintaining a stoic expression. In her arms was a small infant, a boy swaddled in white blankets, his tiny arms reaching up toward his mother. He had dark hair already apparent on his tiny crown. A son aptly named Gaetano Lesio Ruggerio, Junior. How fitting it was, Massimo thought, to have this day in the Easter season.

On the command, "PRESENT ARMS!" given again by the old Marine, the procession line of officers, along with the one thousand plus cops in attendance, snapped their white gloved right hands up to the brims of their caps in salute as the surviving widow walked toward the presenting stand. Massimo and the others tried not to but just couldn't help shedding a few tears as Mrs. Ruggerio passed by. As a gesture of thanks, she stopped at each of the officers who helped in her husband's defense and softly touched their cheeks or brushed her hand over a sleeve and stated, "Thank you," to all of them.

After all the attendees were seated, the ceremony began. Several speeches were given, all extending their condolences to his widow, lauding the memory of Ruggerio and promising to seek answers to the troubling number of police suicides in the country. Then the representative from the National Police Memorial Foundation took the podium. The representative was a distinguished middle-aged Hispanic woman who had been a police officer herself in New York City. Her name was Grace Sanchez. She joined in her praise of Officer Ruggerio and offered her sincerest condolences to his widow. Then she told them the special reason she had been sent to this ceremony. Sanchez said that she was proud to announce that Officer Ruggerio's name had been accepted by the board of directors to be added to the list of names engraved on the Police Officer's Memorial Wall in Washington, D.C. This honor, which was normally reserved for those officers killed in the line of duty, was permitted as an exception for this case. Grace Sanchez explained that even though Officer Ruggerio's death was not due to criminal assault, this did not overshadow the honorable fashion in which he comported himself in action. Also taking into account the overbearing stressors that he endured and the length of time that he withstood this emotional strain, it did not abate his professionalism in attempting to clear his name. "For these reasons, Patrolman Gaetano Lesio Ruggerio is eligible for inclusion to the Police Memorial Wall." The crowd erupted with applause at the surprising announcement, all the cops recognizing that this case truly was unique and deserved this honor.

After the ceremony was concluded, the "Ruggerio Cops" decided to hit a bar for a few drinks as usual. It was a good excuse to relax and contemplate the drama that had unfolded over the last several months. Massimo made the suggestion when he saw that his small crew of officers was still hanging around with each other at the cemetery, not wanting to go home. In his mind he equated the feelings that they were experiencing to the high a cop feels after catching a felon in a foot chase or some other dramatic incident that ends successfully. After these types of incidents, the officers involved traditionally need the release of talking out the incident with each other before they can resume their individual routines.

They had all brought with them civilian sport coats and draped them over their uniforms, a lesson learned from the last time they were at this same cemetery. Sitting around a large table inside the mostly empty bar room, a bartender brought two full pitchers of beer over for the group of cops. When they all had something to drink, Massimo raised his glass and gave one of his heartfelt toasts.

"If it were not for the hard work, dedication, skill, intelligence, ingenuity and any other adjective that describes what makes a good cop, from everyone at this table, we would not be here today celebrating the positive result of this unique situation. To all of you," he passed his full glass in a semi-circle in front of him to toast the officers, and then added, "It is damn reassuring to discover so many decent cops still exist these days. Cento anni, which means, one hundred years of good luck. AH, SALUTE!"

Then they all said in unison, "SALUTE!"

Then Massimo sat down and recommended to the group, "Who wants some wings? I'm starving."

Over the next few hours, the off-duty cops ate and drank, and laughed and ragged on each other like close friends do. And it wouldn't be a cop gathering if the war stories were not told one after the other, each party trying to outdo the other. They reminisced about the drama of the case that they had just collectively solved. But after a while they finally started to leave, one at a time, until only Massimo, Tobias, and Diaz were left at the table.

No one was really drunk. They were only sipping at their drinks because they were mostly occupied with talking to each other for the majority of the session. But now, these three individuals who were so intimately involved in this case and who were closest to Ruggerio, sat in silence for a time. Each man sat with his own thoughts, reliving the events of the "Ruggerio Affair," until Diaz spoke. "I've decided something that I want you guys to know."

"You've decided to finally come out of the closet?" Tobias joked.

"Smart ass," retorted Diaz, then continued. "I've decided to resign from the force," he stated with conviction.

"Why? Just because you got shot and almost choked to death, that's no reason to quit being a cop," chortled Massimo as they all chuckled.

"No, I like being a cop but I think I can make more of a difference doing something else," Diaz said sincerely.

"OK, what would that be?" Tobias asked.

"I'm going back to school and finish up my studies in psychology. I think that I want to specialize in police stress research," he said, waiting for a reaction.

Then Massimo looked at Tobias then back at Diaz and said. "I think that would be the best way to honor Guy's memory. I say, go for it kid!"

"Ditto! And the other beauty part would be, I know where to go for a free brain tune-up," said Tobias, giving Diaz a friendly slap on the shoulder.

"Yeah, whenever you want. But wait until I assemble a team of experts before you expect any improvement with that noodle," Diaz responded, joining in the friendly ribbing.

Diaz internally reflected upon his long-forgotten malaise over his career path. He recalled sitting with Ruggerio on that first night, his mind whirling with confusion and uncertainty over his employment situation. But now he was reassured that this confusion was no longer any concern. Taymond Diaz was as positive as a person could be on the direction of his life's journey.

After the laughing died down a bit, Diaz completed his thoughts. "Today only reinforced my decision. There is a real need for more research and maybe even a facility here in Pittsburgh that deals specifically with cops and stress management."

"Yeah, we could have used one about seven months ago. Maybe we could have avoided one hell of a path of destruction," Massimo said.

Tobias put a fresh pinch of Copenhagen in his mouth as everyone nodded agreement to Massimo's assessment. Then he added, "I know. I was thinking about that during the ceremony. I mean the irony of the whole situation is really weird when you think about it."

"What do you mean?" Diaz asked.

"Well this whole thing started with the Jamar Dickson shooting, a "suicide by cop" incident, right?"

The other two both said, "Yeah."

"But then everybody after that fell from some variation of the same thing. G Holland encouraged his own death. Another classic 'suicide-by-cop.' Ruggerio took his own life. You could call that a 'suicide-by-cop.' And then Faust does in his whole career and rest of his life by his own actions, again 'suicide-by-cop.' I mean, you could think of this whole mess as a chain of events that had one common theme connecting it all."

They all sat there for a few moments in silence, contemplating this summation offered by Tobias, then Massimo provided his spin on this analysis. "You could take your conclusions one step further, Toby."

"How so?" asked Tobias.

"The term 'suicide-by-cop' could also be applied to results of the feud between Faust and Ruggerio. The war between them was allowed to fester and grow into a winner-take-all contest. But instead of one defeating the other, their feud ended with the mutual destruction of both officers. There were no winners in this contest," Massimo concluded with the others nodding in agreement.

Then Diaz, reverting to his most fitting word habit, searched his mind for the word that would best describe the events of the last seven months. He settled on the word that Tobias used when he first broached the subject. Nodding his head, he simply stated to the group in a hushed tone, *"Irony."*

THE END

DETECTIVE DENNIS MARSILI

ABOUT THE AUTHOR

Dennis Marsili, a native of Western Pennsylvania, is a 23 year veteran police officer and currently serves as a detective sergeant with the New Kensington, Pennsylvania Police Dept. Detective Marsili is an experienced investigator who has successfully cleared numerous criminal cases, from homicides and bank robberies to fatal traffic accidents and financial fraud incidents. In 1995, then Patrolman Marsili was commended by Calibre Press, creators of the highly acclaimed "Street Survival Seminars," in their winter Survival Selections newsletter for his part in an on duty shooting incident.

He has also been an active police trainer, focusing on subjects dealing with police officer survival. Detective Marsili is also a frequent contributor to the Pennsylvania Police Criminal Law Bulletin as a Research Assistant, in which he writes briefs on recent criminal case law and provides opinion columns on officer survival and procedure. He holds a master's degree in Criminology and has published numerous police related articles as the Pittsburgh Law Enforcement Examiner for Examiner.com. He is an active member of Phi Kappa Phi honor society and the Academy of Criminal Justice Sciences professional association. Excessive Forces is his first novel. He can be reached by e-mail: dennis.marsili63@gmail.com

WA